Wicked Wager

by

Mary Gillgannon

This is a work of fiction. Names, characters, places, and incidents are either the product of the author's imagination or are used fictitiously, and any resemblance to actual persons living or dead, business establishments, events, or locales, is entirely coincidental.

Wicked Wager

Cover Art by *Rae Monet, Inc. Design*

The Wild Rose Press, Inc.
PO Box 708
Adams Basin, NY 14410-0708
Visit us at www.thewildrosepress.com

Publishing History
First Tea Rose Edition, 2015
Print ISBN 978-1-5092-0116-7
Digital ISBN 978-1-5092-0117-4

Published in the United States of America

Dedication

To my dear friends Amanda and Joanne,
for your continued support and encouragement.

Chapter One

It was like taking candy from a baby. Marcus Revington fought to conceal his scorn as he regarded his opponent across the card table. How many times had he seen this scene re-enacted? The arrogant young sharp takes on a real gamester and discovers there's more to winning than luck.

Marcus had disillusioned a few budding high-flyers in his day, but setting down this arrogant coxcomb would be especially gratifying. He didn't like Adrian Withersby, with his cunning blue eyes, his green jacket and yellow waistcoat, his blond hair arranged in a perfect Brutus.

The seeds of the young dandy's destruction had been planted. He was behind by three games and two rubbers; the baize table was littered with gambling vowels. Picquet was a game of skill as well as luck, and Withersby, who was careless in his discards and seemed to have a poor notion of figuring the odds, wasn't an adept player.

"*Capot*," Marcus said as he won the final trick.

Sir James Ludingham, seated to Marcus's right, marked down the points. "Revington takes the rubber. Do you want to continue?"

A hard look came over Withersby's face as he observed the extent of his debt. "I'm not that badly dipped."

"What will you wager?" James asked. "I don't think Revington should accept any more vowels."

"My luck will turn," Withersby muttered. "I know it will."

"Your wager, sir?" Marcus said.

A shrewd look gleamed in Withersby's eyes. "I have property in Hampshire."

James pushed a piece of parchment and quill pen in front of him. "Write down the name of the estate, sir, and make your mark."

Withersby glared at Marcus. "Do you always have your solicitor at hand?"

Marcus smiled blandly. "Ludingham is a friend. I'm certain you'll abide by any promise you make, whether in writing or not."

Withersby signed with a flourish. "Let us resume play."

For a short while, it appeared Withersby's luck had turned. He won three games to Marcus's one and took the rubber. Gloating, he poured himself a brandy and took a deep draught.

Then Marcus's steady skill again took its toll. When he'd won two games in a row, he said, "Perhaps we should call it a night, Withersby. Say this rubber is a draw. You honor your vowels, but keep the property."

Withersby gazed at the pile of parchment on the table. Marcus was offering his opponent an opportunity to walk away with his dignity intact. Although it was unlikely the puffed-up young fellow would avail himself of the generous offer.

As expected, Withersby's face grew hard with contempt. "Coward!" he flung at Marcus. "You're afraid I've mastered the game! You've no right to deprive me of the chance to best you!"

"Don't be a fool," James said. "He's showing you mercy."

"I won't go down like this." Withersby glared at Marcus. "Either we continue to play, or I'll call you out."

Suppressing his disgust, Marcus shrugged. "As you wish."

It seemed as if fate were punishing Withersby, for the next deal went against him. As Marcus scored *carte blanche*, then *quinte* in points, the younger man's disdainful façade cracked. His blue eyes grew hunted, and he tugged nervously at his cravat, ruining its perfect folds.

"*Pic*," Marcus said as he scored heavily in the first tricks.

Withersby gazed at his hand, then heaved his cards on the table.

"Do want to continue?" Marcus asked. "Have you something else you wish to wager?"

Withersby shook his head, glowering.

"Well, then." Marcus stood and flexed his shoulders. "Let's call it a night. Ludingham will be in touch with you regarding the transfer of the estate deed and payment on the other notes."

Withersby got to his feet, beads of sweat glittering on his forehead. "It's not so tidy as that. Although I control Horngate, the estate doesn't actually belong to me. I merely act as guardian."

James seized the note Withersby had signed and thrust it out. "Your signature is here, sir! If you didn't have the right to wager the property, you shouldn't have signed this!"

Marcus stiffened. Would he be forced to challenge the bastard? He had no taste for dueling, but he didn't intend to let Withersby cheat him out of what he'd fairly won.

"Of course I have the right to wager the property!" Withersby said. "I've been responsible for the estate for the past five years. I ought to get something for my trouble." He met Marcus's gaze evenly. "The property is yours, sir, if you're willing to marry the heiress of the estate—my cousin and ward."

Marry! Marcus knew a moment of shock but quickly recovered. Withersby didn't think he'd call his bluff. Well, the fool was about to discover exactly how seriously he took debts owed to him. "A minor stipulation," he responded, unruffled. "As long as the woman agrees. If she doesn't, I will call you out for trying to cheat me out of my fairly-won winnings."

Withersby gaped at him. "You'd marry a woman, sight unseen, to collect a gambling debt?"

"Why not? Once I take control of the property, we can go our separate ways. It will be a marriage in name only."

Withersby didn't react, but James flushed with outrage. "Marcus, you can't mean that! Withersby has no right to offer up his cousin as if she is a piece of livestock that comes with the estate. The woman must have some say!" He glared at Withersby. "Sir, how can you be certain she'll agree to this sham of a marriage?"

Withersby looked nonplussed, but when he answered his tone was defiant as ever. "My cousin will do as I tell her."

James turned back to Marcus. "I must advise you not to go through with this crude, ungentlemanly arrangement. No decent man would consider it."

"Maybe I'm not decent." Marcus had made up his mind. Withersby thought he was trapped. Well, the budding gamester was about to discover what it meant to get in too deep with Marcus Revington!

He met Withersby's gaze with calm implacability. "I'll need directions to the estate. I mean to waste no time in taking possession of my property."

Withersby's mouth twisted. "You're a contemptible blackguard, Revington. You'll be cut everywhere once the word gets out that you've taken a woman to wife as payment for a gambling debt."

"My behavior is no more reprehensible than yours. How dare you make a wager you don't believe can be collected?"

A hint of fear flickered in the young man's eyes, then the disdainful look returned. "You're collecting it, aren't you, Revington? That makes you more of a scoundrel than me." Withersby started for the door. "I'll take my leave now. I wish you every pleasure of married life," he added sourly.

"Here, now." James followed him. "We still need directions to the estate. And then there's the matter of the property deed."

"You may see my solicitor for that," Withersby called over his shoulder.

As Withersby's footsteps echoed down the stairs of the gaming house, James returned to the card table and sat heavily. "Well, I never…in all my days… Have you ever seen a gentlemen behave in such mean, underhanded fashion?"

Marcus's lip curled. "Gentleman? Withersby's no gentleman. That scheming weasel didn't even have the decency to tell me his cousin's name."

"Her name? You don't mean…you can't truly have any intention of pursuing this thing?"

"Of course I have. I've said as much."

"But, I thought you were bluffing!"

"You should have learned by now, James. I don't bluff, except at cards."

"But how can you take advantage of an innocent young woman?"

"What makes you think she's innocent? With a wretch like that for a cousin, she may be the most cunning and unprincipled of creatures."

"All the more reason not to take her to wife!"

"See here, James. Who are you worried for, her or me?"

"Well, I…both of you! You've never met the woman, and now you mean to bind yourself to her for life. This sort of cold, emotionless transaction might be appropriate if we were talking about horses or hunting hounds, but…do you truly mean to wed this woman sight unseen?"

"I've said I will."

"But what about fondness? Affection?"

"I fail to see how this is any different from the usual society marriage. Just because the woman's mama didn't bring her to London and parade her before the rich lords in attendance at Almack's doesn't make the arrangement any more shamelessly mercenary than most marriages among the *ton*."

"If she'd come out during the Season, she would have had a chance to meet you and form an opinion of you as a potential mate."

"Do you think she'll find me displeasing?"

James stared at Marcus a moment. "Well, you are a handsome devil, I'll give you that. But if the woman in question was my relative, I would be very disinclined to have her marry you."

"Why?"

"Because you're a…" James cleared his throat. "You spend all your time in gaming hells and men's clubs. Because you haven't been seen in the company of a decent woman in years. You're what the ladies call a rake, a hellion."

"And that disqualifies me as a desirable husband?" Marcus shot his friend an ironic smile.

The solicitor shook his head. "There's the matter of your reputation. If the circumstances of this marriage are talked around, it's bound to cause a scandal."

"You think I give a damn what the *ton* thinks of me? I intend to marry this woman. I want my future opponents to know I take wagers seriously."

"What if she won't have you?"

A tiny doubt blossomed in Marcus's mind. Withersby might have the power to coerce his cousin into marrying him, but did he really want to wed a woman against her will? Of course, that was exactly what Withersby was counting on. If he declined the marriage in order to spare the woman's feelings, Withersby would have won.

"If the woman refuses me, then it's *his* problem."

James sat back in his chair, looking defeated. Marcus paced across the room and wondered how far the estate was from London. He wanted this unsavory business finished as soon as possible. "Tomorrow you will contact Withersby's solicitor. Find out the location of the property and anything you can about the woman.

Then you'll need to procure a special license, so the marriage can take place as soon as we obtain the woman's agreement."

"If I had any moral principles, I'd refuse to help you," James said, gloomily.

Marcus smiled at him. "You know very well that even if you decline to be part of it, I'll still go through with my plans. This way you can make certain everything is done properly and as befits a transaction between gentlemen."

"*Gentlemen* do not barter off their female relatives to settle gambling debts." James's gaze met Marcus's. "Nor do gentlemen acquire wives simply to enrich themselves."

Marcus felt the familiar bitterness. "Maybe I'm not a gentleman. That possibility has been suggested to me on several occasions, usually by women who can no longer convince me to satisfy their whims, or men who have come out badly after a night of gaming. I don't allow such accusations to trouble me." He gave his friend a grim smile. "There are advantages to being a cold-hearted devil."

****

Penny was putting Juno through her paces when she saw her cousin coming down the trackway. *What the devil does Adrian want now? More money to gamble away, no doubt!*

She dismounted, tied the reins to the fence, and approached him. "'Lo, Adrian. What are you doing here?"

He glared at her. "What do you mean what am I doing here? I'm the guardian of the estate. I have a perfect right to visit and see how things are going!"

She crossed her arms over her chest. "What do you want—more money? Well, there won't be any until we sell off the newest bunch of hunters. And I refuse to do that until they're fully trained and we can get the best price possible. If you're completely dipped, you'll have to look elsewhere for funds."

"How dare you suggest I've come here demanding money! In fact, I made the long trip here for *your* benefit."

"My benefit?" She raised a brow, feeling extremely skeptical.

"Indeed. I've arranged for you to wed a fine gentlemen by the name of Revington. Marcus Revington. I decided I would salvage the family reputation and find you a husband."

She stared at him incredulously. "I don't want a husband. I'm perfectly happy with my life as it is!"

"Nonsense. It's not at all the thing for a woman past eighteen to remain unwed. People will talk, say you're 'on the shelf'."

"I don't care what people say. This is madness, Adrian. I've never done anything to make you think I want to get married. Besides, if I marry, the responsibility for the estate will pass to my husband. I can't imagine any man would tolerate your interference in... Oh!" She paused and stared at him. "That's it, isn't it? You've made some sort of arrangement with some greedy ne'er-do-well like yourself. You want me wed to a man of your choosing, so you can control both of us!"

"Now, Penny, I swear that isn't the way of it at all."

"Oh, really? Don't lie to me, Adrian. I know what

9

you're up to."

His expression turned hostile. "You've always thought the worst of me and never given me a chance. I'm sick of it. I do you a favor, and you act like I'm some sort of manipulative bastard who's coercing you against your will."

Penny told herself to remain calm. She knew how to handle Adrian. "No, I don't think you're coercing me, because I'm not going to do it. I won't wed this man, no matter what!" She turned and started back to the corrals.

He hurried after her. "But Penny...please. Revington's a fine-looking man. And clever. And..." He hesitated. "I imagine he's probably a very good rider."

She turned, shaking her head. "Really, Adrian. If I were ever to wed, I might have some other criteria in choosing a husband than those qualities. I would want a man with a kind nature and a generous heart and..." She thought for a moment. "And someone who enjoys life and loves to laugh."

His face changed. All at once he looked defeated. "But Penny, you don't understand. If you don't do this, I'm utterly done up."

"What do you mean? What sort of trouble are you in now?"

"I-I lost Horngate in a wager."

She gritted her teeth, then said, "No, you didn't, Adrian. You didn't lose Horngate. It doesn't belong to you, so you *can't* lose it."

"Unfortunately, the man I lost it to doesn't see things that way. In fact, he's suggested that if I don't cede the property to him, he'll kill me."

"What? Why, that's extortion! The law will deal with him."

"No, it's the gentlemen's code. If I renege on the wager, he has every right to call me out. And you know I'm a terrible shot. He'll kill me for certain."

"I can't believe this. I simply cannot believe this." She made her way to the fence and sagged against it. She'd always known her cousin was a wastrel. He'd already drained the estate of a good bit of blunt. But she'd never dreamed he'd do anything this foolish. Horngate was all she had. It was home. And it provided the means of doing what she wished with her life, which was training horses. If she lost Horngate, she would lose everything.

If Adrian had to fight a duel and this Revington fellow killed him, it was hardly her fault. But she couldn't do something so heartless. Adrian might be a worthless fool, but he was the only family she had left. She didn't want to live the rest of her life with his death on her conscience.

She straightened and faced him. "Very well. Give me the facts. What does Revington expect? Does he think we'll simply hand the place over to him? Because if I leave Horngate, I have no place to go. If he's any sort of gentlemen, he can't possibly mean to leave me utterly destitute."

"Oh, he doesn't intend that. Nor would I ever allow such a thing to happen. I told him, if he wanted the estate, he would have to marry you."

"Oh, dear heavens, we're back to that!" The sick feeling inside her deepened. Bad enough to have to marry and lose her freedom, but to wed some ruthless blackguard—it was unendurable.

"Don't look so glum, Penny. He doesn't intend for it to be a real marriage. And I promise you, I'll win back the property somehow. Or, we could sell all the horses. Then I'd have the funds to challenge him and win back Horngate…and more besides!"

"Don't be ridiculous, Adrian." She wanted to grab her cousin by his immaculate waistcoat and shake some sense into him. But that would never work. He was a hopeless bacon-brain and selfish besides. Sell the horses? She'd rather go to London and sell her body in a brothel. Somehow she was going to have to fix this. Find some way of making Revington forget Adrian's ridiculous wager. But to do that, she needed to know more about her adversary. "See, here, Adrian, what's this Mr. Revington like?"

He shrugged. "Usual gamester. Hard. Cunning. Arrogant."

Oh, wonderful. "Does he have any weaknesses you can think of?"

"Don't know him well enough to say."

"And his family background—where does his gambling money come from?"

"He's the younger son of a viscount. Suppose he gets his blunt from them."

"He's a gentleman, then?"

"Of a fashion. Fairly well known among the *ton.* But I think many people avoid him because he's so dashed lucky at cards. Always winning, from what I've heard."

"So, of course, you challenged him," she said, coldly.

"I think he cheats." Adrian's face had flushed an unpleasant shade of red. "He's too clever to get caught, that's all."

Penny closed her eyes and took a deep breath. The more she learned about her prospective bridegroom, the more disheartened she felt.

She opened her eyes again. "If he's so 'dashed lucky' as you put it, then he can't be in desperate need of funds. Which raises the question, why is he willing to marry a woman he's never met in order to acquire a modest property like Horngate?"

"I've no idea," Adrian answered. "Maybe he's just so stubborn and proud that he refuses to ever forgive a wager."

Stubborn. Proud. Those qualities could end up being weaknesses. After all, it was Adrian's pride that was *his* downfall. She tried to consider what was the worst thing Adrian could ever experience. Probably it would be to endure some sort of public humiliation. If that was Adrian's bane, then it might be Revington's also.

How could she take advantage of Revington's arrogance and make him back down? Exposing him as a cheat would do the trick, but her cousin had obviously tried that and failed. What other means of embarrassing him might there be?

She glanced down at her scuffed hessions, and then at the worn, dirty buckskins and much-mended linen shirt she'd borrowed from Tad when the groom outgrew them a few seasons ago. Adrian was always telling her how disgraceful she looked. How she dressed like a street urchin and acted more like a stable boy than a lady. She assumed he said such spiteful things in part because he was jealous of her skill with horses, but there was probably some truth to his words.

Which meant a London gentleman like Revington might consider her less than desirable as a wife.

A plan slowly unfolded in her mind. What if Revington met her and was so appalled at the thought of marrying her that he decided Horngate wasn't worth it? Adrian was right. Revington couldn't simply turn her out. He had to marry her if he wanted the estate. All she had to do was make that course of action so unappealing he would agree to settle for some other form of compensation. If she could get him to wait until fall and sell off the latest bunch of hunters, she might have enough to satisfy at least part of the debt. She'd certainly rather owe him the estate's profits for the next few years than marry him!

"I have an idea," she told her cousin. "It's a simple plan, but it might work."

****

As the coach drove down the long gravel drive to Horngate House, Marcus gave a low whistle. "Even if my wife-to-be is as homely as sin, marrying her will be worth it to acquire this place."

"It looks rather rundown," James said. "And there's no telling how much of this pastureland and woods belong to the estate. I didn't have a chance to look at the deed before we left London. It might include no more than the house and the grounds immediately surrounding it."

Marcus gestured to a pasture in the distance where a several chestnut mares and their foals grazed. "Someone is raising horses on the property. I can't imagine a wastrel like Withersby would be involved in such an endeavor."

"All the more reason to think the land we're

passing through belongs to some neighboring landowner."

As they progressed down the drive and neared the house, Marcus knew an intense satisfaction. The house itself was a fine old dwelling, built of grayish stone with a slate roof and high mullioned windows. "If I ever have a fancy to retire to the country, this would be the perfect place," he mused.

"I can't exactly see you as a country gentlemen."

"Quite true. But it might be entertaining to come up in the fall and do some running to the hounds. That is, if the estate still retains hunting rights."

The phaeton rolled to a stop in front of the house; the two men climbed out and stretched. "I wonder if there are any grooms or footmen about. The place looks deserted," Marcus said.

"Perhaps Miss Montgomery heard you were coming and ran away. I can't say I would blame her under the circumstances."

"She'd better not have disappeared. If she has, I swear I'll find Withersby and call him out. He promised her consent would not be a difficulty."

James sighed. "I have to say one more time that I don't like this above half. The whole arrangement seems quite uncivilized."

Marcus regarded his friend with a lazy smile. "I know, James, I know. That's why you're the solicitor and I'm the gamester. With your fine moral sense, you wouldn't last a week in the circles I frequent."

They both turned at the sound of hoof beats. A huge stallion barreled down the drive, its rider bent low over the withers. Halfway to the house, the rider reined in the magnificent animal. Blowing and snorting, the beast slowed to a trot and, finally, a walk. As horse and rider approached, Marcus couldn't help gaping at the young woman controlling the stallion. He'd never seen a female ride like *that* before!

She halted the stallion and, before either of them could assist her, leapt down and faced them. The woman was dressed in soiled men's clothing, and her brown hair hung down in messy wisps around her face. "So, which one of you is the London bloke I'm supposed to wed?"

James gestured to Marcus. "This is Mr. Revington. I'm James Ludingham, his solicitor."

The woman extended a grimy hand to Marcus. "Pleased to meet you."

Marcus stared at her in astonishment "You're Miss Montgomery?"

"Yes, but you can call me Penny, everyone does. The house is there, see." She pointed. "Mrs. Foxworthy will offer you something if you knock. I really can't be bothered with playing hostess. I've got to get back to the stables. We're gelding the colts today, and they need me to do the cauterizing. Good meeting you though, Mr. Revington, Mr. Ludingham." She turned and mounted the stallion, then cantered back down the lane.

"Hmmm," James said. "What were you saying about marrying the woman sight unseen?"

Marcus swallowed, trying to get over his shock. "I'll allow she is a bit eccentric, but that hardly matters. It's really quite simple. She'll go her way and I'll go mine." His words belied the uneasy feeling in the pit of his stomach. Gads! The chit was an utter hoyden. He'd encountered Covent Garden orange girls who had more polish than Miss Montgomery. But at least she wasn't unattractive. Despite the dirt and her disheveled hair, she had huge blue eyes and pert, pretty features, and the masculine clothing only served to emphasize her leggy but clearly feminine form.

"There is the small matter of the marriage ceremony," James reminded him. "Unless you think to get a clergyman to perform the rites in the barn, you may have a problem."

"Well, she's bound to come back to the house sometime. We'll discuss the details then. Meanwhile, I'm starved. Let's hope this Mrs. Foxworthy is a bit more hospitable than her mistress."

****

"Damn! He's still here!" Penny grimaced as she and Tad walked up to the house and saw the phaeton in the driveway.

"At least he had the decency to have someone unhitch the horses and take them to the barn," Tad pointed out. The dark-haired youth went to examine the carriage. "Fine rig, too. Think he drove it here himself?"

"Probably. He looked like he could handle a team easily enough." That was an understatement. She'd been expecting some dandified tulip like Adrian. It had been a shock to discover Revington was a very different sort of man. The lines of his immaculately tailored coat emphasized his well-formed, muscular physique. And with his striking jet-black hair and dark eyes, he managed to seem both elegant and formidable. If he'd been a stallion, she'd have bought in on the spot.

"What now?" Tad asked.

She turned to the house, chewing her lower lip.

"Let's sneak in and see what we can find out about our adversary."

Tad nodded. The two of them went around and entered by the servants' entrance. Mrs. Foxworthy had put their guests in the drawing room. As they approached and heard voices, Penny nodded in satisfaction to her companion. She and Tad crouched near the open door and listened.

"Grand old place, isn't it?" a man remarked in a rich, baritone voice. "I wonder what year it was built."

"That's Revington," Penny whispered to Tad.

"It's not bad, I suppose," the other man responded. "But think of the work and the investment it would take to get it up to civilized standards. You hardly have time for such an endeavor."

"I suppose you're right. The main thing is to get the chit in front of an altar and settle this business. I can worry about what to do with the property later."

"You're incorrigible, Marcus. You still mean to go through with this? The woman obviously has no manners. To barely greet us, then rush off to the stables." He tsked loudly.

"I don't care a fig for her manners. It's not as if I intend to have her presented at court."

"But you will have to spend some time with her. There is the matter of the…er, uh…consummation of the marriage."

Penny felt her face flush. She moved farther back from the doorway.

"You really think that will be necessary?" Revington asked.

"Oh, absolutely. Withersby's just the sort to cry foul if you don't go through with all the proper legal details."

"I suppose you're right. Well, it shouldn't be much of a hardship. She's obviously got all the proper female parts, despite her outlandish clothing. And I actually thought she was rather appealing, under all that dirt and scraggly hair. Quite lovely blue eyes, did you notice?"

Penny stiffened. He'd called her hair scraggly, the bastard! But then, that had been her aim. Besides, he'd also said her eyes were lovely.

"Yes, I suppose she's got potential, just as the house does." The other man sounded irritated. "But do you really have time for any of this? Shouldn't you be getting back to London? If you're gone too long, the deep-pocketed players will find someone else to lose their money to."

"Will they? In only a day?" Revington's voice rang with sarcasm. "Why don't you stop fighting me, James? It's no use. You know how stubborn I am."

James sighed. "So, I do. But dash it, you're also usually impatient. Are you really going to sit around here all day waiting for the chit to show herself?"

"Of course not. We'll give her a little while longer. If she's not back before three, we'll walk down to the stables and fetch her."

Penny motioned to Tad that she'd heard enough. They crept back down the hall and out the way they'd come.

"I, say, what are you going to do now?" Tad's freckled brow furrowed in concentration. "You could hide from him. Horngate is big enough that you might elude him for a few days."

"Hide from him?" Penny shook her head. "I'm mistress here. I won't sneak around like an errant child

19

avoiding punishment."

The groom shook his head. "He's a greedy bastard. You can hear it in his voice. And stubborn, too. Said so himself. It's not going to be easy to convince him to give up Horngate."

Penny was having the same thoughts, but she refused to give in to them. "It's far too soon to admit defeat." She squared her shoulders. "I'm going up to change. The second phase of my scheme is about to begin."

Chapter Two

"Given up yet?" James put down his cup and jerked his head toward the clock on the mantel.

Marcus grimaced and got to his feet. "I suppose I'll have to fetch her."

The next moment, Miss Montgomery entered the room. She was dressed in a hideous green day dress at least ten years out of fashion. It hung on her slender form like a sack. She'd made some attempt to arrange her hair, but it was an inept effort at best. Wisps floated around her face in wild disarray.

She smiled at them, then hurried to the refreshment table. "Cook makes the best cherry tarts, don't you think?" She stuffed one into her mouth, juice dribbling down her chin. "And these cucumber sandwiches... Mmmm...divine."

As she gobbled down several, Marcus watched in amazement. The chit was more than eccentric. She was downright batty. Or maybe she'd never been taught the manners of a lady. Stuck away in the country, orphaned at a young age, she might have had no one to teach her.

But Mrs. Foxworthy, the housekeeper, appeared gracious and polite. Odd that a servant would seem more well-bred than her mistress. Was he being gammoned here? Had Withersby convinced his cousin to present herself as an ill-mannered, awkward gapeseed so he would back out of the marriage? But the

21

woman appeared so innocent, those wide blue eyes incapable of deceit.

She turned from the table, still chewing. "So, when do we leave for London? I can't wait to see all the sights. The opera, the balls and parties, Almack's." She approached him, smiling ingenuously. "And if it's possible, I would very much like to be presented to the Prince Regent. It's my fondest wish."

For a moment, Marcus couldn't speak. He cleared his throat. "Miss Montgomery...I—that is, there's no reason for you to come to London at all. You see, under the circumstances, this marriage is really a business arrangement. While it is necessary that we exchange vows in order for me to...um, take ownership of the property, it really isn't going to be a marriage in the true sense of the word."

Something flashed in her eyes, a hint of pure fury. Then it was gone, her expression as wide-eyed and guileless as ever. "Oh. Adrian didn't tell me any of that. He made it seem that you...that we..." She looked as if she was going to cry.

James cleared his throat, and although Marcus refused to look at him, he knew his solicitor was regarding him with profound disapproval.

Guilt wrapped around Marcus's neck like a noose. If this woman was even half as innocent as she appeared, he was using her badly. And then there was the matter of consummating the marriage. If, as James suggested, Adrian was going to insist on that legality, his explanation to Miss Montgomery was inaccurate. A business arrangement did not generally involve sexual intimacy.

"Miss Montgomery, I'm sorry that your

cousin…that he misled you regarding the terms of our…relationship. You see, having not even met you, I assumed that—"

Dabbing at her eyes, she broke in, "I may be an unsophisticated country miss, but every woman dreams of her wedding day, of wearing a beautiful dress and being feted and admired. I know I have no right to ask it of you, but I really do desire a proper wedding."

Marcus took a deep breath. What could he say? "Of course, you have the right. I didn't really think…about any of this. You should come out of this arrangement with something. It's only fair…"

She smiled at him through her tears, and something inside Marcus twisted. Despite the horrible dress and untidy hair, she was one of the loveliest creatures he'd ever seen. Those huge blue eyes, elegant arched brows and temptingly full lips. She made him want to kiss all her tears away. "I-I'm certain something can be worked out. If you really desire to come to London for the wedding… And you should have some new clothing." He motioned to the green garment. "I'm hardly an expert in that sort of thing, but really, that gown doesn't do a thing for you."

She looked down at herself. "I'm afraid it's all I have. I'm always been so busy with the horses I never have an opportunity to dress up. I would love a chance to purchase a new wardrobe. I've heard that in London, a woman must wear something new nearly every day. Day dresses, riding costumes, pelisses, shoes and hats."

Marcus felt a stirring of unease. How much would all this cost him? Miss Montgomery was a substantial heiress, but her assets were likely tied up in the horse operation and the estate. When it came to purchases in

London, it would be *his* money she spent.

"I'm certain something can be arranged." Despite the sinking feeling in his gut, he told himself it would be all right. He might have to spend some money to properly dress Miss Montgomery, but it would be worth it to possess Horngate. For someone who'd lived in rented houses for the past ten years, the idea of owning property was thrilling. And he wasn't about to give up what he'd fairly won. Miss Montgomery was simply a complication in his plan. A most startling and unpredictable complication.

Once again, he searched for a hint of Miss Montgomery's true character beneath her artlessly pretty countenance.

Was she simply a naïve country girl who'd been taken advantage of by her scheming cousin? Or was there more to her? It bothered him he was so affected by her appearance. He couldn't seem to think clearly around her. She distracted him, a dangerous situation for a gamester.

But then, she wouldn't be around long. She'd stay at his townhouse a few days while she was appropriately outfitted and saw some of the amusements of London. Then they'd be married and he would insist she return to Horngate. If she did take a fancy to the London social whirl—which he could hardly imagine, given her obvious passion for horses and farm life—he would explain he was seldom invited to parties. In fact, as a gamester who'd won considerable sums of money off members of the *ton*, he was generally avoided by the upper echelons of society.

"A London wedding it is," he said. "You can ride back with us today, then stay at my townhouse until all the arrangements can be made."

"You want me to leave today? But what about my responsibilities here?"

"Now, see here, Miss Montgomery, I'm a busy man. I'm not going all the way back to the city, then return in a few days to fetch you. If you want the marriage to take place in London, you'll have to find a way to come with me now." Harsh, but necessary. He wouldn't let this chit, appealing though she might be, dictate his life.

She pursed her lips, an extremely provocative gesture, then nodded. "I suppose I could get Mr. Hareton to take over with the horses. But it's already late in the day. By the time I get a few things together, it will be nearly dark."

"We'll travel as far as we can, then stay in an inn for the night."

"But is that proper, sir, given that we're not wed?"

"Bring a maid with you, if you're concerned about the proprieties." He was getting irritated. The woman seemed to be wracking her brain for reasons to delay.

"I'll go pack," she finally said, then moved toward the door with aggravating slowness.

As soon as she was gone, James addressed Marcus in a smug voice. "So, it's going to be a one-day affair, is it? A quick visit to the country to get married, then back to London and your normal routine?"

"Perhaps it's more complicated than I thought," Marcus responded. "But I can handle this, have no doubt of it. It's just like cosseting a child. Distract them with a few treats and they'll willingly go along with your plans. I'll purchase a few gowns for Miss Montgomery, take her around to see the city. After that, she'll go to the altar quite eagerly."

"A child, is she? I think you underestimate Miss Montgomery."

Remembering the flash of keen intelligence he'd glimpsed in her eyes, Marcus wondered if his friend wasn't on to something. "Do you think this is all pretense? Her hoydenish behavior when we arrived? The disgraceful manners? The wretched gown? Maybe Withersby put her up to this. He might think I'll be so appalled at the prospect of marrying her that I'd hightail it back to London and forget about the wager."

"Perhaps," James said thoughtfully. "If that's the case, do you really want to be wed to a woman who'd do something so conniving?"

"Dammit! I don't want to be married at all! I'm only going through with this to collect the debt owed me." Marcus raked his fingers through his hair. What if Miss Montgomery was playing him for a fool? His resolve hardened. He'd faced clever opponents many times before and always managed to outsmart them. "Maybe she is a shrewd little minx. It really doesn't matter. I still intend to have my way in this."

****

"What happened?" Tad demanded as soon as Penny met him behind the house.

"Nothing. He seems as determined as ever to marry me."

"The gown? Stuffing your face with food? None of it scared him off?"

Penny shook her head. "He's so consumed with greed, I think he could have discovered I was bald and toothless and he'd still marry me."

"Well, that's part of the problem. It's not easy to

make someone like you look ugly."

Penny gazed at him in surprise. "Really? You think so?"

"Of course. All the fellows do. But we can hardly make a fuss over you under the circumstances. You're our mistress and far above us."

"Bosh. That's nonsense." Penny felt herself blushing. The stable hands were her friends. She worked side-by-side with them. She didn't want them to think of her as some snobby, nose-in-the-air miss.

"Anyway, I suspect that's part of the trouble. Revington can see you're worth having, and he's not about to let go of his prize."

"Well, I've put him off for a while. Although I had to change tactics. I told him I've always dreamed of a big, fancy London wedding. He fell for it, but something like that's bound to take time to arrange. Now I'll have a week or two to convince him just how much trouble I would be as a wife. Problem is, I'll have to pursue my plan on my own. He insists I go to London with him today."

"Can't you talk him out of it? Tell him to go and make the arrangements, and you'll meet him there in a week?"

"I doubt it. He was very firm about my coming today. Besides, while such an agreement might buy some time, it wouldn't accomplish our objective. I need to be around him, a constant source of difficulty and irritation. It's going to take a lot to drive him to the point where he's willing to give up Horngate."

"Well, dash it, I wish I could go with you."

She smiled at Tad. "I wish you could, too. Maybe I'll ask him. That might unsettle him a bit, to think that while I don't have a maid, I'm quite cozy with my groom."

****

Marcus and James waited in the drawing room. And waited. When the clock on the mantel struck five, Marcus stood. "I'm going up and see how her packing is progressing."

"You can't do that," James protested.

"Watch me."

He rounded the corner to the stairs, just as Penny was coming down. She'd added a straw hat covered with garish purple flowers to her unflattering costume and carried a small valise. "I'm ready," she said as she reached the bottom. "Although I would like to ask another favor of you. I was hoping Tad could come with us. We've always been inseparable. It's going to be hard to get along without him."

"Tad?"

"He's one of the grooms from the stables." She flashed him a charming, little-girl smile. "We're ever so close. And I'm afraid I'll be lonely in London all by myself."

Good heavens! This chit really had no notion of the proprieties! Exactly how "close" a relationship did she have with this fellow? A spark of jealousy flashed through Marcus. "I'm sorry, Miss Montgomery." He sought to make his voice gentle and concerned-sounding. "But such a thing simply isn't done. Now, if you have a female servant or relative you would like to accompany you, that's another matter altogether."

"I really have no one." Tears glittered in her expressive eyes. "No family at all, and Cook and Mrs. Foxworthy are the only female servants at Horngate. I

28

could hardly ask one of them to accompany me. They're needed here."

"Well, I'm certain we can employ a maid for you from one of the agencies, so you won't be altogether alone. Besides, you won't be in London that long. Only a week or so, enough time to have the wedding and to settle business matters."

"But what about the banns? Isn't there a waiting period before we can be wed?"

Marcus tried not to let his smile become too smug. "I've purchased a special license. We can have the ceremony as soon as we purchase your dress and I can arrange things with a clergyman."

"Oh." This set her back a bit, he could tell.

"We can discuss things further in the carriage," he said firmly, then took her valise. "Is someone bringing down your other luggage?"

"This is all I have. Nothing else is fit for London. And you did say you would buy me a new wardrobe."

First it was a wedding dress and a few things. Now it was a whole wardrobe. Marcus gritted his teeth as they left the house.

She paused before the carriage. "Wait! I must say goodbye to Tad." She ran off, skirts raised to her ankles, looking as fleet and graceful as a deer.

"So, who is this Tad fellow?" James asked as Marcus secured the valise on the back of the vehicle.

"A groom from the stables. It appears Miss Montgomery is quite taken with him."

"Are you jealous?" James teased.

"Don't be absurd. Even if she's shared a few kisses with the fellow, why should it matter to me?"

"Because she'll soon be your wife. I suspect that

once she becomes Mrs. Revington, you'll discover you're not as detached as you thought."

"That's preposterous. I'm not about to get emotionally entangled with a woman, any woman."

"Who's to say you'll have any control over the matter?"

Marcus shook his head. "James, you've been out in the sun too long. One minute you're complaining I'm a cold-hearted, mercenary devil. The next you're warning me not to fall in love."

"I'm merely trying to point out that there may be other pitfalls to this arrangement. Pitfalls you may not have thought about."

"Ah. I see your plan. If you can't convince me of the impropriety of this marriage, you mean to try to frighten me out of it. Well, it won't work. I'm not some lovesick fool. I've said this is a business arrangement, and that's all it's going to be."

"What about taking her to bed? That's hardly a business endeavor. It isn't going to be a matter of simply servicing her, as if you were a stallion and she a mare. At least I *hope* you approach the matter with a bit more finesse than that."

James's words aroused enticing images in Marcus's mind. Miss Montgomery was a spirited little filly—long-limbed, sleek, and wild. What would it be like to tame her? To feel her lithe, yet undeniably female, body beneath his, shuddering and bucking with excitement... Bloody hell! He had to stop thinking like that!

"I'm sure I'll manage, when the time comes." He fixed James with a look meant to suggest that further discussion of the subject would take place at the peril of his physical wellbeing.

At last Miss Montgomery reappeared. Marcus helped her into the carriage, then took his place in the driver's box. Let James match wits with her for a while. He needed a rest from trying to figure out the puzzling Miss Montgomery.

****

"Miss Montgomery." Mr. Revington's companion nodded to Penny, then sat back against the squabs. "Since Marcus has been remiss in making formal introductions, let me tell you about myself. I'm Marcus's solicitor, but also his friend. We went to school together. My family has known his family for generations. Since you're apparently going to marry Marcus, I think it would be perfectly proper for you to call me James."

"Thank you, James." Penny flashed him her most charming smile. If she'd read things right, this man was her ally. "And you must call me Penny."

"Delightful. Tell me about yourself, Miss...that is, Penny."

"I'm afraid there's not much to tell. I've lived at Horngate all my life. My parents died of a fever when I was sixteen. Since then I've managed on my own, with the help of the farmhands and servants, of course."

"How sad to be orphaned at such a young age. And your guardian, I take it that would be Mr. Withersby?"

"Indeed." She found she couldn't quite control her bitter smile.

"Ah," James said. "How much do you know about the...er, the arrangement between your cousin and Marcus?"

Penny felt a twinge of warning. She dare not

Mary Gillgannon

appear too shrewd. Even though James seemed to be on her side, it was possible he was testing her. "Of course Adrian told me that Mr. Revington and I were to marry. It would have been very awkward if you arrived at Horngate with me having no foreknowledge of your purpose there."

"Quite. And what did your cousin tell you regarding Marcus?"

"Only that he'd found a gentleman he thought would be a good match for me, and that he would be arriving within a day or two."

She felt James's eyes on her, weighing and assessing. "What do you think of Marcus, Miss Montgomery? Your honest opinion, not what Adrian may have told you to say."

Careful, careful. Penny made her eyes wide, and slipping back into her role as ill-mannered hoyden said, "Why, I hardly know the bloke, do I? How could I possibly have an opinion about him?"

"But you're willing to marry him anyway? Even though you profess to know little of his character?"

"Adrian says he's a fine gentleman and well-regarded in London."

"You trust your cousin's judgment, do you?"

She'd been caught out. Her contempt for Adrian showed too clearly. Somehow she had to soften it. "Well, not about finances or horses, no. But he is my closest relative, and I don't think he'd marry me off to some blackguard or scoundrel." She jerked around to face her coach companion, feigning anxiety. "What are you trying to tell me, James?" She cast a nervous glance at the man in the driver's seat and lowered her voice to a whisper. "Is there some reason I shouldn't wed Mr. Revington?"

"Why, no." James cleared his throat, a mannerism that suggested he was very uncomfortable. He also glanced toward the driver's box, then back at her. "He's a fine gentleman. I value his friendship a great deal. And as I've told you, his family and mine have been acquainted for years."

"Oh, thank goodness." Penny collapsed against the squabs. "For a moment, I thought you were trying to warn about Mr. Revington's motives. As an heiress, I must be careful. It's possible some fortune hunter would seek my hand in marriage solely for the purpose of acquiring Horngate and my other assets."

"Yes," James said gravely. "That's entirely possible."

Silence reigned for a time, as Penny struggled to control her expression. Poor James. He was obviously an honorable man who'd been dragged into this awkward situation through no fault of his own. She sensed his turmoil. He didn't want her to marry Revington, but his loyalty to his friend prevented him from saying so. His attitude was something of a relief. A man like that wouldn't associate with anyone who was a complete fiend. Revington must at least have some redeeming features.

Like a blindingly handsome face...and an impressive, athletic build... No! She couldn't allow herself to be distracted by such superficial attributes. Revington was a calculating, ruthless fortune hunter, the exact sort of man of which she must be wary. She had to continue with her plan. If she made his life utterly miserable, a spoiled, shallow London swell like Revington would eventually give up and move on to easier quarry.

James cleared his throat again. "Tell me about your horses, Miss Montgomery, the breeding and training operation you manage at Horngate."

Penny took a deep breath. She must try not to be too enthusiastic. No need to hint at the sort of money the estate was making—and Adrian was losing in the gambling hells. "We've been breeding jumpers for ten years now. My father began the line with Hero's sire. That's the horse I was riding when you first arrived. The market for carriage horses is more dependable, but you don't make as much as with hunters. And frankly, it's more of a challenge to train horses for running game. They must be fast and know how to jump, but also have stamina..."

She went on until James's eyes glazed over. No doubt he would warn Revington not to ask her about horses. No matter. She'd find some opportunity to bore him with endless details just the same. A horse-mad hoyden with no manners and no sense of style—why would any wealthy London gentleman want to marry a woman like that?

"The business sounds profitable," James said when she finally ran out of mind-numbing equestrian detail. "It appears Horngate has done well these past few years."

Penny tensed with warning. She didn't want him to guess how well. "Oh, Adrian handles all the business interests of the estate," she said off-handedly. "I don't know much about the farm's income."

"Don't you at least know how much the horses you raise sell for?"

"No. A man in the village handles all that and

reports the income to Adrian."

"So, you never personally participated in the actual sale?"

"Adrian always told me that no man would buy a horse from a woman. He said we'd get much better prices if we had his man handle the transaction."

"I suppose there's something to that." James fell silent again, as if he'd apparently run out of topics for small talk. Penny took this opportunity to yawn and stretch back against the squabs. "I'm a bit sleepy. Do you mind if I nap?"

"Of course not."

She wasn't tired at all, but it was a strain to live by her wits. Besides, she needed time to plan her strategy once they reached London. Her main scheme was to be so profligate in her spending that Revington would become convinced having her as his wife would cost him more than the income Horngate could provide. She'd seen the look on his face when she'd mentioned buying a new wardrobe. He obviously hadn't considered that having a wife might be expensive. Well, the greedy gamester was about to learn otherwise.

Chapter Three

"Miss Montgomery, wake up. We've arrived at the inn."

Penny feigned awakening. "What station is this?"

"It's Petersfield, miss," James said. "I hope they can accommodate us. It looks rather crowded."

In the purplish twilight, she made out the dark shape of the inn, with lights winking from nearly every window. The barouche pulled into the yard full of carriages and rigs, and an osteler came up to hold the team. Revington jumped down from the driving box; James climbed out of the carriage and offered his hand to Penny.

Revington scarcely glanced at her before striding toward the inn. James took her arm. "Allow me to escort you, miss."

****

"One room? That's all you have?"

The innkeeper shook his head at Marcus. "'Fraid so, sir. You're lucky I saved it back for someone of quality like yourself. Could have filled it several times over, but I guessed there might be someone coming along who'd be willin' to pay extra for their accommodations."

The balding man gave him a shrewd look and Marcus felt a muscle twitch in his jaw. The bastard was going to charge him double; he knew it. "But there's three of us." He gestured to Penny and James, who'd just come in. "I really don't see how we'll manage."

"Oh, it's quite a large room, sir. With an adjoining parlor. The gentleman and his wife…" He nodded to Penny and James. "They could take the bed, and you could sleep on the settle in the parlor."

"The lady is with *me,*" Marcus corrected him.

The innkeeper shrugged. "Then you and she can have the bed and the other man takes the settle."

"I suppose so," Marcus snapped. He was rather dismayed with the idea of sharing a bed with Penny, but it was certainly preferable to sleeping with James.

He returned to where Penny and James were waiting. "The innkeeper only has one room left. Apparently there's some sort of fair going on, and the place is crammed full." He looked at Penny. "He says it's a big room, with an adjoining parlor where James can sleep. But it means we'll have to share a bed. It's a bit awkward, since we're not wed yet, but…"

"I'm sure we'll manage." Penny shrugged.

Marcus motioned. "If you'd like to go up and change." Remembering that she only had one dress, he added, "Or at least tidy up a bit. I'll have the innkeeper show you the way. James and I will wait for you in the taproom."

****

Penny felt unsettled as she followed the innkeeper's wife up the stairs. She'd agreed to share a bed with Revington because she could tell the idea discomfited him. But she was none too happy about it. She didn't think he'd attempt intimacy—not with James in the next room. But even so, she wasn't comfortable with the thought of being so close to him. To have his big male body mere inches from her own. How would she ever sleep?

Of course, having to sleep with her would be another inconvenience for him. Perhaps with what else she had planned, he'd finally give up and take her back to Horngate. *Please, please let this work! Let him realize what a trial it would be to have me as his wife!*

****

"Admit it, Marcus, it feels good to relax and drink a brandy." James settled back into his chair in the taproom. "We're too damned old for such foolishness as driving all night."

Marcus gave his friend a black look. "You're not the one who has to negotiate the awkwardness of sharing a bed with her."

"You might as well get used to it, since she's going to be your wife."

"Most married couples of my acquaintance have separate bedchambers, let alone beds," Marcus responded icily. "The only time they're forced into such close proximity is for the purpose of begetting an heir."

"Are you going to attempt to consummate the marriage tonight, or wait until you're officially wed?"

"Wait, of course. There's no reason to take things to that point until it's absolutely necessary. Besides, you'll be sleeping in the adjoining parlor."

"From your tone, you'd think it was going to be a great trial to bed Miss Montgomery. Frankly, I don't understand your distaste. Her wretched attire aside, she's actually very attractive."

"Yes, she is," agreed Marcus.

"You needn't look so glum about it." James laughed.

Marcus leaned back and shook his head. "Frankly, this whole marriage business has been disconcerting."

"Well, you aren't committed yet. In the morning, you could return Miss Montgomery to Horngate and forget the whole thing."

"Yes, I could."

"You're considering it?"

"Don't look so bloody hopeful, James. But you're right. I have considered abandoning the whole notion of collecting on Withersby's debt. You know why I won't?"

"You're so taken with Miss Montgomery that you can't imagine living without her?"

Marcus raised his brows. Some remarks didn't deserve comment. "I'm going through with this for two reasons. I refuse to let a worthless wretch like Withersby get the best of me, and second, I've decided Horngate is exactly what I've been missing in my life."

"Horngate, *not* Miss Montgomery?"

He let this pass as well. "I've earned a fair amount of money gambling, and I'm able to live well, if not extravagantly. But I've never owned property. My townhouse is rented, as were my apartments previously. As long as my brother Reginald lives, I have no claim on the family holdings, not even a hunting lodge or cottage. Horngate is likely the only chance I'll ever have to own property free and clear."

"You could buy a townhouse, or even a small estate. Or you could gamble for another property."

"No, it's Horngate I want. It feels like a-a home."

"It is. It's Miss Montgomery's home. What about her? Do you intend to banish her to the barn once you're wed?"

"Of course not. It's a good-sized house, and she appears to spend a great deal of time off with the horses. We'll share."

"A business arrangement, as you've said."

"Exactly. All I have to do is get through with the awkward marriage business and the rest of it will fall into place."

"I have a suspicion it isn't going to be quite so easy."

"What makes you say that?"

James shrugged. "I don't know. Something about talking to Miss Montgomery. She's no fool."

"You think she has some clever plan to convince me not to marry her?"

"Maybe. And I can't truly blame her. Withersby has used her badly in this."

"Which is all the more reason she'll be better off once she's married to me," argued Marcus. "I'll deal with her much more fairly than that bastard has!"

"Perhaps you should discuss the matter with her. Negotiate her capitulation, if you will."

"There's no need for that. She's agreed to the marriage already."

"Has she?"

"Why, yes. All she's asked is that it takes place in London, be a proper wedding, and that I purchase her a new wardrobe."

James raised his brows skeptically. "I don't know. I think you're making assumptions that may end up being proven wrong."

"I see. A few minutes of conversation with Miss Montgomery and you claim to know her mind. Expert on women, are you, James?"

"No, certainly not. I merely think that this marriage business is much more complicated than you believe it is."

Marcus was getting irritated. It didn't help that Miss Montgomery hadn't come down yet. She only had one change of clothing. How long could it take for her to ready herself for dinner? He turned back to his companion. "So, tell me, how do *you* intend to approach the matter of matrimony?"

"Well, when I do marry, it won't be to settle a gambling debt. I'm going to find the perfect wife."

"And what qualities will this paragon possess?"

"I prefer fair hair…and blue eyes. She should be well, smaller than Miss Montgomery and with some"— he cleared his throat—"nice curves here and there."

"Miss Montgomery has nice curves."

"Indeed she does," James agreed. "Those trousers she wore when we met made that quite obvious."

Marcus felt a stab of jealousy. Once Miss Montgomery was his wife, he wouldn't let her go around in such shameful attire. He didn't want the whole world to know what a nicely rounded bottom she had. And those long, long legs… With effort, he forced his mind away from the thought. "What else?" he asked James. "What other attributes do you seek in a wife?"

"Well, she doesn't have to be rich, but a nice income or some property would certainly be welcome. And I don't require that she be proficient at music or art, but I insist she know how to manage a household. She should also be frugal. I don't want a woman who runs up outrageous bills." James gave a shudder. "I can't abide profligate women."

"Well, I'm fortunate in that way, aren't I? My new

wife is clearly not a spendthrift, at least in regards to clothing or personal effects."

"Either that, or she's had no opportunity to purchase things for herself. If Withersby controls all the finances for the estate, he may have her on some pitiful allowance."

Marcus frowned. It disturbed him to think his bride-to-be had been ill-treated. It also alarmed him to realize she might make up for past deprivations with *his* money.

They continued to discuss James's requirements in a spouse. As his friend recited his prerequisites in exacting detail, Marcus began to enjoy himself. He'd wager odds ten to one that James would end up marrying a woman who was nothing like his ideal. It should be amusing to watch his fantasy crumble away.

Then his thoughts turned to his own future spouse. "Where can she be?" He got to his feet. "I guess I'll have to fetch her."

"I'll wait here." James hoisted his second glass of port.

Marcus climbed the stairs and went down the hall to the door the innkeeper had directed him to. He knocked softly. There was no answer. He knocked again, more briskly this time. Again, no answer. He took a deep breath and opened the door.

The parlor was empty. He entered the adjoining bedchamber. There was no one in that room either. *What the devil!*

He went to the water closet down the hall and knocked. Nothing. Miss Montgomery had vanished. He hurriedly retraced his steps down to the taproom. "She's gone," he told James.

"Gone?" James rose unsteadily. "How can that be? Are you certain you didn't miss her?"

"If she isn't in the room and she isn't down here, then where the hell is she?" He was angry, but also a little worried. What if something had happened to her? He really should have gone up much earlier and escorted her down to dinner.

James echoed his fears. "I hope someone didn't accost her on the way to the dining room."

"Damn," Marcus muttered. "I'll go talk to the innkeeper."

The innkeeper hadn't seen her. Nor had the innkeeper's wife. Marcus decided to go outside and speak to the ostler. The man nodded in response to Marcus's query. "Aye. I seen her. A young woman, tallish, in a green dress, headed down to the stables, she was."

Marcus got a lantern from the osteler and circled behind the inn to the outbuildings. He found her in an open area between the stalls, talking animatedly with a group of stable hands. Seeing him, she smiled and stepped forward. "Are you looking for me? Sorry. I came out to look at the horses and got caught up talking. I'll come in now, of course."

For a moment, he couldn't think what to say. He'd been beside himself with worry. Now, to find her calmly conversing with a group of roughly dressed stablemen... "You're damned right, you'll come in now," he muttered as she moved beside him. "What were you thinking? Don't you have any common sense or decency? Anything could have happened to you!"

"We were merely discussing horses. I've spent most of my life around men like that. I can assure you they would never do me any harm."

"What of your reputation!" He felt his face growing hot with fury. "If we're to be wed, you must understand how a lady should behave. And that doesn't include openly associating with servants, especially of the male sex!"

For a second, he sensed her resentment, then she smiled sweetly. "Of course. I had forgotten I'm soon to be Mrs. Revington. It does take a bit of getting used to, you know."

They were outside now, with only the lantern for illumination. The light from it caressed the planes of her face, the high cheekbones and wide-set eyes, her slightly parted lips. James was right. She was very attractive. No, beyond that. At this moment, he'd have to describe her as beautiful. He reached out wanting to touch her face, then quickly caught himself and moved his hand down to grasp her arm. "It's time to come in now. If we don't join James for supper soon, he'll drink himself into a stupor."

Neither of them spoke as they returned to the inn. Marcus felt like a tongue-tied fool. This woman had the most startling effect on him. He'd been genuinely panicked when he couldn't find her.

And furious when he found her with a group of stablemen. Could this fierce, raw feeling inside him be jealousy? But how was that possible? Miss Montgomery was nothing to him, merely a means to an end.

****

Walking beside Revington, Penny couldn't help recalling how, for a moment, the lines of his normally harsh face had softened, and his fierce eyes had become warm and tender. He'd looked as if he meant to kiss her!

This whole scheme to have him find her in the stables and be horrified had gone completely awry. Instead of disgusting him, her actions had somehow made him more possessive. Even now, the way he held her arm as they walked made clear his claim upon her.

They turned the corner, and their bodies brushed. She felt his hard strength. Once again she was reminded of Hero, and the exhilarating and yet comforting sensation of powerful muscles responding to her own movements as she rode him. Would it be like that when Revington took her to bed?

At last they were at the doorway to the inn, and she could pull away to enter ahead of him. She sighed with relief.

James was waiting for them in the taproom. The solicitor did look a little bleary-eyed. "There you are," he said. "I'd 'bout given up on you."

Marcus didn't respond. Neither did Penny.

Dinner was a quiet affair. James appeared on the verge of nodding off, while Revington was coldly silent. Penny couldn't help watching him surreptitiously as she ate, admiring the dusky smoothness of his skin glowing in the candlelight, the graceful movements of his strong hands. She also couldn't help remembering the feel of his hand on her arm.

Dangerous, that's what Marcus Revington was. Not only because he had the power to take Horngate away from her, but because he had the means to weaken her determination to thwart him. Her goal was to convince him not to marry her. To do that, she must keep to her plan. She couldn't melt when he looked at her as he had in the brief moment outside the stables. Nor could she allow him to kiss her.

Still, she couldn't quite keep from imagining what such a moment might be like. His well-shaped lips pressed against hers, his strong arms around her, her body held against the warmth of his. The image her mind formed was tantalizing, intriguing…and it had the potential to lead to her utter ruin.

She took a deep breath. This last escapade of going off to the stables had angered him, but she doubted it was enough to cause him to give up on marrying her. Perhaps an awkward night sharing the bed would do the trick, although that was unlikely. Revington wasn't easily discouraged; it looked like she had to go to London with him after all.

She finished eating, then rose and announced she was going up to bed.

"Goodnight," responded Marcus. "I'll be up in a while." James also bade her goodnight.

As Penny made her way to room, she considered the next part of her plan. Once they were in London, she'd start by spending an exorbitant amount of his money in the shops. Then cajole him into taking her to places where they'd be surrounded by people. In those public circumstances, she should be able to convince him that as a wife she would be an embarrassment and a nuisance. He was a practical man. He would see the light and send her back to Horngate.

****

"Waiting for her to fall asleep, are you?" James asked as soon as Penny was gone.

"And for my temper to cool," responded Marcus. "I can't believe what she did." He shook his head.

"When I found her, she was conversing with a bunch of stablemen. Even for a sheltered country girl, her lack of awareness of her social position is appalling. I blame Withersby for that. He obviously encouraged her hoydenish ways in the hopes she'd never wed, and he could retain control of Horngate."

"If that's true, you shouldn't be angry with *her*."

"I'm not. I know it's not her fault. But I will be glad to get her to London where I can surround her with the proper influences to help her realize her status as a lady."

"Hmmm," said James, rising. "I thought you were sending her back to Horngate as soon as you're wed."

"I am, of course," Marcus retorted.

James rose. "I wish you the best in that regard. For now, I'm going to bed. I hope the parlor settle isn't too dashed uncomfortable."

"Goodnight," Marcus responded.

After James left, he finished his brandy and mulled things over. He had to admit James was right. There was no reason to be distressed by Penny's behavior. She would be his wife in name only. He must not let her affect him so much. His response to finding her alone with a group of men had been ridiculous. She'd been perfectly safe.

He couldn't understand why she upset him the way she did. Even now, thinking of sharing a bed with her, he felt an odd disquiet. How absurd. It was merely a practical arrangement. If the bed was of reasonable size, their bodies need never touch.

Of course, he'd have to consummate the marriage eventually. James was right. It would be dangerous to give Withersby any sort of loophole he might use to void the agreement. The thought of what Penny would look like naked flashed into his mind, and he was immediately aroused. *Damn! This was no good.* He'd have to stay here and order another brandy, and keep his thoughts away from Penny.

A while later and another brandy finished, he stood and decided to face the inevitable. He left the taproom and climbed the stairs. Reaching the room, he eased open the door and moved through the parlor where James was sleeping. Taking a deep breath, he opened the door to the bedchamber and went in.

A candle burned on the washstand; he could see she was abed. He sat on the chair near the washstand and took off his boots and stockings, then stood to remove his coat and undo his cravat. Although he disliked the idea of sleeping in his shirt and trousers, he simply couldn't imagine lying beside her all night in nothing but his smallclothes.

Before blowing out the candle, he approached the bed, wanting to see her. The next moment he regretted the impulsive action. Penny's silky brown hair was spread around her face, and in repose her features were almost angelic. The delicate line of her cheek and jaw, her creamy skin and plump, rosy, slightly parted lips— every detail made him long to kiss her. To nuzzle her long, elegant neck. To slide down the thin, nearly transparent, night rail she wore and mouth the plush curves of her breasts.

With effort, he drew away, wondering why she affected him so much. Perhaps it was because he knew that he would soon have the right to touch and kiss her…and everything else. Indeed, once they were wed, he would be *compelled* to make love to her. As uneasy as his mind was with the thought, his body was supremely eager to do exactly that. He was hard again. Now, how was he supposed to lie beside her and go to sleep?

He glanced around the room, seeking an alternative to that frustrating option. The straight-backed chair would be impossible, and he wasn't about to stretch out on the uncarpeted floor. He had no choice but to climb into bed.

Resigned, Marcus blew out the candle and again approached the bed. At least she'd fallen asleep on the far side, and he wouldn't have to climb over her. He drew the covers back and eased himself in beside her. Staring up into darkness, he told himself he'd eventually fall asleep.

****

At last! Penny shifted slightly and rubbed her nose, which had been itching ever since he entered the room. He'd taken forever to come to bed. The worst part was when he stood there looking at her. That had been agony, knowing she dare not move a muscle or he'd realize she was awake. Although she didn't know why it mattered if he knew. It might actually be less awkward if they'd exchanged "goodnights" before going to sleep.

Of course, she doubted if she'd sleep much at all. She couldn't stop thinking about him. Even though her eyes were closed, tantalizing images of the man beside her filled her mind. At dinner, she'd admired his dusky skin glowing in the candlelight, his dark piercing eyes, and hard yet sensual mouth. And then there was the way his well-tailored clothes emphasized his long, muscular legs, broad shoulders, and trim torso.

An involuntary shudder swept through her at the memory, and suddenly she felt him move beside her. She went very still as he pulled the blanket up over her shoulders. He wasn't asleep yet either.

Maybe she should forget the pretense of being asleep and speak to him. But what to say? If only she knew what he was thinking. His gesture in covering her was tender and caring, rather like how he might behave with a child. Was that how he thought of her? She'd been intent on making him see her as a hopelessly gauche country girl. It seemed her acting had succeeded. But now, having done what she'd intended, why did she feel so disappointed? What was this foolish yearning to have him see her as a desirable woman, rather than a difficult child?

****

Damn but this was miserable! How was he to sleep when his member was rock-hard, and his whole body ached with longing for the woman beside him? In the darkened room, he couldn't see her, but that didn't stop his imagination from running wild. In his mind's eye, he was peeling off her thin nightgown to reveal her slender womanly form. He was kissing those pert, perfect lips, then her breasts and then lower…

He suppressed an involuntary groan at the thought of what he wanted to do to her. Somehow he had to think of something else or he'd never sleep. Maybe he could try to recall the details of Horngate, the estate that would soon be his.

A moment later he'd given up on the technique. It seemed whenever he thought about a certain building or facility of the estate, he immediately imagined making love to Penny there!

Chapter Four

Penny woke the next morning, feeling stiff and gritty-eyed; Revington was already gone. She dressed quickly, splashed water on her face, and pinned her unruly hair up into a knot. Staring into the looking glass above the wash table, she repressed a sigh. If she wanted to convince Revington she was an uncouth hoyden, she certainly looked the part. While her obvious unattractiveness served her purposes, she couldn't help feeling a bit dismayed. The next moment, she told herself not to be such a fool. Her goal was to repel Revington, not attract him.

She found James eating breakfast in the public taproom. He rose as she approached the table. "Miss." He gave a slight bow, then helped her sit. Penny dove into the plate of eggs and biscuits placed before her. "Where's Revington?" she asked after a bite or two.

"You should get used to calling him Marcus," James said. "He's already eaten and is seeing to the horses. You know how anxious he is to get back to London."

"Why is he in such a hurry? I mean, I know London is his home, but I don't understand why he's racing back there."

James shrugged. "I think he's got it into his head that the place will fall apart without him." He grinned at her.

Penny toyed thoughtfully with her food. "He said he had business interests there. What sort of business is he in?"

"He's a gamester. Makes his money off cards, dice, and other sorts of wagers. It probably doesn't sound like quite the thing to a country miss, but it's completely acceptable among the *ton*. In fact, Marcus's skill is much admired. He's made a fortune at it. His father's a viscount, but Marcus's older brother is the heir. Marcus was left with a modest allowance, and he's managed to parlay that into a substantial living."

At that moment, Revington strode into the taproom, cracking his riding whip against his thigh. He gave the vaguest hint of a bow. "Good morning, Penny. As soon as you're ready, we'll set off."

She started to rise, but James said sharply, "No need to rush her. We've plenty of time."

Revington shot his friend a hostile look and then sat on the bench beside her. Penny suppressed a smile. Revington was clearly an impatient man. It should be easy to drive him to distraction.

She took her time with breakfast, then rose and followed James and the glowering Revington out to the carriage. James appeared to have run out of small talk, and Penny decided not to attempt conversation either.

It was a fine, bright morning. The carriage seemed to fly effortlessly along the country roads. Even more than the day before, Penny was impressed by Revington's driving skill. Adrian's cowhandedness with a team had always seemed indicative of his weak character, while Revington drove with an assurance that suggested a strong and confident disposition. While Penny admired those qualities, she realized she didn't necessarily favor them in an adversary.

They passed through several villages and finally reached the edges of the city itself. Penny noticed a pall of smoke hanging in the air. When she mentioned it, James told her it was from the coal cooking stoves and was much worse in the winter, when coal was also burned for heat. While he didn't seem perturbed by the haze, Penny couldn't help contrasting it with the clean fresh air of Horngate.

The smoke had left a layer of grime over the buildings. Indeed, everything seemed dull and gray. Even when they finally reached Mayfair, which James said was the nicest part of the city, and drove past some huge houses, Penny wasn't impressed. "Give me a meadow cloaked in wildflowers or a forest glen bright with autumn colors," she murmured. "The country possesses more true beauty than this."

"Perhaps you would like riding in Hyde Park or the visiting Vauxhall Gardens," James suggested. "They're a bit more rustic."

"Oh, that would be delightful." Then, remembering her plan, she shouted up to Marcus, "James said you could take me to Vauxhall Gardens and riding in Hyde Park!"

Marcus muttered something unintelligible. Penny had to struggle to keep her expression from growing smug.

A short while later, Revington brought the chaise to a halt in front of a modest two-story dwelling. Turning back to face them, he motioned to James. "Take Penny into the house. I'll drive the rig around to the livery stable."

James helped her down, and as Revington drove

off, they headed for the door. James knocked sharply. A moment later a stiff-necked manservant in immaculate dress opened the door. "Hello, Bowes," said James. "Marcus and I are just back from the country."

"Very good, sir," responded Bowes.

As the butler's gaze alighted on Penny, James added, "This is Miss Montgomery, Marcus's fiancée."

Bowes stared at her, clearly startled. "His fiancée?"

"Yes. Marcus plans to wed Miss Montgomery as soon as everything can be arranged."

"I see," Bowes responded. Although clearly, he did not. In fact, he looked appalled.

"I presume Marcus will have a footman bring in her valise," James said. "Until then, I'll take Miss Montgomery up to the master suite."

Bowes's eyebrows shot up. "She's staying *here*?"

Penny knew a twinge of satisfaction. The butler's obvious distress implied Revington wasn't used to entertaining female visitors.

"I presume so," said James. "At least until the wedding."

"I see." Bowes frowned. The butler drew James aside and spoke in low urgent tones. Although Penny couldn't hear all that was said, she caught the phrases "no one to wait on her" and "really not proper". In response to the butler's concerns, James merely shrugged and smiled. James clearly anticipated her presence in his Marcus's life would inconvenience his friend and was amused by the situation.

Despite the butler's doubts, in a few moments James was escorting Penny up to the second floor of the town house, where he led her into a large bedchamber. The room was furnished with deep, understated colors that made it clear a man resided there. Everything was of the finest materials, from the dark gold brocade draperies to the rich brown, green, and cream Turkish carpet.

"It's a bit masculine, isn't it?" said James. His eyes twinkling, he added, "Perhaps you could suggest that Marcus have it done over. Brighten it up with some lighter colors and more delicate furnishings."

Although she guessed where James was heading, she couldn't help saying, "I actually like it. It rather reminds me of being in an autumn forest."

She walked to the table by the bed, where a half-dozen ivory dice were lined up, along with neat stacks of gambling counters. She started to finger the objects and then stopped. "I guess I shouldn't touch anything. Gamblers are supposed to be nearly as superstitious as horsemen."

"Marcus isn't. In fact, I'm not certain he believes in luck. He's arrogant enough to think he's so successful simply due to his own skill."

"But surely he realizes that some of it is chance. Even in horse racing, fate plays a part. I've seen good riders go down through no fault of their own, and sometimes a horse will perform completely against your expectations. There must be similar factors in gambling."

"I don't think Marcus believes in fate either," James answered. "He likes to think he has complete control over his destiny."

Oh, he does, does he, Penny thought with amusement. Well, they would see about that! She turned back to James. "Besides Vauxhall Gardens and Hyde Park, what other sights would you advise me to ask Reving…Marcus to take me to see?"

"From what Marcus has said, you won't have much time before the wedding for gadding about London. But I presume he will take you shopping on Bond Street."

"Oh, yes." She smiled broadly. "You must tell me where I should purchase my wedding trousseau."

A wicked look brightened James's countenance. "I've heard Madame Dubonet is the finest modiste in London. Quite pricey, I'm sure, but Marcus can afford it." He gave her a quick smile. Penny almost laughed aloud. Marcus Revington didn't know it yet, but he'd gotten himself in deep this time.

****

"You've got to find her a maid." James took the brandy Marcus held out. "It's not proper for her to stay in this house without some sort of female companion, especially since you're not married yet."

Marcus sat in his usual chair in the drawing room and took a swallow of brandy. He'd hoped imbibing some spirits would improve his mood, but James's reminder of his responsibilities canceled out the warm glow the brandy gave him. He was trying to avoid thinking about tonight, when he'd have to sleep on the hard, narrow bed Bowes was having made up in the spare bedchamber. Now James reminded him of another difficulty he faced with his prospective wife. "Well, I don't imagine I can hire a maid today," he answered irritably. "It's nearly tea time. All the agencies will be closed by now."

"At the very least, you must have one of the servants help her undress and see that her clothing is laundered. Otherwise, the poor thing will have nothing to wear when you take her shopping tomorrow."

Marcus groaned.

"You know it can't be helped. Until she has a maid to escort her, you'll have to do the honors. And as badly as she needs new clothing, you can't afford to delay."

"The only woman I have employed here is Maggie, the cook."

"Well, have *her* see to Penny then. If we eat late, it won't be the end of the world."

Marcus rose slowly. "I guess I'll go talk to Maggie. Bowes would only make a muddle of it. He doesn't seem to get on with her."

"I'm not surprised," James said, dryly. "Bowes is a bit full of himself. You should have seen him look down his nose at Penny when they first met. You would have thought he was the Prince Regent and she a grubby street urchin."

"Dash it! She didn't notice, did she?"

"Oh, I think she did."

Marcus's tension increased as he started for the door. He felt enraged at the idea of Penny being treated rudely. He must insist that every member of his household give her the respect she was due as his wife. It was the least he could do for the chit.

He went downstairs to the kitchen, where Maggie was cutting up vegetables. The Irishwoman gaped at him when he told her what he wanted. "You want me to wait on your wife?" She shook her head, coppery curls bobbing under her mop cap. "I don't know nothing 'bout waiting on ladies."

"She isn't a lady. That is…she is, but she's been living out in the country without female companionship for so long, she doesn't have any notion what a lady's maid is supposed to do. Assist her with whatever she needs. Undo her dress, help her take down her hair, comb it out." He gestured helplessly. "She only has the one gown, so it'll have to be washed."

"Washed, sir?"

"Surely, you know how. You must attend to your own laundry."

"Of course, but while I'm doing all this, who will see to supper, sir?"

Maybe it was the lack of sleep, or thinking about all the things he must do to get his wife settled in, but he was getting a megrim. "Don't worry over it. I don't care how late I eat. As a matter of fact, I'll take a meal at the club. You'll only have to feed her and the other servants, and I'm certain she's used to plain food."

The cook stared at him a moment longer, then wiped her hands on her apron. "I'll try, sir, but this is all most irregular. If you'd given us some hint you were going to take a wife, we could have managed much better."

Marcus was about to say that the arrangement was more a business venture than a marriage. Then he realized how cold and condescending that would sound. He must start treating Penny with a little more deference or the servants would never come to respect her. Of course, that didn't really matter. She'd be going back to Horngate soon enough.

The thought eased his mood but didn't completely reassure him. He'd known Penny a little more than a day, and she'd already turned his life upside down. He'd begun to suspect that James was right. Collecting on his wager wouldn't be a simple matter.

This thought was reinforced when he returned to the library. "So, since Penny's in your bedchamber, where are you going to sleep tonight?" James asked him. "Or are you going to share a bed with her again?"

"Certainly not! I'm not sharing a bed with Penny until we're properly wed. For now, I'll have to make do with whatever Bowes has found for me sleep on in the spare room." Just the thought of it made him grimace.

"It's your own fault," James remarked. "You never bothered to do up this house properly. You have only a skeleton staff and a handful of rooms that are really livable."

Marcus shook his head. "I never expected that a wife would be so much trouble."

"Are you still determined to get the wedding over with and then send her back to Horngate?"

"Of course. Why would I have changed my mind?"

James shrugged. "No reason. Just thought you might be having second thoughts. Getting tired of being inconvenienced and all that."

"Horngate is worth a few days of trouble," Marcus snapped.

****

"Miss?"

Penny opened her eyes. At first she didn't know where she was. Then she looked up and saw a young woman with startling red curls and a freckled face leaning over her and remembered Maggie, the Irish servant who helped her undress the night before.

"I'm sorry to wake you, miss," Maggie murmured. "But Mr. Revington said to get you up. I guess he means to take you to the dressmaker for some new frocks." She motioned to a cup on the table beside the bed. "I brought you some chocolate."

Penny sat up and yawned. Picking up the cup, she

took a swallow. "Oh, lovely."

"I'm glad you like it, miss. As soon as you're finished, I'll help you get dressed and do your hair."

"Oh, my hair." Penny ran her fingers through the tangles and sighed. If she kept to her plan, she'd have Maggie put it up into her usual messy knot. But she was tired of appearing gauche and unkempt, and she really didn't want to present herself that way in London. "I wonder if there might not be a way to curl it."

"Well, the one parlor maid who worked here last fall did leave some curling tongs behind, so we could try," said Maggie. "But I'll warn you, I never done no hair curlin' before. You might say it would be the last thing to come to my mind." As she motioned to her own head of springy curls, Penny couldn't help laughing. She felt quite comfortable having Maggie wait on her. The maid appeared to be a good-hearted sort, for all her lack of experience as a lady's maid.

Between the two of them, they got Penny dressed. Then Maggie went down to get the curling tongs while Penny brushed out her hair. Maggie returned, and after heating the tongs in the fireplace, approached Penny, seated on the bed. "Here goes, miss."

Maggie grabbed a strand of hair and wrapped it around the tongs. "How long should I hold it?"

"I've no idea," said Penny. A few moments later, the distinctive smell of burning hair floated to her nose. "That's enough, I think!"

Maggie removed the tongs and they both stared at the slightly singed curl that resulted.

"I'm not sure…" Maggie began.

"It's fine," said Penny. "Let's try another one."

This curl turned out a bit better. But the tongs

cooled quickly and Maggie had to keep reheating them. When they had Penny's hair only about half curled, a sharp knock sounded at the door. "Penny, are you ready yet?" Revington called.

"Not…not quite," she answered.

"What the devil are you doing in there? It smells like burning feathers."

Penny suppressed a giggle. The doorbell rattled. "Give us a moment, sir," called Maggie.

They heard a sigh of aggravation, then footsteps receding down the hall.

"Don't you fret," said Maggie. "We'll manage this yet. Mr. Revington's a real impatient bloke, but he'll be pleased as punch when he sees you. The curls really do wonders for you."

Penny got up from the bed and went to look at herself in the glass over the dresser, turning her head so she couldn't see the uncurled part of her hair. Maggie was right. She actually looked rather attractive. The next moment she felt a twinge of uncertainty. If her goal was to disgust Revington so he'd give up on marrying her, she shouldn't be trying to make herself look nice. But she couldn't seem to help herself. Her wretched cousin Adrian had always acted as if she was utterly repulsive, and a part of her was determined to prove him wrong.

Maggie returned with the tongs and Penny sat again so she could finish. As soon as she was done, Penny grabbed her pelisse and reticule and started downstairs. Revington was waiting for her in the library. He jumped up when he saw her. "There you are. I have the phaeton waiting outside. The groom's been walking the horses."

He took her arm and led her briskly toward the door. Penny felt a flash of irritation. *He hasn't even noticed my hair!*

But as he helped her into the phaeton, he glanced at her and his eyes widened. "What have you done with your hair?"

"I had Maggie curl it. Do you like it?"

"Like it?" A strange expression crossed his face. "Why...yes. It seems quite flattering." The next moment he frowned. "I was going to engage a maid for you, but perhaps you could get by with Maggie." His gaze shot up to meet hers. "Since you won't be in London long."

"That's perfectly fine with me." Even as she said the words, she realized she should have insisted he get her a maid. She must remember her goal to inconvenience him as much as possible. And also cost him as much money she could. She felt irritated with herself. What was it about this man that made her want to appear agreeable and pleasing?

As they set off, with Marcus driving, she asked, "Do you drive everywhere you go?"

"Usually. I like to take charge of my circumstances and not rely on anyone else."

His words echoed what James had told her. Revington liked to feel in control. If she could make him feel as if marrying her would cause his life to spiral *out of control*, he would almost certainly give up the idea.

On the way to Bond Street, they passed numerous stylish open carriages. Revington nodded to many of the occupants, as if he was acquainted with them. While the men took little note of Penny, the women regarded her with frank curiosity. She wondered if Revington was embarrassed to be seen with her. Glancing at him, she saw that he appeared cool and distant, his usual demeanor.

They reached a street full of shops. Revington pulled the team to a halt and handed the reins to a waiting osteler. He helped Penny out of the carriage and they started down the street. As they drew near to a sign proclaiming Madame Dubonet, Modiste. Penny recalled what James had said, and exclaimed, "Can we go in here?"

Revington halted, frowning. "I suppose so. This is probably as good a place as any."

A striking red-haired woman met them coming out, her low-cut gown revealing an expanse of lush white cleavage. "Marcus," the woman said. "How lovely to see you!" Gazing at his face, she gave a lilting laugh.

Revington appeared startled at first. Then he smiled tightly and bowed. "Elizabeth."

The woman turned and stared pointedly at Penny. Marcus cleared his throat. "Ah, yes…. That is…" He took a breath. "Elizabeth, may I introduce my-my fiancée, Penelope Montgomery."

The woman stared at Penny, her blue eyes wide. Then she smiled, an altogether false smile. "Charmed, I'm sure." She turned back to Revington. "What happened? Did your famous luck finally desert you? If you were that desperate for blunt, you could have sought out your friends. There was no need to get leg-shackled."

"That's not the way of it at all, Elizabeth," Revington snapped.

"Of course not." Elizabeth gave another trilling

laugh. "I'm sure it's quite a love match." Nodding to Penny, she added, "Congratulations, Miss Montgomery. I wish you every happiness." She moved away, still laughing.

Penny clutched her reticule, feeling insulted and something else, something like…jealous.

"Paid no heed to her." Revington guided her into the shop.

They were greeted by a petite, impeccably groomed woman Penny guessed was Madame Dubonet. "What may I do for you, *monsieur, demoiselle*?" the woman said, bowing.

"My…fiancée." Revington gestured to Penny. "She needs some new clothing. Dresses, and, er…everything that goes along with them."

"Everything, *monsieur*?"

Revington glanced at Penny, frowned, and then turned back to Madame Dubonet. "I suppose so."

The modiste beamed. "'Twill be a pleasure, *monsieur. Demoiselle* is a natural beauty, but we can make her absolutely stunning. Does *monsieur* have certain colors or styles in mind?"

Revington looked startled. "I'm afraid I'm completely out of my element in this." He motioned vaguely. "Whatever you think will be suitable. The main thing is, she needs at least one change of clothing as soon as possible."

"*Oui, monsieur.*"

Marcus started toward the door. All at once, he seemed to remember himself. He glanced at Penny, then at the modiste. "I'll be back in two hours. Will that give you enough time?"

"*Oui, monsieur.* She'll be ready."

As the door shut behind him, Madame Dubonet gave a delighted laugh. "*Demoiselle* is most fortunate."

Penny was still thinking about Revington's interaction with Elizabeth, and the familiar, almost intimate way she had spoken to him. She turned her attention back to the modiste. "I'm sorry. What were you saying?"

Madame Dubonet beamed at Penny. "I was saying how fortunate you are. Many men are not so indulgent. They set the cost they will endure and refuse to spend any more. But *monsieur* has left that all up to us."

"Oh, indeed he has." Penny suppressed a smile. The modiste obviously felt Penny could spend as much as she wished, and Penny wasn't about to tell her otherwise.

Madame Dubonet drew Penny into the light by the window. "You have lovely skin, and your features are quite refined. With a little effort, we can make you an *incomparable*."

Penny smiled, feeling uncomfortable. This was likely part of what made Madame Dubonet so popular. She knew how to flatter her clients and make them feel attractive. Of course, *she* was under no illusions. While she might not be as awful to look at as Adrian implied, she was certainly no great beauty.

"Now, we must get started," Madame Dubonet exclaimed. "Two hours is not long. First we must measure you, then pick out fabric. Come into the dressing room, *demoiselle,* and we will get started."

She led Penny to a small chamber with looking glasses on every wall. Penny was stripped down to her shift and pantaloons, and Madame Dubonet began to measure her. "A pity that the classical silhouette is all the rage, as it favors the well-endowed woman rather than slender figures such as yours. But with careful fitting, we can make the most of what you have."

The modiste's words made Penny think of Elizabeth. She said, "As we were coming in, there was a red-haired woman leaving. My fiancé greeted her as Elizabeth. I wondered who she is."

The modiste gave her a shrewd look. "Ahh, that would be *Demoiselle* Valant." She patted Penny's arm. "Don't trouble yourself about her. She's what is known as demi rep."

"What's a demi rep?" Penny asked, then immediately felt embarrassed by her lack of knowledge. "I afraid I haven't been in London long, and I don't know what everything is called."

"A sweet young thing like you wouldn't know, of course." Madame Dubonet raised her brows meaningfully. "A demi rep is a woman of questionable reputation. Someone who trades sexual favors for…gifts from gentlemen. Sometimes such a woman will only have one wealthy patron. Others, like *Demoiselle* Valant, may have several. If you are concerned that Monsieur Revington might enjoy the company of such a woman, don't trouble yourself. *Demoiselle* Valant could never compete with someone like you."

"I wasn't concerned, merely curious."

"Of course, *demoiselle*." The modiste snapped her fingers and a young girl with golden curls appeared from behind the curtain. "Giselle, if you would bring me a bolt of mauve muslin. And the blue sprigged batiste as well."

Penny's neck and shoulders grew stiff as Madame

draped, pinned, and arranged. Giselle brought several more bolts of fabric, as well as a selection of ribbons and lace that Madame said would be used to trim the garments.

Penny had plenty of time to contemplate what Madame Dubonet had said about Elizabeth. Was it true that Revington was one of many men who'd been intimate with *Demoiselle* Valant? If so, why did it matter so much?

It didn't matter, of course. She had no interest in Revington. None at all. Indeed, if she succeeded in her plan, she'd never have to see him again.

At last, the fitting was over. As the modiste was helping her dress, Penny asked hopefully, "Are we finished?"

"I'm afraid not. Monsieur implied you needed a whole new wardrobe. We still need to select undergarments. We stock several fashions. Long and short pantalettes. With lace and without."

"I had no idea there would be so many choices!"

Madame Dubonet shrugged, smiling faintly. "Perhaps several of each style then, since you can't decide?"

Penny nodded. "Yes, I think that would be ideal."

"And of course after you leave here, you will need to purchase slippers, hats, and reticules."

"Of course." Although she was frankly sick of shopping, she mustn't lose sight of her goal. She followed the modiste into the public area of the shop.

Marcus was waiting near the entrance, impatiently tapping his driving whip against his thigh. "Ready?"

"Yes," Penny said.

"When will her things be delivered?" he asked the

modiste.

"I will have at least one of the gowns finished and sent 'round tomorrow."

"Well, that's finally over," Revington exclaimed as they left the shop.

"Not quite," Penny said. "Madame Dubonet pointed out that I must have new shoes and perhaps a hat or two."

Revington grimaced. "I suppose you're right. But it will have to wait until another day."

Chapter Five

Marcus tried to quell his irritation as he escorted Penny back to the phaeton, which he'd left some distance down the street. He couldn't believe how much time all this was taking…and heaven knew how much money. But he supposed James was right, and it was churlish of him to be so resentful. After all, he was getting some fine, valuable property out of the arrangement, while Penny was essentially losing her independence.

As he helped her into the rig, he felt a stab of guilt. If Adrian weren't such a worthless wretch, Penny might have married quite well. She was very attractive, and Horngate was a decent dowry. But now, thanks to the worthless Withersby, she'd been robbed of any choice in who she married.

Not that he would be such an awful husband. He wouldn't mistreat her or seek to control her. Indeed, once they were wed, she could go back to training horses, if that was what she wished.

He tossed a halfpence to the boy holding the team, then climbed in beside her and took up the reins. Before setting off, he cast a glance at Penny. With her new hairstyle, she looked quite appealing. If he had to marry, he could do much worse. He was really coming off quite well in this. Under the circumstances, the least he could do to buy her a few new things.

****

Was her plan working? Penny couldn't tell. Although Revington appeared quite irritated at the shop, the look he just shot her wasn't one of aggravation or distress. Indeed, there'd been a kind of longing in his expression.

What would she do if she couldn't dissuade him from marrying her? She might have to consider the possibility. Not only was he clearly a stubborn, determined man, but despite all her efforts, he didn't seem averse to her company. She should never have had Maggie do her hair. That was a mistake. All these clothes she'd just been fitted for wouldn't help either. Madame Dubonet obviously knew what she was doing; Penny's new garments would make her appear as attractive as possible. She should have stuck to her original plan and retained the look of a gauche, disheveled country maiden. Somewhere she'd gotten off track. She'd have to think of a new plan.

She was so caught up in her thoughts that before she knew it, Revington was helping her down from the phaeton. "By the way," he said as they started up the brick walkway to the house, "I asked James to find a clergyman to marry us. That way, as soon as your new wardrobe is finished, we can have the wedding and everything will be settled."

Penny nodded politely, although the news hardly pleased her. *It looks like my wretch of a cousin is going to get his way!*

As soon as they entered the townhouse, Bowes announced, "Mr. Ludingham is waiting in the drawing room."

Turning to her, Revington said, "I'm certain you're

tired from shopping. Why don't you rest until dinner?"

"Of course."

Upstairs, she sat on the bed and tried to sort out her thoughts. Somehow she had to find out more about her future husband and what motivated him. A sudden thought came to her. It was rather audacious, but it seemed like the only way to learn more about Revington.

After changing from the sensible half-boots she'd worn to go shopping into a worn pair of slippers, she crept down the stairs. She glanced around for Bowes and then made her way to the doorway of the drawing room. From here, she could just barely hear Revington and James's conversation.

"As soon as the wedding is over, I'm heading to Horngate," Revington was saying. "Things looked fairly well kept, but I'd like to make some improvements to the house."

"You intend to reside there?" James asked. "What about making a living? The deep players are here in London. Horngate is quite isolated. Even in the village, I doubt you'll find many men willing to play cards for money. If you do, there'll not be much for you to win."

"I've been frugal these last few years. I've enough saved up to live on for a while, even if I make some improvements to Horngate. Also, this horse-breeding business might potentially be very lucrative."

Penny could barely suppress her gasp of dismay. Bad enough that Revington planned to reside at Horngate, but to learn he wanted to involve himself with the horse business outraged her. *Whatever was she to do?*

"Really, Marcus, I never saw you as a country

squire. I truly don't understand what's got into you. Why would you want to give up your comfortable life here in London to live out in the sticks and raise horses?"

"My 'comfortable life' here in London has gotten quite boring the past few years. The men I spend time with are usually fools like Adrian Withersby, hardly the wittiest or most accomplished members of society."

"I see," James said, sarcastically. "You're moving to the country because you seek intellectual stimulation. I'm sure you'll find the horses at Horngate an endless source of intelligent conversation."

Penny couldn't help smiling. Revington's reasoning did seem rather flawed.

But his response was crisp and confident. "I'm sure a successful horse-breeding operation requires much serious effort and planning. Although I know gentlemen are supposed to be above such things, I actually savor the idea of doing real work and facing a challenge greater than guessing what card my opponent will play."

"Gads, don't let anyone in your current circle know you feel this way. Real work—the idea is quite appalling."

Penny couldn't tell if James's horror was real or feigned. But Revington was clearly serious. So far, she hadn't known him to jest or make jokes. She'd expected Revington to be a typical shallow and self-involved nobleman—what Tad and the other stablemen called a "swell". In fact, he appeared to be cut from a different sort of cloth altogether.

"I don't give a damn what people think," Revington said. "I have little respect for most members of the *ton*. They're a bunch of overgrown boys and top-lofty blowhards. Of course, my cynical attitude probably results from the circumstances in which I associate with them. Gambling doesn't tend to bring out the best in people."

"It's probably just as well you have no concern for your social standing," responded James, "since you're marrying Miss Montgomery and someone like her is unlikely to attract positive notice from the old tabbies and snobbish matrons who dictate who is worthy of acclaim."

"I'm not convinced Penny would be an utter failure in Society. I suspect if she was properly turned out, she might surprise you. This morning, Maggie curled her hair, and the result was rather startling. Penny looked like a different woman, and a strikingly pretty one at that."

At Revington's words, conflicting emotions flared inside her. While gratified to think he found her attractive, improving her appearance might well work against her best interests.

"It sounds as if you're becoming rather fond of Miss Montgomery. For all that this marriage began as business transaction, perhaps it will end up being a love match."

"Love!" Revington gave a harsh laugh. "Tell me, James, do you know any marriages that are love matches? At any rate, I'm certainly not the sort for such foolishness. There's as much likelihood I'll fall in love with Miss Montgomery as there is I'll become enamored of the orange girl who sells her wares on the corner."

"Well, my parents were fond of each other. And I

think there's something to be said for having a *tendre* for one's spouse. I hope to at least *like* the woman I marry."

"I see you've added another requirement to your long, long list of the attributes your future wife must possess. I can't wait to meet this paragon, James. I doubt there's a woman in London who'll measure up to your standards."

"Well, then, perhaps I'll remain unwed," James responded.

"Perhaps you will," Revington agreed. "Or perhaps your natural tendency for romance will induce you to fall in love with a woman who's nothing like your paragon."

"My natural tendency for romance? I can't think what you mean."

"You insist I'll come to care for Penny. But it's really nothing more than a business arrangement. I'd never even have looked at her if it weren't for Horngate. The property is what I desire, not the woman."

"Is that so?" said James. "If you're so certain, then there's no reason not to make a wager. I'm not normally a gamester, but I'd be willing to bet that if you spend one month in London with Penny, you'll fall in love with her."

"One month?" Revington let out a groan. "That will seem like an eternity! What the devil are you offering that would possibly make me endure such a trial?"

"If you end up going through with this and residing at Horngate, you'll need someone in London to look after your business interests. I'd be willing to do that, at no cost to you."

"It's true I'd need someone to keep an eye on things here. I'd have to continue to rent this house, so I'd have somewhere to stay when I did come to the city. And there are the other investments that would need looking after. I suppose it would be worth my while to agree to this nonsense, especially since I'm quite certain I'll win. But what about you, James? If I should somehow manage to lose this ridiculous wager, what do you want in exchange?"

"That's simple enough. If you come to care for Miss Montgomery, you must forgive her cousin's debt and release her from any commitment to marry you."

"But that's absurd! If I were to—perish the thought—actually fall in love with her, then there would be no reason for us *not* to be wed!"

"Unless she doesn't want to marry *you*. It would be her decision then, you see."

"I don't understand, James. What the devil are you up to?"

"I just want to make things fair for Miss Montgomery. She's been a helpless pawn in this whole business. I want to make certain she has a say in her future."

"Why? Unless you're in love with her yourself, in which case we have a real problem, as I'm not about to give up Horngate. Even for you!"

"My motivation isn't love, but compassion. I feel sorry for Miss Montgomery. She seems like a nice person who's been used badly by her cousin."

Penny winced. While it was touching that James was so concerned for her, she didn't like being pitied.

"It's true you've always had compassion for the

downtrodden and oppressed. An admirable enough quality but hardly practical. If there's anything my upbringing's taught me, it's that a man has to look out for himself."

"Quite true for men, but women don't always have the same opportunities. I'm merely trying to give Miss Montgomery some say in her life."

Both men were silent for a time. Then Revington said, "Before I accept the wager, I want to know how you intend to determine which one of us has won. How, exactly, do you intend to gauge my feelings for Penny?"

"I presume you'll be honest and honorable. And even if you do try to lie, I think I'll be able to discern your true feelings."

"Very well. I'll accept the wager, even if I find the whole matter quite ludicrous. I have no doubt I'll win."

There was another bit of silence when Penny guessed they were shaking hands to seal the agreement. She was on the verge of slipping away when Revington said, "I presume the requirement that I stay in London with her means I must do everything I've agreed to already. Take her to see the sights and all that?"

"Of course. You must continue to escort her to places and circulate in society. Go through all the motions of courting her properly."

Revington groaned. "This is going to be a dashedly long month."

Penny tiptoed away from the door and made her way up the stairs. Once in the bedchamber, she sank down on the bed, her thoughts spinning. James had offered a way out of her predicament. All she had to do was make Revington fall in love with her. Then, when he asked her to marry him, she could refuse and he'd be bound by his agreement with James to give up Horngate and set her free.

Was such an outcome possible? The notion of Revington falling in love with her—or with anyone—seemed too nonsensical to contemplate. He was a hardened, cynical gamester, and he'd made his motivations quite clear. He wanted Horngate, and nothing would dissuade him. And his feelings for her were equally clear. He dreaded having to spend a month in her company. Absolutely dreaded it.

She shook her head, feeling a bit put out by his obvious distaste for her. Of course, she was at least partly responsible for his outlook. But now it was time to change tactics. Instead of scaring him off, she somehow had to induce him to fall in love with her.

She got up restlessly. If, by some miracle, her plan were successful, then rejecting his offer of marriage would be quite cold and unfeeling. She would have cruelly manipulated him for her own ends.

On the other hand, he hadn't considered her feelings in this. Since he'd been so heedless of her wishes, why should she worry about hurting him?

If only Tad were here. He'd be able to convince her to do whatever was necessary to save Horngate and the horse operation. He'd also remind her that Revington was a cold-hearted, selfish "swell" who deserved whatever fate befell him.

She caught a glimpse of herself in the looking glass above the bureau. Who did she think she was fooling? She wasn't a sophisticated, elegant beauty like Elizabeth Valant. She probably had as much chance of getting Revington to fall in love with her as Maggie did!

As she had the thought, there was a knock on the door. "It's Maggie, miss," the cook called. "Is there anything you need before I start the evening meal?"

A thought came to Penny. Although Maggie might not have much experience with curling hair, she struck Penny as someone who was a good judge of character. She might well have some insights into how to induce Revington to fall in love with her. "Come in, Maggie. There is something I need."

"Aye, miss." Maggie entered and stood waiting.

Penny thought a moment, trying to figure out how to phrase her request...and also how to explain it. Finally, she said, "You know, don't you, that Mr. Revington and I are to be married?"

"Aye, miss."

"I'm afraid he's marrying me so he can take control of my property, a farm called Horngate. While it's common for men of his class to marry for practical reasons, my own parents were quite fond of each other. I'd like to have something similar with my own husband. What I'm saying is...well, Maggie, I guess I want to know if you have any suggestions on how to get Mr. Revington to have feelings for me, rather than simply marrying me for my property."

Maggie wrinkled her freckled nose in thought. "I can't blame you for wanting your husband to care for you. But I worry it's going to be difficult for you to win Revington's affections. He's not the sort to go all sheep-eyed over a woman."

"Do you think it's hopeless?" Penny asked, feeling discouraged.

"No, not hopeless. You're quite pretty and

sometimes good looks can turn a man's head. But it's usually not sweet, girlish beauty that gets them, but something a little more—"

"Sophisticated?" Penny offered.

Maggie nodded. "You do know the sort of woman I mean, don't you?"

"Yes, yes I do." Penny recalled Elizabeth Valant and her generous expanse of cleavage. "Your point's well taken. In fact, you've given me an excellent idea."

Madame Dubonet had said Elizabeth Valant wasn't a great beauty, but that she knew how to "turn herself out." If it was simply a matter of knowing how to dress and present oneself, then there was no reason she couldn't adopt some of Elizabeth's methods for herself. No reason at all.

"Thank you, Maggie. You've been most helpful."

"Any time, miss. But now I must see about dinner."

****

"There's no need for you to go shopping with me for the rest of the things I require for my wardrobe," Penny announced when Revington met her in the breakfast room the next morning. "I can go by myself. Then you won't have to endure waiting for me while I shop."

Revington shook his head. "I'm afraid you can't go by yourself. You must have an escort of some sort. I really am going to have to call an agency and get you a lady's maid." He repressed a sigh. One more duty—and expense—he'd been trying to avoid. This wager with James had disrupted all his plans.

"What about Maggie?" Penny suggested. "Couldn't she act as my maid?"

Marcus stared at her. The chit didn't know anything about the rules of proper society. "But she's *Irish*. A proper lady's maid must be French, or at least English."

"But she's done lovely things with my hair. And when I discussed some of the gowns being made for me, she seemed to have a genuine interest in colors and fabrics. Not to mention that we get on quite well. I enjoy her company. Isn't that also a requirement of a lady's maid?"

"Even so, Maggie hardly has an appropriate wardrobe for a lady's maid. While a maid certainly isn't expected to be as well-turned-out as her mistress, she must blend in with polite society. Maggie's mob cap and dark, plain clothing would look quite out of place on Bond Street." What was Penny thinking? She seemed to have no sense of the natural division between the well-born classes and those who served them.

"Perhaps I could purchase some nicer clothing for her. Or, that is, *you* could." The look she gave him was so sweet and winsome, Marcus felt himself weakening. He had to admit Maggie had done wonders with Penny's hair. The striking young woman standing before him bore little resemblance to the messy hoyden he'd first encountered. And not having to deal with an agency would save him quite a bit of time. Although if he made Maggie Penny's maid, he'd have to hire a cook. But Bowes could take care of that.

"Very well," he said, "Maggie may escort you. And you have my leave to purchase her a few *inexpensive* garments." He fixed Penny with a stern look. "Given that your wardrobe is probably costing a fortune, I trust that you will be frugal with hers."

"Of course. Thank you!"

The smile Penny gave him was so luminous he almost regretted his harsh tone. Really, a few gowns and furbelows were a small price to pay for a property like Horngate. And they *would* be wed, James's bizarre wager notwithstanding. What the devil was his friend thinking, betting that he would fall in love? The very idea was absurd. Penny might be fetching, but that didn't mean he was about to lose his head over her. He might grow fond of his future wife, but that was all.

With that comforting thought in mind, he went to get Bowes and talk to him about hiring a cook.

****

"You really want me to serve as your lady's maid? Truly?" Maggie's eyes were wide with astonishment.

"Yes. There's no reason for Revington to hire someone else. After all, you did quite well at curling my hair."

Maggie clutched her hands together, looking distressed. "But I don't have no clothes, that is, *any* clothes appropriate to being a maid."

"I intend to remedy that. I have leave from Mr. Revington to purchase what's required."

Maggie smiled. "Blimey, but you're a miracle worker. Mr. Revington's normally right tight with his money. You should see how he's on me about buying provisions at the market. Always reminding me that it's just him I'm cooking for and not to be extravagant." She straightened abruptly. "The market! Who's going to buy the food and cook it if I'm busy waiting on you?"

"Revington's hiring another cook. I suspect he thinks it will be cheaper to pay for kitchen help than for a lady's maid."

"Ah, so that's how you done it." Maggie nodded knowingly. "You're right clever, miss. You appear to have the master all figured."

"I wish that were true. Frankly, every time I think I understand what he's about, he does something to surprise me. At any rate, you and I are going shopping today. Until we get you some new garments, you can wear my old pelisse." She scrutinized Maggie. "And we have to do something about your hair."

"What do you think?" Maggie asked, smiling broadly. "Perhaps we should curl it?"

Penny laughed. "Probably not. But I do think we should try putting it up. Take off your mop cap and sit down." She motioned to the chair in front of the dressing table.

Maggie frowned. "It don't seem right for you to wait on me."

"It's no bother. Just pretend I'm your sister."

Maggie dutifully sat in the chair. As Penny started brushing out her curls, Maggie sighed. "I wonder how my sisters are getting on these days. I haven't seen them in nearly a year."

"How many do you have?"

"Four sisters…and three brothers."

"I envy you. I haven't any siblings."

"It's just you then? What about your parents?"

"Both dead. The only close relative I have left is my cousin Adrian, but I'd rather not talk about him. What about Mr. Revington? Do you know anything about his family? I understand he has an older brother who's the heir. Has he ever visited here?"

"Not that I know of. The master is not much for

having people to the house. Except for Mr. Ludingham."

"Ah, Mr. Ludingham. What do you know about him? He seems like a very nice gentleman."

"Aye. He's a right genial sort. Spends a lot of time with Mr. Revington, he does."

Penny's thoughts again turned to the wager the two men had made. What was James's purpose in betting against Revington falling in love with her? Had he done it simply for his own amusement, or was he truly concerned for her?

As soon as Maggie's hair was finished, they set out for Bond Street in Revington's carriage, with the footman Jeremy driving. When they reached the fashionable district, Penny said, "Before we shop for you, I want to go back to Madame Dubonet's. She's the modiste who's making my wardrobe."

"What should I do in the meantime, miss?"

She didn't want Maggie to hear her conversation with the modiste. "Perhaps you could wait outside. I shouldn't be long."

Madame greeted Penny as soon as she stepped into the shop. "*Demoiselle*! How lovely to see you again. I'm afraid your clothing isn't quite finished yet. But it shouldn't be more than another day or so."

"The thing is, I was hoping to make a few changes before then."

Madame raised her perfectly arched brows in surprise. "Has something happened? Have you discovered you are *enceinte*?"

Penny, who knew the term meant expecting a child, felt herself blushing furiously. "No, that's not it at all." She glanced away, collecting her thoughts. "You recall when I was last here I mentioned meeting Elizabeth Valant?"

"*Oui, demoiselle.*"

"And we discussed her…ah…appeal for men."

"Indeed."

"Well, the thing is…I would like my new clothing to be more in line with what she might wear."

"You seek to present a more sophisticated appearance?"

"Yes, that's it."

Madame Dubonet nodded. "The day dresses you ordered are almost finished, but there's no reason we can't adjust the necklines a bit. For your more formal attire, we'll have to use altogether different styles and fabrics to obtain the effect you desire."

"Thank you. I expected you would know what to do."

Madame Dubonet smiled warmly and patted Penny's arm. "Don't worry, *demoiselle*, we will dress you in a way that will make certain your new husband won't look at another woman. But to do this, we must have another fitting. If you would please come with me."

"I didn't think we'd have to do that again," said Penny, feeling dismayed. "The thing is, my maid is waiting for me outside."

"She must come in then. We can't have her waiting in the street."

Penny went out to fetch Maggie. "I'm afraid this is going to take more time than I anticipated. I must be fitted again."

Maggie nodded and followed her into the shop.

"This is Maggie," Penny told Madame Dubonet.

"She's recently become a lady's maid and doesn't have an appropriate wardrobe yet. Mr. Revington has agreed to pay for some new garments for her. Certainly they can't be newly made, but perhaps you have something in her size that's already done up?"

Although Penny had worried Madame Dubonet would be condescending to Maggie, the modiste nodded politely to the Irishwoman. "If you would be so good as to take off your wrap, *demoiselle*, so I could see your figure."

Maggie removed the pelisse and stood awkwardly as Madame Dubonet examined her. After a moment, the modiste nodded. "*Oui*, I think we have something that will fit her." She snapped her fingers and dainty Giselle appeared. "Please search the storeroom and see if you can find a daydress or two that would fit Maggie." She gestured to the maid.

Madame Dubonet took Penny back to the fitting room where Penny removed her daydress and put on one of the new ones. The modiste lowered the neckline so that it barely covered Penny's zona and then pinned it in place. "You're fortunate your maid is of a similar size and shape. Eventually you'll be able to hand down your clothing to her."

Penny nodded even as she told herself that if her plan succeeded, she wouldn't need a maid or new garments. *Please let this work. Please let Revington fall in love with me so I don't have to marry him.*

Chapter Six

Marcus sat up and rubbed at the crick in his neck. He really should give in and purchase another bed. Or perhaps a whole bedroom suite. Even after he'd married Penny, they'd inevitably visit London on occasion and when they did, they'd need separate bedchambers.

Of course, right now, he'd happily share a bed with her. He got up and paced across the spare bedchamber to get his dressing gown. He'd been looking forward to that part of being married. She was quite an appealing female. He liked that she was no frail, delicate creature but fit and healthy. She rode a horse as well as any man he knew and yet when she climbed down from the horse, she moved with an elegant grace that was very, very female.

The tantalizing memory of Penny wearing breeches aroused him, and he let out a groan. He didn't want to wait a whole month to bed her. Why the devil had he agreed to such a ridiculous wager? He wasn't short of blunt, and he could afford to pay James to manage his affairs. But if he tried to get out of the agreement now, James would taunt him mercilessly and claim he was canceling the wager because he was afraid he'd lose. How ridiculous! Of course he wouldn't fall in love with Penny.

It was true she was much more appealing than he'd anticipated. He found he liked her, which was remarkable, given how little use he usually had for women. But Penny was so practical and no-nonsense; it was quite refreshing. She obviously had a good head on her shoulders or the horse operation wouldn't be so prosperous. That idiot Withersby clearly wasn't responsible for that. It had to be Penny.

As he put on his dressing gown, he considered what an intriguing contradiction his prospective wife was—intelligent and capable but also touchingly naïve. He found her artless innocence quite arousing, and he was looking forward to teaching her all the finer points of lovemaking. Growing up on a farm, she obviously knew about sex. But he doubted she knew anything about the delicious pleasures the experience could offer.

Damn. At this rate he'd never be able to get dressed. He could hardly call in Bowes while he had a raging erection that even his dressing gown wouldn't hide. For that matter, putting on trousers while he was in this state would be very uncomfortable. He must think of something besides Penny.

He'd focus on Horngate. The thought of taking control of the property aroused pleasure of another sort. He wished now he'd taken the time to look around and have Penny show him the horse operation. There was no reason to be in such a hurry to get to London. But at the time he'd been so keen to get the wedding over with that he hadn't wanted to bother with such things.

And then there was the startling way he'd met her. He recalled the shock of seeing her come tearing up on that enormous stallion, her hair flying around her flushed, lovely face and her blue eyes sparkling. The graceful way she'd dismounted and then the striking picture she'd made in a man's shirt and tight breeches.

Ah, the breeches…

Bloody hell! He was doing it again! He'd have to think of something else. Something tedious and annoying. Like the fact that since he was stuck in London for a month, he might as well try to win some more blunt while he had the opportunity. But that would have to wait. Today he'd promised Penny he would show her the sights.

At last, with his thoughts suitably subdued, he rang for Bowes.

****

"What do you think?" Penny took a step back from the looking glass so Maggie could get the full effect of her new attire.

Her new maid shook her head. "I can scarce believe it's you, miss. You're a bloomin' vision, you are."

Penny shared her maid's astonishment. She scarcely recognized herself either. Madame Dubonet had skillfully fashioned the dress to make the most of Penny's modest bosom; a remarkable amount of cleavage showed above the rose-colored ribbon framing the gown's deep neckline. The color was also skillfully chosen. The pale pink made her skin seem to glow. She gave a delighted laugh. "Now all we have to do is add the rest of the ensemble, and I'll be all ready to go sightseeing with Mr. Revington."

"You're going to wear that now, in the daytime?"

"Well, it is called a daydress," Penny responded to the Irishwoman's shock. "Believe it or not, the gowns I'm meant to wear for evening events are even skimpier."

Maggie's copper-colored brows shot up. "La, miss,

you'll look like an opera dancer or an actress!"

Penny couldn't help a small smile. "Do you think Mr. Revington will approve?"

"Approve may not be the particular word I'd use. But I'm quite certain he'll take notice of you."

"That's the idea, Maggie. I want Revington to see me as a woman, rather than an awkward country miss he has to marry in order to acquire Horngate."

Maggie frowned and drew near. "I hope you won't think I'm too forward, miss, in bringing this up. But I do think there's something about your plan you may not have considered. When he sees you in this gown, Mr. Revington's likely to want to take you to bed, whether you're wed yet or not. And while that might be the very thing to encourage his 'fondness', are you willing to go along? Because if you put out the bait..." She nodded toward the dress. "Then you have to deal with what you catch. Otherwise you'll make Mr. Revington angry rather than pleased with you."

Penny frowned and chewed her lower lip. What was she going to do if Revington decided to exert his marital rights before they were married? Maggie was right. If she refused him, he might be angry. And did she truly want to refuse him? The thought of being intimate with Revington filled her with foreboding, but also a shivery expectation. He was like no other man she'd ever known, so masculine, fierce and implacable. A stallion among a herd of geldings.

Suddenly aware of Maggie watching her, she responded, "I suspect you're right. But if I'm to wed him, I'll end up being intimate with him anyway, so there's no reason not to go through with it now. As far as society goes, since I'm staying in his house without a female relative or a proper chaperone, I'm ruined anyway."

Maggie smiled, showing her dimples. "They say the way to a man's heart is through his belly, but there's no sign that works with Revington. Perhaps it's another part of his person you must appeal to."

****

He might have known she'd take hours, Marcus thought with irritation as he waited in the drawing room. Offer to take a woman somewhere, and she fussed and fiddled half the day. He'd thought Penny was more practical than that, but it appeared she was as tardy as other members of her sex. A pity if she'd already been corrupted by Madame Dubonet and lost that ingenuous charm of hers. He rather liked the grubby hoyden he'd met in the drive of Horngate. She'd been a delightful change from the coy, manipulative women of the *ton*.

He paced across to the window to check on the phaeton and team. Hearing a faint sound, he turned. For a moment, he couldn't believe what he was seeing. His gaze moved down Penny's slender form, then returned to the expanse of lush creamy flesh exposed by the low neckline of her dress. He swallowed hard, then choked out, "What the devil are you wearing?"

She gave him an innocent smile. "It's my new daydress. Do you like it?"

Gone was the sweetly pretty young miss he'd brought to London. She'd been transformed into a sensual, sophisticated, breathtaking…goddess. It wasn't just the lush décolletage the gown revealed, but the color of the fabric. Some subtle shade of pink that made her look edible. He longed to kiss and lick and nibble every inch of the silken, creamy skin the garment exposed. And then move on to the parts concealed by the soft, shimmery fabric. The very thought made him instantly aroused.

He took a deep breath and tried to focus on Penny's face. "The dress is fashionable, I'm certain. But if you don't want to catch a chill, you'd best put on your pelisse."

Penny hurried to do as he suggested. Despite having carefully planned this moment, when it actually came time to appear before Revington in the skimpy gown, she'd experienced an attack of nerves. It had taken all her willpower to walk boldly into the drawing room, despite feeling half-naked.

Revington's expression had turned quite strange, almost savage. But then a moment later, his normal reserve had prevailed and he'd carried on in his usual impatient style.

She donned her pelisse and started for the door. Then she remembered the other part of her plan. Turning, she said, "I wondered if rather than driving today, you could have footman take the reins and sit in the carriage with me. That way you'll be able to tell me about the sights as we travel through the city."

A muscle twitched in his jaw; she wondered whether he disliked the thought of spending time with her. Too bad, she thought stubbornly. For her plan to work, she needed to force him into close proximity.

****

As the carriage wound through the vivid spring greenery of Hyde Park, Penny tried to assess the mood of the man next to her. He'd said very little since they set out, answering her questions, but volunteering nothing. Trying again, she said, "So this is Rotten Row, where the fashionable go riding?"

"Yes."

Not much she could do with that. His refusal to contribute to the conversation was getting rather aggravating.

A moment later, they pulled up next to an open carriage. Penny couldn't help gaping at the extremely heavy-set man wearing a daffodil yellow waistcoat. Was that how fashionable men dressed in London?

The man lifted a gloved hand. "I say there, Revington, you old dog." He gave a terse order to his driver and the vehicle halted. Apparently taking his cue from the other driver, the footman driving Revington's rig also pulled the team to a halt.

"Bloody hell," Revington muttered. Then the next moment he said in a perfectly cordial voice, "Good day, Lord Haversfield. You're looking well."

"As are you, Revington." Haversfield raised a quizzing glass and scrutinized Penny. "And who is that with you?"

Revington cleared his throat. "Lord Haversfield, may I make known to you Penelope Montgomery, my...er...fiancée."

Haversfield removed the glass. He gazed at Revington a few moments, then chortled, "You don't say, Revington. Wherever did you find her? She's quite a fetching creature. A diamond of the first water."

Revington cleared his throat again. "Our families recently became acquainted. Found we had some business interests in common."

"Gads, but you're a sly one, Revington. Why, if I'd known such a luscious bit of muslin was available on the marriage mart, I might have been tempted to get leg-shackled myself."

"I rather doubt it. You're not known for romantic gestures, Harry."

"For that matter, neither are you. What's the story here, Revington? Is she an heiress as well as a beauty? Have you finally decided to seek your fortune by less chancy methods than cards and dice?"

Revington's voice became even crisper. "None of your business, my lord. And if you think I've lost my touch, how about a game or two. Say tonight at White's?"

Haversfield shook his head. "I'm not that much of a fool. You've fleeced me for all you're going to get."

"Sorry to hear that, your lordship. Good day to you." To the driver, Revington said, "Move on, Benjamin."

"Good day to you as well," Haversfield called as their carriage pulled away. "I'm charmed to make your acquaintance, Miss Montgomery. Hopefully I'll be seeing you soon."

"Like hell you will," muttered Revington under his breath.

"Do you dislike Lord Haversfield for some reason?" Penny asked as they left the other carriage behind.

Revington shot her a hooded look. "He's no better or worse than most of his kind. Bit of a lecher though. If we go out in society, he's the sort of man you need to steer clear of."

"I would like to attend a party or two," Penny said. In fact, she rather dreaded the notion, but having observed how Haversfield's keen regard had aroused

Revington's jealousy, she decided she should take advantage of this weakness. "Given that I have a whole new wardrobe, it seems a waste not to make use of it. In addition to several daydresses similar to this one, Madame Dubonet insisted I must have at least two gowns for evening functions."

"Of course," Revington said tightly. He fell silent again, and a short while later suggested they return to the townhouse.

She agreed, with a stab of irritation. They'd been out driving barely an hour. Did he think that constituted seeing the sights?

Of course, going back to the townhouse suited her goals better than driving around the city, especially since he was practically ignoring her. Her plan was to seduce him so he would warm to her and possibly fall in love. It seemed rather far-fetched, but she had no other ideas. Having sex with him was bound to help her cause. It would force him to see her as a woman, rather than the unpleasant encumbrance he'd acquired along with Horngate.

Although the logic of her plan was clear, she felt apprehensive about carrying it out. The thought of being close to Revington, of being naked with him, filled her stomach with butterflies. She'd never even kissed a man, other than her father. As for the rest of it, well...she knew the basics, but not much else.

Her mind filled with images of Hero at stud. It didn't appear that enjoyable for the mares, and she suspected they only allowed it because they were in season and nature drove them to do it. Did female humans tolerate it for the same reason—because it was some basic drive? Or did some, like Elizabeth Valant, enjoy it?

An image of Revington and Elizabeth flashed briefly into her thoughts, and Penny's body reacted with a surge of tingling warmth. It began between her legs and quickly spread. Despite her mind's doubts, her body seemed convinced that being naked with Revington and having him touch her would be quite enjoyable.

But how was she to seduce him? As soon as they arrived at the townhouse, he'd likely disappear into the library. She had to find a way to keep him from dismissing her. To reignite that flare of interest she'd seen in his eyes when he first saw her in her new daydress.

Unfortunately, said dress was now quite covered by her pelisse, and with the cool weather, it would seem odd if she suddenly removed her outer garment. But perhaps, if she loosened it and leaned toward him he might catch a glimpse of her modest décolletage.

She waited until he was looking away, then carefully adjusted the neckline so it was even lower. Unbuttoning her pelisse, she let it fall away from her body. As they left the park, she leaned toward him. "The lilacs are lovely this time of year, don't you think?"

"Mmmm, quite," he muttered.

Penny touched his arm. He turned toward her. His gaze shifted downward and fixed on her chest for long intense seconds. She sensed his quickened breathing and sudden arousal. When he raised his gaze, she was transfixed, pinned in place by his dark eyes. Long moments passed. Finally he said, "Although the view is delightful, I would suggest you adjust your attire."

Looking down, she realized what he meant. In pulling down her bodice, she'd managed to completely expose one of her breasts. She gave a little gasp and covered herself. "Thank you. Madame Dubonet failed to prepare me for the uh…risks of wearing fashionable attire."

"Indeed." He turned away.

The heat of a blush moved up her neck. She was mortified. The next moment, she was angry. *If Elizabeth Valant had exposed herself to him, he would not react with such cool detachment!*

She blinked hard, her anger and embarrassment bringing sudden tears to her eyes. What a fool she was to think she could entice a man like Revington. He was a hardened, cold-blooded…She searched for a term harsh enough to reflect her mood. *A bloody bastard*, that's what he was!

She fumed for a short while, nursing her resentment, then gradually sought to force it aside. It was absurd to be so upset. She'd known from the beginning that getting him to respond would be a challenge. He was a jaded, cynical gamester. Hardly the sort to fall for an unsophisticated country girl. She'd have to think up some other scheme to avoid having to marry him. But what? In this game, as she supposed he did in many others, Revington seemed to hold all the cards.

When the townhouse came into view, she let out a small sigh. The last few minutes had been agonizing—sitting beside him while he blatantly ignored her. Was he angry? How dare he be! He wasn't her husband, at least not yet. Besides, she'd revealed only a tiny bit more flesh than Elizabeth Valant had displayed outside

Madame Dubonet's. Remembering the incident, she decided it was outrageously hypocritical of him to appear so offended.

Penny fought to hold on to her anger, but underneath it, a gnawing gloom threatened. Revington hadn't seemed even a tiny bit aroused by the sight of her breast. Did that mean he had no interest in her as a bed partner? She knew she wasn't beautiful or her figure particularly impressive. But other things had led her to believe she was reasonably attractive. Tad had said so, and with the other servants at Horngate, she'd always felt they not only approved of her but felt a sense of pride that she was their mistress.

No. She would not act like a mewling milk-and-water miss and feel sorry for herself. She was an heiress to a fine estate. She deserved better than the scorn and disapproval Revington's attitude reflected.

At the thought of Horngate, new determination filled her. She *would* find a way to make Revington see her as a woman, and use that weakness to keep him from running roughshod over her.

At the townhouse, Revington climbed out and reached up to help her from the carriage. She considered pretending to slip and fall against him, but couldn't make herself do it. He thought her awkward and embarrassingly unsophisticated as it was. No need to reinforce that outlook by acting like a graceless ninny.

As soon as they were inside, Revington gave her a terse bow. "I enjoyed your company today, Penny. I look forward to seeing you at dinner."

Despite his gracious words, there could be no doubt she'd been dismissed. Penny smiled tightly. "I enjoyed today as well." She turned and started up the stairs.

Chapter Seven

Marcus gritted his teeth as he made his way to the library. Damn, he was still aroused! Penny was driving him to madness. The whole way back to the townhouse he'd had to fight the urge to dismiss the driver, drive the carriage to a secluded area of the park, then lay her down on the carriage seat and have her right there!

And it wasn't merely the provocative glimpse of her beautiful breast that threatened to push him over the edge. It was the awareness that she had no idea of her effect on him.

If Elizabeth had exposed herself to him in such a fashion, he'd have laughed at her and told her not to be such a greedy slut. He'd be aroused, but would have no real desire to act on it. Elizabeth's shameless cock-teasing could get tiresome. There were times he almost felt used, knowing he was only one of many men she engaged to satisfy her.

But with Penny, things were different, he mused as he poured himself a brandy. She was so fresh and sweet, so charmingly unaware of her beauty. Along with intense desire, he felt a longing to protect her, to keep her from being corrupted by the harsh, crude world of London society. He wanted her to remain the way she was when he found her.

At the same time, he longed to introduce her to all the delights of lovemaking. To teach her the pleasures her body could experience. He fancied himself a good lover, taking as much time and care with a woman as necessary to bring her to her peak. His ability to be patient and subtle was wasted on someone like Elizabeth, who wanted it hard and fast. But with Penny, skill and tenderness might actually matter. He would make it good for her, even the first time.

He took a deep swallow of brandy, reminding himself that he would never be able to do that in his current state of arousal. If he bedded her now, he'd lose control and make a botch of the whole thing. Somehow he had to get himself in a more relaxed state of mind first.

On the other hand, he shouldn't have been so terse with her. Recalling the almost chiding way he'd responded to the sight of her exquisite breast, he winced. She must think him a cold bastard. Gads! There was no excuse for his behavior. What was it about her that brought out the worst in him?

He took another swallow of the brandy and grimaced. He was well aware of his faults. Numerous women had pointed out that he was prone to appearing distant and uncaring. With Penny, his behavior was even worse. The more she affected him, the more he found himself drawing away. Having made up his mind that he wanted quite badly to take her to bed, he'd done everything he could to push her away. He'd cut short the sightseeing trip. Ignored her on the way back to the townhouse. Then curtly dismissed her when they arrived.

Soon they would dine together. Somehow he must overcome this uncharacteristic nervousness and regain his poise. Do something to take the edge off his rampant lust. Maybe he should visit Elizabeth. A quick furious tumble with her would be just the thing.

His conscience tweaked him. It probably wasn't appropriate to bed another woman a few hours before attempting to seduce one's fiancée. But if he didn't do something, he suspected he'd make a complete bungle of things with Penny.

He checked the water clock on the table. Half past three. He certainly had time to see Elizabeth. Or, if she wasn't home, he could always go to the house of Venus several of his acquaintances had recommended.

He rang the bell for Bowes. "Have the phaeton brought around. I'm going out. Not for long. Indeed, I'll be back in plenty of time to join Penny...Miss Montgomery for the evening meal."

"Very good, sir."

****

"You look like an utter fool," Penny muttered, staring at her reflection in the dressing room mirror. Not only was the mauve gown low-cut, the sheer fabric gave more than a hint of her naked form beneath it. "You should forget this nonsense and put on something sensible." Thing was, she didn't have anything sensible. Madame Dubonet had designed nothing like the plain, high-necked green gown she'd worn to London. And she couldn't wear that. It was truly awful. Indeed, she'd chosen it exactly for that reason.

"There really is no help for it," she told herself firmly. "You don't have a better plan."

She went to the window and tried to gauge the time of day. It was at least an hour until the evening meal. She didn't know what to do in the meantime. Although she'd started a novel, it wasn't holding her interest. Life in London was quite boring. Other than shopping or riding around, there didn't appear to be much to do during the daytime—a stark contrast to her usual existence at Horngate, where there were always a dozen things demanding her attention. And if she finished with the most pressing tasks, she could always go riding.

A sharp pang of longing shot through her. She didn't want to give up the life she loved at Horngate. Lord Haversfield had referred to marriage as being "leg-shackled". The term sounded perfectly appropriate. She didn't want to be tied to Revington, to be forced to go along with whatever he wanted. Which meant that somehow she had to find a way to make him fall in love with her so she could avoid marrying him and everything could go back to the way it was before.

And she didn't want to wait hours to put her plan into action. There was no reason she couldn't see Revington now, rather than waiting until dinner. If she meant to seduce him, there was no time like the present.

Pushing aside the doubts and worries crowding her mind, she strode briskly to the door. She kept up her bold pace all the way down the stairs, slowing only as she neared the library. *Oh, dear, this is it, the moment of truth!* Taking a deep breath, she squared her shoulders and opened the door.

All the expectation and tension drained out of her. The room was empty. Had he gone up to change for dinner? Or left the townhouse altogether?

She headed toward the foyer. Seeing Bowes, she immediately guessed the truth. "Mr. Revington has left, hasn't he?"

For a fraction of a second, the butler's gaze dipped

to her décolletage, then swiftly returned to her face. "Indeed, miss. But he did say he would return in time to dine with you."

Penny longed to ask the butler if he knew where his master had gone, but she doubted if Bowes would tell her. "Very good. I'll come back down as it gets closer to the dining hour."

She started up the stairs, fuming. Revington was clearly avoiding her. He'd rushed back to the townhouse, dumped her off and left again. It was obvious he considered spending time with her a great trial, and only did it when politeness forced him to do so. Under the circumstances, her scheme to seduce him seemed utterly futile.

****

Marcus drove the phaeton around the block for the third time. It had seemed simple enough earlier, but now that he was actually here, outside Elizabeth's townhouse, he couldn't bring himself to go in. This wasn't what he wanted, not at all. If James were here, he'd be certain to tell him what a horrible plan this was, to bed one woman when he was actually longing for another.

Indeed, thinking about Elizabeth, the idea of bedding her suddenly seemed distasteful. He was repelled by her vulgarity, her selfishness. Once he'd suggested they slow things down and get to know each other a bit, perhaps share a meal or take a drive around the city. She'd responded scornfully that she didn't need a companion and had no interest in him except as a lover.

Heading back home, he realized that what he'd proposed to do with Elizabeth was exactly what he should do with Penny. Before he bedded her, she needed to get to know him. Before consummating the relationship, he must court her.

At the townhouse, he changed and went down to the dining room. Penny was already seated. As she looked up, he repressed a gasp. She looked absolutely spectacular in another low-cut gown, this one a pale, purplish-pink shade, with a band of black lace around the bodice. The mere sight of her made him want to pull her from the chair and ravish her. Instead, he stiffly took a seat opposite. "You look lovely tonight, Penny."

"Thank you."

Now what the hell did he say? Recalling his plan to court her, he searched his mind for a topic that might interest her. *Ah, yes, Horngate. The horses.* Clearing his throat, he said, "So, you grew up at Horngate?"

She gave him a startled look. "Yes. In fact, I was born there."

"No siblings?"

"I'm afraid not. I had a brother, but he died in infancy."

"I'm sorry." He took a drink of his wine. He was already making a muddle of things, bringing up matters she likely wanted to forget. He tried again. "I'm very interested in the horse operation at Horngate. You seem quite knowledgeable about breeding. Did your father teach you the business?"

"Yes, it was he who started raising horses."

"And you said you raise both hunters and carriage horses?"

As he continued to ask about the horse operation, he realized he'd blundered again. Her expression grew guarded and her voice, terse, almost expressionless.

Damn! He had no idea how to deal with her.

Thankfully, the footman served their soup and for a time they could pretend to be occupied by eating.

He still hadn't come up with anything to say, when she broke the silence. "We've discussed my background. But what about you? James says you make your living at cards?"

Caught off guard, he answered. "Why, yes. I've been quite successful with my wagering. But it isn't luck. It's a matter of learning the odds of getting a certain hand. And knowing when to keep playing and when to stop. That's the mistake most people make. When they start winning, they lose control and bet even more. It's essential to keep to a rigid plan and remain completely unemotional."

"So, that's your secret? You refuse to get caught up in the moment, to lose control?"

Marcus nodded and took another bite of his fish. He didn't like talking about these things. While he had no fear she would turn his methods against him—it was unlikely they'd ever play cards together—he was still uncomfortable revealing his methods.

She gave him an arched look. "Given your skill, I'm not surprised you won Horngate from Adrian. My cousin has always been one to lose his head."

He nodded, thinking she didn't like her cousin much. He couldn't blame her. Withersby was a bastard. He needed to move the conversation in a different direction. But what should they talk about? No wonder he'd never associated with women in situations where he would be required to converse with them. This was dashedly hard work!

They ate in silence. As the footman brought the

meat course, Marcus tried again. "Did you enjoy yourself today?"

At last, a bit of a smile. "Yes, I did. I liked Hyde Park especially. All the trees and flowers. I'm afraid I'm already homesick for the country."

"You didn't care for the rest of it, the Carlton House and the other fine buildings?"

"I'm afraid not. Of course, merely driving by, I'm certain I didn't get a true sense of the real splendor of the city." She paused, then added, I would still like to attend some balls or soirees. I must take advantage of my new wardrobe."

At the mention of her wardrobe, he immediately glanced at her décolletage. She caught his gaze and frowned. What had he done wrong now? Given that she was wearing a gown that revealed a good portion of her bosom, he didn't understand her reaction. Unless she was remembering what happened in the carriage.

Oh, damn, that was it! Recalling the curt, almost rude way he'd addressed her, he gritted his teeth. He must make it up to her. Treat her like a lady, rather than an object of his lust. It wouldn't be easy. But he had to try.

He took another swallow of wine. "I'm certain we can find some sort of social event where you can make use of your new wardrobe. Although I'm not invited to many functions these days. Most of the society matrons have given up on me."

"Oh, why is that?"

"I suppose in the past I so seldom accepted invitations that they've written me off as hopeless."

"You don't like parties or balls?"

He hesitated. While the fact was, he hated them, it

was probably unwise to tell her this. Given that she'd just expressed the desire to attend one of these functions, it would be quite rude of him to make his real feelings known.

"It's not that...exactly. It's more...I suppose I've always been so occupied with pursuing business matters that I've ignored the social opportunities that have come my way. But now that I have Horngate, it would behoove me to mingle more in society. After all, we'll need to find buyers for the horses bred at the farm." He shot her a smile as he said this. Surely this would please her. She'd have an opportunity to enjoy London society and at the same time, talk about her beloved horses.

Again, she reacted unexpectedly. She gave him a look that could only described as hostile and responded in clipped tones. "That sounds delightful. And of course, I would also like to go to Covent Garden and the theatre. I've heard the shows are something to see."

"Indeed."

What the devil did she want! The woman was impossible to please! He took a deep breath and focused on the trifle the footman had brought. The next month would be grim indeed. Especially if he didn't find a way to take her to bed. His attraction to her hadn't ebbed, but had grown fiercer. Perhaps it was the wine. In his distraction, he'd drunk his first glass quite quickly and already started on a second. She'd hardly touched hers. He definitely needed to get her to imbibe more.

As the footman cleared away their plates, Marcus said, "Perhaps we should take our wine into the library."

What a surprise, Penny thought sourly. He was actually going to spend time with her, rather than abandoning her as soon as he'd fulfilled his minimum obligation! Could it be he was warming to her?

She should be pleased, but she wasn't. She was still furious about the way he'd talked about finding buyers for *her* horses. No matter how she sought to distract him, Horngate always remained on his mind. The man was as cold and single-minded as James had portrayed him! Their whole conversation during dinner had been a disaster. She'd had to struggle not to snap at him as he gloated over the success of the horse operation.

But now she had to get hold of herself and remember her goal. This was it, her chance to seduce him.

Revington called Bowes and asked the butler to prepare the room for them. A few moments later, they both rose from the table, and Revington escorted her to the library. Although the fire had been lit, it was still a bit chilly. She couldn't quite suppress a shiver as they entered. He apparently noticed, for he said, "Here, drink some of your wine. It will help warm you."

He held out her glass, which he'd carried along. She accepted it and took a quick swallow. He was right. The ruby red liquid burned a pathway of heat down to her stomach. She took another swallow, gradually getting used to the taste. Wine wasn't a beverage to which she was accustomed.

"There. That's better, isn't it?" He was watching her intently.

Her anger and determination vanished, replaced with a sense of panic. He was so close. The expanse of the dining room table had served as a comfortable barrier, but now there was nothing between them. In many ways. She was uncomfortably aware of the sheerness of her gown. It made her feel vulnerable, like helpless prey.

****

She was driving him to madness. His cock was rock-hard and his whole body on fire. To be so close to her...to the alabaster perfection of her skin, her slender and yet sensual body. Her sweet mouth. Those huge blue eyes.

With effort, he forced himself to glance away. He took her glass from her and went to pour more wine from the bottle Bowes had brought in. "Have a bit more. It's a fairly good vintage." He carried the glass back to her.

She nodded and obediently took a swallow. He watched, entranced as the dark red liquid stained her lips. By god, he wanted to kiss her in the worst way!

She took another swallow, then looked up and saw him staring at her. "What is it?" She gazed at him, blue eyes wide. "What's wrong?"

All this polite conversation was going nowhere. He had to act...now!

She drew in her breath sharply as Revington took her glass of wine. His dark eyes focused on her with an intensity that was frightening. He carried both of their glasses to the table and set them down, then came back to where she stood. She was on the verge of again asking what was wrong when he seized her.

His arms surrounded her, pressing her against his hard chest. His mouth came down on hers. Despite the ferocity of his embrace, the kiss was tender. He caressed her lips with his own. Subtle. Sublime.

Delicious warmth shimmered through her. Her body seemed to melt. She could smell him. Then, as he coaxed her lips apart, she could taste him. Sweet. Heady. Male.

Unthinkingly, she pressed her body against his. She wanted to be closer. To merge with him. The joining of their mouths sent shockwaves down her body. She was keenly aware of her nipples as hard, aching points. Of a throbbing, yearning sensation in her lower abdomen.

The kiss deepened. She felt his tongue in her mouth and met it with her own. Their tongues danced. Mated. Drowning in a sea of sensation, Penny finally came up for air. As he raised his head, she let out a low moan.

He looked almost savage, ferocious. But she wasn't afraid. She felt drawn to his wild intensity. He kissed her again, more forcefully this time. His mouth possessed hers. She melted. Dissolved. His hands were on her buttocks, pressing her against him. She could feel the hard ridge of his phallus through the thick wool of his trousers. The sensation made her squirm, wanting, needing, something more.

She was writhing against him, begging for it. He felt almost dizzy with desire. Her ardent response almost undid him. But he reminded himself she was a gently reared virgin. He must slow down if he wanted to make it good for her.

He raised his head…and nearly lost control again. She looked so beautiful. Her eyes were deep blue pools of yearning. Her lush pink lips parted in invitation. Her expression was not one of innocence, but frank sexual need. Somehow he had to satisfy her and yet not fall into the abyss of his own arousal.

With trembling fingers, he slid down the strap of her gown, exposing one of her breasts. He cupped her opulent, creamy flesh and lowered his mouth to taste her delectable pink nipple. Suckled. Nibbled. Caressed her sweet delicate flesh with his teeth. Then, adjusting her dress, he transferred his attentions to the other side. She sighed and let out a soft moan.

He was intoxicated, overwhelmed with desire. But some part of his mind remained aware, reminding of him of the lack of privacy. With great effort, he drew away and murmured, "We should go upstairs."

She was frowning. Damn! When faced with the reality of what they were doing, she seemed to have lost her nerve. He shouldn't have broken things off, but just laid her down on the settle and had her. Bowes would never have dared disturb them and it wouldn't have been too awkward. But, strangely, he didn't want it to be like that with her. That was something he would do with Elizabeth—tumbling her on the floor or a piece of furniture. Penny deserved more care and consideration.

****

With effort, she fought off the mind-numbing haze of desire. He wanted to go upstairs. Once they did that, there would be no turning back.

Not that she wanted to turn back. Her whole body ached with longing and unfulfilled desire. But her mind remained wary. Did she really want to do this—give herself up to this man who affected her so intensely? It seemed dangerous to lose control, especially with someone she was trying to manipulate. What had he said about winning at cards, that the important thing was not to get carried away emotionally?

Penny turned away from him. Was there some way

to let him know she desired to continue things, but not yet? She could hardly tell him she wanted to wait until they were wed. That would ruin her whole plan. She must be careful not to give him that idea. There was nothing she could do except go upstairs and continue.

Steadying herself, she turned to back to him, smiling sweetly. "Yes, we should go upstairs. That's exactly what we should do."

Chapter Eight

Revington stared at her a moment, then gestured toward door. "After you."

She left the library. Revington followed, carrying their wineglasses and the half-empty bottle. She was grateful for his foresight. They might both need to imbibe more spirits to get through this.

Her heart raced as she went up the stairs. The dazed, almost trance-like state she'd experienced had been replaced by a mixture of terror and excitement. Her breasts and private parts tingled with longing, but the idea of what would happen next panicked her. If his kisses and caresses could cause her to slip into a kind of wild delirium, how would actual consummation affect her? Would she would lose all sense of reason and completely forget the plan? She dreaded being so vulnerable. But what choice did she have? She could scarcely back out now.

****

He decided that having Penny walk upstairs ahead of him had been a bad idea. A very bad idea. As if he wasn't aroused enough, the sight of her pert little bottom swaying provocatively nearly pushed him over the edge. He loved her slender elegance. Her tall graceful form perfectly rounded in all the right places. Her sheer gown revealed much of those delicious curves, while his memory of her in riding breeches supplied the rest. Soon he would be able to see all of her. How would he maintain control?

He took a deep breath, glad his hands were occupied with the glasses and the bottle. He must focus on practical things. Hopefully, his bedchamber would be warm enough without a fire. Should he start undressing immediately? Was she ready for that? He was unsure how to go from making polite conversation to making love. In the library, he'd simply grabbed her and kissed her. Such blunt behavior showed a lack of finesse. But he didn't know how they'd ever get to the next step unless he took direct action.

The problem was, he didn't know her. They'd exchanged superficial information about their lives, but never revealed themselves to each other. In playing cards, discretion and secretiveness were essential, but it didn't seem appropriate in a marriage. He didn't want to always be guessing what she was thinking, to never truly know her mind.

But maybe sexual intimacy would lead to more openness between them in other ways. Even as his mind worried over these things, his body had no such qualms. He wanted her as badly as he'd ever wanted a woman.

When they reached the bedchamber, he put the two glasses on the small escritoire and quickly poured them each a substantial portion of wine. It was clear she was nervous. She stood by the bed, looking like a startled deer, set to flee at any moment. Indeed, she had the same delicacy and ethereal beauty as a lovely doe: long legs, graceful neck, wide, expressive eyes. Although hers were deep blue rather than brown.

But as he approached and handed her the wine, he was keenly reminded that she was a woman, not a hind.

His eyes lingered on her décolletage, remembering how those softly rounded, luscious breasts had felt in his hands. The taste of her tender pink nipples.

With effort, he returned his gaze to her face. As she took a swallow of wine, he was overwhelmed with the memory of kissing her. The splendor of her mouth. The feel of her body in his arms. He took a sharp breath, struggling against his almost painful arousal. He couldn't endure this much longer.

Finishing his wine, he reached for her nearly empty glass. She handed it to him, and he set the two goblets on the table. Returning to her, he smiled. "Now, where were we?"

You were kissing me senseless, was the response that sprang to Penny's lips, although she didn't speak the words. In a heartbeat, he closed the distance between them. He took her face in his hands. The tenderness of the gesture shocked her. She could only wait helplessly, silently begging him to bring his mouth to hers.

And then he did.

It was even better than their first kisses. She knew now how to open her mouth and respond to his teasing, tantalizing tongue thrusts. As their tongue-play grew more passionate, she leaned into his solid warmth and strength and let her body meld to his. Her breasts were crushed against his hard chest and her stomach rested against the provocative ridge of his arousal. The unmistakable evidence of his masculinity made her weak with longing.

Seized by a sudden restlessness, she pressed herself against him. Her body knew exactly what she needed. If only he would touch her…soothe that tormenting ache.

****

He could scarcely believe how responsive she was. The awareness nearly pushed him over the edge. He wanted to rip off their clothing and push her down on the bed. With effort, he forced himself to continue with foreplay, kissing her neck, then moving his hands down to cup her buttocks. As he pulled her against him, she made soft mewling sounds. He kneaded her delicate flesh through her gown and then pulled up the thin silk, exposing her sheer muslin pantaloons. Dragging them down, he touched bare skin. *Mmmm. Pure bliss.*

He stroked and fondled, then slid his fingers along the cleft of her bottom, seeking paradise. She moaned as he touched her tender essence, her response making him fight for control. She was so wet. So small and tight. He could barely get a finger inside her. Somehow he must slow down, take his time to ready her.

He edged her toward the bed where he broke off their kiss and helped her lie down. She rested on her elbows facing him, her eyes wide and helpless, her kiss-swollen lips parted. He pulled off her slippers and stockings, then pushed her dress further up and took her pantalettes completely off. For a moment, he admired her naked beauty. Then he gently spread her thighs and lowered his mouth to kiss her sweet, intimate flesh. She let out a cry of mingled delight and shock.

****

Dear heavens! She'd been on the verge of begging him to soothe her savage need, but she'd never guessed he'd do it this way! The pressure of his mouth both soothed and tormented her. She writhed and raised her hips as a fierce heat built inside her. She could not. Help. Herself. Could. Not…

A wild cry escaped her lips as a fierce energy burst inside her and exploded.

Gradually, she floated back to earth and opened her eyes. Revington was leaning over her. His mouth glistened with moisture and his dark eyes watched her. She felt her face heat with a blush at the thought of what he'd done to her. And this was only the beginning. They had not yet...

She took a deep breath, anticipating what was to come. The aching, heated sensation again built inside her. How could that be? He'd taken her to such heights of feeling. Could there really be more delights to experience?

But as he started to undress, she felt a twinge of panic. A few moments before, she'd been quite sure of herself. But that was before she realized just how intimidating he would be without his clothing. His bare shoulders seemed twice as broad and his naked torso much more muscular.

He sat on the chair by the bed to remove his boots. Once they were off, he stood and pulled down his trousers and small clothes. She stared. She hadn't anticipated that his male member would be so...

She brought her gaze back to his face. If she didn't look down there, she might regain her nerve.

But, having seen him, she couldn't get the image from her mind. She told herself he wasn't as large as a stallion, that there was no reason to be intimidated. But he was certainly larger than she'd anticipated. She couldn't imagine how they were going to...

He seemed to guess that his nakedness unsettled her. Moving quickly, he climbed onto the bed, pulled her into his arms and kissed her.

Once again she gave into the delights his lips and tongue and teeth could arouse. By the time he'd kissed and nibbled her neck and shoulders, she was helpless with desire. As he mouthed her breasts, the yearning ache between her legs grew urgent. She clung to him as he eased her farther onto the bed, feeling nearly blind with desire. The feel of him on top of her, his heated flesh against hers...Oh!

And still he kissed her, plundering her mouth, then nuzzling her earlobes and neck. She writhed and moaned, feeling as if she would burst into flames. Helpless with need, she spread her legs and lifted her hips, seeking something, seeking *him*. In response, he rubbed his phallus against her, making her feel the hard, heated length. Holding himself above her, he rubbed his member against her belly and then lower. As the soft, plump tip stroked her intimate parts, she opened herself to him, desperate to be filled, to have the raw, fierce ache inside her soothed and satisfied.

****

At last, she was ready. His own control was near the breaking point. As she thrust her hips up to meet him, frantically seeking penetration, he used his hand to guide himself, pressing his cock against her sweet slit. For a few seconds, there was resistance, then he was inside her. She let out a gasping moan, and he felt her body tense around his. The pressure nearly did him in. He closed his eyes and gritted his teeth, fighting the desperate urge to thrust deep.

Reaching between them, he found the top of her cleft and sought the tiny tender nub at the center of her pleasure. She reacted by moaning and shifting her hips, allowing deeper access. He continued to stroke her, not touching the sensitive spot but circling around it. She arched her body and cried out. As she went limp, he thrust harder and faster, finally giving in to the implacable needs of his own body.

She was caught up in a whirlwind of mindless sensation. Once, twice, three times she reached some pinnacle of feeling, partially recovered, then found herself climbing the heights again. As he dragged her to the summit, his breathing was harsh and fast in her ears, while his body pulsed inside hers with some ancient rhythm. She could only hold on while they galloped toward their soul-shattering destination. Close...closer...His deep groan echoed her own intense release.

He collapsed upon her, breathing hard. She held him tight, feeling a deep tenderness. As he raised his head and looked at her, she saw perplexity in his expression...and something else, a sudden wariness. Triumph surged through her. She'd reached him. For a brief time, the mask of the cold, hardened gamester had fallen away and she'd forced him to actually feel something for her.

But along with that realization came another thought. In the process of drawing him out, she'd stripped away her own protection. If she'd made him care for him, then it was balanced by a sudden surge of yearning in her own heart.

She struggled for control, telling herself she couldn't give up her own goal and let her emotions overrule her wits. The pleasure he'd shown her was fleeting. She had the whole rest of her life to consider.

****

It would be so easy to fall asleep here. His body

felt replete with sexual satisfaction, his whole being, languid and content. The next moment he reminded himself that he'd already let Penny get too close. He dare not fall asleep next to her silky feminine warmth, or what reason and resolve he had remaining would dissolve.

He forced himself to get out of bed, taking care not to touch her or look at her as he did so. Somehow he had to regain his poise, his normal sense of himself. He gathered his clothing, but even that action brought his thoughts back to Penny, reminding him how he'd practically torn off his garments in desperate need to join his body with hers.

Damn! He must remember not to go so long without having sex. Yes, that was it. He'd simply waited too long, allowed himself to become too desperate. That was why he'd wanted her so badly.

He jerked on his trousers and hastily buttoned his shirt. Now that the deed was done, he needed to move on, to get back to his normal mode of living. He needed some distance from his response to her, the way her body felt in his arms. Her scent, her taste…

Hurriedly putting on his stockings and boots, he made up his mind. He'd go to the club. Have a few brandies and look for a game. After all, that was his business, his livelihood. He'd neglected it far too much as it was. Grabbing his coat and cravat—he'd have Bowes retie it—he hurried out the door.

****

Penny sat up at the sound of the door shutting. As Revington dressed, she'd been in a kind of daze. She hadn't thought he'd leave so abruptly, and without saying a word.

120

She got out of bed and went to the adjoining water closet, then returned to the bedchamber. Her sense of repletion vanished, and she felt bereft and melancholy. She was obviously wrong to think lovemaking would influence Revington's feelings for her. If such a blindingly intense experience didn't affect him, nothing would. Her whole plan was a waste of time.

Even worse was the knowledge that what they'd shared had changed her feelings for *him*. They'd been so close, as if they were one person instead of two. How was she to forget that and go back to despising him?

Restless, she grabbed her clothing and dressed. But even as she clothed herself, she couldn't help thinking about the way Revington had kissed her. A wave of emotion swept through her and she bit her lower lip, feeling as if she might weep. What was wrong with her? Why did she long to have him come back and hold her in his arms?

She forced off the mood, finished dressing and redid her coiffure as best she could. Downstairs, she peeked into the library but found it empty. She sought out Bowes in the foyer. "I'm looking for Mr. Revington."

"He's gone out."

Feeling irritated and depressed, she went to the library and tried to read. She glanced up frequently, watching time creep by on the mantel clock. When the hands pointed to eleven o'clock, she slammed the book shut.

Where was he? With Elizabeth Valant? Bitter jealousy clenched her jaw. How dare he treat her like this? She was his fiancée. She deserved some respect and consideration. The next moment, her anger slipped away and she felt almost despairing.

Disgusted with herself, she left the library. Bowes was in the foyer. "I'm going to bed, Bowes."

"Very good, miss."

As she started up the stairs, her fury returned. Did the whole staff guess Revington had bedded her and then left like a man fleeing for his life?

Thinking of the staff made her remember Maggie. She could certainly use some company now, not to mention some advice. Returning downstairs, she asked Bowes, "Is Maggie still up?"

"I'll go and see. Should I send her up if she is?"

"Yes, but if she'd gone to bed, don't wake her."

She went back upstairs and changed into her nightrail. A few minutes later, there was a knock on the bedchamber door. "Miss? Did you need help undressing?"

She opened the door and Maggie entered. Penny stared helplessly at her a moment, then said, "I did what you suggested. I seduced Mr. Revington." Maggie gave her a startled look, and Penny felt her face flush with embarrassment. Turning away, she began to pace.

"Afterward he left. Ran out of here like a man fleeing for his life. And he hasn't come home yet." She again faced Maggie. "What do you make of that?"

"Perhaps he remembered some sort of business he must attend to. His behavior might not have anything to do with you."

"You don't truly believe that, do you, Maggie?"

Maggie looked thoughtful. "I suppose not. But even if he left because of you, it doesn't necessarily mean anything bad. He might have been so affected by what happened between you that he needed to get away."

"I suppose it's possible." Penny recalled the expression on Revington's face immediately after they'd made love. The look he'd given her had been almost tender. But for all she knew, she'd imagined it. She sighed. "The thing is, where do I go from here? What do I do now?"

Maggie gave her a tentative smile. "He's bound to come back some time, miss. When he does, you can insist he spend time with you, take you around the city. He did promise he would."

Penny nodded. Maggie's advice was sound. Even if their first experience of lovemaking hadn't affected him, that didn't mean all hope was lost. The real problem was, by the time she'd broken through his cold reserve, she feared her own emotions would be in tatters.

****

"Marcus! What the devil are you doing here? It's nearly midnight. Why aren't you with Penny?"

Marcus grimaced as James greeted him in the library of his townhouse. "I spent the day with her! That should be enough."

"Testy, aren't we?" James responded. "What did she do—insist you go shopping with her?"

Shopping—if only that's all they'd done. Heated memories filled Marcus's mind. *Penny lying on the bed, naked. The feel of her skin. Her taste…*

No. He wouldn't think about it. Moderating his voice to blandness, he said, "Obviously, I can't spend all my time with Penny. I have to earn a living."

James arched a brow. "I just don't want you to

forget the terms of our wager. You did promise to behave like a proper fiancé."

Dash it all! Why had he ever agreed to this? He could easily afford to pay James to manage his affairs. There'd been no need to make this ridiculous wager. It was only that he'd been so certain he'd win. Now he wasn't certain of anything any more.

"Lord Wendover is having a party tomorrow night," James added when Marcus didn't answer. "I'm sure Penny would enjoy the opportunity to experience the London social whirl firsthand."

Marcus wished he could say he hadn't been invited. But he knew that was unlikely. Despite what he'd told Penny, every week he received a half-dozen invitations to soirees, routs, and other gatherings. As a single man, he was in great demand by hostesses eager to balance out their guest lists. Of course, he wasn't a single man any more, or he wouldn't be as soon as he and Penny were married.

Attending the ball wouldn't be so bad. There'd be such a crush he'd scarcely have to speak to Penny. Indeed, taking her out in public might be the ideal solution to his dilemma. He could appear to be spending time with her, and yet keep things formal and distant.

"Of course, I'll take her. We have to make a public appearance at some point."

Chapter Nine

Here they were again, Penny thought glumly. Sitting across from each other at a meal, this time in the breakfast room. And things were even more awkward than last night. She found it difficult to eat. Her stomach seemed tied in knots, and every time she looked at him, the memories rushed in like a wild tide that threatened to capsize her. It was unfair. How could he appear so remote and detached? Didn't what they'd shared have any effect on him?

Of course not. He was a man. He probably couldn't even remember all women he'd taken to bed. And most of them were likely experienced seductresses like Elizabeth Valant, rather than awkward virgins like her.

Stop it! You can't let self-pity interfere with your goal. There had to be some way to crack that formidable reserve. She just needed to use her wits, rather than acting like a sniveling milk and water miss.

Penny was so caught up in her agonized thoughts, she started when Revington cleared his throat and spoke, "Lord Wendover is having a ball tonight. I was wondering if you'd like to go."

He was actually suggesting they do something together. She'd better take advantage of it! "Of course, I'd like to go." She gave what she hoped was a winsome smile.

He nodded, looking utterly unmoved. "Very good.

I'll let Maggie know we won't be here for dinner. Instead, she can spend her day helping you get ready. Is there anything you need for a formal affair like this? Perhaps another visit to Madam Dubonet is in order."

She certainly wasn't turning down an opportunity to get out of the townhouse. "I think I have a gown that might serve. But I could use some new slippers and a reticule to go with it."

She expected him to look pained at thought of her spending more of his money. But he merely nodded. "Maggie can escort you. I'll have the barouche brought around after breakfast."

****

She and Maggie were nearly finished shopping and had just left a milliner's when a familiar voice called, "Penny, what are you doing here?"

Turning, she faced her cousin. "I'm shopping, Adrian. That's what people normally do on Bond Street."

Adrian approached, his eyes narrowing as he looked her over. "I'd never have guessed that London would turn you into a fancy slut."

Maggie gasped. Penny took a deep breath before responding. "What exactly do you mean, Adrian?"

He motioned to her new pelisse. "All done up like a society miss, aren't you? And here I thought you actually cared about Horngate and the horses."

Penny took a step toward him, glaring. "I *do* care about Horngate and the horses. How dare you imply otherwise?"

Adrian shrugged. "Looks to me like you forgot them as soon as Revington offered to buy you some new clothes." He drew near and lowered his voice. "I thought we'd agreed you were going to convince him not to marry you."

"I'm doing my best!" Penny snapped. Then remembering herself, she added in more discreet tones. "My original plan wasn't working, so I had to come up with another scheme."

"This one had better succeed," warned Adrian.

"Or what?"

He leaned so close she could tell he'd been drinking spirits, gin most likely. "Once you're married and he has control, Revington will sell off all the horses like that!" He snapped his fingers.

Although she realized he was probably right, defiance caused her to say, "Are you certain? You hardly know him."

Adrian shook his head, his expression implying she was an utter fool. "Do you really think a London gamester like Revington is going to settle down in the country and raise horses?"

"But I could take care of the horse business on my own. He wouldn't have to do a thing."

"Oh, indeed. Revington's going to let his wife run around in trousers and spend all her time in the stables with a bunch of rough, hired men. Even if he doesn't care a jot for you, he has his reputation to uphold. He's an arrogant bastard."

She took a deep breath, fighting for calm. Adrian, curse him, was right. If she didn't find a way out of marrying Revington, she would lose everything. Still, she wasn't about to let Adrian see her distress. Facing him with a haughty expression, she said, "I told you, I have a plan. Now, if you would be so good as to let us pass, I'll carry on with it."

Adrian gave her a sneering look, but finally stepped aside. As they passed, he muttered, "You'd better not fail me, Penny."

"What was that all about?" Maggie asked as soon as they were down the street.

Penny shook her head in exasperation. "My wretched cousin. He's the whole reason I'm in this mess. He lost Horngate in a card game with Revington, even though it wasn't his to lose. Now I have to find a way to get out of marrying Revington or I'll lose everything I care about—my home, my horses, my freedom." She let out a sigh.

Maggie stared at her, her pert, freckled features scrunched into a frown. "I don't understand, miss. I thought you said you wanted Mr. Revington to come to care for you. Now it sounds as if you don't want to marry him."

She'd been caught out. Oh, dear. Could she trust Maggie? She gave the maid a searching look.

"What is it, miss?" Maggie asked.

"You have to understand. The horses, the farm— they mean everything to me. I can't bear the thought of losing all that."

"But why should you lose it? If the horse business is prosperous, I can't imagine that Mr. Revington would sell it off."

"He may not sell it off, but I doubt he'll let me have any involvement with it once we are wed."

"Why is that?"

"Because he won't want his wife to spend her time in the stables." Penny gave a frustrated sigh. "You should have seen him on the way to London. We stopped at an inn, and I went out to see the horses.

128

When he found me there talking to the stablemen, he was livid. And if he was angry then, I can't imagine he'll be willing to let me do such a thing when I'm his wife."

"Perhaps he was jealous to find you talking with a group of men. That might be what upset him as much as anything."

"Jealous? But why? He scarcely knew me back then."

"But he knew he intended to marry you. So, for him to find you talking to other men, regardless of their social class, it probably made him feel a bit possessive." Maggie frowned at her. "I still don't understand, miss. If you don't want to marry Revington, why are you trying to get him to care for you?"

Penny chewed her lower lip for a moment and then said, "Mr. Revington made a wager with his friend James that he won't fall in love with me, even after a month in London. If he does fall in love, then he has to ask me to marry him in the proper way, and if I refuse, he must abide by my wishes. Regardless of any arrangement he may have made with my guardian, he'll have to give up Horngate."

Maggie raised her auburn brows. "So, you're hoping to get Mr. Revington to fall in love with you?"

Penny nodded.

"And then you'll refuse to marry him?"

Again, she nodded.

Maggie shook her head, copper curls bobbing. "I'm sorry, miss, but I can't approve of your plan. To deliberately make Revington fall in love with you and then refuse to marry him seems quite cold-hearted."

Maggie was right. Her plan did seem very unkind. But was it any worse than what Revington had done to her? He'd given absolutely no thought to *her* feelings when he sought to take over Horngate. At no point had he asked if she wanted to marry him. All she was doing was paying him back in his own coin.

She shrugged and gave a light laugh. "Honestly, Maggie, I don't see why you're so worried. I'm not going to break Mr. Revington's heart. You know as well as I that he's quite unlikely to fall in love with me. A man like him...well, he's hardly the romantic sort. I can't think I'm going to sweep him off his feet, no matter what sort of provocative attire I wear. My plan is likely futile. But the thing is, even if Revington wins the wager with James and I end up marrying him, it won't hurt if he softens a bit toward me. If I can get him to at least see me as a woman rather than simply an inconvenience, then that's all to the good, isn't it?"

"I suppose so," Maggie agreed, although her expression remained dubious.

"So, you'll help me?"

Maggie sighed. "Aye. I'll help you."

Chapter Ten

"You look lovely," Marcus said as he met Penny in the foyer. *That wasn't the half it. She looked beautiful. Simply beautiful.*

"Thank you."

"Ready, then?"

She nodded. He took her arm and led her out to the waiting barouche.

Once inside the vehicle, Marcus struggled to think of a topic of conversation. Being around Penny seemed to reduce him to the level of a green boy, so overcome with longing he was tongued-tied. He'd avoided her all day, hoping that by keeping his distance he'd get over this wild infatuation. But the moment he saw her tonight, everything came rushing back: The way she'd felt beneath him. Her scent. Her taste.

He took a deep breath. Somehow he had to regain his composure and behave like a civilized man, rather than a lust-crazed fool. With effort, he cleared his throat and said the first thing that popped into his mind. "Did you have a pleasant day shopping?"

"Why, yes. It was most pleasant. And you, sir, how did you occupy yourself today?"

"Business, of course. I'm trying to tie up things here in London so that once we're wed I can focus my attentions on Horngate."

"I see. And what are you plans for Horngate?"

He hesitated. The last time he'd discussed the estate, she seemed to grow angry. But having brought up the topic, he had no choice but to respond. "The estate seemed a bit rundown. I'd like to make some improvements."

"I'm glad to hear you're planning ahead," she said. "But tonight I'm not interested in discussing Horngate. My thoughts are on the upcoming party. I'm curious about our host. Is Lord Wendover an important man?"

There was something in her tone, a kind of forced cheerfulness. He wondered what she was really thinking. Grateful for a safer topic, he said, "I suppose you could say Wendover is important. He has some political clout, if not much money."

"If he hasn't much money how can he afford to give a ball?"

"Lots of the nobility live beyond their means, incurring bills they have no intention of ever paying."

Penny looked startled. "And people find this acceptable?"

"I'm sure the shopkeepers don't care for it. But even so, ignoring your debts is fairly common. If a man, or woman, has a lofty enough title, no one refuses to do business with them. The Prince Regent is thousands of pounds in debt, but no merchant would ever turn down his business."

"That seems so...dishonest."

She *was* naïve. Which was part of her irresistible charm. He smiled. "After you're in London a while, you'll learn the usual rules of behavior don't apply to members of the *ton*. If the man is important enough, he can get away with almost anything."

"In your business dealings, do you ever have men

refuse to pay you?"

Why was she asking about his business again? It made it uncomfortable. "Not often. Although the Quality may not pay their bills or loans, gentlemen are expected to pay their wagers."

"And if they don't?"

Was she referring to his arrangement with her cousin? And where was that leading? If she hoped to soften him up regarding the wager, she was wasting her time. "If the risk of social ruin isn't enough, I have other means of forcing men to honor their debts." Shrugging, he added, "If you think me harsh, consider that I'm quite careful about my gaming associates. I don't play with green boys or men too inexperienced to realize the stakes involved. And when the wagers go beyond a certain point, I always give my partners a chance to get out. Your cousin, for example. I warned him he was getting in over his head. But he was too arrogant to heed me."

"That sounds like Adrian," Penny answered.

****

So, Adrian wasn't lying. Penny leaned back against the squabs of the carriage, feeling unsettled. If she refused to marry Revington, he intended to make her cousin pay. Even if Adrian deserved whatever happened to him, she didn't want to see him physically injured.

She shot a glance at the man across from her. Was Revington truly ruthless enough to do something like that? The idea made her repress a shiver...and also heightened her determination. Somehow she had to cause Revington to lose his bet with James. Somehow she had to get him to fall in love with her.

The idea wasn't completely ridiculous. Revington must feel *something* for her, or he wouldn't have made love to her so passionately. But since then, he'd gone back to dealing with her with the same cool detachment he'd exhibited when they'd first met.

She must do something drastic. Maggie had suggested the way to recapture Revington's interest was to make him jealous. That meant at this ball tonight, she should seek out the company of other men and flirt with them.

The idea of flirting made her uneasy. Especially given the gown she was wearing. If anything, it was even more scandalous than the mauve one from yesterday. She'd worried Revington would make her change if he saw her, so she'd worn her pelisse downstairs. But at some point she would have to take it off and then everyone would see her dress, or lack of it.

She bit her lower lip, telling herself she had to do whatever was necessary to save Horngate and her horses.

A few moments later, the carriage rolled to a stop. "We're here." Revington climbed out, then took her hand to help her alight.

As they started toward the house, Penny could only stare. Although it wasn't even dark yet, lights glinted from every window in the huge mansion. "It's...spectacular."

"An absurd waste of fuel," Revington responded. "But yes, it is impressive." Taking her arm, he guided her up the brick walkway.

They were greeted by two footmen dressed in bright blue velvet. After escorting them into the large foyer, one of the footmen took Revington's hat while the other helped Penny out of her pelisse. As her dress was revealed, Revington sucked in his breath. An impish urge made her ask, "Do you like it?"

"I don't think 'like' is the right word. I'm sure it's all the fashion, but still…" A muscle twitched in his jaw. A moment later he jerked his gaze away and took her arm to guide her down the hall after the footman.

****

Bloody hell! She looks like a Cyprian! Marcus could hardly control his dismay. Considering what she'd worn the day before, he should have expected this. But no one had seen her in that gown except the servants. Now she was on display for all of London society. The thought made him grit his teeth as they climbed the stairs to the ballroom.

He told himself there were undoubtedly women here wearing much more scandalous attire. Madame Dubonet catered to the most fashionable of London women, so there was really nothing improper about the dress. And Penny did look stunning. Once again the modiste had managed to make the most of Penny's natural beauty. The blue color made her skin look like ivory silk and set off her eyes. The tight, low-cut bodice highlighted the perfect shape of her breasts and her elegant neck. And the narrow column of the skirt emphasized her long legs and clung to her delicious little bottom. She looked like a wet dream come to life. Merely the sight of her made him yearn to find an empty bedroom and spend the rest of the evening ravishing her.

But he could hardly do that. She was his fiancée, not his mistress. While a number of sexual liaisons would undoubtedly take place in the bedrooms over the course of the ball, they would be between married women and their lovers. It would be completely inappropriate for him to do the same thing with the young woman who was to be his wife.

Besides, she'd said she was looking forward to this ball, and it would be inconsiderate of him to interfere with her enjoyment of the event. With that thought in mind, he sought to ignore his body's response and follow through with his proper role.

They reached the ballroom. Marcus gave their names to the footman and led Penny into the room.

****

She'd never seen so many candles. Two huge chandeliers and several candelabras arranged around the room cast a brilliant light on the assemblage. Everyone was beautifully attired in shimmering silks, sheer muslins, and sumptuous woolens. Jewels sparkled on necks, fingers, wrists, and earlobes while feathers adorned exotic-looking headdresses. Penny wouldn't have thought it possible, but she felt positively underdressed. At the same time, she was relieved to discover her gown wasn't the sheerest or most low-cut in the room. Not by any means. She would blend in quite well. Of course, blending in wasn't part of her plan. To arouse Revington's jealousy, she needed to attract the interest of other men.

In grave tones, the butler announced them: "Mr. Marcus Revington and Miss Penelope Montgomery." A few people turned their way, but many others continued on with their conversations.

Revington led her through the throng, nodding politely and occasionally stopping to introduce her to someone. Penny found herself clinging to his arm for dear life and telling herself to smile. *Smile and nod. Don't think about the fact you're an awkward, gawky miss from the country. At this moment you're Revington's fiancée, and he appears to be acquainted with many of the guests.*

Despite her admonishments to herself, her heart seemed to be fluttering in her chest like a trapped bird as she responded to the people they met. There could be no doubt she was being shrewdly evaluated, her importance quickly assessed. Several women narrowed their eyes, as if seeing her as competition, which meant she must appear reasonably attractive. But the majority of the women glanced at her briefly and then looked away. The men were a bit more positive. Many of them gave her interested or even frankly lustful looks.

She tried to take note of which men seemed likely prospects to help her carry out her plan. Unfortunately, most of the men they encountered were either elderly or very young. She could hardly expect Revington to become jealous of a man old enough to be her grandfather, or a spotty-cheeked boy, either.

She finally felt a spark of hope as they neared a tall fair-haired man who was openly perusing her body.

"Hello, Charles," Revington greeted the man in cool tones.

"Marcus," Charles responded. "And who is this beauteous creature?"

"My fiancée, Miss Penelope Montgomery." Revington seemed to force the words out, as if being civil to this man was a chore.

"Charmed, Miss Montgomery." Charles bowed, his gaze lingering on her décolletage. He turned to Revington. "Getting leg-shackled, are you, Marcus?

Well, well. I suppose if a man must lose his freedom, it should be to a luscious chit like this one." Once more, he looked at Penny, his green eyes so intent, she felt herself blush.

"Indeed." Revington's hand gripped her arm tightly as he drew her away.

"Who was that?" she asked as soon as they were out of earshot.

"Charles Lambson."

"I couldn't help noticing that you seem to be...not on the best terms. Is there some reason you dislike him?"

"The man is an arrogant cockscomb. I'd advise you to stay well clear of him."

Penny nodded agreeably, although she realized she must do the exact opposite. Regardless of Revington's opinion of the man, he was the only one who'd shown serious interest in her, and she was running out of options if she was going to find a way to arouse Revington's jealousy.

****

*If that bastard Lambson didn't quit gawking, he had half a mind to call him out! M*arcus took a deep breath and told himself to let it go. Lambson could gawk all he wanted. Penny was marrying *him*.

At the thought, he felt a stab of intense possessiveness. Penny was indeed a "beauteous creature" and he was very fortunate. If he could just get through the next few weeks, he'd not only fulfill his dream of owning property, but have the additional bonus of a beautiful and desirable wife. It was quite remarkable really. Few men, especially younger sons, were ever so fortunate.

But as he glanced at Penny again, a warning sounded in his head. He couldn't allow himself to feel this warm glow of affection every time he looked at her. This was the response of a man who was close to being smitten. He had to put his emotions in perspective. What he felt for Penny was no more than simple gratification at his auspicious circumstances, and the normal response any man would have to an attractive woman. Her effect on him was no different than the one she had on Lambson, or any of the men here who had eyes in their head.

Maybe the only way to quell these intense feelings was for him to get away from Penny for a time. But if he was going off by himself, he needed to find some place where she'd be safe from the worst of the lechers in attendance. He'd take her to the refreshment room where he could pretend he was being solicitous by making certain she had something to eat and drink. As soon as she was settled with a cup of punch and a plate of food, he'd excuse himself and go to the library where the other men who were avoiding dancing and gossiping with the ladies were gathered.

****

The man was so predictable! Penny thought with a surge of irritation as she glanced around the refreshment room. Once again, he'd abandoned her. After handing her a cup of lemonade and gesturing toward the several tables spread with delicious-looking food, Revington muttered something about needing to track down someone regarding a business arrangement. Then he vanished.

But she shouldn't be upset. Revington was giving her exactly the opportunity she needed. She finished her lemonade, then placed the cup on a tray held out by a footman and started back to the ballroom.

The musicians were playing, and she paused inside the doorway to watch the couples moving gracefully across the gleaming parquet floor. She searched the spectators gathered around the edge of the room, looking for Mr. Lambson. She finally spied him talking to an elegant dark-haired woman with white feathers in her hair. Watching the woman smile at Lambson and observing him smiling back, Penny wondered if she would have to find some other man for her scheme. But then Lambson looked in her direction and saw her watching him. He turned to the other woman, spoke a few words, and excused himself with a bow.

As Lambson made his way through the crowd, clearly headed her direction, her heart beat wildly. What in the world was she doing? She didn't have a clue what to say to him. Besides, her plan would only work if Revington saw them, and at this moment he was nowhere to be found.

"Miss Montgomery." Lambson took her hand, then executed a low bow. "I'm stunned to find you alone. A great beauty such as you should be surrounded by admirers. Whatever is your fiancé thinking, to leave you unattended?"

"I…he had some sort of business to attend to."

"Ah, business." Lambson's green eyes bored into her. "How very like Revington, to put business before pleasure. But his loss is obviously my gain. Would you care to dance, Miss Montgomery?"

Although she'd done some dancing at the local village parties and knew the basic steps of country-dances and the quadrille, she was not skilled enough for such sophisticated company. "I-I'm not an accomplished dancer. I fear I'll step on your feet."

Lambson laughed, showing strong white teeth. "I doubt that very much. You strike me as a woman who's far too naturally graceful to step on a man's foot."

"But even so, I worry I'll embarrass myself." She sought to smile winsomely. "Perhaps later in the evening, when there aren't so many people watching."

Lambson smiled back at her. "Of course. We'll dance later." He leaned nearer. "For now, perhaps we could find some quiet place to talk."

Warning bells rang in her head. Revington had advised her to avoid this man, and her instincts also told her to be wary. Lambson's manner was so practiced and smooth. No doubt he frequently sought out inexperienced women to seduce.

"I really shouldn't wander too far from the ballroom. My fiancé expects to find me here."

"Ah, your fiancé." Lambson smiled sourly. "Typical behavior for Revington, you know. Goes off on his own at the first opportunity, but expects you to wait for him. Do you truly want to appear so dutiful and predictable?"

"I suppose not." Penny pretended to play along. "It might be fun to worry him a bit."

Lambson beamed at her. "Precisely." He took Penny's hand. "Come along then. I know just the place."

Penny allowed him to lead her from the ballroom, telling herself she mustn't let this cunning and manipulative man take her anywhere too isolated. He led her down the hallway, but when he started for the upstairs, she balked. "I don't think I should leave the public areas."

For a second, Lambson's eyes gleamed with annoyance. Then he regained his poise. "Of course. I'm certain we can find a private place down here." Still holding her hand, he led her back to the ballroom and through the crowd. Penny knew a surge of satisfaction. This was ideal. Someone was bound to notice them. Then when Revington came back and asked around...She repressed a smile, thinking about how angry he would be.

The next moment, she experienced a twinge of doubt. Her goal was to make him jealous, not irate. What would he think when he found she'd left with a man he'd explicitly warned her against?

As they reached the other side of the ballroom, Penny pulled from Lambson's grasp. "If all you want to do is talk, we can certainly do that here."

Again she observed a crack in Lambson's aura of agreeable charm. "I thought you wanted to make Revington sweat a bit. Surely you're clever enough to realize you can't allow him to take you for granted if you want him to have any interest in you at all."

"I do realize that. But going off alone with you is not the best means of gaining his regard."

Lambson regained his silky-voiced charm. Gently retrieving her hand, he said, "You're quite right, Miss Montgomery. But there's no reason we can't step outside for a moment. It's so stuffy in here."

Penny nodded and allowed Lambson to escort her through a doorway at the far side of the room. At the end of the hallway, a pair of wide double doors opened out onto a veranda. As they reached it, Penny let out a sigh. It was much more pleasant out here, with a soft breeze cooling her heated skin. She turned to look at the mansion, admiring the way the lights gleaming from the many windows contrasted with the velvety darkness all around.

It was a lovely, romantic setting. If only Revington were here, holding her hand in his firm calloused grip. She imagined his tall form beside her. His subtle scent of leather, wool, and maleness drifting to her on the night air. His strong arms around her and his mouth on hers.

With a shiver of longing, she sought to shake off the thought. The next moment, Lambson drew her tightly against his body and lowered his mouth to hers.

"Sir!" She jerked away. "I thought we came out here to talk!"

"You're so lovely. I simply can't resist." He fingered a curl that had escaped from her chignon, then lightly caressed the nape of her neck.

Despite the gentleness of his touch, the determined look on his face filled her with anxiety. She should never have done this. If Revington found them, he would be enraged. He might even challenge Lambson to a duel. The thought of Revington dying or being injured panicked her.

"I must get back!" Penny twisted away. Lambson caught her wrist and pulled her hard against his body. She struggled. "Let go or I'll scream!"

"Then what?" Lambson sneered. "Everyone saw you go out here willingly."

She was trapped. He was much stronger. But that might not matter. Recalling something Tad had told her years ago, she stomped on Lambson's instep as hard as she could.

He let out an exclamation of pain. His grip loosened; she whirled away and dashed through the double doors and down the hall. Behind her, he shouted, "Vicious little bitch!"

Near the entrance to the ballroom, she slowed and sought to compose herself. She must pretend nothing had happened. Pretend she'd never left with Lambson. Instead of entering the ballroom the way she'd left, she'd go around to the other doorway.

She moved swiftly, practically running. At the corner, she halted. Revington approached, a murderous-looking expression on his face.

There she was, thank god! Relief flooded Marcus, but instead of easing his anger, knowing she was safe made him even more furious. "Where the devil have you been, Penny? I've been looking everywhere for you!"

"I...uh, I went out for some fresh air."

"With Lambson?" he asked, incredulously.

Her flushed cheeks and the guilty look in her eyes told him it was true.

Bloody hell! She'd been alone with Lambson! He gazed at her in shock for a moment, not trusting himself to speak.

When Lady Dunnett had informed him rather gleefully that his fiancée had left with Lambson, he'd been certain the shrewd old tabby was lying. It would be just like her ladyship to try to stir up trouble. But if it was true, then Penny had deliberately ignored his warning!

He continued to stare at her, trying to figure out her reason for doing such a thing. Did she seek to humiliate him in front of London society? Did those innocent blue eyes mask a manipulative and cold-hearted nature? Perhaps she was much more like her cousin than he'd guessed. But if she'd deliberately set out to disgrace him, then he didn't think she'd look as she did now, flushed and trembling.

He had to know the truth. Find out her true motivations.

But not here, where anyone might see them. He was probably already the laughingstock of the party. No need to seek out further embarrassment.

"I think it's time to leave." He grabbed her arm and led her down the hall.

He expected her to protest, or perhaps give him some excuse for her actions. But she said nothing. Realizing she wasn't going to defy him, he relaxed his grip. They would pretend that all was well between them. If they left on obviously cordial terms, perhaps it would dispel the worst of the gossip.

Their departure proceeded smoothly. They said goodbye to their host, then waited in the foyer for their carriage to be brought around. Marcus sought to regain his usual detached manner, but inside his emotions roiled. This woman had the most astounding—and troubling—effect on him. He considered himself calm and levelheaded. But around Penny he always seemed to be on the verge of losing control. She made him furious…and almost mindless with desire.

Even now, he wondered if he would be able to restrain himself once they reached the privacy of the coach. He didn't know what he was more likely to do: Rage at her like a crazed maniac or seize her and ravish her senseless.

Chapter Eleven

Penny took a deep breath, trying to quell the anxiety building inside her. Revington hadn't said a word since she'd encountered him in the hallway. Although obviously furious, he quickly regained control. He led her back to the ballroom and said goodbye to their host, then escorted her out to the waiting carriage. Now he sat across from her in the vehicle. Although she couldn't see his expression clearly in the faint light filtering in through the coach windows, his rigid posture suggested he was still beside himself with anger.

She wasn't certain what to do, whether to try to explain or hope his anger would cool. Somehow it didn't seem right not to make some comment. She didn't want him to think she'd defied him out of spite. Nor did she want him to believe anything had happened between her and Lambson. She had to make that clear.

But what could she say? How could she explain things in a way that would ease his anger? She could hardly reveal that she'd hoped to make him jealous. Or could she? Not only was it a logical explanation but it would indicate to him that she cared what he thought about her.

Clearing her throat she said, "I'm certain you're angry with me, and I can't blame you, but you should know that I—"

Revington leaned across the coach and pressed his mouth to hers in a savage kiss.

Her body seemed to explode with delight, as if to say, *Yes! Yes! This was what you were waiting for! This is the man you desire!*

She wrapped her arms around his neck, giving in completely. Their lips and tongues mated and danced. Eventually he drew away so they could both catch their breath. He moved to sit beside her and pulled her onto his lap. His lips were warm against her neck, licking and nuzzling, making her shiver and sigh. He tore away the pelisse and sucked and nibbled at her shoulders and cleavage. Then he pulled down her gown and mouthed the nearest breast. His lips encircled her nipple, drawing in the tender flesh. Kissing. Sucking. Until she was limp and moaning with pleasure.

She felt she was drowning, pulled under by a wild tide of passion. A piercing need built in her core. A yearning so deep it almost hurt. Just when she thought she would die of it, he rucked up the skirt of her gown and fondled her private parts through the thin fabric of her pantalettes. She writhed and twisted, lifting her hips to press herself against his tormenting fingers.

So intense was her lust that when he drew away, she almost cried out. She waited, breathless and horrified as he thumped on the roof of the carriage. As the vehicle rolled to stop, she scrambled to cover herself.

"No need for that," he murmured. The next moment, he cracked open the window and called out, "Jeremy, we're not ready to go home yet. Take the route through the park."

He shut the window, and the carriage started

forward, Penny let out a sigh of relief. The next moment, he was kissing her again and lightly stroking her breasts. Her desire surged back, as strong as ever. He raised the hem of her gown, pulled off her pantalettes, and tossed them aside. She waited breathlessly as he adjusted his own clothing. A part of her was aghast at what they were about to do—having sex in a carriage! But as soon as the heated flesh of his phallus pushed against her own desperate wet opening, every vestige of doubt vanished. She welcomed him, urging him deeper and deeper still.

He filled her to the point of pain, and she moaned helplessly as he moved inside her. Gradually her taut flesh yielded, and she leaned back against the carriage squabs and tried not to scream from the pure pleasure pulsing through her. He clutched her, thrusting wildly. Their bodies were so close. Their sweat mingled. His mouth found hers as they climbed the precipice together. Then thundered off the cliff...falling into mad, swirling ecstasy.

Marcus disengaged himself from her exquisite, cushioning flesh and adjusted his garments. A sudden rush of emotion made his hands tremble as he buttoned the placket of his trousers. He'd never felt like this way about a woman before. This poignant, yearning...tenderness.

As she dressed herself, the realization of his own vulnerability filled him with panic. He'd always prided himself on being in control. But with this woman, he most certainly was not. She beguiled and suborned him. Around her he was helpless. At the mercy of his own feelings. He didn't know what to do. How to deal with this. He wanted desperately for things to return to the way they had been. Maybe if he pretended not to feel anything, this gnawing ache inside him would go away.

Yes. That's what he must do. It was unthinkable that he let this crack in his defenses deepen any further. He had to squash these feelings. Shove them aside. Bury them deep.

He moved back to his side of the carriage, thankful it was dark and he couldn't see her. If he looked at her beautiful face right now, he would waver. The most basic courtesies of lovemaking demanded he appear pleased and content with what they'd shared. For him to draw away and coldly proceed as if nothing had happened was bound to hurt her. But it couldn't be helped. If he weakened even a little, he would be lost.

He thumped on the roof of the carriage again. This time, when it halted, he opened the window and called out, "Take us home, Jeremy."

The ride to the townhouse seemed interminable. The silence, heavy and suffocating. He held his hands tight against his thighs, struggling against the urge to reach out for her. He could hear the sound of her breathing and smell the lingering scent of their shared desire. What was she thinking? Had their lovemaking affected her as profoundly as it did him? What did she feel for *him?*

All at once he remembered what had brought him to that state of agitation. *She'd gone off with that bloody bastard Lambson!* His anger returned, gradually banishing the pathetic longing that had overcome him. He wanted to grab her again, but this time instead of kissing her, he longed to shake her and demand to know why she'd deliberately defied him. She was so headstrong and stubborn. Such an independent, aggravating woman.

And he was going to marry her and bind his life to hers. The thought of it filled him with anxiety. Maybe he should get out while he could. Break off the engagement and give up Horngate.

But he could hardly do that now. He'd taken her maidenhead and introduced her to all of London as his fiancée. For him to cry off now would be unforgivable. If he did such a thing, Withersby would have every right to call him out.

Of course, the puling coward would never do that. Withersby would be more than happy to slither out of the arrangement. He would get to keep Horngate, which is exactly what the bastard wanted. But Penny would be ruined and humiliated. No doubt she would feel hurt and angry, but would she also be disappointed? Marcus wondered if she felt anything for him. Was it merely lust that made her respond so passionately?

He couldn't understand her. How could she melt in his arms and surrender so completely only a day ago, then turn around and go off with Lambson? Was she no different than Elizabeth? Now that Penny had discovered sex, was she willing to do it with any man she found attractive?

The thought made him grit his teeth. Confound her! He wasn't the jealous sort. How dare she make him feel like this!

Marcus repressed a sigh. Here he was, back where he started, wondering how he'd ever gotten himself into this mess. Somehow he had to figure things out. And soon. He wished he could discuss the situation with James, but that was out of the question. If he revealed how he felt about Penny, James would accuse him of being in love with her. And that couldn't be true. Love didn't make a man feel as he did now. This doomed, sick feeling in his stomach couldn't be love. Love was supposed to make a man happy and content, not turn him into a raging lunatic!

****

Penny heaved an inward sigh of relief as the carriage halted. In another few moments, she'd be able to escape this hellish situation. Get away from Revington, escape to the bedchamber and give in to her emotions. But what exactly was she feeling? Did she want to cry? To scream? Or to hit something very hard, over and over?

She felt as if she was losing her mind. Once again, Revington had drawn away from her, becoming that cold, infuriating nobleman she encountered that first time at Horngate. It had to be a false persona. She simply couldn't believe it was his true nature. Someone so cold and haughty wasn't capable of making love with such passionate abandon.

Or was he? She knew little about men, but she had been led to believe that when it came to sex, they were significantly different than women. Maybe Revington really was able to demonstrate such tenderness with his body and yet keep his emotions completely in check.

As he helped her out of the carriage, his demeanor was as distant as ever. If only she could do the same. It seemed like every time he touched her, another piece of her defenses crumbled away and she was left exposed and vulnerable. Try as she might, Penny could no longer hate him, or even dislike him. Her resolve to escape this marriage was weakening. Even though she knew she would lose everything she cared about if she didn't win this battle of wits, she no longer had the will to fight him.

Bowes met them in the foyer. "Good evening, sir. Miss Montgomery."

Revington didn't respond, but strode down the hall and into the library.

As he helped her out of her pelisse, Bowes asked, "Did you enjoy the party, miss?"

"Yes," she answered automatically. "The house was beautiful. And the food...the music...everything was exceptional."

"Very good, miss." Bowes bowed to her, and Penny started up the stairs. At this moment, she felt like screaming. No. What she actually felt like was turning around, following Revington into the library, and forcing him to speak to her. But the problem was, she had no idea what to say. She must untangle her own feelings before confronting him.

In the bedchamber, she went to sit on the bed. A moment later, there was a knock on the door. "It's me, miss," Maggie called. "Do you need help?"

"Yes. Come in."

Maggie hurried in, copper curls bobbing, blue eyes bright with curiosity. "How did it go, miss? With Mr. Revington, I mean."

Penny let out sigh. "I have no idea. None." Seeing Maggie's questioning look, she continued, "I followed your advice. There was a man who seemed interested in me. I left the ballroom with him, hoping to make Revington jealous. I don't know if I succeeded, or simply made him angry. He scarcely spoke to me on the way home."

Maggie moved behind Penny and unhooked the

back of her dress. "Sounds as if it worked. Revington's the sort to turn silent as a statue when he's upset."

Her gown slipped to the floor and Penny stepped out of it. "The plan may have succeeded, but I don't see how it's going to aid me. Revington was distant and difficult before. I don't see how anything is improved."

"Give it time." Maggie picked up the gown and frowned. "It looks as if something got spilled on your dress. I'll have to see if it will wash out."

Penny felt an acute wave of embarrassment. She'd tried to use her handkerchief to clean herself before putting on her pantalettes, but... "It must be punch," she responded quickly.

Maggie folded the gown and left it on the bed, then went to fetch a clean shift from the bureau. As she helped Penny into it, she said, "I do think our plan will work. As Mr. Revington sees other men are interested in you, he'll realize he's quite fortunate to have you. He might be angry now, but that doesn't mean he isn't coming to care for you. And if we succeed, Mr. Ludingham will lose the bet, and you'll be able to get out of the marriage...if that's what you still want, that is."

"Of course, it is," Penny answered. But inside, she knew it was a lie. She no longer had any idea *what* she wanted.

When Penny didn't answer, Maggie motioned to the chair by the dressing table. "If you'd like, I'll take down your hair."

****

He really should go to bed, thought Marcus, staring gloomily into his brandy. But what would be the point? He'd end up tossing and turning all night anyway. Since he wasn't going to sleep, he might as well stay here. He leaned back in the horsehair chair and stretched out his legs. It felt as if there was a war going on inside him. A fierce battle between his rational mind and his emotions. He was filled with a deep yearning to go to Penny and tell her that if she didn't want to marry him, she was free to return to Horngate.

But his mind argued that doing such a thing would be witless. He'd won Horngate fair and square, and he'd be a fool to give it up. After all, it wasn't as if he were condemning Penny to a life of misery. Once they were wed, she'd be free to do as she pleased. He wasn't the sort of man who sought to control the actions of his wife. *As long as she was faithful to him.*

Although it was the fashionable thing for both parties to have affairs, he had no interest in doing such a thing, and he'd never be able to endure it if Penny had sex with other men. That's what had upset him so much and why he'd behaved so rashly. The thought of her and Lambson… It was not to be borne.

Why had she done it? Was it simply an act of defiance? His earlier fear reawakened. Having discovered the pleasures of sex, was she now eager to explore those pleasures with other men? Maybe she thought Lambson would please her better than he had. The thought made him feel sick inside.

He let his mind linger on the possibility, then finally decided that lust was unlikely to be the motivation for her actions. He must not let his experience with Elizabeth make him think all women were like that. Sheer defiance seemed unlikely to be the reason either. Penny might sometimes appear a bit childish, but it was an innocent kind of childish rather than the petulant sort.

So, why had she done it? He was back to that. If she didn't seek to aggravate him or desire to have an affair with Lambson, then what was it about?

All at once, it came to him. *Maybe she hoped if she pushed him far enough, he would decide she was too much trouble and abandon his plan to marry her.*

That thought led to another. The consistent thing in all her actions had been that she was trying to shock him. From her dramatic arrival on the huge stallion, her gauche and hoydenish behavior at Horngate, which he now knew was an act put on for his benefit. Purchasing an extravagant and outrageous wardrobe... Everything she'd done was calculated to convince him she would be a difficult and aggravating wife.

She didn't want to marry him. He could see that clearly now. Which meant that if he cared for her at all, he should forget the wager and give up Horngate.

Hadn't James warned him of this all along? And wasn't that the point of his wager? James wanted Penny to have a choice; he'd known from the beginning what she would choose. She'd done everything in her power to get him to change his mind about making her his wife.

Which brought him back to where he started.

He got up and poured himself another brandy, then returned to the chair. The path ahead seemed very clear. And yet, he didn't see how he could bear to go through with it. To not only give up Horngate, but to give up Penny herself... It would feel as if something vital had been torn out of him.

****

Penny sat in bed and gloomily surveyed the

bedchamber. For a few hours she'd found respite from her dilemma in sleep. But now it was morning, and she was faced with the same problem as yesterday. After spending nearly a week trying to convince Revington not to marry her, she now realized that of all the men out there, he was the one she truly wanted as her husband. After all, he clearly had no intention of selling Horngate, and he seemed interested in continuing to breed horses. Whether he would allow her to be as involved as she would like was more uncertain.

Of course, it was possible she'd so angered him the night before that he'd never want to have anything to do with her again.

Restless, she climbed out of bed and went to the dressing room. She was going mad thinking about these things. Somehow she had to clear her head. If only she could go riding. That always helped.

Maybe she could. She recalled seeing horseback riders along Rotten Row in Hyde Park. They'd all been men, but that didn't mean she couldn't do it. Revington might not approve, but then after last night, could she really make things worse?

Of course, there was still the problem of what to wear. Madame Dubonet suggested having a riding costume made, but Penny rejected the notion. The idea of a cumbersome skirt, not to mention riding sidesaddle, dismayed her. That was hardly riding at all!

She searched the back of the closet for the garments she'd brought from Horngate. Even knowing how unlikely it was that she would ever wear them, she'd brought a pair of riding trousers and an old shirt.

She took them out and laid them on the bed. Compared to the clothes she'd been wearing the past few days, the woolen trousers and linen shirt looked terribly crude and unfeminine. But their plain familiarity was reassuring. This was how she'd dressed for much of her life.

Penny put on the clothes, then her old riding boots. Now, she faced her next dilemma. How was she to get a horse suitable for riding? Surely one of the footmen would help.

She crept downstairs making certain Revington wasn't around, then made her way to the servants' quarters. The young footman, Jeremy, appeared shocked to see her. When he heard what she wanted, he was even more surprised. "You want to go riding, miss? Dressed like that?"

"I know Revington wouldn't approve. But he doesn't have to know, does he?" Penny made her expression pleading.

A frown darkened the young man's thin face, and his blue eyes grew troubled. She could tell he was weighing his decision, trying to decide what Revington would do to him if they were found out. Finally, Jeremy gave her a crooked smile. "He did say we were to accommodate you in any way possible since you were soon to be his wife and the mistress of the household."

"Exactly." Penny breathed a sigh of relief.

She waited impatiently until Jeremy returned, all the while worrying that Maggie would appear. With luck, the maidservant was busy in the kitchen. As far as she knew, Revington had never gotten around to hiring a new cook.

At last Jeremy returned. He led her out the back way, to where a lovely chestnut gelding waited, fully saddled. Patting the animal's neck, he said, "This is

Nero. He's a real goer. I feel sorry for him, always having to be part of a team and pull a rig."

"Now, how do I get to Hyde Park?" Penny asked.

Jeremy gave her directions and helped her mount. As she found her seat on the animal, he nodded approvingly. "Looks like you know what you're about, miss."

"I do. Don't worry. I won't get hurt. I'll be back here in an hour or so. Revington will never be the wiser."

With that reassurance she set off.

****

He felt even more hellish than usual this morning, Marcus decided as he made his way downstairs. That would teach him to fall asleep in a chair in the library. He'd awakened very early in the morning and made his way to the guest bedchamber to sleep the last few hours, but even so, he'd wakened with a crick in his neck and a nagging headache, although the latter discomfort was likely due to all the brandy he'd imbibed as much as where he'd slept.

He wasn't in the best frame of mind, especially since he still hadn't decided what course of action to take with Penny. But he had realized he couldn't continue to ignore her. After what they shared, it would simply be too cold-hearted to act as if there were nothing between them. With that thought in mind, he braced himself to enter the breakfast room.

It was empty, except for Bowes. Marcus was surprised, as he'd distinctly heard Penny leave her bedchamber and head downstairs. It had been some time ago, but he thought she'd still be at breakfast.

Bowes approached him. "Good morning, sir. I was

158

waiting for you to call me to help you dress."

"I'll change clothes later," Marcus responded. "For now, I thought I'd have breakfast with Penny. Has she already finished?"

"Miss Montgomery never came to the breakfast room. I thought she must still be abed."

"I'm sure she's not. I heard her come downstairs some time ago." Marcus felt a stab of regret. He should have gotten up right away, instead of lying in bed trying to work up his nerve to face her.

"Indeed," said Bowes. "I wonder where she's gone."

Marcus turned and left the breakfast room. Bowes followed. Although it seemed unlikely she would be there, Marcus checked the library, the dining room, and the drawing room. When he failed to find her in any of those places, he started up the stairs. "I suppose it's possible she returned to her room," he called down to Bowes.

He knocked softly on her bedchamber door. When there was no answer, he slowly opened it, wondering if she'd gone back to sleep.

But the room was empty. "Maggie. She must know where she is."

He took the stairs rapidly and swept past Bowes to make his way to the kitchen, where he found Maggie kneading bread. "Where's Penny?"

Maggie looked startled. "I don't know, sir. I went up a while ago to see if she needed help with dressing, but she wasn't there." Seeing Marcus's expression, she continued, "I know I should have checked on her sooner, sir, but it is a challenge to serve as both cook and lady's maid."

"I know, Maggie. I promise to have Bowes hire a cook today."

Marcus frowned as he left the kitchen. Penny must have gone out. More distressing, she'd apparently done so by herself. The familiar anger suffused him. Hadn't he told her repeatedly she must have an escort when she left the townhouse? Was she deliberately trying to upset him?

The next moment, he regained control. He wouldn't jump to conclusions with Penny, but deal with her in a civilized and rational fashion. But as hard as he tried to regain his composure, the more agitated he felt. *Where could she have gone? Was it possible she'd arranged to meet Lambson?*

She wouldn't, would she? *Oh my God, it doesn't even bear thinking about!*

He started for the servants' area, panic and rage tearing through him.

Chapter Twelve

By the time he found Bert polishing tack in the carriage house, he'd managed to calm himself, at least enough to speak. "Have you seen Pen—Miss Montgomery?"

"No, sir. Perhaps Jeremy has."

"Where might I find him?"

"He's in the house, sir. Maggie asked him to bring in more coal."

Marcus hurried, taking long strides. In the kitchen he found Jeremy and Maggie. The footman was standing on a stepstool, getting something from the tall cupboard.

"Jeremy! Have you seen Miss Montgomery?"

The footman climbed down and turned to face him. As soon as Marcus saw the young man's expression, he knew. He glared at Jeremy, his fists clenched at his sides. "You have, haven't you? Where has she gone? Where's she meeting him?"

The footman's eyes, which had looked guilty and anxious before, went wide with astonishment. "Meeting who, sir?"

Marcus took a deep breath and forced himself to relax. No point letting the servants know Penny had made a fool of him. "I...what I meant was, where has she gone?"

The guilty look was back in Jeremy's eyes. He

seemed almost panicked. "I-I'm sorry, sir. But you did say that the staff should to try to please her. That she would be our mistress soon, and we should seek to accommodate her in any way possible."

"What is it? What has she done?" He felt almost faint. It was unthinkable his staff would help Penny arrange a liaison with another man. Surely they weren't that dense!

Jeremy grimaced. "I meant no harm, sir. She promised me she wouldn't get hurt. I don't think she will. She appeared quite experienced."

The stunned, numb sensation spread. He wasn't certain his mouth would work if he tried to speak.

Jeremy ducked his head. "She's very hard to refuse, sir. Surely you must know that. But you're right. I shouldn't have done it. Or, at least I should have gotten her a tamer mount. Nero can be a handful."

"Nero?" Somehow he managed to get the name out. *Who is Nero? Is there another man he didn't know about?*

"Nero's one of the carriage horses, sir. One of the team I usually get from the livery stable. Although as I told Penny, he's wasted as a rig horse. Henry down at the stables says he can really fly. Not that he's supposed to race the horses, of course. But he does need to try them out a bit. That's part of his job."

"A horse? What did she want with a horse?"

"To go riding, of course, sir. She was dressed all for it. Breeches and riding boots. None of that silly riding habit nonsense that most ladies wear."

"She went riding? Alone?" He knew he sounded like an idiot, but he simply had to know, to be certain.

"Aye, sir. But there will be plenty of people there

this time of day. All the grooms will be out exercising the horses. If anything should happen, there'll be all sorts of experienced fellows to help her."

"Happen? What do you mean?"

"If she should fall or something, sir. Although she assured me that wouldn't happen. And she did seem to know what she was about. Nero settled down as soon as she was on him. Like he knew she was someone he could trust."

Marcus was suddenly aware of the desperate expression on the groom's face. Jeremy was babbling on, behaving like a condemned man trying desperately to explain as he's dragged to the gallows. Meanwhile, Marcus felt his own self-imposed sentence lifting. *She isn't meeting Lambson, or any other man. Of course not. She's simply gone riding. It is exactly what Penny would do. Exactly.*

He hadn't misjudged her. He *did* know her. She was still the lovely horse-mad hoyden he met that first day at Horngate. But for all her experience with horses, this was London, not the countryside. What if something startled her mount and she was thrown?

"Where did she go? Rotten Row?"

Jeremy nodded.

"I'll need a horse. Any sort will do. I just want to get there. To make certain she's all right."

"Of course, sir. I'll meet you in back by the livery stable."

****

This was hardly the sort of riding she was used to, Penny thought as she cantered to the end of the track. Rotten Row couldn't be much over a mile in length, and riding on the surface of gravel and tan wasn't nearly the same as racing over the countryside. She also had to watch out for other riders. She'd encountered a half dozen or so, all grooms exercising their master's mounts. Still, it was better than nothing. At least she was out in the relatively fresh air and comfortably dressed for a change. And, as always, riding was such a pleasure. The feel of the powerful animal between her thighs, the exhilarating sense of freedom.

The horse also seemed to be enjoying himself. Jeremy was right. Nero was wasted as a carriage horse. Pulling up, she leaned over to pat the gelding's neck. "That was wonderful, Nero. Thank you. Unfortunately, we should be getting back."

Turning the animal, she started the other direction down the track. She could just imagine Revington discovering where she'd gone and shouting at Jeremy. She would have to make it clear that Jeremy was simply accommodating his mistress. Her stomach lurched a little at the thought of confronting Revington. He always unsettled her so much. How could they be so close, so intimate in some ways and such strangers when it came to everything else?

She sighed. Maybe she wouldn't go back quite yet. She might not have another chance to ride for a long time.

She decided to put the horse through some of the training drills she used at Horngate. Slow walking, then speeding into a trot. Slowing again. As she neared the end of the track, she turned the animal in a tight circle and then around in a figure eight.

As she finished the maneuver, she heard several whistles and a shout of "Well done!"

Flushed with satisfaction, she trotted to where

several of the grooms were gathered, holding the reins of their mounts. As she reached them, a couple of the older fellows moved to help her dismount, but she waved them off. "No need. I'm used to being on my own."

"We can see that," said one of the younger grooms as she slid to the ground. The black-haired youth grinned at her. "I've never seen a mort ride like that. Where'd you learn all those fancy moves?"

Penny shrugged. "I've been training horses for a half-dozen years. I'm not sure where I picked some of it up."

The youth gestured to Nero. "Who does the horse belong to? Did some gentleman actually hire you?"

Penny grinned, amused by his assumption that she was a groom. "The horse is from a livery near here. He's the one for hire, not me."

"Don't be a bacon-brain, Frankie," said one of the older men, his brown eyes watching her warily. "She's a lady. Can't you tell?"

Frankie stared at her, blushing furiously. "My pardon, miss, I thought..."

She smiled to put him at ease. "No need to apologize. I'm actually quite flattered. I'm pleased to think I appear skilled enough that you thought someone would actually hire me as a groom."

"But how...I don't understand. How did a lady like you ever learn to ride like that?"

The next moment Penny found herself telling them all about Horngate and her horses.

****

The whole way to the park, Marcus fought to control his emotions. He reminded himself Penny had been riding a spirited stallion when he first met her. If she could control that beast, she should easily deal with a carriage horse. And this time of day, there was little traffic in this part of this city. There was nothing to worry about.

As for the idea she was using the horse to meet another man—that was even more preposterous. If she intended to meet Lambson, she'd hire a hack. And it was unlikely she would arrange a liaison first thing in the morning anyway.

No, this incident was nothing more than Penny being homesick for her life at Horngate. She'd wanted to go riding, and with typical ingenuity, she'd arranged to do so.

By the time he reached the park, he was feeling much better. He no longer imagined Penny lying injured on the trackway or tucked away in Lambson's carriage engaged in a bout of passionate lovemaking. But when he reached Rotten Row, he was once again thrown into turmoil. Penny stood on the trackway surrounded by a group of men!

Even as his body reacted with instinctive and primal jealousy, his brain recognized that the males were hired horsemen, and not a threat in any way. They would never dream of touching Penny, except to help her dismount.

Even so, his jealousy didn't entirely ease. He couldn't help but be struck by how happy and relaxed she appeared. She never smiled and laughed like that when she was with him.

But then, when had he ever given her anything to smile or laugh about? Their encounters had been marked by either cold formality or desperate passion.

There was nothing light or relaxed about any of it.

As he watched her, he felt something else. Pride. The stances and expressions of the men around her reflected respect and admiration. They were taking keen note of her every word and treating her as an equal. It was quite remarkable. No matter what he did, he doubted he'd ever be able to earn even the grudging respect of these men. They would always dismiss him as a top-lofty nobleman.

That was what was so special about Penny. She was real and genuine. Her warmth and passion for life shone through, giving her a beauty with which even the most exquisite courtesan couldn't compete.

Longing filled him. He'd possessed Penny's body, made her sigh and moan with ecstasy, but they hadn't ever come close to attaining the simple and honest connection she shared with these men. And he wanted that. Wanted her to be his friend, a companion rather than simply a bed-partner.

As if she felt his yearning, she glanced his way. The abrupt change in her dismayed him. She tensed and her expression turned guarded, as if she expected him to chastise her...or worse.

****

As soon as Penny saw Revington, she felt a kind of breathless panic. She couldn't forget how angry he'd been when he'd found her talking to the stablemen at the inn in Petersfield. This time it would be worse. Not only would he be angry about finding her with a group of stablemen, he'd also be upset with the way she was dressed and the fact she'd gone riding by herself. She could easily imagine what he would say: "What were you thinking? Going riding in a public place...and dressed like that!"

As he approached, she braced herself. She didn't think he'd strike her, not in front of all these men. But she dreaded a tongue-lashing almost as much. These men were treating her as their equal. They respected her skill and her knowledge of horses. It would be humiliating to have Revington deal with her like a recalcitrant child.

He halted a few paces away. After nodding curtly to the men, he spoke. "I was a bit worried when I found you'd gone riding. But I realize now I shouldn't have been concerned. You obviously know what you're about."

Penny felt her mouth drop open. *Is it really possible he's praising me?*

"But you should come home and have some breakfast now," he continued. "I did promise to take you around the city. What would you think of a boat ride down the Thames this afternoon and then the theatre tonight?"

"I…that would be lovely," she mumbled.

One of the horsemen helped her mount Nero, and she simply followed after Revington, still struggling with her sense of disbelief. Was it possible he'd expressed confidence in her ability with horses? That he'd treated her as his equal, someone whose opinion he cared about?

She could tell his reaction had impressed the horsemen. Like her, they'd expected him to be angry, or at least condescending. When he'd seen fit to be polite and gracious, they could hardly believe it. She very much appreciated his courtesy. She valued the opinion of those men. They might be servants and by the standards of society, beneath her, but she'd rather have their regard than that of most gentlemen and ladies.

Just thinking about what he'd done made her feel strange. She'd longed for some hint of warmth or kindness from Revington. For him to react to her with something other than cold politeness or unbridled passion. At last he was finally doing so, and Penny found herself unnerved by the way it made her feel. It was as if the ground beneath her feet had shifted. She didn't know what to think or feel.

When they reached the townhouse, he dismounted, then helped her down from Nero. "I'll take care of the horses while you go inside and have some breakfast."

Penny nodded, wondering if she could eat. The events of the morning were unsettling enough; the thought of spending the day with Revington made her even more nervous and excited.

She entered the townhouse, nodded to Bowes, then continued on to the kitchen.

As soon as Maggie saw her, she asked, "Did the master find you, miss?" From the maidservant's expression, it appeared she had also expected the worst of Revington.

"Yes, he did. And you'll never believe how civil and polite he was. Not to mention that he asked me to spend the day with him. We're to go boating on the Thames and then to the theatre." She gave a nervous laugh, grinning at the maidservant.

"What did I tell you, miss?" Maggie grinned back.

"Can you see fit to get away from your tasks here and come help me bathe and dress?"

"Of course, miss. I'd be delighted."

"But first you should eat something."

Both Penny and Maggie turned to see Revington in the doorway. Penny felt herself flushing. How long had he been standing there? Had he heard her speak with disbelief about him being civil and polite?

"I'll fix something to bring up to you, miss," Maggie said, quickly. "Give me a moment and I'll be right there."

Penny started toward the door. Revington moved aside as she reached him, but she still had to pass near him. Being that close to him made her feel breathless.

She hurried up the stairs, trying to decide what to wear.

****

This was what he wanted, Marcus thought as Penny dashed up the stairs. He wanted her to be excited and happy, to return to being that charming, free-spirited miss he'd met at Horngate. Caught up as he was in his own plans back then, he hadn't appreciated her at the time. But now he found her exuberance delightful.

Careful, came the niggling thought. *At this rate you're likely to fall in love with her.*

****

"Not much to look at, is there?" Revington gestured as the waterman rowed the small sculler past the London docks. "As we get upstream a little farther, it will become much more scenic."

Penny actually thought the waterfront from the boat was quite interesting. She enjoyed seeing the tall ships and sailing vessels. Ahead was London Bridge. Although she'd crossed it in a carriage, it was much different to see it from this perspective. As the boat passed beneath it, she marveled at the amount of work it must have taken to build the huge stone structure.

Then they were out into the sunlight again. Penny blinked at the sudden brightness. Revington sat facing her, with the waterman behind him in the prow, smoothly rowing as they traveled upstream. For a change, Revington looked relaxed and almost happy. The faint frown line between his eyebrows had disappeared, and his mouth wasn't set in a grim line. Seeing him like this, she thought again how handsome he was, his features sensual and finely made.

She felt a twinge of embarrassment as he caught her staring. The usual tension between them returned, and she struggled to think of something to say, some small talk to break the mood. She knew very little about this man, other than he made a living gambling. That thought gave her an opening: "You know all about my family. What about you? Do you have any siblings? Are your parents still living?"

He raised his brows, as if surprised by her question, then responded, "My parents are still alive. They mostly stay at the family estate in Hampshire. Don't come to London often. I also have a sister. She's married and lives in Hereford. My older brother, of course, is the heir."

Speaking of his family, the tension returned to his face. Although Penny regretted disrupting his pleasant mood, she was also intrigued. Why did talking about his brother make him look as if he'd tasted something foul? "Do you ever visit them?" she asked.

"Not often. They don't approve of me…the way I live."

"Why is that?"

His voice was acid. "While gambling is an

accepted pastime for a gentleman, apparently making your living from doing so is frowned upon. I don't know what they expect me to do, live on the pitiful allowance my father's willing to pay me?" He shook his head. "I'm not about to take a halfpenny from him. I'll earn my own way, thank you. Even if it is doing something disreputable like gambling."

Penny was a bit surprised by this side of Revington. He was obviously quite proud of being independent. And bitter about his family's attitude.

He met her gaze briefly. "I'm one of the unfortunates known as the 'younger son.' Not a lot of choices for men like me. I can either marry well, live off my family, or live as I wish and not pay my bills." He raised his brows. "There are plenty of men who do so."

Marry well. That was where she came in. She felt a twinge of resentment. This was the reason he wanted Horngate.

As if he guessed her thoughts, he said, "You may think in wedding you, I've chosen the first course of action. But it's truly not like that. The fact is, I *earned* Horngate through my own hard work and skill. Once we're wed, I'm not going to live off your inheritance, but work hard to improve the estate. My family thinks being a gentleman is an excuse to be lazy and worthless, but I have no respect for that sort of man. Nor do I have any intention of living like that myself."

Even though his mention of earning Horngate rankled a bit, the rest of his comments pleased her. Like him, she had no respect for men who did as little as possible and benefited from the hard work of others. The men she respected were usually servants and commoners like the grooms and stablemen she'd met this morning. Despite his background, Revington was much like them in that he took satisfaction in working hard and being good at what he did. Indeed, if it wasn't for her fear that he would take everything away from her, she found she was coming to actually like and admire Revington.

She quickly pushed the unwelcome notion into the back of her mind. No matter what he said, Revington had no right to Horngate.

They both were silent for a time, as the boat moved slowly up river. As Revington had promised, the shoreline was becoming more scenic. The clutter of buildings gradually turned to trees and bushes. The sounds of the city: voices, the clatter of wheels and hoof beats, gave way to birdsong. It even smelled better, the scent of meadowland replacing the less pleasant odors of people living in close confinement. Penny began to relax and revel in the natural beauty all around. The red campion and wild hyacinth growing along the river. The sweet call of the thrush and warblers in the trees. The warmth of the sun on her face.

She closed her eyes and leaned back. Although she was probably getting sunburned, she didn't care. This was lovely, simply lovely.

****

How different she was from the other women he'd known, Marcus thought as Penny relaxed in the sunshine. Most women would be worried about ruining their complexions or the breeze blowing their hair into disarray. They'd never lean back without a hat or parasol and soak up the sun like a contented cat. Penny clearly missed the outdoors. He couldn't imagine her living in the city. Which was just as well, since he intended to spend most of his time at Horngate as soon as they were wed. He was beginning to think they'd get on very well together once they were married.

And he was certainly looking forward to the time when he would have the right to take her to bed any time he wished. Just looking at her aroused him. Today she'd worn a simple printed dress, not formfitting or low-cut at all. But that didn't stop him from recalling her slim, supple and elegantly sensual body. The feel of her in his arms... Beneath him... How it felt to be inside her... He'd planned for them to have a picnic somewhere along on the shoreline, but with the boatman nearby, there would be no real privacy or chance for him to make love to her. He'd have to wait until they returned to the townhouse, and that seemed a long time off.

Patience, he told himself. He'd planned this day so they could get to know each other better. And that meant conversing with her instead of lusting after her. With that thought in mind, he scanned the shoreline, seeking a place for the boat to put in so they could have their picnic.

****

Penny floated in a haze of contentment, lost in memories of lazy summer days at Horngate. All at once she realized the boat had stopped. She opened her eyes to see Revington disembarking. He held out his hand. "Here, I'll help you out."

His strong grip pulled her ashore, then he returned to the boat and retrieved the basket of food he'd brought. After saying something to the boatman, he took her hand to lead her up the bank. "I thought this looked like a pleasant spot for a picnic."

The feel of his strong hand and the warm huskiness of his voice sent a thrill down her spine. She almost wished that instead of eating, they were planning to satisfy other appetites!

They walked to a grassy field dotted with oak trees and scatterings of cornflowers and poppies. Revington headed to the largest of the trees, where he let go of her hand and spread a blanket packed on the top of the basket. They sat and he took out the food.

"It seems you're well acquainted with picnics," she said. "Do you do this sort of thing often?"

To her surprise he colored. "Hardly. I haven't been on this sort of outing since I was a child."

"Who did you go with then?"

"My sister. My brother was older, and he would have none of it."

"Did you get along well with your sister?"

"I suppose so. She liked to involve me in her games." He met her eyes, looking sheepish. "When I was very small, she even made me play dollies with her."

Penny couldn't help laughing. "I can hardly picture that."

He shrugged. "She's five years older so I had very little say in the matter."

"You don't see her much these days?"

"Not much. She's busy with her family and seldom comes to London."

Is that what he would want her to do if they were wed? Penny wondered. Stay at home and tend their children? The thought of it reawakened her resentment.

In this relaxed setting, she'd begun to think it might not be so bad to be wed to him. But she had to remember what he would expect of her as his wife. He'd inevitably end up trying to control her. While it would be more pleasant to have him as her gaoler rather than Adrian, she would still lose her freedom.

"What of you?" he asked. "It must have been lonely for you, growing up without any siblings."

"It wasn't so bad. Some of the staff had children, and the servants themselves were always willing to entertain me."

She saw him raise his eyebrows and guessed he was thinking that her unusual upbringing was the reason she saw fit to socialize with servants and working people. He clearly didn't approve. Well, too bad for him! She wasn't going to change. Most of the time she preferred the company of ordinary folk to her own class. They were much more genuine and kind, and often more interesting as well. She'd rather discuss horses with a bunch of grooms than make polite small talk with someone like Lambson. And she was certainly more comfortable with Maggie than she'd ever be with a "lady" like Elizabeth Valant.

****

Penny had gotten her back up again, he could tell. She knew he didn't approve of her familiarity with service staff. Well, it was unseemly. He could only imagine what his mother would think of the way Penny treated everyone as nearly her equal.

His mother. Just the thought of her provoked him. He'd always despised the way she ran his father's life. He had no intention of tolerating such behavior in *his* wife. Which was why Penny's defiant, independent attitude irritated him so much. Yes, she was lovely and desirable, but he couldn't let her manipulate him the way his mother had his father. Once they were wed, he would see to it that she deferred to his wishes, rather than the other way around.

They'd finished eating, and he could see no point in lingering. He gathered the remains of the meal. "I guess we should get back to London. I'm certain you'll want to change and freshen up before we go to the theatre."

A look of surprise crossed her face, followed swiftly by a frown. She'd probably like to stay here a bit longer, but he truly hated to be idle, and as far as he was concerned, he'd indulged her long enough. Not to mention he was giving up his evening to go to the theatre with her.

As he stood and started back to the boat, he felt a stab of resentment. He'd be glad when they were wed, and he didn't have to engage in this sort of nonsense.

****

Penny followed him to the boat, feeling disappointed and a bit angry. They'd been getting on so well, but then Revington had reverted to his usual distant, impatient demeanor. What had changed his outlook? Was it because she'd reminded him she enjoyed the company of service staff? Did he fear her lack of snobbery would embarrass him? Was that what all this was about—his blasted pride? Well, too bad. If he was going to be a pompous, stiff-necked idiot then he deserved to be embarrassed!

But as he helped her into the boat, she sought to put aside her anger. She had to remember her goal, to make him fall in love with her. If she could only hide her resentment long enough to win him over, then she could get out of this marriage and go on with her life. She'd never have to see him again.

Of course, while her mind might rejoice at the thought of that, her body felt a sharp stab of dismay. What they'd experienced together physically was quite sublime. She doubted any other man in the world would ever make her feel that way.

Oh, why did this have to be so difficult? Why couldn't the magic they shared when they made love carry over into the rest of their lives? How could a man who was such a tender, passionate lover be such a cold, arrogant bastard the rest of the time?

As the boat moved swiftly downriver, Penny watched the passing scenery with growing frustration.

Chapter Thirteen

"Bowes, please have Maggie go up and check on Miss Montgomery. Have her tell Miss Montgomery that it's time to leave for the theatre."

"Of course, sir."

Marcus glanced around the library, trying not to pace. What was taking so long? Was it possible she'd changed her mind about going? They'd hardly spoken on the return boat trip or in the carriage ride to the townhouse. That was his fault, no doubt. He shouldn't have let the unpleasant memories of his upbringing get the best of him. In fact, Penny wasn't much like his mother at all, and he doubted her actions were directed toward controlling him. Curse it! Why had he let his problems get in the way of enjoying the afternoon?

He would have to do better this evening, try to be pleasant and courteous. Spending time with Penny was hardly a trial. She was intelligent and straightforward, exhibiting none of the coy, simpering foolishness that many young misses indulged in. He was most fortunate to be marrying such a sensible and appealing woman.

Appealing, yes, she was certainly that. What he really wanted was to get all this courtship business out of the way so he could take her to bed! Maybe that was part of the reason for his short temper this afternoon. What he yearned to do was take her to some private glen, lay her upon the blanket and make love to her until they were both limp with contentment. Instead, he'd been forced to sit beside her chatting politely about their childhoods. The strain had gotten on his nerves and he'd been much shorter with her than he intended. Now he must make it up to her.

"I'm ready."

He turned to the doorway, and once again her beauty took his breath away. She was dressed in a gown of vivid blue silk. It wasn't particularly low-cut or elaborate, but it made her fair skin glow and her eyes sparkle like sapphires.

"You look quite fetching," he said.

She smiled, a bit tightly he thought. "Thank you."

"Have Bowes get your wrap and we'll go."

"It's here, sir," Bowes responded. The butler helped Penny put on a silvery shawl. Marcus took her arm and escorted her out the door and to the waiting carriage.

****

Does he really think a trite compliment can make up for his earlier cold disdain?

Thinking about it made her clench her jaw. Well, she wasn't about to forgive him so quickly. At least she hoped she wouldn't. Why was it that the mere sight and touch of him seemed to cause her resentment and anger to dissolve? It was maddening that she couldn't despise him. Indeed, most of the time she struggled to even dislike him. But she would give it a real go this evening. She'd not make it easy for him!

"I understand the play we're seeing is quite good." He spoke cordially and his dark eyes regarded her with warmth. "Sarah Siddons is in it. You may have heard of her. She's said to be very talented."

Penny gave him a chilly nod.

"Due to her reputation, I expect it will be extremely crowded. I should have asked around to see if anyone I knew had a box available. On the other hand, if we sit up front, we'll be close enough to see the performance."

"Do you often go to the theatre?" She imagined him attending with Elizabeth Valant, the two of them alone in one of the box seats, kissing or perhaps indulging in even more scandalous activities. The idea immediately aroused a stab of jealousy.

He smiled almost sheepishly. "The truth is, I've never been to a performance before."

"Truly? All this time in London and you've never gone to the theatre?"

"I'm generally not much for such entertainments."

"What do you do for diversion?" she asked, archly. "Surely you don't gamble and engage in business *all* the time."

"I've been known to go to the country for hunting or other sport. And sometimes I go to the horse races at Newmarket."

Penny nodded. "I've heard about the Newmarket races. I've wondered how Hero would do."

"Hard to say. I'd have to see him in an all-out gallop. And even then it's not easy to predict how an individual horse will perform in a race. Unless the animal's been raced before, it's usually risky to bet on them."

"Is that why you go to Newmarket? To bet on the races?"

"No. I prefer cards. With them I can better control the outcome. There's an element of skill to winning at cards, while in horseracing it often comes down to luck as much as anything."

"Don't you believe luck plays a part in cards?"

"Not really. I've found you have to make your own luck. You also have to know when to quit. That's the real key to winning. You can't be greedy."

"I would like to go to races at Newmarket sometime," she said. "It sounds very exciting."

"It is thrilling to see the animals run." He gave her a look that could almost be called warm. "Perhaps we could attend one weekend."

"I'd like that." She felt her animosity toward him slowly trickling away. The next thing she knew she'd be smiling at him.

The carriage slowed and then stopped. "Have we arrived?" she asked.

"The theatre is still some distance away. This traffic is probably from all the carriages headed there."

Penny turned so she could look out the back window. A long line of carriages trailed behind them. Although she couldn't see in front, it was probably the same. The carriage crawled along. Finally Revington said, "We might as well get out here. We probably can't get much closer."

He rapped on the coach ceiling. A few moments later, Jeremy opened the door. "Watch your step, miss," the footman warned as he helped her out. Revington quickly followed.

She could barely see the theatre for all the people. In addition to those waiting to get in, there were all sorts of vendors. Some of them had carts, while others carried baskets of oranges, flowers, and various kinds of foods.

As they waited in a queue outside the theatre entrance, Penny took in the crowd. There were elegantly dressed ladies wearing colorful cashmere shawls, hats trimmed with feathers, ribbons and faux fruits, jeweled necklaces and earrings. The gentlemen wore tall beaver hats and fine frockcoats. There were also more plainly dressed individuals. To her surprise, Penny spied Dickie, one of the grooms from Rotten Row the day before. She recognized him despite the black and gold livery he was wearing. Without thinking, she waved at him. He gave her an uncertain look before waving back.

"Who's that?" Revington asked, an edge to his voice.

"That's Dickie. I met him when I went riding. I must say I'm a little surprised to see him here."

"He's probably saving a seat for his employer. A lot of the grooms do that so the more top-lofty sorts don't have to wait in line. But there are plenty of ordinary folk who are here for the show. The price of admission to the gallery is still only a shilling, so even clerks and working fellows can afford it."

Finally, the line moved and they slowly made their way into the theatre. Revington paid their admission and bought a program from a young woman with a basket full of them. As Revington led Penny through the crowd, the orchestra started to play. She could hardly hear them over all the people talking.

Revington greeted several acquaintances, but it was so crowded he had no chance to introduce Penny, although several times she heard him murmur, "my fiancée." More than a few people gave them curious glances. Penny could tell they were surprised to see

Revington here. One man leaned near to Revington and muttered, "My wife dragged me here, but I didn't expect to see you. Gotten yourself leg-shackled, have you?"

Revington nodded curtly, then led Penny on, firmly guiding her through the crowd. They finally found seats halfway back from the stage. Penny sat, sighing in relief. "All these people…it's a bit overwhelming."

"I agree, but most of the people here aren't bothered by the crowds. In fact, seeing who is here and who they're with is the main reason many of them come."

The orchestra quieted, the curtain rose, and the play began. But all around them, people continued to talk, making it difficult to hear the performance. Even so, Penny enjoyed watching the actors with their extravagant costumes and their ability to make a character come to life with their voices and movements.

Following the shorter play after the main performance, they rose to leave the theatre. Once again they were borne along with the mass of people. Penny felt like a sheep in a large herd. The air was thick with the odors of various perfumes, not to mention less appealing smells from so many people crowded together. It was a relief when they reached the fresher air outside.

Revington said, "I told Jeremy to bring the coach around, but I don't know how close he'll be able to get." He stood on tiptoe and strained to see down the street. Turning to Penny, he said, "Wait here, I'll try to find him."

Although she felt uncomfortable with people all around, Penny nodded.

Gradually, the crowd thinned, and she became aware of a man and woman arguing nearby. The woman sounded so distraught Penny couldn't help moving closer. When she saw the woman was carrying an infant, she drew even nearer.

"You bastard!" the woman cried. "How dare you suggest the child belongs to someone else? You're the only man I've ever been with. You knew I was a virgin and still you ruined me!"

"The brat's not mine!" the man retorted. "And if you don't get away from me, I'll take drastic action."

"She *is* yours," the woman persisted. Her eyes were wild and her face tear-streaked. She took a step closer. The man responded by striking her with his walking stick. The woman cried out and fell backward.

Penny pushed her way through the crowd. Reaching the woman, she helped her to her feet. As soon as the woman and child were righted, Penny whirled to face the man. "What sort of beast are you, striking a woman holding an infant!"

"Meddling, interfering bitch! This is none of your affair," the man sneered.

The cold hatred in his eyes made Penny's breath catch. Her heart pounded with dread. Would he strike her? Despite her fears, she held her ground. "It *is* my affair. Even if no one else cares about this woman, I do." As she spoke, she shot an outraged glance at the people standing around, seeking to shame them into action.

All at once, the man seemed to realize the scene he was making. He flushed crimson and took a step nearer and spoke so only Penny and the woman could hear him. "I'll make you pay for this, you worthless

185

whore...and your little brat, too. As for you..." His gaze alighted on Penny. "Mind your own business, you meddling bitch." He stalked off, the crowd parting to let him pass.

Penny turned her attention to the woman. "Are you hurt?"

The woman shook her head. Her face was tear-streaked, her eyes bleak. Penny felt a desperate urge to do something for her. "My fiancé should be back soon. He has a carriage. Is there somewhere we can take you?"

"I've nowhere to go. My family has disowned me. I used my last shilling to come here, to try and get him to help me." The woman gave a convulsive sob.

Although she wasn't certain Revington would agree, Penny found herself saying, "You can stay with me...at least for now."

The crowd drifted away and eventually Revington appeared. "I found the carriage. It isn't far." He took Penny's arm.

"Can we take this woman with us? Please?"

"Of course," Revington responded. He inclined his head politely to the woman. "Madam. Where can we convey you?"

Penny put her hand on Revington's arm. "I've asked her to come back to the townhouse with us. She has nowhere else to go."

****

As they rode home, Marcus felt a sense of disbelief. Seated across from him was a woman with an infant in her lap. What had happened to his comfortable bachelor life? First, he was engaged to be married. Now it looked as if he was going to have a woman and a baby staying in his home. He couldn't imagine where he would put them. There wasn't another spare bedroom. But he could hardly say no to Penny. Or leave this young woman—Penny said her name was Lily—and her baby in the street. Especially not after Penny explained what had happened.

What sort of man struck a woman, especially one holding a baby? He had half a mind to call the bastard out. But an unprincipled blackguard like that wouldn't necessarily behave honorably in a duel. Marcus had heard stories of men getting killed because their opponent shot too soon. Although he considered himself a decent and compassionate man, he didn't fancy getting killed over a woman he scarcely knew.

He would have to investigate this man, Brakestoke, and find how dangerous he was. He'd have James get started on it first thing tomorrow.

James! Of course. That's where this woman and her child could stay. James's townhouse was quite spacious, and fully furnished.

His mind made up, he rapped on the carriage roof. Jeremy halted the vehicle, climbed down and opened the door. Marcus announced, "Take us to Mr. Ludingham's townhouse."

"Of course, sir."

When Penny gazed at Marcus in surprise, he motioned to the woman. "Lily will be safe there. James has plenty of space. She'll be quite comfortable." When Penny still looked dubious, he continued. "I think we all need a good night's sleep. First thing tomorrow, we'll put our heads together and decide how to deal with this."

"Thank you so much, sir," Lily murmured. "I'm

ever so grateful."

"You're welcome." Seeing her desperate gratitude, his anger returned. Brakestoke was truly a monster.

When they reached James's house, Marcus helped Penny and Lily from the carriage and escorted them to the door. He rapped loudly. James's butler, Vincent, opened the door.

"Is James still up?" Marcus asked.

"He's in the library. Please come in and I'll fetch him." Vincent shot Lily and the baby a curious glance as he left them in the spacious foyer.

A moment later James appeared. He greeted Marcus and Penny, then turned expectantly to the young woman.

"Lily, this is James Ludingham," Marcus said. "James, this is Miss…"

"Wilson," Lily supplied.

"Charmed, I'm sure." James inclined his head.

"Lily is in rather dire circumstances. I was hoping she could stay here for a day or two."

James's eyebrows shot up. "Here?"

"Yes. I really don't have room at my townhouse."

James frowned. He shot a glance at Lily, then looked back at Marcus.

"I'll explain in a moment," Marcus said. "For now, perhaps you could have Vincent show Lily…Miss Wilson, upstairs to one of the bedchambers. I'm sure she's quite dead on her feet."

"Of course." James turned to the butler standing nearby. "Vincent, if you could be so good as to take Miss Wilson to the blue bedroom."

As soon as they were out of earshot, James said, "What the devil is this all about, Marcus?"

Marcus looked at Penny and realized how pale she was. "Let's go into the library. I could do with a brandy, and I suspect a small glass might be just the thing for Penny as well."

****

Penny sipped her brandy as Revington explained to James everything that had happened at the theatre. As she watched Revington, she was keenly aware he was exhibiting the behaviors that both attracted and unsettled her. On one hand, she was impressed by how he'd taken charge and gone out of his way to help Lily. At the same time, she was wary of his forceful, controlling manner.

He hadn't asked James if he was willing to have Lily stay there. He'd simply made it happen and then set about convincing James he had no choice. She supposed that since James was—in a sense—employed by Revington, maybe Revington's behavior wasn't quite as high-handed as it appeared. Still, she couldn't help feeling a little sorry for James. Whether he wanted it or not, he was suddenly stuck with houseguests, including an infant.

At one point, she'd almost suggested Lily and the baby stay in her room. But that meant she either slept on the settle in the library or shared Revington's bed. She was fairly certain he wouldn't allow her to sleep in the library, and although the thought of sharing a bed with him was tantalizing, it also terrified her. She needed some distance from this man, some way of staying aloof from him. As it was, her resolve to convince him not to marry her weakened every day.

She was impressed he hadn't hesitated to help Lily. Of course, the idea of having a baby in his household had clearly given Revington pause, which was why they were here. He'd found a way to keep Lily safe without being inconvenienced himself. But at least he'd done something. He hadn't walked away.

And it was obvious from the way Revington was talking to James that he felt genuine compassion for Lily. He wasn't merely doing this to please Penny, but because he believed it was the right thing to do. James had put up only a token defense, quickly agreeing that Lily and the baby could stay at his house and then shaking his head in dismay at the thought of someone striking a woman carrying a baby.

"Brakestoke's a real piece of work," James was saying now. "From what I've heard, this isn't the first time he's done something like this. He has a reputation for debauching young women."

"Someone should make him pay for what he's done," said Revington. "While it horrifies me to think of Miss Wilson being married to such a man, Brakestoke should at least be forced to make some sort of settlement to care for the child."

"How are we going to manage that?" responded James. "Since he's a peer, he thinks he can get away with anything. He probably can, too."

"There must be some way to force him to do the honorable thing," Revington mused. "I'll have to think on it."

"In the meantime, what do we do with Lily?"

"I thought we'd agreed she could stay here."

"For tonight, yes," said James. "But this will take some time to sort out. While I'm as compassionate as the next fellow, I really don't think—"

"I'll compensate you financially, if that's what

you're worried about," Revington broke in. "Although I can't imagine that a young woman and an infant can cost that much to maintain."

"No, I don't suppose so." James was still frowning. "But the idea of it…a young unmarried woman staying with a man she doesn't know?"

"I hardly think we have to worry about her reputation," said Revington. "Once a woman's ruined, she can hardly be ruined any further."

"I suppose not."

Penny sensed James was coming around. Revington obviously knew what to say to sway his friend.

"It's settled then." Revington rose. "I'll be around tomorrow to discuss this further."

James also rose, looking panicked. "You mean you're leaving now?"

"Well, yes. It's been quite a night. I think it's time I got Penny home."

James shot Penny a frantic look.

"It will be all right," she told him. "Just pretend Lily is your sister. I'm sure you'll get on perfectly well."

They returned to the carriage. Revington appeared deep in thought as they rode back to the townhouse. Penny asked, "Are you trying to decide what to do about Lily?"

"I'm thinking about Brakestoke. The man's an unprincipled villain. Someone needs to make him face up to his responsibilities."

The next moment he seemed to shake off the mood. He turned and smiled at her. "Tonight didn't exactly turn out as planned. I'd hoped we would have a pleasant evening at the theatre and then return to the townhouse for a relaxing dinner. We're rather late. I hope it isn't ruined by now."

"I'm sure Maggie kept the food warm."

"It's not Maggie who's preparing the meal, but the new cook. Bowes finally hired someone. Now Maggie can concentrate on waiting on you."

Penny nodded. Revington seemed to be going out of his way to please her. His solicitousness made it even more difficult to harden her heart against him. As always, his mere physical presence made her long for him to make love to her. Although she was a bit hungry, what she really wanted was to skip dinner and indulge another sort of appetite. She wondered if there was some way to convey this, to make him realize how much she desired him.

****

As they rode home, Marcus told himself he had to stop obsessing over Brakestoke. There was nothing he could do this night, and he should be concentrating on Penny. He cast a surreptitious glance at her sitting across from him, wondering what she was thinking. As always, the mere sight of her aroused him. She was so beautiful. So provocatively lovely. Just a glance made him yearn to return to his original plan for this evening. After indulging her wish to go to the theatre, he'd hoped she'd be eager and willing to let him make love to her.

They arrived at the townhouse. He helped her down from the carriage and took her arm to escort her into the house. The feel of her slender body so close to his was almost tormenting.

Bowes greeted them at the door. "Have you eaten,

sir? Miss?"

"Not yet." Marcus turned to Penny. "Did you want to freshen up before we dine?"

She touched his arm. "Perhaps you could escort me." Her manner seemed somehow seductive. He told himself he must have imagined it. But when they reached the bedchamber door, she did it again. Her eyes were wide and yearning as she said, "Perhaps you could come in and undo the back of my dress."

Feeling slightly breathless, he followed her into the room. She stood by the bed and turned away from him. He undid the hooks on her dress, his gaze taking in her long elegant neck, the delicate tendrils of hair curling at the nape, the smooth ivory skin of her shoulders. He wanted to kiss and caress every inch of her.

As soon as he'd undone the hooks, she turned around. Her blue eyes were bright, her cheeks flushed. With a faint smile, she said, "I don't think I'm that hungry after all."

Chapter Fourteen

Although he was on fire with arousal, Marcus wouldn't allow himself to touch her. Not yet. First he wanted to feast his eyes on her. To drink in his fill of her beauty.

Either she guessed what he wanted, or she was desperate, but when he didn't immediately reach for her, she drew down the top of her gown. Another subtle movement…and the garment slid to her waist.

She was wearing a zona, the strip of thin muslin fabric wrapped tight against her breasts. Although it was sheer enough that he could make out her nipples, he still wanted to see her naked. Again, she either guessed his unspoken desire or she was yielding to her own, for she turned around. "If you wouldn't mind."

He unfastened the hooks of her undergarment. It fell to the floor. Very slowly, she turned back to face him.

His breath caught. She looked good enough to eat. To devour. Softly rounded breasts, their exquisite delicate shapes tipped with pale pink nipples, as enticing as some sweet, creamy confection. His gaze took in her graceful shoulders and arms, slender waist. His eyes were drawn back to her breasts. He was on the verge of giving in to his urge to kiss and suckle when she let out harsh, impatient breath, then grasped her gown and slid it down her body, wriggling her hips to pull it over her pantalettes. She stepped out of the dress and Marcus watched entranced, staring at the thin fabric that shielded the shadowy triangle of her maiden hair.

****

She couldn't believe she was being so bold. So shamelessly seductive. But the fact was she simply didn't have the patience to wait any longer. She knew he wanted her, could tell he was enjoying every moment as she revealed herself to him. His gaze burned streaks of fire into her flesh.

Yes, this was what she wanted. To be alone with him, to have him touch her, kiss her, make love to her. Her hunger for this was much greater than for food. All day there had been this tension between them, this yearning. Now her longing for for him had become an almost painful ache, pulsing through her.

The delicious throb of desire, the craving, was keenest between her legs. When his gaze caressed her there, his eyes focusing on the burning core of her, she felt as if she might burst into flame.

Slowly, breathlessly, she drew down her pantalettes and stepped out of them. She could feel the wetness between her legs. He could take her now and she would be ready. But would he? Or, would he stand there, fully dressed, and stare at her until she succumbed to madness? "Please," she whispered.

He nodded, his eyes dark and gleaming. She waited for him to begin to undress. Instead, he reached for her, pulling her against his fully clothed body. His mouth came down on hers. Firm. Insistent. She opened her mouth, welcoming his tongue. The slightly rough feel of his clothing against her body enflamed her. She rubbed her taut, aching nipples and her hips against him, seeking, seeking... Would he never touch her, never soothe her agonized need?

Finally, when she could bear no more, he slid his hands down her body and cupped her buttocks. His hands gripped her sensitive flesh and pressed her even more tightly against him. She broke off the kiss to let out a moan. His fingers followed the cleft of her bottom and finally reached the excruciatingly tender place between her legs. She let out a frantic cry of delight. Burying her face against his shoulder, Penny dissolved into whimpering moans as his skilled fingers teased, tantalized and finally found the perfect rhythm. She gave into the wild pleasure whirling around her, sucking her down into a violent maelstrom.

****

Her intoxicating feminine scent...The feel of her, soft, wet and eager... His senses reeled. With effort, he shook off the bewitching sexual miasma, released her and began to undress. As he fumbled with fabric, buttons, and hooks, he cursed the social conventions that made men's clothing so cumbersome and difficult to remove. Freeing himself from each garment, he threw it to the floor: ascot, jacket, shirt.

For his boots and trousers, he had to sit down. While he fought with leather and wool, she sat on the bed and watched him. The thrill of baring himself for her eyes aroused him even more. By the time he was fully naked, he was near to exploding.

He'd taken it slowly so far, drawing out their foreplay until they were both mindless with desire. Although he'd given her some satisfaction, he'd had no relief for his own arousal. Now the needs of his body overtook him. He pushed her onto the bed and thrust into her. She lay back, legs spread, hips lifted, meeting him with an eagerness that inflamed him. Her moans and cries echoed in his ears, mingling with his own groan of ecstasy as he peaked.

Then it was over and they were two people again. Sweaty, disheveled and a bit uneasy with each other. He wasn't certain what to do. What he longed for was to throw back the covers and climb into bed with her. To lie beside her all night. To have her delicate scent and the sound of her breathing lull him to sleep. But that seemed too intimate. It was presumptuous of him to expect such a thing. They weren't even married yet. For all he knew, they might never be legally bound. Because the blunt truth was that he'd have to admit to James he had lost the bet and fallen in love with her.

He could find no other explanation for his irrational actions. The way his response to her veered from exasperation to fury to wrenching tenderness. When it came to dealing with Penny, he'd utterly lost his wits.

The thought filled him with panic, a breathless dread that propelled him to rise from the bed and begin dressing.

****

He's leaving. The awareness filled Penny with an aching sense of loss. She wanted him to stay for a while. To have him hold her in his arms so she could savor his nearness. His warm, rich masculine scent. His sleek hard body. To lay her head upon his broad chest and feel safe and cared for.

What a ridiculous notion. Revington wasn't the sort of man from whom she could expect cuddling and tenderness. He was a man who maintained his control and reserve at all times.

Well, that wasn't strictly true. He'd had little enough control when he pounced upon her a short while ago, thrusting into her with wild abandon. Thinking of it, she felt a twinge of satisfaction, and was forced to hide the smile the memory brought to her lips. Revington might fancy himself in control at all times, but the truth was, she knew how to get past his damnable aloofness, to shred his detachment and interfere with his perfect command of himself.

Thinking of it gave her a heady sense of power. Too bad that her effect on him was so short-lived. As soon as they finished making love, he returned to his usual cool demeanor.

Even now he was once again hiding his sensual masculinity behind the stiff woolen garments of a gentleman. Of course, there were little details that gave away what he'd been doing. His retied cravat lacked the elegant perfection of Bowes's handiwork. And his thick black hair was a bit mussed. She thought of mentioning it, then decided not to. His slight dishabille made her feel as if what had transpired between them wasn't merely some sort of waking dream.

Another moment and he was at the door. She expected him to leave without a word, but to her surprise, he turned. There was uncertainty in his expression, a kind of vulnerability. "Dinner's probably ruined by now, but if you're hungry, I'm certain the new cook can come up with something."

"What of you?" she asked. "Are you planning to eat?"

His expression softened even more. "I must admit I'm a bit hungry. And since we've already gravely insulted the new cook, we might as well complete the business by forcing her to come up with a late night repast." He grinned suddenly, revealing a dimple on his right cheek she'd noted on a few other occasions.

"I'd better dress then." Penny got up from the bed.

"A pity you have to," he said in husky, provocative tones. "I'd like to dismiss all the servants and dine with you looking like that."

"I hardly think that's practical." Although his words tantalized her, she truly was hungry, and she felt certain that if she didn't get dressed quickly, eating would be forgotten.

"Probably not," he agreed. "But sometime I'd like to try it."

Penny nodded. This playful side of him intrigued her. She had been wrong. He hadn't totally reverted to his usual unapproachable reserve.

She grabbed her gown and began to dress. He watched her, his expression unreadable. As she met him at the door, he said, "I know it's all the fashion to have separate bedchambers, but I don't see the point of it."

She went out before him, feeling his eyes on her like a caress. With effort, she repressed a shiver of mingled yearning and dismay. How had she come to feel so tenderly toward this man she'd been so determined to reject? She'd once been consumed with getting Revington out of her life. Now the idea of never seeing him again was almost unthinkable.

Her thoughts were in turmoil as they walked downstairs.

****

She is so quiet! What does that mean? Marcus felt a spasm of anxiety. Once he'd been absolutely confident Penny was going to be his wife. He hadn't considered she had a choice, and if he had, he would have assumed she would be pleased to be marrying him. Now he was terrified she would reject him.

No, he told himself. That was ridiculous. He simply couldn't think like that. He knew he'd pleased her sexually. She obviously desired him. He had to make use of that. By the time she faced the decision of whether to marry him, she would be so eager to continue sharing his bed that she would readily agree.

Or would she? He might please her as a lover, but maybe she wanted something more from a husband. Obviously, he must continue to woo her. To show his best side and try to make her happy. Unfortunately, he knew little about this sort of thing. He must ask James for advice.

All at once he remembered Lily and the baby. As they headed for the dining room, he said, "I wonder how James is getting on."

"I'm sure James is fine," Penny responded. "It's Lily and the baby I'm worried for. What are they going to do? Since her family has turned her out, they have nowhere to go."

"I suppose not." Marcus helped Penny into her seat at the table.

"Unless someone can force Brakestoke to provide for her. Is there any way to do that? Are there any laws that protect a woman in Lily's circumstances?"

"Normally, it would be up to her male relatives to press the issue with Brakestoke. But it doesn't appear they'll be much help."

"It's appalling. She said her family acts as if this is all her fault." Penny shook her head, looking very aggrieved.

"I can look into Brakestoke's circumstances. Find out if he has any family members or associates who can be convinced to pressure him to do the right thing."

She nodded, then a moment later, frowned. "I'm not sure I want you to pressure Brakestoke after all."

"Why not?"

"If he's a danger to Lily, he might also be a danger to you."

She is worried about me? He couldn't decide whether to be insulted or touched. While gratified that she cared enough to concern herself with his wellbeing, he wondered whether she thought he couldn't handle himself in a risky situation.

"In my business I've gotten on the wrong side of some very hardened fellows," he told her. "The most important thing is to not lose your head. To maintain control and deal rationally with the situation. Also, to make certain you're not alone with them."

She nodded, still looking troubled. He saw merit in her concerns. This wasn't a dispute over the results of a card game, carried out in a public setting. If he were to confront Brakestoke, he'd probably have to do so in the man's own home, where he wouldn't have anyone to back him up.

"So," he said, "if we don't pursue Brakestoke, what other plan would you suggest?"

"If Lily had family to help her, they would probably find someone to marry her off to, someone who would care for her and her child."

"It won't be easy to find a man willing to take on the burden of a wife and child. Most men of means are looking for a wife who will better their circumstances," he reminded her.

"But Lily is quite fetching. It's not impossible that some man would want her as his wife. It need not be someone wealthy, just a man of moderate means."

Marcus regarded her dubiously. He'd forgotten that Penny had been raised in a sheltered world and was innocent of the more brutal facts of life. She seemed to think a pretty face was enough to cause a man to make the irrational decision to marry a woman who would be more burden to him than asset. Her naiveté struck him as charming, but certainly not realistic.

He said, "I know some of the popular novels make much of love as a reason for marrying, but in real life, that seldom happens. Most men marry to improve their own circumstances, or they marry someone with a family connection. They don't marry because they lose their heads over an attractive woman."

"Of course. I don't know what I was thinking. *Obviously,* fond feelings and sexual attraction have nothing to do with marriage. That's strictly business."

Clearly, he'd put his foot in it and offended her by the reminding her of his own motivation for marrying her. Well, it *was* the reason he intended to wed her. That he found her irresistibly attractive was a delightful bonus, but it was not the main reason.

But in light of her cool response, it seemed he should soften his remarks. "That's not to say it's *impossible* some man might want to wed Lily. But I don't know quite how to go about finding this individual. We could take her to a few parties and see what sort of man takes an interest in her. But really…" He shook his head. "The men I associate with…I'm afraid it's very unlikely. What we need is to find someone in trade, a craftsman, someone of more humble circumstances. And I'm not certain how to arrange for her to meet men like that."

Penny nodded, chewing her lower lip in the way she often did. At least she no longer appeared angry with him. This was his chance to turn the conversation a different direction. "Lily's problems aside, what did you think about the play?"

They discussed the theatrical production as Bowes and Jerome brought in the late supper: cold roast beef, tomatoes and boiled eggs.

After eating, they started upstairs. As he walked her to the door of what was formerly his bedchamber, he wanted to ask her if he could come inside. But he'd heard Bowes say he was sending Maggie up to help Penny undress. Again he wondered at the conventions of his class that a woman was normally assisted in undressing by her maid, rather than her husband. He gave her a kiss on the cheek and wished her goodnight, then set off down the hall to the spare bedchamber.

****

Penny paused inside the door of the bedchamber, frowning. It was ridiculous. She'd spent nearly all day with Revington and at one point they'd been as physically close as two people could be. Despite that, she really didn't know his mind at all. Before saying goodnight, he'd lingered near the door, as if he wanted to come in. Was it possible he wanted to make love to her again?

She wouldn't have been averse to the idea. Her body yearned for his. It was as if she couldn't get enough of being close to him.

With a sigh, she dismissed the idea. A moment

later, there was a knock on the door. "It's Maggie, miss. Bowes sent me up to help you undress."

Good thing she and Revington hadn't yielded to their urges! "Please come in, Maggie."

Maggie entered, beaming broadly. Inside the door, she stopped and gestured to herself. "My new clothes came. What do you think? Do I look like a fashionable lady's maid?"

"You do indeed," said Penny, smiling back. The muslin dress was simple but showed off Maggie's voluptuous figure to great advantage. Instead of her usual mob-cap, Maggie wore her coppery curls swept away from her face and gathered in a knot on top of her head. While she didn't exactly look like a lady—her many freckles prevented that—she did look very attractive in a wholesome sort of way.

"I'm impressed," Penny told her. "I especially like what you've done with your hair."

"It's a bit of challenge." Maggie preened. "Takes a lot of time and dozens of hairpins. But I think the result is worth it."

"It is indeed."

Maggie approached Penny, back to her no-nonsense self. "Shall I help you undress now, miss?"

Penny nodded and turned around so the maid could undo the hooks at the back of her dress.

"So," said Maggie. "How did your day go? Bowes said you went to the theatre."

Sensing the maid's eagerness to hear the details, Penny described the play and the incident with Lily and Brakestoke afterward.

Maggie's cheerful mood vanished. "How terrible! That man actually struck her, even while she carried his babe in her arms?"

"He did, indeed." Just talking about it made Penny angry all over again. "Then when I stepped in to defend Lily, I thought he was going to strike *me*!"

"He didn't, miss? Did he?" Maggie looked aghast.

"No. I think he realized that would be going too far. But he did threaten me. Said he would make me pay for interfering."

Maggie gasped. "Does Mr. Revington know this?"

"No. And I don't want him to." Penny gave the maid a stern look. "This man—Brakestoke—I think he could be dangerous. Not merely to me but to Mr. Revington."

Maggie frowned. "I think you're wrong, miss. Mr. Revington strikes me as a man who could take care of himself."

"If the conflict was fair, yes. But I very much fear Brakestoke might do something underhanded and devious. A man who would strike a woman carrying an infant obviously has no sense of honor."

Maggie nodded. "I suppose you're right, miss. But I still think Mr. Revington should know this man threatened you."

"He probably reacted in the heat of the moment. I doubt he truly means to pursue the matter. If anyone is in danger from him, it would be Lily. And I believe she'll be safe at James's."

"Mr. Ludingham's house? That's where she's staying?"

"It was Revington's idea. He pointed out that James's house is larger than this one. It makes sense. Lily and the baby need their own room."

"I wonder what Mr. Ludingham thought of that."

"I think it will be good for James. He's nice enough, but rather stuffy at times. Having a baby around might help him relax and enjoy himself."

"Perhaps that's what Mr. Revington needs as well. Having a baby around might be just the thing for him."

Penny tried to imagine Revington with a baby. It was almost as amusing as the thought of James having to deal with Lily's child. But maybe she was underestimating her fiancé. She'd never have guessed he was such a skillful and considerate lover. What other ways might he surprise her if she gave him a chance? "Perhaps," she said.

She looked up and suddenly realized how Maggie was looking at her. The maid wasn't talking about Lily's child, but about *her* having a baby with Revington. "We aren't even wed yet," she informed Maggie sternly.

"Ah, but you will be. I can see how you've softened toward the master. At one time you were scheming every minute, trying to get him to forget about marrying you. Now, here you are, worrying about him."

It was time to change the subject. "I'm not the only one who's distracted by a man these days. I saw you and Jeremy together the other day, looking quite cozy."

Maggie blushed so intensely, her freckles almost disappeared.

Chapter Fifteen

As she made her way downstairs the next morning, Penny thought about Maggie's remark. It was true; her attitude toward Revington *had* changed. Although it had only been a few hours since they'd parted, she couldn't wait to see him again. Just the thought of being in the same room with him made her breath quicken.

When she reached the breakfast room and he wasn't there, she felt a rush of disappointment. Had he already left the townhouse?

As Jerome helped her into her seat, she asked, "Have you seen Mr. Revington?"

"No, miss. I'm not sure he's come down yet."

Maybe he'd risen late. He might be tired after everything that happened the day before. She repressed a smile as she recalled their vigorous lovemaking.

A few moments later, Revington entered the room. She felt ridiculously pleased to see him.

"Good morning, Penny."

"Good morning."

He took the seat across from her. As Jerome served them, Revington said, "What would you like to do today? Do you want Jerome to get some horses so we could ride in the park?"

He was genuinely trying to please her. A great change from the controlling, inconsiderate man she'd first met. She wondered at the reason for his transformation. Was it because of the intimacy they'd shared in the bedchamber, or was it something else? Could it be he was actually coming to care for her?

"A ride in the park sounds delightful. But I really think we should see how Lily and the baby are faring."

"I suppose you're right."

"And James," Penny added with a smile. "He seemed a bit overwhelmed last evening."

****

What bachelor wouldn't be overwhelmed with a woman and baby landing on his doorstep, Marcus mused as he took a bite of egg. Having Penny here had turned his life upside down. He couldn't imagine how much the addition of a baby would change it. Of course, if Penny and he kept having sex, there was every reason to think they *would* have a baby to disrupt their lives.

The idea made him feel strange. A tiny creature who was part him and part Penny. What would the child be like? He rather fancied having a girl, as long as she looked like Penny. His mind's eye was filled with the image of a slender, blue-eyed girl, graceful as a wood sprite.

He reminded himself that such an event was long in the future. Penny and he weren't even wed yet. He was as bad as some of the fools he gambled with, counting his winnings before the game was over. The thought aroused the memory of his wager with James. He didn't like losing. Maybe with the distraction of Lily and the baby, James would forget their discussion.

Little chance of that. James never forgot anything. But maybe he could bargain with James. Find some way of taking care of this difficulty of Lily and the baby. Maybe that would be enough to sway him.

They ate breakfast, talking of things of little consequence. Afterward, Penny fetched her wrap and he called for the carriage. A short ride later, Vincent welcomed them into James's house. "Mr. Ludingham is in the library," he announced as he led them down the hall.

"Probably hiding out," Marcus muttered.

But when they reached the library, they found James pacing back and forth with the baby in his arms. James transferred the infant to his left arm and held a finger to his lips. "Little mite just fell asleep," he whispered.

Marcus stared at his friend in astonishment. James continued to move around the room, swaying slightly, rocking the baby. Finally satisfied the infant was asleep, he started toward the door. "I'll put him to bed," he murmured as he moved past them.

"He seems to have things well in hand," Penny said after James had left.

"Indeed. I'm rather astonished. I had no idea he knew what to do with an infant. Frankly, I'm terrified of babies and small children."

Penny smiled at him. "I am, too, I'm afraid. Having had no younger brothers and sisters, I haven't had much experience with infants, at least the human kind. I've bottle fed a few foals over the years."

"Bottle fed?" asked Marcus. "You can do that?"

"There's no other way if the mare dies or is too weak to let the foal nurse. It's exhausting, but if several people take turns, it's not impossible. Believe it or not, that's what we did with Hero."

Marcus had an image of a young Penny holding a bottle for a small black colt to suckle. No matter what she said about being afraid of babies, he could tell she'd be a wonderful mother.

James returned. "Charles isn't much for sleeping at night. Poor Lily's exhausted."

"Charles?" Marcus asked.

"That's what she named the baby. I guess she hoped that by giving the child Brakestoke's Christian name, it might help him accept him as his son." James grimaced. "Apparently there's no chance of that."

"Indeed," Marcus said. "That's what we came to discuss."

"It's very good of you to help Lily like this," Penny said.

James shrugged, "I had four younger brothers and sisters, so I'm fairly well-acquainted with babies."

"I'd have never guessed it," Marcus said.

"Other than tired, how is Lily?" Penny asked.

James's expression grew harsh. "Still a bit shaken. I can't believe that beast actually struck her. What sort of man hits a woman? Especially when she's holding a baby!"

"Brakestoke's a black-hearted fiend," Penny agreed.

"Someone needs to make him pay for what he's done," James shot back. "I have half a mind to call him out!"

Marcus was astonished. While he'd initially had the same reaction, he was surprised at his friend's vehement response. "Penny and I actually discussed my doing that very thing. We decided a direct confrontation with Brakestoke might end disastrously. He's hardly a man of honor. If it did come to *pistols at dawn*, what's to stop him from shooting before his opponent's ready?"

"I suppose you're right. But it makes me furious just the same. Lily is a sweet, decent young woman. She deserves far better." James's face was flushed, his eyes bright with outrage.

Marcus regarded his friend with a mixture of astonishment and amusement. Who would have guessed that mild-mannered James could be aroused to such heights of emotion?

A sudden thought came to him. Penny and he had decided that the best way to help Lily was to find a man to marry her. *Why not James?*

Why not, indeed? James was a gentleman, but his background was modest, which meant there wasn't any pressure from his family to marry well.

Marcus glanced at Penny. From the faint, satisfied smile on her face, he wondered if her thoughts weren't moving along similar pathways. A moment later, she said, "Perhaps once Lily is rested, I could take her shopping. I'm sure she could use a few things. And she'll need supplies for the baby as well."

"An excellent idea," James said. "It's been rather difficult. Cook came up with some rags to use as nappies, but poor Lily has nothing but the clothes on her back. Apparently, her family threw her out, blaming her for her disgrace." He shook his head. "I can't understand the callousness of some people. Lily is an innocent young woman who was cruelly used by Brakestoke. There's no reason to blame her."

"Of course not," Penny said. "She deserves a chance at a decent life. And so does the child."

James nodded, still frowning.

"Perhaps you should go and check on her," Marcus

suggested. "See if she's awake yet."

"Yes, I'll do that."

As soon as James left, Marcus said, "James seems quite taken with Lily."

"Yes, he does."

Marcus gave her a conspiratorial look. "Perhaps this will resolve itself on its own."

"What do you mean?"

"Perhaps James will decide to marry Lily and adopt the infant."

Penny grinned at him. "You're as bad as some sly, matchmaking old tabby."

Marcus felt he must defend himself. "It all seems perfectly logical to me. Lily needs a husband, and James would suit quite well." He ticked off the reasons on his fingers: "He's well-off enough that he doesn't need to marry for money. He has a comfortable relationship with his family, so they wouldn't gainsay his choice. He appears to like Lily, and she's the sort of woman he finds attractive."

"How do you know that?" Penny laughed.

"Because he told me he favors women who are fair-haired and relatively petite, but with a shapely figure. Lily appears to have all those qualities. Of course, he did say he wanted a wife who was sensible and frugal. While I have no reason to think Lily is a spendthrift, I suppose having an affair with Brakestoke isn't exactly something a sensible woman would do. But I'm sure she learned her lesson and will make future decisions more carefully."

"It seems you and James have discussed exactly what you're looking for in wives. What sort of woman did you tell him *you* had in mind?"

"When James and I had this discussion, I believe I told him that the only requirement I had of a wife was that she possess property and wealth."

"Of course." Penny's smile faded, and Marcus suddenly wished he'd answered differently. He should have told her what a fool he'd been back then, and now what he desired in a wife was exactly the qualities she possessed: courage and loyalty, intelligence and beauty.

Before he could amend his comment, James entered the room. "Lily's awake and tidying up. Then she must feed the baby. But once Charles is taken care of, she should be ready."

Feed the baby. Thinking of it, Marcus was rather embarrassed for Lily. In his experience only lower-class women nursed their infants.

James must have noted his expression, for he said, "I know it's not exactly the thing, but when I suggested getting a wet nurse, Lily rejected the idea." He shrugged. "It's the natural way, certainly. Not to mention cheaper and more convenient, for everyone but Lily, that is."

All at once, Marcus had the image of Penny with a baby at her breast. Like the thought of having a child together, the image aroused an odd throb of hope and longing in his midsection.

****

If we have a child together, will Marcus object to me nursing the baby myself? Recalling the look on his face when James talked about Lily feeding the baby, Penny couldn't help wondering. She wanted to tell him she understood exactly how Lily felt. Animals bonded with their offspring while nursing their infants. If she ever had a child, she would want that sort of closeness, even if it weren't fashionable.

Once again, she was reminded of the differences in the way she and Revington had been raised. He'd been brought up with all the values of his class, which meant marrying for money and having a wife who was expected to do very little except look decorative. In his world, wives weren't partners, except sexual ones, and then only until an heir was conceived. If a man sought real passion and intimacy, he kept a mistress.

Considering these things, a sudden thought came to her. What if instead of them marrying, he agreed to make her his mistress? That way she could keep her freedom, and preserve her relationship with him as it was now.

Such an arrangement would be perfect. The only problem was whether Marcus would agree.

Marcus. When had she started thinking of him as Marcus, rather than "Revington"? The change in her thinking unsettled her. By thinking of him as Marcus, she was acknowledging him as someone she was close to, a lover.

Her troubled thoughts were interrupted when Lily entered the room. Penny had thought she was attractive the night before, but now, no longer tear-stained and disheveled, Lily's loveliness was even more apparent. With her golden hair, cornflower blue eyes and curvaceous figure, it shouldn't be that difficult to find her a husband. Marcus obviously favored James, but was that what Lily wanted? Penny decided she would find out.

"I'm ready to go whenever you are," Lily announced.

"Excellent," said James. "I'll have the carriage

brought around."

When James left, Penny approached Marcus. "Shall I charge the items to your name?" she asked in discreet tones.

Marcus looked startled. Frowning slightly, he responded, "Yes. Unless you want me to go with you."

"I think I'd like to talk to Lily alone."

He nodded.

James returned. "The carriage should be here momentarily. What about you, Marcus? Will you be leaving or do you want to wait here?"

"I'll wait here."

****

"This is terribly generous of you," Lily said as soon as they were in the carriage.

"You can thank Marcus. He's paying for your new things."

"I will, of course." Lily took a sharp breath, appearing almost near tears. "You've all been so kind. I don't know what I'd have done without your help. I dare say I'd have ended up on the street and who knows what would have happened to Charles then."

Penny patted her arm. "Don't think about it. You're both safe now."

"But what of the future? I can't stay with Mr. Ludingham forever."

You could if you married him. "What do you think of James?" Penny asked.

"Oh, he's wonderful. Such a gentleman. And to see him with Charles—he's just lovely with him."

"Indeed. I think he'll make a fine father...and husband." Penny gave Lily a meaningful look.

Lily immediately shook her head. "No, don't even

mention it. I'm ruined. A man like that—he'd never be interested in me."

"Don't be so certain. I saw how he looked at you."

Lily sighed. "I've learned the hard way that arousing a man's interest is far different than attracting a husband. But there is one thing I did think of," she added, her face brightening. "I did consider he might be willing to make me his mistress."

"But you have a child, and that child needs a name. If you become some man's mistress, you'll be much less marriageable. And that means Charles will grow up a bastard."

"You're right, of course. But I fear finding someone who will provide for me and Charles is the best I can expect. I can hardly imagine any man would want to give his name to another man's son. I have no dowry, and you know as well as I that most men marry for money and property."

Indeed, thought Penny. That's exactly what Marcus was planning to do. "We don't need to resolve your situation today. For now, let's concentrate on finding you some clothing." Although she didn't say it, Penny thought that once Lily was properly turned out, her other problems might resolve themselves. After all, Marcus knew James quite well. If he thought James might consider marrying Lily, then Lily's prospects were far better than the young woman thought they were.

****

"It's such a shame," James said as he and Marcus sat in his library. "Lily's a lovely woman. If not for Brakestoke's villainy, she could have had her pick of suitors, ended up marrying well and living a life of comfort and leisure."

"There's no reason she can't still have those things."

James frowned. "Really, Marcus, it's not like you to ignore the truth, unpleasant though it might be."

"Which is?"

"What sort of man is going to marry a woman whose reputation is utterly ruined? One who has a child as a result of the liaison? And no dowry, income, or settlement of any sort?"

"Not a young man with a title, certainly," agreed Marcus. "But perhaps a prosperous business man...or an older man who already has an heir, but who is looking for companionship. Someone who's willing to look beyond the obvious and see what a charming woman Lily is and what a fine wife she would be."

James nodded. "I suppose it's a possibility. Lily *is* quite fetching. But I don't think we can allow her to marry just anyone. We must make certain the man will treat her well and accept Charles as his son."

"We should try to think of acquaintances who might consider such an arrangement," Marcus suggested.

James waved dismissingly. "I'm sure there will be time for that. For now, she needs to recover from her ordeal."

"And you have no objection to her staying here?"

"Well, I..." James shrugged. "I guess I don't. As horrified as I was last night by the prospect of having a young woman and a baby in my household, I've found it to be quite...quite..."

"Entertaining?" suggested Marcus.

"I suppose it does kind of brighten things up. It

also gives me a purpose, a reason to get up in the morning. My life was getting rather dull."

"No chance of that with Lily and a baby around!"

"No, indeed." James smiled broadly.

Poor James, thought Marcus, also grinning. His friend had no idea he might end up falling in love with Lily. Of course, *he'd* also been convinced he would never fall in love with Penny. And here he was, quite smitten. Love did strange things to a man.

Love, there was that word again. Was it truly love he felt for Penny? He very much feared so. And somehow he had to keep it from James. How ironic that by falling in love with Penny, he might well end up losing her. Talons of anxiety dug into him. If he gave Penny a choice of whether to marry him or not, he still worried she would choose her freedom. Despite the pleasure they'd shared in the bedchamber. Despite the fact he was trying desperately to please her. He'd simply have to try harder...and hope James was too distracted by Lily to notice how things had changed between him and Penny.

****

"Nothing fancy or expensive. I merely need a few practical day dresses and some new undergarments," Lily explained to Madam Dubonet, as she nervously twisted the strap of her reticule.

Catching the modiste's glance, Penny said, "Simple things, of course. But of good quality. Mr. Revington will expect your usual fine work."

"I understand, *demoiselle*," Madam Dubonet, responded, although from her questioning look, it appeared she didn't. Turning to Lily, the modiste said, "Come with me. Let us get you measured." She guided

Lily into the back of the shop.

When she returned, the modiste said, "*Mademoiselle* Lily is quite pretty. It seems a pity to waste such beauty. Are you certain you want only plain, simple garments made for her?"

"I'm not certain at all." Penny smiled. "She must have some practical things, of course. She recently had a baby and currently doesn't have a lot of occasions for dressing up. But I'm certain she will need at least one dress suitable for an evening out. And for her everyday attire, I trust you will choose colors and styles that complement her natural beauty and charming figure."

At the mention of Lily's figure, Madam Dubonet smiled and nodded knowingly. "*Oui, demoiselle*. I understand what you mean. She may be a mother, but she is still a woman."

"And since she is as yet unmarried, it couldn't hurt to make certain the gentleman she's staying with was aware of that fact," Penny added.

Madam Dubonet nodded and smiled broadly in response.

The modiste returned to the back of the shop while Penny sat to wait. She'd only been there a moment when there was a tapping sound. Startled, she got up and was shocked to see her cousin Adrian through the shop window.

She hurried outside, feeling uneasy. "What are you doing here?"

He gave her a sneering smile. "Is that any way to greet your dear cousin?"

"What do you want?"

His expression turned even colder and more mocking. "My, my. You're getting quite above yourself these days. Forgetting where you come from and who's looked after you the past three years."

"I'll ask again: Why are you here? Did you follow me?"

He drew near, put his hand on her arm and squeezed. "I thought it was time to make certain you were looking out for *our* interests."

"What interests might those be?"

She sought to pull away from him, but he held on tight. "Why, Horngate, of course. I thought you cared about your heritage. But from the way you're cozying up to Revington, I've begun to wonder if maybe you aren't enjoying the comfortable life of a fine lady so much you forgot all about Horngate and your precious horses."

"Of course, I haven't forgotten about Horngate! I'd go back there in a moment, if I could. How dare you imply I'd ever forget? It was your foolishness and greed that got me into this predicament in the first place. You have no right to imply I've become shallow and greedy!"

"Well what other reason do you have for throwing in with Revington if it's not for the nice life that comes with marrying him?"

She spoke quite precisely: "I've found Mr. Revington isn't quite the villain you made him out to be."

Adrian's fingers tightened on her arm, and his blue eyes gleamed with fury. "If you think you can join up with him and cut me out of everything, you're very mistaken!"

"Why? What will you do? You lost any right to Horngate when you gave away the estate in a card game!"

He leaned nearer. She could smell his breath, rank with the scent of gin, although it wasn't yet afternoon. "Something could happen to your precious Revington. Not everyone likes the bastard as much as you do. I'm certain I can find someone who would be pleased to help me get him out of the way."

Penny felt a sudden frisson of fear. She'd never been concerned for her own safety at Adrian's hands. After all, it was only through her that he had any claim to the estate. But Marcus was another matter.

"Penny? What are you doing out here?" Lily stood in the doorway of the modiste's shop, her eyes wide.

Adrian's grip on Penny's arm immediately relaxed. He stepped back and said in a normal voice, "Delightful to see you, cousin. As always. I'll be in contact to see how things are progressing."

The next moment he was gone, walking swiftly down the street.

Lily approached Penny. "Are you all right?"

"I'm fine."

"Is that really your cousin?"

"Yes...and my guardian. At least until I marry Mr. Revington." Seeking to lighten the mood, Penny laughed. "He's a bit of a bully at times, but essentially harmless."

"Are you certain?" asked Lily. She touched Penny's arm in a protective gesture. "I thought the same of Brakestoke. But it turned out I was wrong. You can't always judge a man based on how he's behaved in the past."

Indeed, thought Penny. This was a side of Adrian she'd never seen before. If he was truly that desperate, it was hard to tell what he might be capable of.

She turned to Lily and forced a smile. "Anyway, what are you doing out here? I thought you were being fitted for some new gowns."

Lily's face regained its normal color. "I wanted your opinion on this one dress Madame Dubonet was describing. I don't see that I'll ever have anywhere to wear something so fancy. But she said you suggested I was to have at least one gown suitable for formal occasions."

Taking Lily's arm, Penny guided her back into the shop. "You never know. Perhaps some night, we'll get one of the servants to watch Charles and the four of us will go to the theatre."

Chapter Sixteen

"There they are!" James jumped up and rushed out of the library. Marcus followed at a more sedate pace.

By the time he reached the foyer, James was standing next to Lily as she animatedly described the shopping trip.

"I take it everything went well," Marcus whispered to Penny.

"Yes." She gave him a quick smile.

"And you were able to have some garments made that properly show off Lily's beauty?"

"Yes. I expect Madame Dubonet will work her usual magic."

"Madame Dubonet? Isn't there a less expensive modiste you could have taken her to?"

"I'm sure there is, but you must consider this an investment in the future." Penny leaned near and lowered her voice even more. "If our plan works and James ends up marrying Lily, it will all be worth it."

Easy for you to say, Marcus thought with a twinge of irritation. *It isn't your money.*

He immediately suppressed the ungallant thought. Penny was right. They had to find Lily a protector. Besides, with James distracted by Lily, he would be less likely to think about the wager.

Distracted—that was certainly an apt description for James's current behavior. He was standing close to

Lily, seemingly entranced by her description of her new wardrobe. Marcus could scarcely believe the transformation in James. Seeing his staid, practical friend gazing worshipfully at a woman as she nattered on about fabric, styles, and colors was rather amazing.

He turned to Penny to say something to that effect and discovered her deep in thought, a slight frown creasing her forehead. "What's wrong?" he asked.

"Nothing," she answered. "Nothing at all."

He studied her face, searching for some hint of what was troubling her.

Feeling his gaze on her, she smiled and motioned with her head toward James and Lily. "They make a lovely couple, don't you think?"

****

What am I going to do about Adrian? The thought weighed on Penny all through the dinner. As Marcus, James and Lily made small talk she struggled to keep her mind on what they were saying. She couldn't forget Adrian's threat. He'd implied he was willing to resort to murder to regain his control over her. Adrian was desperate, and desperate men did terrible things. And he was right. In the business he was in, Marcus had undoubtedly made some enemies. If Adrian allied himself with one of them…Someone who had money and resources…

A shiver went through at her. The next moment she sought to shake off the ominous mood and pay attention to the dinner conversation.

They were discussing the play she and Marcus had seen. Had it truly been only the night before? Penny said, "Perhaps once Lily's new clothes are ready, we could all go to the theatre together."

"An excellent idea," said James. Turning to Lily, he asked, "Would you like that?"

"Of course!"

In the carriage on the way home, Marcus asked, "What deep thoughts have you so occupied, Penny?"

She glanced up and gave him a quick smile. "I'm mulling over Lily's situation, of course."

"I thought we'd settled things, at least for now. Although it still angers me that Brakestoke's going to get away with what he's done. I have half a mind to inquire around the clubs and find out a bit more about him. The man undoubtedly has enemies, I can't help wondering—"

"No! Don't do that!"

"Why not? The man's a monster who preys on young women and ruins them. Someone has to stop him."

She reached out and touched his knee. "But not *you*. You don't have to be the one to stop him."

"Are you still worried Brakestoke is dangerous? I've dealt with considerably more treacherous individuals than him. In my business, it's impossible to stay on the good side of everyone. A lot of people don't take kindly to losing. But I know how to take care of myself. As long as I don't directly challenge Brakestoke, nothing's going to happen."

"Do you have a lot of enemies, Marcus?"

"Not a huge number. But I'm not on friendly terms with every man in London."

And it only took one. If Adrian found someone who had a grudge against Marcus. Someone with money and resources...

Marcus grasped her hand and gently squeezed.

"Don't worry about me, Penny. I can take care of myself."

"Of course you can," she answered. *I hope so. I truly hope so.*

What should I do? Should I tell him about Adrian's threat?

She couldn't stop agonizing. If she told him, there was a good chance he would scoff and tell her not to worry. She'd like to believe that was true, but couldn't convince herself. There was something different about her cousin today. A frantic aspect to his manner. Recalling the way he'd squeezed her arm, the wild intensity in his blue eyes, her sense of dread increased. All her instincts told her Adrian *would* resort to murder to get what he wanted.

She glanced at Marcus. He was looking at her, his expression tender. She glanced away, her throat suddenly tight with emotion. How had this happened, that she'd fallen in love with this man and begun to worry about him? And now that she felt like that, how could she protect him? There must be an answer, some way of compromising.

What if she asked Marcus to make some sort of financial arrangement with Adrian so he had an income from Horngate? Would that satisfy Adrian? For that matter, would Marcus agree? He appeared to be quite ruthless about insisting people honor their debts. Would he make an exception in this instance?

It seemed unlikely. Unless she asked him to do it as a favor to her. Her stomach tightened at the thought. Although Marcus appeared to be developing fond feelings for her, she had no idea how intense those feelings were. She might be in love with *him*, but that didn't mean he felt the same. He was a man, and not a particularly sensitive or emotional one. If she'd contemplated the idea of him falling in love with her even a few days ago, she'd have found the idea laughable. It probably was.

Her thoughts were going around in circles. Thankfully, they'd reached the townhouse. Now she could go up to her room and not have to hide what she felt. Unless he wanted to...

She shot another glance at Marcus as he helped her out of the carriage. The warm, almost burning look he gave her suggested he had other ideas in mind than simply going off to their respective bedchambers.

"Tired?" he asked as they walked up to the house.

"Yes." Should she have said that? Did she really want to discourage his attentions? Especially if she intended to ask this favor of him.

"I'm a bit, too. I was thinking of just going up to bed. Or did you want to have a nightcap first?"

She had a fairly good idea where a nightcap would lead. If only she didn't feel so nervous and unsettled. "I think I'll just go up to bed." She saw the disappointment on his face. Her body responded with an answering regret. But her mind was relieved. She needed to be alone.

They went inside. Penny greeted Bowes, then quickly said goodnight and started up the stairs.

****

"She's tired," Marcus said to Bowes.

"Of course. And you, sir?"

"I'm not quite ready for bed." He motioned to Bowes to indicate he was going into the library, where he poured himself a brandy and sat staring into the unlit fireplace, wondering if he would ever understand Penny. Would it always be like this? That one minute he would think she felt what he did and the next he would be agonized with doubts? Maybe once they were wed, things would be more settled between them.

But would that ever happen? Eventually James would remember the wager they'd made and call him on it. He'd have to admit he was in love with Penny. Then he'd have to ask her to marry him properly and abide by whatever she decided.

His stomach twisted. If he couldn't tell whether she wanted to go to bed with him, how was he to guess whether she would marry him? That she seemed worried for his safety was a good sign. But even if she cared for him, that didn't mean she wanted to be his wife. She was so independent, so strong-willed. Although he liked that about her most of the time, in this instance her self-sufficient nature terrified him.

****

This isn't helping. My thoughts are spinning in circles.

Penny climbed from the bed and fumbled in the darkness for her dressing gown. Finding it, she stripped off the nightrail and pulled on the silk dressing gown. She carefully opened the door and crept out. The hall was even darker than her room—which at least had the summer twilight filtering in through the windows. She made her way by feel to the guest bedroom. "Marcus," she called softly.

When there was no answer, she opened the door. A candle burned on the nightstand, but the bed was empty. Chagrined, she shut the door and went the other direction. She made her way downstairs and tiptoed to the library and knocked on the door.

"Yes, Bowes. What is it?" Marcus called.

She slipped into the room, closed the door behind her, and locked it. Slowly, she turned to face him. He was seated on the horsehair settle near the fireplace, a nearly empty glass in his hand. His nostrils flared as she approached. His dark eyes seemed to grow darker still, the pupils gleaming in the light from the candelabrum on the table beside the settle.

"I couldn't sleep," she said.

He placed the glass on the table and got to his feet. She felt his gaze upon her, keen as a caress. As he drew near, her nipples tightened as she realized he could see them through the thin silk of her wrap.

He halted a few inches away. With practiced fingers, he undid the tie of her wrap and slid it off her shoulders so it pooled on the floor around her. Her breath caught as he cupped her breasts in his warm hands and stroked her nipples with his thumbs. Fire streaked down her body, striking an inferno in the sensitive flesh between her legs.

He leaned down, and still cupping her breasts, licked and nuzzled first one nipple and then the other. She let out a moan and her knees grew weak. He straightened and drew her into his arms. He kissed her neck and licked her ear. As he thrust his tongue inside the sensitive hollow, she melted against him.

His clothing felt hard and rough against her nakedness and the sensation aroused her further. She let out a low moan. Still holding her close, he reached down to fondle her buttocks. His strong, firm hands squeezed and kneaded, making her writhe against him.

When he abruptly released her, she wanted to cry

out in frustration. But then she realized he was undoing his trousers. *Yes! Yes! Don't bother undressing the rest of the way. Take me now!*

She thought he would push her down upon the settle, but instead, he drew near and again stroked her bottom. As he lifted her, she instinctively grabbed his shoulders and wrapped her legs around his waist. Holding her tight, he made his way to the table and boosted her onto it. With her balanced on the table's edge, he stroked her between her legs, delicately parting her soft folds. She cried out and thrust against his fingers, on the verge of begging him to enter her. Then she felt the hot, deliciously plump tip of his phallus replace his fingers. She opened herself to him, letting out a throaty, plaintive cry as he penetrated her.

He is so deep! I can scarce bear it! Violent pleasure fanned out from the place they were joined. Sizzling. Incinerating. All thought and reason seemed to vanish as she was swept into a wild, churning whirlpool. He rocked against her, thrusting deeper and deeper. She fought the urge to scream. Struggled to remember to breathe. Sparkling lights flashed before her closed eyelids, as vivid as fireworks.

A final thrust and he let out a husky groan and collapsed against her.

****

Marcus closed his eyes and savored the moment: the feel of Penny's soft, silky body in his arms, the satisfying sense of being so intimate, so close. She stirred and he realized she must be uncomfortable. He released her and helped her down from the table. As she retrieved her dressing gown, he admired her beauty. Her body so slender and graceful. Her long, loose brown hair gleaming with soft golden highlights.

After slipping on the dressing gown, she turned to face him, her expression tender and somehow wistful. "I'm going to the necessary. Do you want to meet me in my—" She hesitated and smiled. "In *your* bedchamber?"

He nodded, smiling at her. That was exactly what he wanted, to sleep all night with her. To have a chance to hold her close and breathe in her delicate feminine fragrance.

You are far gone, he thought as Penny left the library. How had he become such a moonsick fool? Men weren't supposed to fall in love with their wives. But she wasn't his wife yet. He still had to ask her properly. Then he could go to James and admit he'd lost the wager, but it didn't matter because Penny had agreed to marry of her own free will.

Surely she would say yes, he thought as fastened his trousers. If he felt this way about her, she must have some fond feelings for him. If she didn't, she wouldn't be so eager for lovemaking. Would she?

Recalling Elizabeth's lustful demands, his anxiety returned. Elizabeth was certainly proof a woman could enjoy sex without falling in love. Although it was hard to imagine Penny being as cynical and detached as Elizabeth, he couldn't be certain what Penny felt for him. She'd put on quite a performance when he first met her. He recalled her attempts to convince him she was a gauche, unattractive hoyden. Clearly, she was capable of subterfuge and deceit.

As he left the library, he fought against his doubts. Maybe she wasn't in love with him yet, but there was still hope. He'd simply have to try harder to convince her. With that thought in mind, he started up the stairs.

When he reached the bedchamber, Penny appeared to be soundly asleep. Although a little disappointed—he'd hoped to hold her and cuddle her for a while—he could see the wisdom of getting some rest. There would be time for more lovemaking in the morning.

****

Penny grasped Marcus's arm and gently moved it off her hip. When his breathing remained deep and even, she slid to the side of the bed and stood up. The first hints of dawn showed in the window as she tiptoed across the room, ducked into the dressing room and put on her clothing. When she was dressed except for her shoes, she tiptoed to the door, and carrying her slippers and reticule, slipped out.

She felt a twinge of guilt as she made her way downstairs, through the house and down the additional flight of stairs to the servants' quarters. She hated leaving him like this, but it was nothing compared to the fear that gripped her whenever she thought about Adrian's threat. Somehow she had to work out an arrangement with her cousin. She couldn't live like this worrying Marcus's life might be in danger every time he went out.

She found Jeremy and the new cook having a quick breakfast before they started their day. After telling Jeremy what she wanted, she waited nervously outside the door to the townhouse for him to bring the carriage around. Thankfully, she hadn't encountered Bowes. If she had, she wasn't certain what she'd tell him. It was too early for shopping and she wasn't dressed to go riding.

Jeremy finally came around with the carriage.

"Where to, miss?" the footman asked as he helped her in to the vehicle.

She gave him the address she'd always used when corresponding with Adrian, and they set out. Penny had worried her cousin might live in some disreputable area of town, but the part Jeremy took her to was quite near where James lived. No wonder Adrian had been able to follow her so easily.

But when she inquired at the townhouse where he was supposed to reside, the servant who answered the door told her that Adrian Withersby no longer lived here.

"You do know of him, don't you?" she asked.

"Yes, miss. He did reside here for a time. But he was unable to pay the rent and had to move out."

"When was this?"

"About two weeks ago."

Two weeks. About the time he lost Horngate to Revington. "Do you have any idea where I might find him?"

"You might check the various gambling hells near St. James and Pall Mall. He spends a lot of time in that area."

"But surely he doesn't sleep in a gambling establishment," she pointed out.

"No, miss. But he might have met someone who offered him a place to stay."

Penny returned to the carriage, deep in thought. Finding Adrian was more difficult than she'd thought. And once she found him, it would be even more challenging to arrange a financial settlement that would satisfy him. Adrian was clearly having money problems. Indeed, he was probably "deep in dun territory" as Marcus referred to it.

Not knowing where else to go, she told Jeremy to take her to Pall Mall Street.

The footman raised his eyebrows at this. "Are you certain, miss? Begging your pardon, but that's not a part of the city appropriate for a young woman to be visiting."

"Is it a dangerous neighborhood?" From listening to Marcus and James, she knew there were areas of London even they would be uneasy visiting.

"Not exactly," answered Jeremy. "But unmarried ladies don't usually frequent such locales. I'm certain Mr. Revington wouldn't approve."

"I've already done a number of things of which Mr. Revington doesn't approve. I doubt one more will matter. I have no intention of staying long. I merely want to make a few inquiries."

"What sort of inquiries, miss?"

"I'm looking for someone. A man named Adrian Withersby, my cousin and guardian. I was told I might find him at an establishment in the Pall Mall area."

Jeremy nodded. "I'll take you there...if you'll let me make the inquiries. I suspect people will be more likely to talk to me than you, anyway."

"That's probably true."

Jeremy drove the carriage to Pall Mall, then came around. "Wait here. I'll be as quick as I can."

Penny leaned back on the squabs and let out a sigh. This errand was taking much longer than expected. By the time she got back to the townhouse, Marcus would almost certainly be up and looking for her. If she'd been in the bed when he woke, he'd probably have made love to her again. At the thought, her body throbbed with regret. She told herself there'd be plenty of mornings for that. It was more important that she find a way to work things out with Adrian.

As a new wave of anxiety assaulted her, she scooted to the window of the carriage and peered out. The street was quiet, and there wasn't much to see. With no one around, it shouldn't matter if she got out to stretch her legs and ease the tension in her shoulders.

Opening the door, she climbed out. She paced back and forth, then went to the front of the vehicle to stroke the horses. All at once, someone came out of one the buildings. *Brakestoke!* Her breath caught. What was that villain doing here?

Not wanting him to see her, she hastily climbed into the carriage and sat there, heart pounding. What if Brakestoke was meeting with Adrian? What a dreadful alliance that would be.

She told herself it was unlikely the two men even knew each other. But she couldn't get the thought out of her mind. Adrian had warned her there were plenty of men who had grudges against Marcus. Brakestoke might be one of them. And she'd already seen what he was capable of.

Jeremy came out a little later. His expression was grim. "I found out where Mr. Withersby is staying."

"You must take me there."

"I don't think so, miss. I've heard some things about Withersby. Apparently he's not very trustworthy or honest."

"That's true, but he would never hurt me, I'm certain. If anything happens to me, he loses all claim to the estate." Jeremy still looked dubious. "Please. We've come this far. I simply have to speak to him." She thought of insisting it was a matter of life and death. But if Jeremy knew about Adrian's threats, he would be even more disinclined to take her to see him.

"Very well, miss. But I'm going to insist Withersby come out to the carriage to speak to you. There's no way I'm letting you meet with him alone, even if he is your kin."

They set off again. They hadn't traveled far when Jeremy stopped the carriage. He came around to the carriage door. "Wait here."

Penny let out a sigh. Her stomach was full of butterflies. What if she couldn't convince Adrian to accept some sort of financial settlement? Even if he did, how could she ever get Marcus to agree to it? Perhaps she could have James convince Marcus that this was the best course of action. James was a sensible man. Surely he would be her ally in this.

She shifted restlessly on the carriage squabs. *What is taking so long?*

Finally, Jeremy appeared with Adrian. Penny was shocked by her cousin's appearance. His clothes were disheveled and he badly needed to shave and comb his hair.

He approached the carriage door and peered in at her, his blue eyes bloodshot and wary. "Why are you here, Penny? I told you what you had to do."

"Please get in." Although she dreaded being close to her cousin, she didn't want Jeremy to listen to their conversation.

Adrian climbed in and sat sullenly across from her. He reeked of spirits, as if he'd been drinking all night. She wondered if he'd even been to bed.

"I've been thinking," she said. "While there's no

way Revington will give up Horngate, that doesn't mean you have to come out of it with nothing. What if I got Marc—Revington to agree to give you an income from the estate? I can tell him you helped build up the horse business. That you found the buyers and arranged the sales, so it's only reasonable you should be compensated in some way."

"An income? A pittance, you mean." Adrian practically spat out the words, and Penny experienced the full force of his gin-soaked breath. He grabbed her arm, squeezing so hard she gasped. "I'm not giving up Horngate! I won't do it!"

Penny's stomach twisted. She'd been worried this would happen. Adrian could be so stubborn. But she had to remain calm and figure out a solution. "When you first told me about this, you said if I refused to marry Revington, you feared for your life at his hands. Now you say that if I marry him, you'll do something to him. I don't understand what's changed. Once you were afraid of Revington. Now you're threatening him."

"I wanted you to go along with him in the beginning, but I never thought you'd be so stupid and womanish as to fall in love with him!"

Penny thought about protesting that she wasn't in love, but she didn't think Adrian would believe her, especially since she didn't believe it herself. She said, "My attitude toward him may have changed, but that doesn't explain your ultimatum."

Adrian's expression turned sulky. "I don't have to explain myself to you."

Penny faced him squarely. "Yes, you do! Tell me what's going on, Adrian. I insist!"

He regarded her warily. She glared back at him,

determined. Finally, the sneering arrogance left his face and he looked defeated and miserable. "I'm in trouble, Penny. This time I've tangled with someone who means it when he says I must pay up or face the consequences."

"Go on."

He looked away, and for once Penny had the sense he was being absolutely truthful. "I was trying to win enough to buy back Horngate. I was so close…so very close…" He sighed heavily.

"What were you wagering with?" asked Penny, although she had a horrible thought she already knew.

He gave her a stricken look, then glanced away again. "Horngate. I was wagering with Horngate."

Penny stared at him, aghast. "How could you? How could you be so foolish?"

Adrian grimaced. "I was desperate. I'd lost everything to Revington, the cheating bastard. I had to win Horngate back. I had to."

Penny took a deep breath. "Instead, you lost it a second time." She shook her head. "Oh, Adrian, you are hopeless!"

He shot her a bitter look. "I'm more than hopeless. I'm *dead*. If I don't make good on this wager, this fellow will kill me." He grabbed her arm again and brought his face close to hers. "But before you think you've found an easy way to get rid of me, rest assured that before he comes after me, he'll take care of Revington." He sat back. "So, you see, if you care for Revington at all, you'll have to break things off with him."

She stared at him disbelievingly. "You want me to marry this other man, the one you've lost Horngate

238

to…a second time?"

Adrian nodded. "It's the same as before. You have to marry this fellow so he can take possession of Horngate."

"What fellow?" Penny demanded. "Who is this murderous devil who's willing to kill two people to get his hands on Horngate?"

Adrian crossed his arms over his chest. "I'm not going to tell you. I'm not going to bungle things this time by letting you meet him until the wedding is all set to take place."

"You can't think I'll consent to marry a man I've never met!"

"Very well. I'll let you meet him. But not until you've broken things off with Revington."

"What about Revington? I thought you said if I didn't marry him, Revington would kill you."

Adrian smiled smugly. "We both know Revington wouldn't do that. He'd never do anything so harsh as to murder his future wife's cousin. Apparently, he's not the hardened gamester I thought he was. Otherwise, he'd have married you immediately and not let things drag out like this." Adrian made a disgusted face. "For that matter, I doubt you'd have come to fancy him if he was a cold-blooded killer. You always were the squeamish sort, the kind to waste your time nursing the runt of the litter."

Penny felt her anger growing. She'd never realized what an awful person her cousin was. The world would probably be better without him. But worrying about his wellbeing was no longer the issue. It was Revington she had to protect. But how?

What if she told him about Adrian's threats?

Perhaps they could think up some plan where she pretended to break things off with him, and then when Adrian introduced the man he now wanted her to marry, Marcus could work out some arrangement with *him*. After all, Adrian was the villain in this. He'd foolishly lost property he didn't even own, not once but twice, and then proceeded to blackmail and scheme and plot to save his own neck while ruining her life!

Her fury must be showing on her face, for Adrian grabbed her chin and jerked her head around so she faced him. "Quit your scheming, you little minx! I'm not letting you undermine me this time. If you go to Revington and get him all riled up, you'll be signing his death warrant!"

Penny pulled away and glared at him defiantly. "Is that so? How can I be certain there is another man? This could all be a bluff. Obviously, you were bluffing last time. How do I know you're not making up this story?"

"Oh, there's another fellow, all right. And he's not as honorable as your precious Marcus. He won't think twice about killing to get what he wants."

"You never know. You may be underestimating Marcus. I hear he's a crack shot. In a duel, he might just come out the victor."

Adrian let out a cold, sinister laugh. "Who said anything about a duel? Some men don't like to leave things to chance. No, what Revington has to watch out for is something unexpected: a carriage accident perhaps, or tainted food. Or some ruffians might attack him one night when he's out gambling. London is full of danger."

Penny's blood ran cold. There was no way to

protect Marcus from a truly determined murderer.

"I see you're finally catching on to my meaning. 'Bout time, Pen. You need to understand that I've got nothing to lose if Revington dies. Nothing. While you..." He leaned near again, his gin-soaked breath hot on her face. "If you play along nicely, you can always take Revington as a lover after you've wed. I doubt your new intended will care what you do once he takes control of Horngate."

"What about you, Adrian? How do you benefit by seeing your cousin and ward married to a murderous rogue?"

"I told you, I get to stay alive. Besides, I'm certain I can convince the gentleman to let me handle the horse business. He's a city boy. He knows nothing about livestock."

Neither do you, you worthless fool, thought Penny. But she didn't say it. Right now all she wanted was to be away from Adrian and his evil plotting.

Chapter Seventeen

He dreamed of Penny, her soft skin, her silky warmth...He reached out for her...

Opening his eyes, Marcus immediately felt bereft. The other side of the bed was empty. Penny was gone.

He knew a sharp stab of disappointment. His plan had been to lie abed with her this morning and make love to her slowly and leisurely. Then he would simply hold her close for a time, savoring the wonder of knowing she was his.

Except she wasn't. Not yet.

He got up and went to the chair where he'd left his clothing. His shirt and cravat were hopelessly wrinkled. And he needed to bathe. Lovemaking may make Penny smell more delectable, but he doubted the same was true of him. He pulled on his small clothes and trousers, then his shirt, leaving it unbuttoned. Barefoot and carrying his jacket and boots, he left the room and returned to the spare bedchamber where he'd moved most of his clothing. After ringing for Bowes, he changed into a dressing gown.

Bowes knocked, then entered.

"Have a bath drawn, Bowes." As an afterthought, he added, "I suppose Penny's already down at breakfast?"

"Actually, sir, she left without eating."

"Left?" Marcus gazed at the manservant in

surprise.

"Yes, sir. It appears she had Jeremy bring the carriage around at least an hour ago."

"Did she say where she was going?"

"No, sir, she did not."

"She's probably off to James's to see Lily and the baby."

"That would make sense, sir."

After a quick breakfast, Marcus also headed to James's townhouse. He was a bit irritated he'd had to take a hired hack. Penny might have waited for him. Or woken him to let him know her plans.

When reached the townhouse, he paid the driver and marched up the walk. Vincent greeted him at the door. "A pleasure to see you, Mr. Revington. If you'd like to wait in the withdrawing room, I'll let Mr. Ludingham know you're here."

"And Lily and Penny as well."

"Miss Montgomery isn't here, sir."

"She's not?"

"No, sir. We haven't seen her since yesterday."

"I see."

While he waited for James, Marcus puzzled on where Penny could be. He couldn't imagine where she might have gone in the carriage, especially so early in the morning.

"Good morning," James entered the room and greeted him. "You're out and about early."

It might be better not to let James know I've come here looking for Penny. "I wanted to see how Lily and baby were getting on."

"Charles seems to be settling into more of routine. Slept most of the night. Where's Penny? I'm sure Lily

243

would like to see her."

There was no help for it; he'd have to admit the truth. "I don't know where she is. I was wondering if Lily might have some idea."

"We can ask her when she comes down. Ah, here she is," James added as Lily joined them.

Lily smiled warmly at Marcus. "Good morning, Mr. Revington. I have to thank you again for all you've done for me. It's so generous of you to buy me new clothing. I hope someday I can find a way to repay you."

"You're welcome, Lily...and do call me Marcus. By the way, when you were with Penny yesterday, did she say anything about having plans for today?"

"Why, no. That is, she didn't mention anything. I'm surprised she's not with you now. She said she would come over today so she could see me in my new garments as soon as they arrive."

"I'm sure she'll be here soon." Marcus was truly puzzled now. The only time Penny had gone anywhere without telling him was when she went riding. But she wouldn't take the carriage if she were riding.

"Maybe she went back to the modiste's," James said. "She might have seen something she later decided to purchase. I know my sisters are like that. They go shopping and fall in love with something and then go back for it."

"The modiste's? I wonder..." murmured Lily.

"Did you think of something?" asked Marcus.

Lily gave him a strange look, then smiled quickly. "Oh, no, nothing at all."

Marcus stared at her, feeling certain she *had* thought of something. Why was she pretending otherwise?

"Have you eaten, Marcus?" Lily asked. "When I came down, Vincent said breakfast was ready to be served."

"I had a light repast before I left the townhouse," Marcus answered.

"Well, I'm hungry," said James. "Let's go into the breakfast room. I'm sure we can find something to tempt you."

Although he had no appetite, Marcus ate some coddled eggs and toast. He didn't want James to realize how concerned he was about Penny.

They were almost through with breakfast when Vincent appeared at the door and announced, "Miss Montgomery has arrived, sir."

"Send her in, of course," responded James.

Penny came in, smiling broadly. "What a delightful day. I just had Jeremy take me for a turn in the park. You should see the hyacinths in bloom. They're simply stunning."

"You've been at the park all this time?" asked Marcus.

Penny glanced at him briefly. "Of course."

"You might have waited for me to go with you."

"I suppose I should have." She met his gaze for a bare heartbeat, then looked away.

She lying. Just like Lily. What are the two of them hiding?

Penny joined them at the table but ate little. Marcus's suspicions grew. If she'd skipped breakfast to take a turn in the park, she should be hungry now.

There was easy way to get to the bottom of this, he decided. He'd simply question Jeremy.

Marcus got his chance a short while later when several boxes from Madame Dubonet's arrived and the two women went upstairs so Lily could try on her new garments. Marcus excused himself and went out to the carriage where the footman was waiting. The young man snapped to attention. "Good morning, sir."

"I hear you had an early one. Took Penny for a ride in the park."

Jeremy hesitated, then responded, "Is that what Miss Montgomery said?"

"Yes. But I know it isn't true. I don't believe she'd get up so early merely to take a drive in the park. And if she did decide to view the early summer foliage, I'm fairly certain she'd do it on horseback rather than from an enclosed carriage."

A muscle worked in Jeremy's jaw. "Yes, sir."

Marcus moved so he was directly in front of the footman. "Where did you take her, Jeremy? And before you respond, you might recall that I'm the one who pays your wages."

The footman let out a sigh and shook his head. "She went looking for her cousin, sir. A Mr. Adrian Withersby. When she didn't find him at the address she had for him, she asked me to take her to the club area of Pall Mall."

"You took her there?" He felt a surge of anger.

"I took her there, yes, but don't worry, sir, I didn't let her leave the carriage. I made her wait while I went in and found Mr. Withersby."

"When you brought him out to her, what did they discuss?"

"I didn't hear, sir." He gave Marcus a helpless look. "I thought since he was her cousin…" He sighed and then continued, "I would never knowingly take her into danger. I hope I didn't do wrong, sir. But you did tell us Miss Montgomery was to be our mistress, sir. And that we are to try and please her and accommodate all her wishes. I didn't think there was any harm—"

Marcus put a hand up to halt the footman's agonized explanations. "I don't blame you, Jeremy. I know Miss Montgomery can be very convincing. How well I know that."

Marcus left the footman and walked back to the house, deep in thought. Last night, he'd accepted that he was in love with Penny and told himself she was coming to care for him, too. But now he wasn't nearly so certain of her. The thought of her being in contact with Withersby unnerved him. From everything she'd said, she disliked her cousin and avoided him as much as possible. What could she possibly have to discuss with him?

As he returned to the library, he decided to take the matter up with James.

His friend looked up from the desk where he was doing paperwork. "What have you been up to, Marcus?"

"I learned something rather disturbing from my footman. I found out Penny met with Adrian Withersby this morning."

"Her cousin? That wretch you won Horngate from?"

"Indeed. The very one."

"But why? What could she have to say to him? I thought she heartily disliked the man. And who can blame her, after what he did to her?"

"Exactly." Marcus turned and paced across the

room. "It makes no sense. Unless what she told us about her relationship to Withersby was false."

"What do you mean?"

Marcus turned and paced the other direction, deeply disturbed by the thought that had just come to him. "You remember how Penny behaved in the beginning. How she went to great lengths to discourage me from marrying her, presenting herself as a gawky, mannerless hoyden who would be an embarrassment to me?" He paced back the other way. "Obviously, that was mostly pretense. While Penny is hardly a sophisticated city deb, she's nowhere near as naïve and gauche as her behavior suggested."

"That's true. Although we've never discussed it, Penny's attitude toward you has definitely changed from what it was in the beginning."

"Exactly. I must admit I never questioned the change," said Marcus. "If I thought about it at all, I assumed her behavior had altered because she no longer abhorred the thought of being my wife, but had actually began to embrace the idea." He met James's gaze. "Perhaps it was conceited, but I assumed as she'd gotten to know me better, she'd stopped thinking of me as the ogre she was forced to wed and begun to warm to me. But maybe my assumption was wrong. Maybe her behavior changed because her plans have changed."

"In what way?" James asked.

Marcus paced back and forth before answering. He hated to voice these thoughts, as if saying them aloud would make them more real. "What if Withersby was the one who told her to convince me not to marry her, and now he's changed his mind?"

"Why would he do that? Once you marry Penny,

you gain control of Horngate. Withersby can't possibly want that."

"No, I suppose not." Marcus stopped pacing. "But something's going on. Something that involves Withersby."

"Maybe Penny met with him for some reason that has nothing to do with you."

"Then why did she lie about it?" Marcus retorted, feeling even more agitated. "If the meeting was completely innocent, there would be no reason for her to make up this story about going to the park."

"Hmmm. I can see your point. Still, I think the simplest way to clear this up is to confront her."

Marcus nodded. "You're right. That's exactly what I should do."

****

"You look beautiful," Penny said as Lily stepped out of the dressing room in the upstairs bedroom and twirled around in her new gown. "In that dress you're bound to turn the heads of all the single men in London."

"I only want to turn the head of one." Lily dipped her head and her cheeks colored.

Penny smiled. "I don't think you need new clothing to make James notice you. It appears he is already quite smitten."

"You truly think so?"

"Yes. I do. But I expect it will take some time for him to get used to the idea. From what Marcus tells me, James has a whole list of attributes he thinks he wants in a wife. It might take a bit for him to realize that lists don't matter much when you fall in love."

Lily came to sit down on the bed next to Penny,

looking troubled. "I'm certain his list doesn't include a ready-made family…or a wife who has no prospects."

Penny patted her shoulder. "James may pride himself on his logic and reason, but he'll ultimately succumb to what's in his heart. But it may take a little while. You'll have to be patient."

Lily nodded. "*My* heart tells me you're right." She turned to face Penny. "If you believe so much in the importance of following your heart, I don't understand why you're not being truthful with Marcus. He obviously adores you. I can't imagine why you think you must keep secrets from him."

"What secrets?" asked Penny, although she suspected she knew exactly what Lily meant.

"About your cousin, for one thing. And also about wherever you went this morning. It's obvious to everyone you didn't go to the park."

"Is it?"

"I'm afraid so. Where were you? What were you doing that you felt you must hide it from Marcus?"

"I was meeting with my cousin."

Lily's eyes widened. "Did he threaten you again? Are you in danger?"

Penny sighed. "I'm afraid I'm not the one who's in danger. It's Marcus." She stood as the anxiety she'd fought to suppress bubbled to the surface. She had to tell someone. She *had* to. Facing Lily, she said, "Adrian says if I marry Marcus, he'll arrange for something to happen to him…something *fatal*."

Lily gazed at her in shock. "That's awful! Simply dreadful! You have to tell Marcus…and James. Between the two of them they'll find a way to protect Marcus from your cousin."

"How can anyone guard against a vague threat of danger?" Penny asked in an agonized voice. "He'll never know when he might be attacked or what to look out for. I don't even know the source of the threat."

"What do you mean?"

"It's not Adrian I'm worried about. I don't believe he could plot Marcus's murder on his own. But he says he's lost Horngate a second time, this time to a man who's determined to marry me and take over the estate."

"I don't understand. What is Horngate? And how can this man marry you when you're engaged to Marcus?"

"Horngate is a farm in south Hampshire, left to me by my parents. But since I'm a woman, the law doesn't see fit for me to manage it on my own, so Adrian was named as my guardian. A few weeks ago, Adrian lost Horngate to Marcus in a card game. That's how Marcus and I came to be engaged."

Lily stared at her, open-mouthed. "But…the two of you…you seem so compatible. I thought it was a love match."

"It didn't start out that way. In the beginning I tried my best to convince Marcus I would be an absolute nightmare as a wife. I was determined to disgust him so much that he would give up any notion of marrying me to gain control over Horngate. Obviously, I failed to convince him, and in the meantime, I decided being his wife might not be so awful. Although I still worry about him interfering with the horse operation, most of the time I think we might be able to work out a tolerable arrangement. I believe there is hope we can function as partners rather than the usual situation of the man making all the decisions and controlling everything."

"Not to mention, you fell in love with him," Lily said.

"I suppose that's true." Penny returned Lily's smile with a rueful one of her own. "Although I'm not sure I'd ever admit that to *him*. I don't want to give him too much power."

"Of course not." Lily's smile widened.

Penny's mood again turned sober. "Unfortunately, Marcus isn't the problem. Adrian is. He says he's lost Horngate a second time. And he assures me the man he lost it to is far more ruthless than Marcus. This man is willing to kill to get rid of any potential rival." She shook her head. "I don't know whether I believe Adrian or not. But until I find out for certain who this man is, the only way to protect Marcus is to call things off with him."

"Which you don't want to do?"

"No, I don't." It was surprising, Penny thought, how little she wanted to get out of marrying Marcus. After going to great efforts to get him to break off the engagement, she now found she was willing—indeed almost eager—to become his wife.

"But you feel it's the only way to make certain this other man doesn't try to murder him?" Lily asked.

"Exactly."

"Maybe Marcus could reason with your cousin and find out who's behind this." Lily suggested.

Penny shook her head. "I think a confrontation between the two of them might make things worse. To find Adrian, Marcus would have to search for him, and in the process he might encounter this other man. He could end up walking right into a deadly trap." She shivered, thinking of Adrian's remark about Marcus being set upon in a dark alley.

"What if he took James and a couple of footmen with him?"

"Adrian would never talk to him then. No, I fear the only way to get the truth from Adrian is for me to call off things with Marcus, or at least appear to. Then Adrian will reveal who this other man is, and I'll find out if he's truly the brutal monster my cousin says he is." She shuddered.

"But if he is a monster, and your cousin forces you to marry him…" Lily stared at her, looking as horrified as Penny felt.

Penny let out a deep breath. "It is a conundrum. To save Marcus, it seems I must sacrifice any chance of happiness for myself. But I feel like I have no choice. I can't bear the thought of him being murdered."

"There must be some way to thwart your cousin's evil scheme. Marcus appears fairly well-to-do, and I'm certain he knows some influential people. Surely someone can help us. I think you should tell Marcus and James the whole story. Marcus could even go into hiding for a time, until we find out who's behind these threats."

Lily's plan seemed like a reasonable course of action, at least from a woman's standpoint. But a man might well find it shameful to hide from a potential threat, rather than confronting the danger head-on. Penny could well imagine Marcus refusing to listen to her concerns and immediately going after Adrian. If there was anything to her cousin's threats, Marcus might end up walking into a deathtrap.

"I don't feel I can risk telling Marcus," she told

Lily. "For Marcus to confront Adrian might be the worst thing he could do. You weren't there when Marcus and I first discussed how to deal with Brakestoke. Marcus was all for challenging him to a duel. And in that instance, it wasn't Marcus's honor at stake but yours, a woman he'd only just met. Think how he might react to a threat directed at him...by a cowardly wretch like Adrian."

"What's the answer, then? If you do as your cousin asks, you could end up wed to a ruthless, violent man. If you do nothing, Marcus might be murdered."

Penny chewed her lower lip in thought. "If only I could be certain Adrian is telling the truth. He might be bluffing. He may not have lost Horngate to another man at all. And even if there is another man, he may not be the murderous monster Adrian says he is."

"How can you find out?"

"I need to have someone spy on Adrian. Follow him and see where he goes and whom he meets. I think I can get Jeremy, the footman, to do it. But to buy time for Jeremy to investigate things, I need to make Adrian think I've ended things with Marcus. But the problem is I'm living at Marcus's townhouse. I can't return to Horngate. If I do, I fear Adrian will follow me there and I'll be trapped. I need to find somewhere else to stay in London."

"You could stay here."

"But what would we tell James?"

"We could tell him the truth, that you're merely pretending to break things off with Marcus because of your cousin's threats."

Penny shook her head. "James will never agree. He'd feel honor bound to tell Marcus what's going on."

"I know a place you could stay," Lily said. "If you have money." Penny looked at Lily questioningly. She continued, "It's where I stayed when my family"—Lily swallowed—"asked me to leave. I thought Brakestoke would pay for it. When he wouldn't, that's when I was forced to confront him. You know the rest."

"I have money," said Penny. "When I left Horngate with Marcus, I planned on returning. I knew I'd need money to travel home. I was also prepared to pay off servants, and anyone else who would help me get out of the marriage." She gave Lily a sad smile. "Back then, I was determined not to have anything to do with Marcus. Now look at me—I'm forced to leave him and it's breaking my heart."

Lily came and squeezed her arm. "Things don't always turn out the way we expect. But sometimes they turn out even better. I'm so happy to have little Charles, regardless of how his birth came about. And James and you and Marcus have been so kind to me. For the first time in months, I actually have hope for the future."

"I believe things will work out for you, Lily, but I'm not so certain about my future. If I leave Marcus now, I doubt he'll ever trust me again. But I've never seen my cousin like this…so anxious and desperate." She sighed. "Even if I can keep this man from hurting Marcus, how can I avoid marrying him? I can't hide forever."

"I wish you would let me tell James about this. I believe he would help you. He's Marcus's close friend. I can't believe he'd do anything to endanger him."

"I fear James is too much like you. He sees the good in people, and he won't believe that someone might be willing to murder Marcus for Horngate. No, for now I have to act as if I'm doing what Adrian wants. He's used to bullying me, so he'll think he has things under control. That will give me some time to make my own plans to get out of this mess."

Lily still looked troubled, but she nodded. Her agreement relieved Penny, but it was tempered by the gnawing awareness of how much her plan would hurt and anger Marcus…and break her own heart.

Chapter Eighteen

"You're certainly quiet tonight," Marcus commented at dinner.

Penny put down her fork and responded with what she hoped was a placid smile. "I'm merely thinking about Lily's situation. James seems quite charmed by her. Do you think there's any chance he might…take things further than simply providing her with a place to stay?"

Marcus raised his dark brows. "Do you mean, do I think he might marry her?"

"Well, yes. Eventually, that is. Once he has time to get used to the idea."

Marcus's dark eyes, bright with emotion, pierced her. "At one time I would have scoffed at such a notion. I would have thought it utterly ridiculous to imagine a sensible man like James deciding to wed a woman with a child and no dowry, income or other prospects. But having learned how powerfully tender emotions can affect even a reasonable person's decisions, I'm no longer willing to dismiss the idea out of hand. James appears smitten, so who can say what he will do?"

Penny could feel herself flushing in response to Marcus's words. He appeared to be discussing his own feelings for her as much as what James might feel toward Lily. It would be easy to interpret his words as his way of telling her he was in love with her. The realization flooded her with an aching dismay. He would feel terribly betrayed when she left him. As difficult as it had been for him to give in to his emotions, he might never get over it.

"I hope for Lily's sake that you're right," she responded. "She seems very taken with James."

"Are you certain she truly cares for him?" Marcus asked. "That she's not merely pretending fondness because James is her best hope for a protector?" Penny started to answer, but Marcus went on, his expression darkening. "I like Lily, but if she's manipulating and using James…I can't abide deceitful women. If Lily breaks James's heart, she'll find out *I* can be nearly as nasty as Brakestoke."

Penny took a bite and struggled to chew. Her mouth seemed to have gone dry. Marcus was making it clear that if she rejected him, he would never forgive her.

When she was finally able to get the food down, she said, "I'm sure Lily truly cares for James. If she felt getting involved with him would hurt him, she would leave before that could happen."

"I don't understand. If she returns his affections, how would getting involved with her end up hurting James?"

Penny shrugged, trying to make her response sound off-hand, yet give Marcus an insight into what she was about to do. "What if Lily thought Brakestoke might decide to do something to James to get back at him for helping her? In that instance, getting away from James might be the best way for Lily to show him how much she cares for him."

Marcus had stopped eating and was staring at her.

"Are you saying Lily has had contact with Brakestoke since the incident at the theater? Has he threatened her in some way?"

"No! Nothing like that! Indeed, Lily told me she's quite certain Brakestoke wants nothing more to do with her. At this point, he's probably thankful to James for getting her out of his life. The situation I mentioned was purely theoretical. I was trying to explain that sometimes people have to hurt the people they care about in order to protect them."

****

Marcus searched Penny's face trying to figure out why she was saying these things. Was she suggesting that if James proposed, Lily would refuse him? Was Penny trying to come up with some excuse for Lily to do such a thing?

Penny gave him a quick, nervous smile. "Don't worry. I don't think Lily will do anything like that. I'm merely saying that if you truly care about someone, sometimes you have to put their interests ahead of your own. The truth is, Lily worries she's not good enough for James. She's concerned his family won't accept her and they'll think he's marrying beneath himself."

"I wouldn't worry about James's family. They don't care what James does. He's got two older brothers who are expected to make good matches, so no one has much interest in what James does. It's exactly like my situation. Younger sons aren't worth bothering about." He knew he sounded bitter, but he couldn't help it. It had always rankled that his family treated him with such disinterest.

"I'm sure Lily will be relieved. She truly cares for James, enough that's she concerned for his future happiness."

Marcus finished his roast beef, keeping his gaze on Penny. She was behaving oddly tonight. He wondered if it had anything to do with her meeting with her cousin. He needed to confront her about that…but later. He didn't want to ruin things between them now, when they would soon be going to bed. He could hardly wait. Even as his mind puzzled on Penny's motivations, his body was focused—as always—on how delectable she looked: her lovely eyes, delicious mouth, long neck and creamy skin. He wanted to devour her, and it was all he could do to wait until it was time to retire and he would finally get his chance to enjoy her charms.

They talked a bit more about James and Lily and the baby, and how well their household was adjusting to the changes. Then Marcus brought up the idea of going to Covent Gardens to enjoy the fireworks and other entertainments. "I'd like to take you tomorrow night, if you'd like to go, that is."

"I'm certain that would be enjoyable," she answered.

"So, we'll plan on it then?"

She didn't respond, but nodded vaguely. Her expression seemed stiff and awkward, which made him uneasy. If she were his opponent in a card game, he'd be convinced she had a poor hand and was bluffing him. But of course, this wasn't a card game, and she was a woman, which meant it was inevitable he would find her moods puzzling and indecipherable.

****

Oh, this is miserable, to constantly be lying to him. How she wanted this meal to be over.

But what was coming next would be even worse.

They'd go to bed and he'd make love to her and she'd experience all that magical passion and pleasure, all the while knowing it might be for the last time. Indeed, it probably *would* be for the last time.

She repressed a sigh. Somehow she had to behave normally, despite her breaking heart. She didn't want Marcus getting suspicious. It would be disastrous if he suspected she was up to something. She had to wear him out with lovemaking so he'd sleep late, as he did this morning, so she could get away. The sooner they went to bed, the sooner they could begin.

Her body yearned for his touch, heedless of what the future held. She might as well have one more night of heaven and try to forget about the hell to come.

****

"Are you finished?" Marcus motioned to Penny's half-eaten meal. She didn't appear to have much appetite tonight. Another sign that something was bothering her.

"Yes," she answered. Marcus nodded to Will, who pulled back Penny's chair so she could rise.

"Would you like another glass of wine?" Marcus suggested. "I could have a bottle brought into the library."

"That sounds lovely." She flashed him a smile.

He went to her and took her arm to lead her into the library. *Ahhh...how good she smells!* Merely to have her lithe, delicate body near was enough to arouse him. At this rate, he wasn't certain he'd survive the hours until bed. Of course, he could always make love to her in the library. But he didn't want it to be like that, as intense and satisfying as that experience had been. Tonight, he wanted to take things slowly, to savor every moment. To leave no part of her body unexplored. To worship every beautiful inch of her.

The thought of it made him almost breathless with impatience. He sought to slow his racing heart and breathe deeply. Hopefully, the wine would relax him…and her as well.

Reaching the library, he guided her to the settle, then sat in the chair across from her. He didn't want to be too close, but he wanted to be able to look at her. To feast his eyes on this dazzlingly lovely woman who would soon be his wife.

If she agreed, that is. The gnawing worry abruptly darkened his mood. He'd been looking ahead to this night as a means of indulging his passion. But it meant so much more than that. He had to please her, to make her so enthralled with his lovemaking she'd be willing to marry him.

He'd always been confident of his performance in the bedchamber, but now, with what was at stake, he felt a twinge of nerves. In the past, when he'd made an effort to please his partners, it had been mostly a matter of pride. And a good share of the women he'd bedded had been experienced and not shy about telling him what they wanted. Penny wasn't going to do that, so he'd have to guess how to please her.

He repressed a sigh, wishing he knew more about women, especially this one!

Penny sipped her wine. She appeared distracted, her thoughts far away. "Is something troubling you?" he asked.

Her gaze focused on him and she smiled, although the expression seemed forced. "Not really. I was merely thinking about James and Lily."

He couldn't understand her obsession with the other couple's happiness. But he knew enough not to say that. Instead, he said, "I'm certain things will work out for them. It all fits together quite tidily, to my way of thinking. Lily needs a protector and a father for her child, and James...I think James is actually quite lonely. He grew up in a large family, and now he lives in that townhouse all by himself."

"You live alone. Does that mean you are lonely?"

He shrugged. "Perhaps I was, but like James I didn't know it. But now..." He leaned closer. "It has been...pleasant having you here." *Pleasant? What a dolt I am! It is far more than pleasant. Why do I struggle so hard to say what I feel?*

She still smiled at him, although her eyes seemed sad. "I thought having me move in was a terrible inconvenience to you, not to mention expensive."

"Did I say that?" *Appalling to think she'd read me so clearly.*

"No, but your actions implied it. You were always frowning and grumbling about things, not to me but to Bowes."

"I'm sorry. I'm afraid I was quite rude. I didn't mean—"

She raised a hand in protest. "Don't worry, I don't hold it against you. And I didn't make it easy for you. In fact, I went out of my way to create problems and make things difficult."

Because you didn't want to marry me. Although she didn't say it, he knew that was what she meant. Lately her behavior had changed. Did that mean she'd changed her mind about marrying him? He wanted to ask, but he was afraid.

"I'm certain it was disconcerting to suddenly have a fiancée," she continued. "Even if it was your choice. You probably felt you were losing control over your life. I can certainly understand that."

What was she saying, that by marrying him, she'd lose control over her own life? Somehow he had to reassure her he didn't mean to treat her the way most men did their wives. He wanted her to be his partner, not his servant. "It can be difficult to get used to considering another person's interests," he said. "But over time…if you truly care about them, you learn to be less selfish." No, that wasn't right. She might be thinking he was talking about her being less selfish. "I was talking about myself," he added. "I think I've changed. I view things differently now."

She nodded. "So do I."

When they talked like this, and she looked at him with that warm, almost tender expression, he felt hopeful. They got along quite well these days. Surely she could see they truly were compatible. Maybe he should ask her to marry him right now, instead of waiting until after they'd made love. But how did he broach the subject?

He'd heard he was supposed to get down on his knees to ask her, but that would make him feel too foolish. It would be too much like begging, as if she should feel sorry for him. He wanted to maintain some dignity at least.

He cleared his throat. "Given that things have changed, I wondered if…" How was he going to do this, when he was so terrified of her answer?

She got up suddenly. "I wonder…that is…maybe we could continue this conversation another time. I'm a bit tired."

He also stood. Had she sensed he was about to propose and sought to head him off? Did that mean she was going to refuse him? But if that was the case, why was she putting it off?

He stared at her. Her behavior was so confusing. A moment before they'd been conversing easily. Now she seemed restless and anxious. Something was bothering her. If only he could figure out what it was.

"I know it's early yet," she murmured. "But I think...perhaps we should go up to bed."

He didn't know whether to be relieved or disappointed. He'd been reprieved from asking the question he dreaded asking. But it bothered him that she seemed to fear it as much as he did. And what did she mean by saying they should go to bed? Was it an invitation to make love to her?

That, at least, he could find out. Smiling, he said, "Bed. Yes, that seems like a fine idea." When she didn't start for the door, he reached for her. As he kissed her, she molded her body against his. Her response emboldened him. He opened his mouth and their tongues mated. She drew closer and their kisses became almost frantic.

He felt his own desire overtaking him and realized this wasn't what he wanted. So much of their lovemaking had been like this, desperate and driven, their need and lust overtaking them. He wanted them to share more than an expression of their sexual hunger. What he yearned for was true closeness, true intimacy, rather than coming together like two drowning people who could only save each other.

He forced himself to draw back. "Should we go

upstairs?"

She appeared a bit disconcerted by his restraint, but she nodded.

He took her hand and led her from the library. They walked together, their fingers entwined. He felt as if he would burst. Not with arousal, but a kind of aching tenderness that built in his chest. It seemed so miraculous, so incredible to be going to bed with this beautiful woman. He could not get over the sense of wonder he felt, that she was willing to share her body with him.

They reached the bedchamber and went inside. It was so early the lamps weren't even lit, and the room was illuminated with only the glow of the summer twilight. He thought about the other times they'd made love in this room. They'd always been so impatient; they could scarcely wait to take their clothes off. This time he meant to make every moment last.

Penny immediately turned her back to him, expecting him to undo the hooks on her dress. Instead, he drew her against his body, and pushing aside the tendrils of her hair, kissed the soft warm flesh at the nape of her neck. She shivered. He licked her ear and nipped her earlobe with his teeth. She gave a soft moan. He cupped her breasts in his hands and continued to kiss her neck. Feeling her yield, he knew a triumphant thrill. At this moment, she was his.

****

Penny sighed and shuddered, giving in to the breathtaking sensations aroused by his kisses and caresses. Her whole body heaved with desire, and it was a struggle not to seem too impatient. He obviously wanted to draw out every enticing pleasure as long as possible. He couldn't know that every moment would be both heaven and torture for her. A part of her agonized at the awareness that what they shared tonight might have to last her a lifetime.

She fought to set aside the bitter awareness and think of nothing except the splendor of this moment. As he undid the hooks at the back of her dress, she concentrated on the tingling heat radiating from her nipples and the yearning ache in her lower belly. Her gown slipped down and he cupped her breasts, stroking them through the thin fabric of her zona. She drifted on a cloud of pleasure as he caressed her.

His expert fingers fondling her nearly bare skin. The sensation of silk and fine cotton gliding over her flesh. The pressure of his warm, skillful fingers. Her body sang with delight, sending waves of quivering heat deep into her core. Her legs failed her and he held her up, the sensation of his hard muscular body against hers arousing her further. Although the eager yearning inside her remained, having him hold her like this made her feel safe and content.

His lips followed where his hands had gone, and she savored his musky, male scent and reveled in his sleek masculine strength. But as hard as she tried, she couldn't deny the desperate need building inside her. She found herself writhing and moaning as his tender, provocative lips brought her to fever pitch. When she thought she could bear no more, he brought his mouth to her cleft, licking and nuzzling her flesh through the fabric of her under-drawers.

She threw her head back and pressed her lips together, fighting the cry of ecstasy that swelled inside her. But she couldn't hold back completely or stop the low, broken murmurs that issued from her lips, matching the shimmering waves of pleasure sweeping through her. She reached her peak with a shuddering gasp, her whole body convulsing. As she went limp, he caught her in his arms and carried her to the bed.

He undressed her. As she lay there, naked and spent, gazing up at his darkly handsome face, she realized she wanted to stroke and fondle and arouse him as he'd done to her. When he drew near, as if to start his exquisite torment once again, she shook her head. "Now, it's my turn," she said.

"What do you mean?"

"I mean, since you've had your pleasure of me, it's only fair I get mine of you." She gestured. "Take off your clothing…all of it."

His eyes darkened and his nostrils flared as he removed his garments. She watched, fascinated as he slowly revealed himself, each glimpse more provocative than the last. Broad shoulders straining against thin white muslin. The thick column of his muscular neck revealed as he untied his cravat. Swirls of dark hair visible as he unbuttoned his shirt. And then the glorious expanse of his chest, so solid and strong. He dropped his shirt to the floor, then paused, letting her feast her eyes on him: dark nipples, taut muscular planes, the intriguing v-shaped pattern of black hair, thinning to a faint line leading down to the mysteries concealed by his trousers.

He moved to the chair to take off his boots and stockings, then stood to undo his trousers. He unbuttoned them slowly, as if deliberately tantalizing her. She watched breathlessly, and as he freed his phallus, she felt the familiar arousal and amazement. It seemed appalling large, and yet, looking at his proud ruddy shaft and recalling the delicious, overwhelming sensation of having it inside her, she realized she reveled in every heated inch.

He slid down his trousers and stepped out of them, naked at last. Her gaze explored his lower body. Narrow hips, dominated by his phallus, thrusting up like a thick, blunt sword. Lean, powerful-looking legs, so different than hers. Hard, defined, hairy.

She stood and reached out to touch him. First, she stroked his shoulders, sliding her fingers over the smooth skin, feeling the hard strength beneath. He watched her with a hooded, provocative gaze as she caressed his chest. Coarse hair. Firm muscle. The pebbly surface of his nipples. She enjoyed each tantalizing texture as she glided her hands over him, massaging gently.

He remained still, but she could sense his breathing quicken. And when she followed the line of dark hair down to his belly, he gasped in expectation.

At the last second she moved her hands to the side, along his hips, avoiding his quivering erection.

"I didn't do this to you," he murmured.

"Do what?" She gently stroked his hips, her hands moving in slow circles nearer and nearer to his buttocks.

"Torture you."

"Ah, but you did," she purred. "And now I'm paying you back."

She'd been watching him so far, enjoying the signs of his heightening arousal, the way the tension in his face increased with each slow caress. Now she closed her eyes and rested her face against his chest as she grasped his buttocks and gently squeezed. He gave a low groan and his body stiffened. His phallus throbbed against her belly, hot and alive, but she concentrated instead on the feel of his buttocks beneath her fingers. "You remind me of Hero," she said. "Touching you, I sense your strength and power."

He grasped her shoulders. "Ah, but *you* ride Hero, while soon I will ride *you*." His words and his hot breath near her ear sent a delicious thrill through her. Oh, she wanted that, she did. But not yet.

She ran her hands down his back, then kneaded his buttocks, imagining the thick muscles flexing as he thrust into her. Her insides felt as if she was melting, and she was so aroused it was almost painful. But as badly as she wanted him, she forced herself to hold back, haunted by the idea that they might never do this again. She must focus on every magical moment before it all slipped away.

But when he gave another agonized groan, she felt pity on him and grasped the pulsing rod of flesh pressing again her belly. He let out a gasp and his body went rigid. She squeezed his warm, solid flesh, experiencing a dazzling sense of power. Each movement of her hands seemed to affect him, and when she fondled the velvety tip she sensed he was on the verge of exploding.

Indeed, the next moment he spoke in a raw, raspy voice. "Please...I wouldn't deny you the pleasure of touching me, but I-I can't bear much more."

"But I've just started," she reminded him. "I haven't yet used my mouth."

He let out a curse and drew away from her his expression agonized. "I promise I will let you do that…after…after I've found release."

She nodded. As enticing as it was to touch him intimately, she couldn't endure much more either.

His expression changed, turning somehow…wicked. "If you're in the mood to explore, we could try making love in a different way."

Although she wasn't certain what he meant, she nodded.

"Turn around and lean over the bed."

She did as he asked, surprised and aroused. At one time she would have considered this position distasteful. But after all the other delightful things he'd taught her, she was intrigued at the thought of doing it the way animals mated. He would be the stallion and she the mare.

She shivered with expectation as he touched her between her legs, stroking subtly. Rubbing her, making her wet. Now it was her turn to moan. She couldn't remain still but found herself moving against his provoking fingers. When he slid one inside her, waves of bliss washed over her. And yet…she wanted more.

Chapter Nineteen

She was almost ready...Almost. He struggled to restrain his own raging lust. Just a little more. He didn't want to hurt her, and a woman might find this position uncomfortable if she wasn't intensely aroused. She was deliciously wet, but he wanted to make her even more so. And he knew exactly how to accomplish that.

He nudged her legs farther apart. Getting on his knees, he brought his mouth to her sweet, secret opening. She cried out and her whole body convulsed. He nibbled and sucked, laving the delicate folds with his tongue, enjoying the way her hips quivered and writhed. She tasted of desire and intoxicating femininity, and he grew more aroused by the second.

When he could endure it no longer, he stood. With one hand on her hip and one on his shaft, he pushed into her. She was very tight, and each inch deeper brought more excruciating pressure. When she made a soft moaning cry and began to tremble, he went still. "Are you all right? I'm not hurting you, am I?"

She shook her head and moaned, as if incapable of speech. In another moment he would be beyond words himself.

He made slow rocking movements, his control beginning to shatter. As much as he wanted it to last, he could not...could not—As he tumbled off the precipice, he heard her wild, piercing cry and knew she was with him as he fell.

When Marcus caught his breath, he drew away and collapsed on the bed beside her. Eyes closed, he floated back to earth. When he could finally reason again, he opened his eyes to the blissful vision of her face next to his. He reached out to stroke her cheek. There were no words to describe what he felt at this moment. This piercing tenderness that made his throat tight and his insides ache with love. He couldn't stop looking at her. He was utterly in awe of her beauty and the magic of what they'd shared.

****

Although he didn't say the words, Penny saw it in his eyes. This man, this hardened, cynical gamester, was in love with her. The awareness broke her heart. What they'd shared was so rare and precious. How could she bear to destroy it? Surely there was some way to work things out with Adrian.

But then she thought of the terrible desperation in her cousin's eyes and the familiar dread returned. She couldn't gamble with Marcus's life and be wrong. Thinking of it, she reached out for him. He drew her close. With her head on his chest, she listened to his heart beat and pretended this moment would last forever.

****

Marcus woke to near darkness, with only a faint hint of summer twilight filtering in the window. At some point they'd gotten under the covers but Penny was still curled against him. The feel of her silky warmth made him almost instantly hard. Should he wake her? He wanted to make love to her again and he'd promised to let her pleasure him more. Mmmm.

What further delightful ways might she find to tease and tantalize him?

But she was sleeping so peacefully now that he hated to disturb her. He lay there a while, listening to the soft sound of her breathing. It felt so right to have her next to him. He wanted to wake up this way every day of the rest of his life. And he would, too, if she would marry him.

Today he would do it. He would tell her about the wager with James, admit he was in love with her and ask her to marry him, not because she was part of the prize he'd won from her cousin, but because he truly wanted her to be his wife.

The idea of it made him anxious, but not nearly as anxious as he'd felt yesterday. Something between them seemed changed. Now when they made love they weren't two strangers drawn together by lust, but lovers expressing their feelings for each other. He'd caught her looking at him with tenderness and warmth. She might not be *in love* with him, but she was at least fond of him. That was certainly enough to build a marriage on. Indeed, it was great deal more than many couples had.

He carefully slid away from her and climbed out of the bed. After pulling on an old robe hanging in the dressing room, he went out and used the necessary. On the way back, he grabbed the night candle in the hallway and took it with him. Bringing it near the bed, he stared at the beautiful woman lying there. She looked so delicate, almost fragile somehow. The deep, protective yearning he felt was stronger than his sexual desire. He would let her sleep. There would be time for more lovemaking in the morning.

He took the candle back to the hallway table, then returned to the bed and climbed in next to her. Closing his eyes, he sought to relax and let the lazy pleasure of having her so near lull him to sleep.

****

Penny woke feeling a deep sense of contentment. Marcus's strong, warm body was right next to hers. But then she remembered what she had to do and the cold despair seeped through her. If only she could wait another day… No, that would only make things worse. Gathering her resolve, she opened her eyes.

It was growing light outside. She'd better hurry if she wanted to get away before Marcus woke. She eased out of the bed, freezing in place as Marcus stirred. Then he turned over and his breathing grew deep and even again. She tiptoed to the dressing room and put on one of the plainer daydresses from Madame Dubonet's. Although she felt guilt for taking the clothing Marcus had bought her, she had no choice. Other than the one worn, ill-fitting green dress, which she'd given Maggie for rags, the only garments she'd brought from Horngate were trousers and shirts for riding.

Once dressed, she grabbed her reticule and the valise she'd already packed and tiptoed to the door. Before opening it, she cast one last longing look toward the bed. Marcus was turned on his side away from her. The sight of his sleek beautiful back and shoulders sent a pang of yearning through her.

She reminded herself she was doing this to keep him safe, then eased open the door and went out.

Downstairs, she quickly made her way to the kitchen and then to the servants' quarters. To her relief, Jeremy was waiting for her. "Is everything ready?" she asked breathlessly.

"Yes, miss. If you're certain you want to do this."

"I told you, I have no choice."

The footman shook his head. "It don't seem right, miss. At least let me take you wherever you're going."

"No, Jeremy, I don't want to involve you, or force you to lie to the man who employs you." She tried to smile. "I'll be all right. My cousin isn't going to do anything to me. I'm the heiress to Horngate."

As Jeremy left to fetch the hansom, she realized that at one time Horngate had meant everything to her. Now her inheritance almost felt like a burden. Of course, Horngate was the reason Marcus had wanted to marry her. And even now, although he might be in love with her, she doubted he would want her for his wife if she weren't an heiress. Without Horngate, the best she could hope for was that he might make her his mistress.

Of course, after what she was doing to him now, he likely wouldn't want her for his mistress either. And unless she found a way to get out of marrying this mystery man to whom Adrian had lost the estate, she likely wouldn't have the freedom to be anyone's mistress.

Her thoughts ran in wild circles again. She had to focus on her plan and find out this mystery man's identity. And convince Adrian she was no longer involved with Marcus, so Marcus would be safe. And finally, she had to come up with some sort of scheme to get out of marrying a man who was capable of killing to gain control of her property. She shuddered at the thought.

A moment later, Jeremy returned. Picking up her valise, he said, "Here, I'll take you out the back. That way Bowes won't see you."

Her nerves taut and her stomach in turmoil, Penny followed after the footman.

It was only when she was safely in the hansom and well away from the townhouse that she could relax. Their first stop was the place Lily had told her about, where she would reside for the time being. It was in what looked like a decent area, although the small, rather shabby houses had been divided up into several living spaces.

She found the landlady, Mrs. Bly, who lived in the lower portion of the house. As she took Penny up to see the room, Mrs. Bly warned, "I don't allow no gentlemen visitors. And the rent must be paid promptly, or I'll have you turned out."

Penny stared at the small, dingy room and imagined living there for weeks or months. Just the thought of it made her feel as if she were suffocating.

"Well?" Mrs. Bly prompted.

"I'll take it," Penny responded. "How much is the first month's rent?"

The amount Mrs. Bly quoted seemed quite high, and Penny realized she should have asked Lily what she'd paid. She suspected the landlady had adjusted the rent upward based on her well-made clothing.

She paid Mrs. Bly, collected the key, then left her valise in the room before returning to the hansom.

"Where to now?" the driver asked.

"Madame Dubonet's on Bond Street."

"Nothing will be open yet, miss," said the driver.

"It's all right. I'm not planning to shop, but to meet someone." She'd had Jeremy take a message to Adrian, asking him to meet her outside the modiste's.

A short while later, Penny stood outside the shop, trying not to pace. What if Adrian didn't come? Should she seek him out at the gambling hell?

At least it was warm and sunny, a truly lovely morning. She thought about how nice it would be to ride in Hyde Park on a day like this, with the sun on her face and Marcus beside her. Another pang of loss went through her, making her want to weep.

"Why so blue-deviled, coz?"

She whirled to see Adrian watching her with a cold, cynical expression. "You know why I'm distressed," she snapped.

"You'll get no sympathy from me. You were raised as a princess, while I've always had to struggle to find my way."

"Well, my life as a princess is about to come to an end, isn't it?" Glaring at him, she added, "I've done what you've asked. I've left Revington. Now you must tell me who this man is you've lost Horngate to...*a second time*."

"Why don't I take you to meet him right now?"

When he took hold of her arm, Penny jerked away. "I don't think so. I'm not going anywhere with you until you give me the information I've asked for."

Adrian glanced around, as if trying to decide if he could get away with taking her by force. Penny tensed, prepared to struggle and scream. The hansom driver was waiting in his vehicle across the street, and if Adrian tried to drag her away, she believed the street cleaners would intervene. To press the point, she said, "If you try to force me to go with you, you'll be sorry."

He met her gaze, his expression sour. "You always were an unnatural, unfeminine creature."

"That's right. I'm a hopeless hoyden, which means I can hold my own against you!" She glared at him. He glared back.

"Why did you ask to meet me here, if you're going to be so bloody stubborn?"

"I asked you here because I wanted you to know I have left Revington. And also because I want to learn more about this man you expect me to wed."

"What difference does it make to you who he is?"

"You can't expect me to exchange vows with a man I've never met!"

"I've told you, I'll take you to him now."

Penny backed away. "No. The first time I make his acquaintance, I intend do so in a public place. Now, tell me his name."

Adrian regarded her with an expression that could only be called cunning. "All you need to know is that he is a viscount. So, you'll be marrying well. It's actually a far better arrangement than the one I had with Revington."

No doubt better for you, Penny thought with bitterness. She was growing more and more suspicious. It especially disturbed her that Adrian wouldn't tell her the man's name. Did that mean he had such an awful reputation Adrian was afraid she'd refuse to marry him if she knew who he was? She thought again of seeing Brakestoke not long before she'd met Adrian on the previous day. And Brakestoke was a viscount.

Somehow she had to get Adrian to give her some clue as to who this man was. "If this man's a viscount, why does he need Horngate?"

"Most of the nobility are deep in debt. The man may have claim to an estate of his own, but it's probably mortgaged to the hilt. Horngate is damned prosperous by London standards."

Penny felt a flash of fury. Adrian had always expressed scorn for Horngate and the horse operation. Now he acted as if it was some sort of great prize.

She pushed aside her anger and focused on getting information. "You say you lost Horngate in a card game. When was that? And what gaming house or club were you in at the time?"

"I told you, none of this is any concern of yours."

"Of course it's my concern! I need to know what kind of man you've betrothed me to. For all I know he's some sort of vile monster!"

"That's ridiculous. You know I'd never marry you off to someone like that."

"Oh, I think you would…especially if there was anything in it for you!" She wondered if Adrian had made an arrangement with this man. Perhaps, unlike Revington, this man had agreed to let Adrian keep part of the profits from Horngate.

She regarded Adrian warily. "Why don't you want me to meet him? What are you holding back?"

"Nothing. I've told you, this is actually a better arrangement than the one with Revington. As for why I'm reluctant for you to meet him, I can't help worrying you'll try to scare off the fellow like you did with Revington."

Penny felt a surge of hope. Perhaps if she met this man and reasoned with him, explained that she didn't want to marry him and that Adrian was trying to coerce her… Looking back now, she realized that's what she should have done with Marcus. Instead of trying to manipulate him and "scare him off" as Adrian put it, she should have told him the truth. Marcus would never have forced her to marry him. He wasn't that sort of man.

But *this* man might be. After all, Adrian had implied her new betrothed was so eager to get his hands on Horngate that he was willing to kill Revington. She stared at her cousin, wondering what was the truth and what was a lie. Somehow she had to find out…and just this moment she'd thought of a way to do it.

Adrian appeared to give in. "All right. It's agreed. You can meet him tonight. As far as a public place goes, what about Vauxhall Gardens? Is that public enough for you? Say tonight at eight?"

"I'll be there," Penny said.

Adrian drew near to her, assuming a threatening posture once more. "You'd better. If you don't show, I'll make certain something happens to your precious Marcus."

Penny watched Adrian saunter away. As soon as he was out of sight, she went to the hansom and told the driver. "If you could please wait here a while longer."

****

Marcus stared at the breakfast food on his plate. The gnawing ache in his stomach made it impossible to eat.

When he awakened and found Penny gone, he'd been surprised and disappointed, but not concerned. Later, when he discovered she wasn't in the house, he decided she must have gone riding in Hyde Park. He was disappointed she hadn't asked him to accompany her, but perhaps she wanted some time alone. Or maybe she hadn't wanted to wake him.

But if she'd gone riding, surely she would be back

by now. *Where is she? Has something happened to her?*

He got to his feet, leaving his food untouched, and went to the kitchen. The new cook gaped at him as he strode past and made his way downstairs to the servants' quarters. Maggie and Jeremy were eating breakfast. They immediately jumped to their feet. "Yes, sir, can we help you?" the footman asked.

Marcus glanced from one servant to the other. "Do either of you know where Pen...where Miss Montgomery is?"

Maggie was the first to respond. "Why, no, sir. She never called me up to help her dress."

"What of you?" Marcus demanded of Jeremy.

"Well, I..."

"Did you get her a horse from the stables this morning?"

"No, sir."

Seeing the guilty expression on the footman's face, Marcus almost lost control. "But you do know where she is, don't you?"

"Not exactly," Jeremy answered.

"What does that mean?" Marcus snapped.

"It means...I...she had me call her a hansom, sir. But I don't know where she was going."

Marcus whirled and left. As he made his way back to the main floor and through the house, he grew more and more agitated. Where was Penny taking a hansom cab so early in the morning?

He found Bowes in the foyer. "Did you see Miss Montgomery leave, Bowes?"

The manservant looked startled. "No, sir. I didn't know she was gone."

"Well, she is. Jeremy says she had him fetch a hansom."

Bowes looked troubled. "I've been here the whole time and never saw any vehicles drive up."

"Well, then she must have gone out the back way." He didn't understand. The night before they'd been so close, as if they were connected in some deep and powerful way. Then today, she left without telling anyone where she was going. Could she be planning some sort of surprise for him? That must be it. It wasn't possible he'd completely misread her.

He told himself to relax. She'd be back soon and the reason for her odd disappearance would be clear.

****

Penny huddled in the shadows in the alley behind the club and watched the back entrance. Although she'd been waiting well over an hour, there was no sign of Adrian. Nor had he been seen by the hansom driver, whom she'd asked to watch the front entrance.

Maybe it was too early for Adrian to contact the viscount. Some of the nobility didn't rise until noon. She'd have to wait a while longer. Eventually Adrian would leave to meet this man and explain the arrangements. Then she would follow him. She had to know who this man was so she could decide what to do.

****

"I'm going to James's house," Marcus told Bowes. "If Miss Montgomery comes back, send Jeremy to get me immediately."

"Of course, sir," Bowes replied.

Marcus hurried to the phaeton he'd had Jeremy fetch. Glancing at the footman, he said, "You'll be certain to come and get me if Penny returns?"

"Of course, sir."

Marcus climbed into the phaeton and headed to James's townhouse.

Vincent met him at the door. The butler barely had time to greet him before Marcus demanded, "Has Miss Montgomery been here?"

"Why no, sir."

"She hasn't been here at all?"

"Not today, sir."

Marcus let out his breath in a sigh. He'd truly thought…

"Would you like to come in, sir?" Vincent asked.

"Yes. And get James for me. Tell him it's urgent. And Miss Wilson as well."

"Very good, sir. Let me take you into the drawing room, and then I'll announce you."

As he waited, Marcus considered having some brandy. But he realized that after scarcely eating breakfast, he'd end up half-foxed if he started drinking this early. He needed to keep his wits about him, in case something had happened to Penny.

Although he told himself it was too soon to worry yet, a part of him was already panicking. After such tender, intimate lovemaking, it seemed extremely odd that Penny would simply disappear.

But according to Jeremy, she'd left the house of her own free will, even sneaking out the back entrance. What could have caused her to do such a thing? Could her wretched cousin be to blame?

"What's this all about?" James entered the drawing room, looking unaccustomedly disheveled. "Frankly, it wasn't a good night with Charles, and we'd hoped to sleep in a bit."

"Its half past ten," Marcus pointed out. "I've never known you to stay abed this late, even in our old days of carousing."

"Maybe I'm getting older and more sensible," James groused.

"The reason I'm here is that I'm looking for Penny. She had one of the footmen fetch a hansom cab this morning, then left by the back way. When she didn't return, I thought she must have come here."

"Haven't seen her." James yawned.

"I'm getting alarmed, James. I worry something's happened to her."

"Why? She obviously left of her own free will."

"It's merely a feeling I have."

"Well, give it a few hours. If she isn't back by this afternoon, we can look into it then."

Lily entered the room and immediately approached Marcus. "You're looking for Penny, aren't you?"

Marcus felt his insides grow tight. "Yes. Yes I am." When Lily regarded him with a look of pity, he grew more distressed. "What is it? What's wrong?"

"She didn't leave you a note?"

"A note? What sort of note?" Marcus took hold of Lily's arm. "What is it? What's happened to Penny?"

"For heavens sake, Marcus!" James approached, glowering. "Let go of her! She doesn't have anything to do with Penny leaving!"

Marcus released Lily. "I'm sorry. But please tell me what's happened. Where has Penny gone? Is she in danger?"

Lily looked away. "I can't..." She heaved a sigh and then met his gaze. "Penny's not in danger. At least not that I know of. That's all I can tell you."

Marcus stared at the young woman. He wanted to find a way to force her to tell him the truth. But James wouldn't allow him to press her. He'd have to find another way.

He gave Lily and James a curt nod and left.

As he drove home, the sick feeling inside him grew more intense. Although Lily said Penny wasn't in danger, something was terribly wrong.

Chapter Twenty

After waiting for what seemed like hours more, Penny finally decided Adrian wasn't going to seek out her prospective husband until later in the day. Perhaps he wouldn't do so until it was time to go to the Gardens. In the meantime, she desperately needed to find a necessary and to get something to eat. She felt almost faint with hunger.

Returning to the hansom, she had the driver take her back to Mrs. Bly's.

She paid the man and asked him to return for her later that evening. She purchased a meat pie from a nearby shop and headed to her rented room. At the top of the stairs, she was startled to find Lily waiting there. "What are you doing here? What's wrong?" she asked.

"Marcus came asking after you. But he has no idea you mean to break things off with him. He thinks something's happened to you, that you're in danger."

"Why would he think that?" Penny asked.

"Because he cares about you! At any rate, you need to write him a note and tell him what's going on."

Penny felt a wave of anguish. "I don't know if I can. How can I bear to write such lies? How can I tell him I don't care about him when it's not true?"

"Well, you need to tell him something so he stops worrying and doesn't go searching for you. He suspects I know what's going on, and he won't rest until I tell him the truth. I know you don't want to break his heart, but if you don't make your intentions clear, he'll suffer in another way."

"And if he seeks me out and confronts me, I'll never be able to convince him I don't love him. I suppose there's no hope for it. I'll have to write him and make him believe this is my choice and I truly don't want to marry him. Otherwise if Adrian finds out, Marcus will be in danger." Penny nodded wearily. "Very well. I'll do it. Come in while I write a note."

She unlocked the door and led Lily inside. After removing a small portable writing desk from her valise, she sat on the bed with the desk on her lap. Every part of her rebelled at what she was about to do. Dipping the pen in the ink, she wrote:

Dear Marcus:

I've made up my mind that I can't marry you. I'm sorry to have inconvenienced you. Despite your agreement with my cousin, I hope you'll respect my wishes. Please don't try to contact me.

Sincerely,
Penelope Montgomery

When she finished, she waved the note in the air to dry the ink, then handed it to Lily.

Lily read it, frowning. "I'm not sure it's harsh enough. You say you *can't* marry him, rather than you don't want to. I think if you intend to make it clear there's no hope for the two of you, you should be emphatic that this is truly what you wish."

"It will have to do," Penny said stubbornly. "Now, how will I get it to him?"

"I'll leave it with Bowes."

Penny nodded. Although she must do this, it still felt like her heart had been torn out.

After Lily left, she struggled to eat the meat pie, but found she had no appetite. She decided to return to the gambling hell, hoping Adrian hadn't already left to meet the unknown viscount. The hansom cab driver was waiting for her when she went out. "Please take me back to Pall Mall," she said.

****

"Sir, Miss Wilson just brought this over."

Marcus looked up as Bowes held out a note. *The little minx!* He'd known Lily knew more than she was letting on. He tore open the note. It was short, taking only seconds to read. Then he read it again...and again.

The anguished doubt he'd carried around with him for weeks had suddenly come true. Or had it? She said she *couldn't* marry him, not that she didn't want to. It was a subtle distinction, but it gave him hope. If only if he could see her...talk to her...hold her in his arms. He felt certain that if he made love to her, he could change her mind.

Unless this wasn't a matter of her choosing, but that she was being coerced by someone. Like her wretched cousin.

He had to talk to Penny. *He had to.* Lily clearly knew where Penny was. Somehow he must *make* her tell him the truth. James would try to protect Lily and keep him from pressing her, so he'd have to speak to her when James wasn't around.

****

Penny waited outside the gambling hell. This time of day, there were numerous men leaving and entering. Penny observed them carefully. That one looked too old, while the next man appeared in a hurry. At last two well-dressed, young gentlemen climbed out of a coach and approach the establishment. Penny took a deep breath, climbed out of the hansom and hurried to the men. After begging their pardon for intruding, she asked if they knew Adrian Withersby.

"Indeed, we do," one of the men answered. He gave his companion a pained look, then returned his gaze to Penny. "What do you want with him?"

Penny sought to smile ingratiatingly. "He's my cousin. I wonder if one of you would be willing to look around inside and tell me if he's there. I don't want to speak to him, just find out his whereabouts."

"Family looking for him, are they?" The man gazed at Penny searchingly. "Don't you have a male relative who could look into this?"

"There's only Adrian, I'm afraid."

The man nodded. "Of course, we'll help you, won't we, Fletcher?"

"Why not?" his companion answered lazily. "We've nothing better to do than aid a damsel in distress."

"Oh, thank you. I'd be so grateful."

The man called Fletcher leaned near, and his gaze moved over Penny assessingly. "Exactly how grateful will you be, miss?"

Before Penny could think of an appropriate response, the man's companion intervened. "Here, now, Fletcher, the young lady needs our help. It would be churlish of us to put conditions on it."

His friend grinned. "You're right." He gave a faint bow. "We'll do this for you simply because we're such fine gentlemen, such noble knights."

"Oh, thank you, sir!" Penny exclaimed. She looked at his companion. "Both of you."

"We'll be back shortly," the first man responded. The two men doffed their hats to her, then went inside.

Penny returned to the hansom to wait. It wasn't long before the gentlemen returned. "He's there," Fletcher responded. "Not particularly foxed, which is unusual for him."

"Foxed?" Penny asked.

"Drunk. Lurched. In his cups. Your cousin has a reputation for it."

Penny pretended to be horrified. "Oh, dear! And I thought his troubles were all ill-advised wagering."

"Oh, he has a reputation for that, too. Heard he lost badly to Marcus Revington a while back. Must have been a substantial amount because Revington hasn't been back at the cards since."

"Who else have you seen my cousin gambling with?" Penny asked.

"Not really anyone," Fletcher responded. "Thought maybe he was so badly dipped, he had to lay off for a while."

"Is he with anyone?" Penny asked.

"No. All by himself," said Fletcher.

The other man spoke: "If you want us to drag him out of there and help you get him home, we'd be happy to do so."

"Oh, no thank you. That won't be necessary. My aunt simply wanted to know where he was and make certain he was safe."

"Your aunt must be a saint to be worried for the likes of him." The gentleman bowed and smiled at her warmly. "Augustus Marsden, Earl of Grandsmere, at your service, miss."

His companion also bowed, and then they were gone.

Penny considered her next move. She'd failed to discover anything about the mystery man. Nor did she have any sort of plan for getting out of marrying him. Perhaps she should return to her rented room and rest. She would need all her wits about her tonight.

****

From his vantage point in a rented coach across the street, Marcus focused his gaze on the door to James's townhouse, waiting for his friend to leave. He'd sent Jeremy to the townhouse a short while ago, carrying a message to James that "Mr. Revington needed to see him right away at his home." Soon Lily would be alone, and he would find a way to make her tell him Penny's location. Then he would go to Penny and convince her to come back and marry him.

His hope faded as the familiar doubts crept in. What if he was wrong and Penny truly didn't want to be his wife? What if what they'd shared meant nothing to her? She hadn't wanted to marry him in the beginning, that was certain. Although he believed she'd come to care for him, he couldn't know what she truly felt. After all, he didn't even know *why* she'd been so against marrying him when they first met.

He'd assumed it was because she didn't know him or like him, but maybe there were other reasons. Maybe she was allied with her cousin. The two of them might have been working together to get him to call off the wedding and give up Horngate. They might think that now he'd fallen in love with Penny, he wouldn't force her to marry him. For that matter, what if Penny somehow knew of the wager he'd made with James?

The thought struck him like a blow to the belly. What if Penny knew and had deliberately tried to make him fall in love with her so he would lose the bet and have to set her free?

He'd barely begun to examine the disturbing idea when James left the townhouse. Marcus waited until his friend was well away, then climbed out of the rented coach and hurried to the door.

Vincent greeted him. "Good day, sir. I'm afraid you've just missed Mr. Ludingham."

"What about Lily?" Marcus asked. "Is she here?"

When Vincent looked surprised, Marcus added, "I want to speak to her about Miss Montgomery."

"Of course, sir. I'll announce you to Miss Wilson."

Lily entered drawing room. "Good day, Marcus." She looked nervous.

"A pleasure as always. I suspect you know why I'm here."

She nodded. "It's about Penny, isn't it?"

Marcus took a deep, steadying breath. "I don't understand it. I truly felt we were becoming close. I even thought that perhaps…she might be growing fond of me. But now…" He sighed heavily. "She's gone off without telling me where she is, and left a note implying things are over between us."

Lily stared at him, clearly upset.

He approached her and took her hands in his. "You must tell me. Do I have any chance with Penny? Is there any possibility she'll come back and agree to be my wife?"

"I-I…don't know what to say." A stricken look came over Lily's face. She slipped her hands from his grasp and turned away. A short while later, she turned back, seemingly more composed. "She didn't want to hurt you, but I think this is worse." A determined look came over her face. "Very well, I'll tell you. I don't know for certain, but it seems unlikely Penny will come back and marry you."

Marcus felt his heart sink. He swallowed hard. "Why not?"

Lily frowned. "I can't tell you. But it-it doesn't have anything to do with you. It's more the circumstances."

"Circumstances? What do you mean?" If Penny's reasons for leaving had nothing to do with him, he could still have hope. All he had to do was find out what the barrier to their marriage was and alter those circumstances.

"It's hard to explain."

Marcus approached her and grabbed her arm. "Try. Try very hard."

"You bastard! You never meant to meet me, did you?"

Marcus let go of Lily and turned to see James in the doorway. His mild-mannered friend looked so furious he was almost unrecognizable. James approached him, blue eyes flashing. "You came here to talk to Lily alone, thinking that if I wasn't here you could harass her into telling you where Penny went!"

"I'm afraid that's the size of it," agreed Marcus. "What are you going to do about it? Call me out?"

Lily gasped, then approached James, her expression placating. "It's all right, James. He hasn't threatened me or hurt me. And you can't blame him. He's so distraught over Penny leaving." She leaned over and whispered something in James's ear. He gave her a startled look, then turned back to Marcus. Slowly, his expression changed from angry to pitying. Marcus's sense of doom returned.

"So you know the truth, too," said Marcus. "Everyone knows but me. It seems devilish unfair. Don't you agree, James?"

James nodded. He looked at Lily. "I'm sorry, but I have to tell him."

Lily looked alarmed. "I really don't think you should."

"No. I think it's better he knows." He met Marcus's gaze steadily. "She found out about our wager, Marcus. She knows if you fall in love with her, you have to give her a choice in whether she marries you."

She knows about the wager. And having guessed I am in love with her, she realized she was free. And so she left me.

"I'm sorry, Marcus," said James. "I never intended for her to find out. But at least this way you were spared the...unpleasantness of asking her to marry you and having her turn you down. She was obviously trying to be kind."

"Kind! You think this was kind! I've been going through hell the last few hours!"

"At least you know she's all right. I know that was weighing upon you."

This was all a nightmare. He could hardly grasp it. If anyone had told him this morning that Penny didn't love him and didn't want him in his life, he would never have believed it.

A sudden thought came to him. "How long has she

known about the wager?"

"I've no idea," answered James. He looked at Lily questioningly. "Lily?"

"A-a while, I'm afraid."

Marcus released his breath slowly, feeling as if he'd taken a blow to the stomach.

Thinking back, it did seem to him her behavior had changed about the time of the bet. She'd purchased her provocative clothing from Madame Dubonet, then one thing led to another and they ended up making love.

"I'm sorry, Marcus," James repeated. "I had no idea things would turn out this way. I thought as you fell in love with Penny, she'd fall in love with you."

Marcus sought to regain his usual reserved, detached outlook. "I don't need your pity, James. I made a mistake. I made a wager I couldn't afford to lose. It's not something I do a lot, and it won't happen again. The thing is, Penny may be 'off the hook', so to speak, but Withersby isn't. He still owes me, and I mean to collect in some way, even if it's only by making him miserable the rest of his life."

Thinking about Withersby's scheming, Marcus felt the hot, bitter anger surge through him. He welcomed it. It was so much better than the misery he'd been feeling a moment before. "Indeed, I think I'll go find him now." He gave a slight bow to Lily, then started for the door.

"Wait!" she called.

Marcus turned around. "What is it?"

Lily's eyes were pleading. "Perhaps it would be better if gave yourself time to cool off before you go out."

"Don't tell me you think Penny actually cares what

happens to Withersby. I can't believe she's that foolish."

"No. No...it isn't that. It's..." Lily glanced at James, as if looking to him for aid. "We-we don't want you to do anything you'd regret. Do we, James?"

"Regret?" asked Marcus. "I doubt I'm going to regret anything I do to that wretched little weasel."

"But you might. That is..." Lily looked at James again. "Tell him not to seek out Adrian, at least not right away. Please."

James was frowning. "Well, I don't see the harm in it."

"What if he challenges him to a duel?" Lily demanded. "What if he's killed?" She looked at Marcus. "Even if you win the duel and Adrian dies, you'll end up losing. You know duels are illegal. You might end up having to leave the country. And if that happened, Penny would..."

"Penny would what?" Marcus demanded.

"I-I'm certain she would feel very bad about it."

"Would she now? She doesn't want me to be killed or forced to flee the country, but she wants no part of me otherwise. Is that about the size of it?"

"I-I suppose so," said Lily, her voice quavering.

"Well, she has no say in the matter. I'll do whatever I damn please." Marcus stalked out of the room. As he swept past Vincent in the foyer and went out the door, he nursed his rage. Curse Adrian Withersby! And curse his devious little minx of a cousin!

****

Vauxhall Gardens was busy this night. Normally, Penny would have enjoyed the sight of elegantly dressed nobles strolling along the graveled walkways and the street vendors selling pastries, nuts, oranges and flowers. But tonight, her attention was focused on Adrian as she followed him through the crowds. He finally neared the rotunda where the orchestra was playing. When he halted, Penny did also, taking a position behind a cart selling meat-filled pies.

She waited, thinking that the mystery man would have to appear soon. Several times a well-dressed man seemed on the verge of approaching Adrian, but then moved past. As the performance ended and the crowd thinned, Adrian remained by himself, frowning and looking around in an irritated manner. The mystery man was obviously late.

As time went on, it looked to Penny as if he was very late. Perhaps he'd changed his mind. But what did that mean? The only way she'd find out was to talk to Adrian.

"About time!" Adrian exclaimed as she approached.

"Where's my intended?" she asked in ironic tones.

"He isn't coming."

Penny took a step back. "What do you mean, he isn't coming?"

"I mean, he couldn't be bothered with this nonsense."

"I told you, I'll only meet him in a public place."

"What are you afraid of, Penny?" Adrian asked, his expression sneering. "That I'll drag you off and force you to marry some disreputable blackguard?"

"Frankly, yes."

"Don't worry. I promise you, the man who'll soon be your husband is a decent enough fellow."

"You may think so, but I'm allowed to have my own opinion." Penny set her feet and faced him challengingly. "I'm willing to meet him only on my terms."

"He lives quite a distance away. Are you certain you want to wait here while I take a hansom to fetch him?"

"What's my alternative?"

"You could come with me. Or follow me, if that would make you feel better."

Penny sighed. She didn't want to stand there for hours by herself. "All right. We'll hire two vehicles."

"I don't have that much blunt on me," said Adrian. "Are you willing to pay?"

"Yes, I'll pay."

There were several hansoms waiting in the street outside the gardens. Penny followed Adrian to them. She gave him some money from her reticule, and he went to make the arrangements. While she waited, she wondered if she was being silly to worry he might drag her away and force her to wed this man.

Adrian returned, and they got into their separate vehicles and started off. Penny watched out the window. To her surprise, she realized they were headed to Mayfair, where the wealthiest of London resided.

A short while later, the hansom ahead of them halted. Penny's driver did the same. Adrian got out and spoke to his driver, then strode to the door of a large, well-appointed townhouse. Penny felt puzzled. Adrian had told her the man he wanted her to marry needed money. If he were low on funds, how could he afford to live in a place like this? Then again, Marcus had told her the titled upper classes often didn't pay their bills.

A butler answered the door and Adrian spoke to him. The butler appeared to nod, then disappeared into the house. Adrian came to the hansom where Penny was and opened the door. "He should be out in a few moments." He climbed in the vehicle and sat beside Penny.

"What are you doing?" she asked.

"Come now, surely you don't expect to have him meet you in the street."

"I suppose not." Penny turned to watch the house. When she glanced back at Adrian, she saw he had his handkerchief in one hand and a small bottle in the other. "What are you doing?" she asked. The next moment, she grew alarmed. But by then, Adrian had grabbed her and pressed the cloth against her mouth.

Chapter Twenty-One

Penny woke to find herself lying on narrow bed in a small drab room. Her wrists and ankles were bound with strips of cloth. Adrian sat in a chair across from her, watching her with a smug expression. "How does it feel now? To have your whole fate and future in someone else's hands? To be helpless?"

Although her head ached and her stomach was unsettled, Penny forced herself to sit up. She swung her legs over the side of the bed so she could face Adrian with some dignity. "So, what *is* my future? Are you going to try to force me to marry this unknown man? Last I heard the woman does have to give her consent, even at Gretna Green."

Adrian approached and brought his gloating face near hers, immediately assaulting her with the potent odor of gin. "There is no other man. I have another plan. A far better plan."

"What is it?" she asked.

"I'm going to make Revington pay a ransom for you."

"What?" Penny recoiled in shock. "Why would you think he'd be willing to pay a ransom when you had me break things off with him?"

"Well, he'd better. Otherwise..." The look in Adrian's blue eyes turned cold and sinister. "Otherwise, you're going down *with* me. If I can't have Horngate, or be properly compensated, you won't have it either."

"What do you mean?" asked Penny, although she suspected she knew the horrible answer.

"Because you'll be dead, you stupid bitch!"

Penny flinched. She'd known Adrian resented her, but she'd never guessed he felt such hatred. Perhaps it was because he was drunk. The cheap gin seemed to be rotting him away from the inside, leaving only a soulless, bitter shell.

She wondered if there was any way to reason with him. "Is that why you had me break things off with Revington, because you wanted an excuse to kill me?"

His expression turned sullen. "I had another plan, but it fell through. There was a man, but he refused to go through with it. He didn't want to be leg-shackled, even to gain control of Horngate."

"So, you did lose Horngate a second time."

Adrian nodded. "This fellow wasn't quite as easy to fool as Revington. He said he would have his blunt, or it would be my neck in the noose. In a manner of speaking, at least. I suspect he'll find a far more painful way for me to die." A muscle twitched in Adrian's jaw, as if he was contemplating the end he might face.

A moment later, Adrian appeared to throw off his anxiety. He glared at her. "But I won't let that happen. I'm going to force Revington to pay ten thousand pounds to keep you alive."

Penny gasped. "Ten thousand pounds? That's a fortune! I'm sure Revington doesn't have that kind of money!"

"But he does." Adrian bobbed his head. "He does. I know about the blunt he's won over the years. Thousands of pounds, fleeced off everyone from green boys to dukes and earls. And he's a cheeseparing bastard, too. Scarce spends any of his brass...until he got hooked up with you. That's why I know he'll pay the ransom. A man who spends money like Revington has on you is surely in love. Although why he fancies such a skinny long meg, I can't imagine."

Penny took a deep, shaky breath. She had to make Adrian see reason. "Perhaps Marcus *was* in love with me. But I ruined all that when you forced me to break off with him. I hurt him and hurt his pride, and I don't think he's the sort of man to forgive that."

"Oh, I think he will. And I'm a far better judge of character than you." His eyes turned flinty. "If he doesn't, then I'll carry through with my threat."

"Which is?"

"I'll inform Revington that if he doesn't pay up, I'm going to kill you. If I don't get the money, you're the one who'll have an 'unfortunate accident'." He jerked his head toward the window. "It's two stories down. I doubt anyone could survive a fall like that."

Penny's churning stomach clenched even tighter. Once she wouldn't have believed Adrian capable of such a thing. But no more. It seemed he truly despised her.

But Marcus wouldn't know that. When he got Adrian's note, he would think he was bluffing. Either that, or he wouldn't care.

Adrian gave her another cold, sneering look, then sat down at a small table in the corner of the room. Uncorking a bottle of ink, he dipped his pen into it and began to write.

When he finished, he stood and waved the parchment to dry the ink. "Now we'll find out if my assessment of Revington is correct."

"How will you get the note to him?"

"I'll pay some little street rat to take it to his door."

He pulled something from the pocket of his jacket and approached Penny. Seeing the handkerchief in his hand, she shrank away. "What are you doing?"

"What do you think? While I doubt anyone in this wretched neighborhood would heed your cries for aid, I'm not taking any chances."

"No, please! I promise I'll be quiet!"

Adrian made a disgusted sound. "I'm not that big a fool."

As he started toward her with the handkerchief, she cried, "Please don't leave me tied up and helpless! What if I have to use the necessary?"

"There's no necessary in a place like this. You'll have to piss in the pot under the bed like a regular wench."

"I can hardly do that when I'm tied up. Please...who knows how long you'll be gone?"

He gazed at her sullenly. "Very well, I'll untie you and let you take a piss. But then I'll tie you up again."

As Adrian knelt to undo the bonds around her ankles, Penny decided to make her move. As soon as her ankles were free, she thrust her knee upward, trying to strike his jaw. But she was too stiff to move quickly and he jerked out of the way in time.

"Damn bitch! Try that again and I'll knock you senseless!" His bloodshot eyes fixed on her, dark with malevolence. "I should just tie you up again and leave you to piss yourself."

"No! Please! I promise I won't try anything."

He gave her another threatening look, then pulled

the chamber-pot from under the bed.

"There. Do your business."

"I can't possibly manage with my hands tied." She held out her wrists and gazed at him pleadingly.

He jerked his head toward the window. "There's no reason I shouldn't toss you out right now. Revington won't know you're dead. He'll still pay the ransom."

His expression was so filled with loathing; Penny feared he might truly do it. "What if Revington wants some sort of proof you have me and that I'm safe? Do you really want to risk killing me until you're certain?"

Adrian stared at her. Finally, he reached out and untied her wrists. He moved swiftly to the other side of the room. Half turning away, he said, "Do what you have to do, and hurry."

Since her need was real, she complied. As soon as she finished, he came over and seized her wrists. She stood stiffly while he tied her again, wondering if she should make another attempt to get away before he retied her ankles. But without a weapon to incapacitate him, it seemed futile. Better to wait until he'd left and see if she could wriggle free and escape. But when he fastened the handkerchief over her mouth, she wished she'd tried harder to get away.

****

"This just came for you, sir."

Marcus glanced up as Bowes entered the room and his heart beat faster. Maybe it was a note from Penny. Maybe she'd explain why she left. But as soon as he saw the handwriting, his heart sank. It wasn't from Penny. Opening the packet, he perused the note. With each line, his anxiety deepened.

"Bad news, sir?" asked Bowes.

"You could say that."

No wonder he'd felt something was wrong ever since Penny disappeared. Curse Withersby! He'd always known Penny's cousin was a greedy, unprincipled bastard. But this… Was he so depraved he was willing to kill her?

Marcus couldn't take that chance. "Have Jeremy bring round the phaeton."

"Very good, sir."

As soon as Bowes left, Marcus went to the escritoire and pressed on a pin beneath the drawer to open the secret chamber. He took out the small key and went to the safe, hidden beneath a picture on the wall where he pulled out several bags full of coins. He reached for a stack of banknotes, then stopped. What was he doing? He couldn't give Withersby his whole savings without some proof he had Penny and that she was safe.

His stomach clenched at the thought of Penny being hurt or in danger. Did Withersby actually mean to kill her? Or was this a bluff?

He replaced the sacks of guineas and relocked the safe. Before he did anything, he had to talk to James.

****

He arrived at James's townhouse, and Vincent took him to the drawing room to wait. James entered, looking decidedly unlike his usual self. "What is it now, Marcus? Did you come to harass poor Lily again?"

"I'm sorry about that, James. But I've found out I had good reason to be worried. Look at this."

He held out the ransom note to James, who quickly skimmed the contents.

"What do you make of that?"

"I'm not certain what sort of game Withersby's playing," James responded. "Or, how big of a fool he thinks you are. Penny's his cousin and his only claim to the estate. If she dies, the property will pass on to another relative, some grandnephew of Penny's mother, who's still a child, I believe. I researched all this when you first got involved with Penny."

"So, you think his threat to kill her is a bluff?"

"He probably thinks you believe he'll inherit if she dies."

"But what if you're wrong about it being a bluff?" Marcus asked. "What if he truly means to do her harm?"

"There must be some way to find out what he's up to. The logical thing to do is hire a Bow Street man to look into it."

"There's hardly time for that. The note says he wants the ransom by tonight!"

"You're not seriously thinking of paying, are you?"

"I don't know. Perhaps if I offered him a portion of the ransom, he'd be satisfied. I can't imagine he thinks I'm going to bring him the whole ten thousand pounds. I doubt I could carry that amount by myself, even if most of it was in banknotes. He might be satisfied with a bag of guineas."

"But even if you pay him, what's to say he'll let Penny go? He might hang on to her and keep bleeding you for more." James shook his head. "I say you shouldn't give in to him. I think it's all a bluff."

"It very likely is," Marcus agreed. "But how can I take the chance? It's one thing to risk money or property in a card game. Quite another to gamble with someone's life." *Especially Penny's.*

As his turmoil increased, Marcus began to pace. He'd believed James would be able to advise him, but his friend was too logical and rational. He couldn't understand how it felt to know the woman he loved might be in danger. Unless...

He whirled to face James. "What if it was Lily who was being held for ransom? Would you be willing to risk *her* life, and take the gamble that her kidnapper didn't mean to harm her?"

James raised his eyebrows. "There's a difference. Lily hasn't been meeting with Adrian Withersby. And Lily didn't suddenly disappear and leave a note that makes absolutely no sense."

"What? You think Penny is a part of this?"

"It's possible, isn't it? She disappeared with no real explanation."

"I can't believe you'd think that of Penny. I thought you liked her."

"Liking hardly comes into it. I'm merely saying that from a logical standpoint, her disappearance, followed by her cousin's ransom note, is highly suspicious."

Was James right? Had Penny played him for a fool? "I don't see what Penny has to gain with this ransom business. She has Horngate and the profits from it."

"Who knows what motivates her? Her behavior up until now hasn't exactly been consistent, or rational, either."

Marcus thought back to Penny's erratic behavior over the past few weeks. He couldn't help wondering whether James was right. Had anything they'd shared been real? Or had she been acting the whole time?

Part of him couldn't believe that. It didn't seem possible she hadn't felt anything when they made love. Women were supposed to be the more sensitive, emotional sex. If he'd found their lovemaking so incredibly moving, how could she not experience it that way?

He turned to his friend. "Maybe I'm a fool, but I can't believe Penny is part of this. Frankly, I'd rather risk losing all my money than risk her being killed."

He started toward the door. James called, "At least make the bastard prove he has her before you pay him anything."

James had a point, Marcus realized. Turning back to his friend, he said, "I'll do that. In fact, I think I'll seek out Withersby right now."

****

He found Withersby at his usual gambling hell, sleeping in the back room. He looked utterly done-up: disheveled hair and clothing, and bloodshot eyes. He reeked of gin, as if he'd been drinking steadily for days on end.

As soon as he saw Marcus, he demanded, "Did you bring the blunt?"

"Before I pay you anything, I'll need proof that you have Penny."

Withersby smiled. He reached under the narrow bed and pulled out a reticule Marcus immediately recognized as belonging to her. "How's this, Revington?"

A chill went down Marcus's body as Withersby opened the purse and withdrew some kid gloves and a handkerchief.

"It did contain a handful of crowns and other

309

coins," said Withersby. "But I had a few expenses."

Marcus's sense of dread was rapidly replaced by the urge to seize Withersby and tear him limb from limb. The villain clearly saw his intent, for he took a step back. "I wouldn't try it, Revington. I've got Penny stashed somewhere nice and secret. She won't last long without food or water. By the time they find her, it will be because of the stink of her dead body."

Marcus sought to swallow his rage. He had to keep his wits about him. No matter what James said, he couldn't risk Penny's life to this madman.

"Is Penny safe?" he managed to get out.

"Yes, perfectly. Now, get the money and we'll talk."

Marcus gave a curt nod and left. Although he still hadn't decided whether to pay Withersby, he couldn't stay in the same room with him any longer or his anger would get the best of him. The thought of Penny at the mercy of this monster made him feel sick. He had to find her, but how? If only he had more time. He could hire a runner to investigate, as James had suggested. Yes, that was it. He'd stall for time. Tell Withersby he needed a few days to raise the blunt.

He made his way back through the hell and again confronted Withersby. "I need more time to get the money. I don't keep ten thousand pounds in my home. I'll have to collect what I can from other sources. Then I'll be back."

"You might want to hurry. Although Penny's unharmed, I imagine she's quite uncomfortable." Withersby gave an unpleasant laugh.

Marcus left the hell, his thoughts whirling. How could he trust a fiend like Withersby? For all he knew,

Penny was already dead. Even if she wasn't, there was no guarantee Withersby would release her if the ransom was paid.

What the devil am I to do?

He thought about returning to James's, but all his friend had done was raise doubts about Penny. He'd implied she was a part of Withersby's scheme and had been gammoning him all along. It was true some of her behavior had been suspicious, but still... He recalled the way she melted in his arms, the passion with which she kissed him, the warmth he'd seen in her eyes when she gazed back at him. Could even the most consummate actress be so convincing?

All his instincts told him no. What had he done for the past ten years but live by his instincts? Although he prided himself on playing the odds and being clever at card games, wasn't the real reason he was so successful because of his ability to size up his opponents? He'd known exactly what Withersby was when he met him. He might not have guessed the extent of the bastard's greed or utter ruthlessness, but he'd known he was a deceitful, cunning little cheat.

In contrast, when he met Penny, he'd been impressed by her guileless innocence. Although it turned out she wasn't quite as innocent as she appeared, he truly believed that at her core she was an honest person. He thought of the care and concern she had for her horses...the kindness she'd shown to his servants and Lily. She'd easily won the affections of Maggie, Jeremy, and even Bowes. If he told his household staff about the ransom note, he had no doubt they'd all insist Penny had no part of it. He might be a fool who'd lost his head over a beautiful woman who given him the greatest pleasure he'd ever experienced in bed, but there were plenty of other people who trusted Penny and believed she was kind and good and incapable of deceit.

At Park Street, the townhouse came in view. Marcus suddenly knew what he must do. He'd collect the money, or at least enough of it to convince the greedy Withersby he'd gotten his hand on a good bit of brass. Then he'd insist Withersby take him to Penny. If he refused, he'd find a way to make the bastard change his mind.

****

Closing her eyes, Penny used all her strength to tear through the strip of fabric binding her wrists. Although she'd managed to rip a portion of her bonds with her teeth, the fabric still held fast. Sighing, she raised her hands. Her mouth felt raw and sore, but she had to keep trying.

She caught a piece of the fabric in her teeth and resumed gnawing. At least Adrian hadn't tied her with rope. Then it would have taken days to get free. As it was, she didn't know how long she had before he returned. It felt as if she had been there for a long while, but it was likely only a few hours. Once Adrian delivered the note to Marcus, he'd have to give him some time to gather the money. That is, if Marcus decided to pay the ransom.

The familiar panic threatened, but she forced it away. She wouldn't depend on Marcus paying up. She'd escape long before then.

Of course, once she was free, Penny still faced difficulties. Adrian had taken her reticule with her money. All she had was the clothing she wore. Where should she go? If she showed up at James's townhouse, would he and Lily help her? If she asked them to take her in, she might well end up endangering them.

She couldn't think about those things; she had to focus on getting free. Seizing the ragged piece of fabric binding her wrists, she chewed fiercely.

****

"I'm back, you little prick. Now, take me to Penny."

Withersby sat up in the chair, looking startled. A moment later, his gaze focused on the valise Marcus was carrying. "That's it? You have the money?"

"What I can carry. Guineas are dashed heavy." Marcus held out the valise. Withersby grabbed it and put it on the bed to open it. He gave a delighted laugh, then reached in and ran his hands through the gleaming coins.

Marcus felt a stir of gratification. He'd filled the valise with the flashy gold coins, guessing they'd please the greedy Withersby, and he wouldn't take time to count them and realize there was only a few hundred pounds there.

Withersby finally looked up, his eyes narrowed. "This is only the beginning payment, of course. I'll need the rest before I take you to Penny."

Half-expecting this, Marcus drew the pistol from his pocket and aimed it at Withersby's head. "You're wrong, Withersby. You'll take me to Penny now."

"Do you expect me to believe you actually mean to use that? Are you prepared to buy off the half-dozen fellows in the gaming room who saw you come back here?" Withersby smirked. "You don't want to risk hanging. The bitch is surely not worth that, is she?"

Marcus clenched his jaw. He might have guessed the slippery little weasel would have an answer for any threat he made. And yet, he was fairly certain that under his cocky, smug demeanor, Withersby was a coward. "I never said I'd shoot you, Withersby. I might just use the pistol to break every bone in your face." Marcus motioned toward the gaming room with his head. "You think anyone out there will care if I do that? Especially when I explain how you've repeatedly sought to cheat me out of the property I won fair and square."

A muscle twitched in Withersby's face. Marcus reversed his grip on the pistol and advanced closer. "Think I'm too soft to hurt you? Think again."

As Marcus raised his arm, Withersby's bravado melted away. "All right. I'll take you to her!"

Marcus nodded and lowered the pistol. He watched warily as Withersby closed the valise and picked it up.

"You first." Marcus motioned with the pistol toward the door.

Withersby gave him a hate-filled look, then left the room, his body bent sideways as he carried the heavy valise.

"I could carry that for you," said Marcus, faintly amused by Withersby's weakness.

"I think not, you bastard," muttered Withersby.

They walked out of the hell, passing through the gaming room, where they received a few curious glances. Marcus had put the pistol back in his pocket but kept a firm grip on the hilt.

They went out to where Jeremy waited with the coach. "Where are we going, Withersby?" Marcus asked. "I need to tell the driver."

Withersby was sweating and his face was red.

Glaring at Marcus, he gave an address off Radcliffe Highway.

Marcus made certain Withersby was in the carriage before telling the footman their destination. Jeremy raised his eyebrows when Marcus told him the address. "That's an evil part of London, sir."

"I know."

"Be careful, sir."

Marcus nodded grimly. Although he felt he could handle Withersby, he worried the wretch might have an accomplice. Even with a pistol, he'd have difficulty dealing with two men. Not to mention that by simply being in this unsavory neighborhood, he might be putting himself at risk to be attacked and robbed.

He got in the carriage. Across from him, Withersby leaned back on the squabs, his expression sullen. Despite his apparent acquiescence, Marcus worried his adversary was still scheming, trying to come up with some way to flee with the money. "It would be easy to shoot you right here," he warned Withersby. "Dump your body in some alleyway and drive off. In the neighborhood we're traveling to, no one would care about how you died or who killed you."

"But you'd never find Penny then. She'd slowly die of thirst and hunger, and it would be your fault." Withersby smiled, seemingly cheered by this thought, while Marcus felt a surge of frustrated anger. *Curse the bastard! What has he done with her?*

When they arrived at their destination, Marcus's unease increased. The street was nearly deserted, except for a group of raggedy children who watched them drive past, their hollow eyes revealing a cold cunning that seemed at odds with their youth.

"This one." Withersby pointed to a narrow, two-story structure that appeared on the verge of falling down. After knocking on the carriage ceiling for Jeremy to halt the vehicle, Marcus climbed out. Withersby followed, carrying the valise. When Marcus gave him a questioning look, Withersby said, "I'm not about to leave it in the rig." He jerked his head toward the children. "This sort of place, they'll rob you blind."

Marcus nodded, then gestured to the building. "You go first, Withersby. And don't forget, I've still got the pistol at the ready."

Withersby opened the door, which was nearly hanging off its hinges. Inside it was dark and stank of damp, urine, and worse. Marcus repressed a shudder, thinking of Penny trapped in such a place.

Withersby started up the narrow stairs. With every step, the floorboards creaked and groaned. Marcus tried to stay close to Withersby and yet move cautiously, lest the stairway collapse beneath them.

By the time he reached the top, Withersby had put down the valise and was turning the doorknob. "Penny?" Marcus called out. "Penny, are you there?"

"She can't answer. I put a gag on her mouth."

"You bastard," Marcus muttered.

Withersby held the door open. "After you."

Marcus breathed a deep sigh. *At last.* "Penny. It's Marcus. Don't worry. I'm here."

Desperate, he started forward. Too late, he saw movement behind him. Then everything went black.

Chapter Twenty-Two

Penny leaned back against the seat in the mail coach, trembling with fatigue and nerves. What an ordeal! Getting loose had been only the beginning. Then she'd had to walk for what seemed like miles, all the while fearing she'd be set upon by footpads or ruffians. What likely saved her was she didn't look like she had anything to steal, which she didn't.

How fortunate that the driver of the first hansom she encountered was a man she'd hired in the past. Because she'd always paid him well, he'd agreed to take her to the mail coach station without charge. At the station, she'd had to convince the mail coach driver that when they reached the village near Horngate, the tavern keeper there knew her and would pay the fee. It helped she was a well-dressed female and obviously alone and in distress.

She took a deep breath, willing the last waves of panic to subside. If she could reach Horngate, she'd be safe. With luck, Adrian would assume she was still in London and had gone to Marcus or James for help. She hoped he didn't threaten them. Her stomach twisted at the thought. As soon as she got to Horngate, she'd send them a message, warning them about Adrian. In the meantime she could only hope that with her gone from London they wouldn't be in danger.

Of course, Adrian would eventually figure out

where she'd gone. But by then she'd be ready for him. She thought of her father's pistols, hidden in the cabinet in the library. She doubted they were loaded, but Tad or Mr. Foxworthy would know where to get ammunition. Then they'd teach her to how to shoot and she'd practice until she was able to hit her target.

She imagined herself holding a pistol, aimed square at Adrian. He'd never believe her capable of shooting him, but he would be wrong. She thought she'd be quite capable of killing him if she had to. Quite capable, indeed.

****

Marcus let out a groan. Damn, his head hurt! What the devil had happened? Where was she?

Gradually, it came back to him. *Penny! I was trying to find Penny!* Withersby had brought him to this place where she was supposedly tied up.

He got slowly to his feet, groaning as his head throbbed even more fiercely. Feeling the back of it, his hand came away damp with blood. Damn! How could he have been so foolish as to let Withersby get the best of him?

Ahead was the room where Penny supposedly was. The door was ajar. He pushed it all the way open. Enough light came through the broken window for him to make out a narrow bed, a table with an empty gin flask and a chair. He went to the chair. Discarded on the floor beside it were some strips of fabric. Marcus bent to pick one up, despite the piercing pain in his head. It looked as if it had been gnawed through by rats. The other pieces, when he examined them, were intact. He felt around on the floor. Halfway under the bed, he found a small button, probably from a woman's glove.

Marcus straightened. It did appear Penny had been here, but now she was gone. Had Withersby set her free, or simply taken her somewhere else? It seemed unlikely he would release her. She was the only bargaining chip he had. He would hang onto her and try to get more money.

In some way, knowing Penny had been tied up was a relief. That meant she hadn't been part of this. The cold farewell note she'd written him had been coerced. If he could find her and set her free, they might still have a life together. But only if he could get her away from her deranged cousin before he killed her.

Goaded by that thought, he left the room and started down the stairs. On the way he suffered a bout of dizziness and had to lean against the wall until it passed. Finally, he made it outside. Squinting into the fading twilight, he saw the coach was gone. He reached into his pocket. The pistol was also missing. Curse the bastard!

Now what should he do? He was alone in east London without a vehicle, a weapon or…Marcus felt in his pocket for his tasseled coin pouch. It was also missing. He had no money either.

He could walk until he found a hansom. But with his aching head and churning stomach, it sounded like a formidable prospect. Yet, there was no help for it. He couldn't stay here.

He started walking, trying not to appear too unsteady. He'd made it a short distance when footsteps approached behind him. Someone was following him. Or several someones. He whirled around and knew a vague relief when he realized he was being pursued by a group of children—four hollow-eyed, raggedy children.

"Evenin' guvnor," called out the largest one. "Out for a stroll, are ye?"

The way the four were eyeing him made Marcus nervous. But surely he had nothing to be afraid of. The eldest one couldn't be more than ten. And he might be able to get some information from them. He was fairly certain he'd seen them on the street when he and Withersby arrived.

"I'm not exactly out for a stroll. Indeed, I was attacked and robbed." He gave the eldest one a hard look. "I'm afraid I have nothing left to for you to steal."

"There's your cufflinks." The boy motioned with his head. "And your fine coat."

"Ah, but even the four of you would have a hard time taking those things from me. Perhaps we could work out some sort of barter instead."

"What sort of barter?"

Marcus crossed his arms over his chest and struck an aggressive pose, even though his head was spinning. "You provide me with information and I'll think about parting with some of my belongings."

"What sort of information?"

Marcus jerked his head toward the dilapidated structure he'd just left. "Did you see a man and a woman around here?" Thinking he should elaborate, he added. "The man would be slender with sandy hair and carrying a heavy valise. The woman is tall and slender and very pretty."

"Aye, I seen 'em. But not together. The mort you're talkin' about left earlier today. The cove didn't leave until a short while ago."

"How long ago would you say the woman left?"

The boy shrugged. Then he turned back to his companions. "'Twas still fair light, it was."

Marcus struggled to process this information. Penny hadn't left with Withersby. Did that mean she'd escaped? But if she had, where she was she now? "Which direction did the woman go?" he asked.

"She set off toward the city."

"Walking?"

"Aye. What else would she be doin'?"

"Thank you. That's exactly what I needed to know."

As the urchin stared at him expectantly, Marcus removed one of his cufflinks and held it out.

The boy seized it. "What about the other one?"

"To earn that one, you'll have tell me a bit more." As the boy glared at him, he added. "I arrived in a rig, driven by a tall, fair-haired footman. Did the man with the valise do something to force the footman to drive off?"

The boy nodded. "He pulled a pistol and aimed it at the tall bloke. He got back in the driver's seat and started to drive off before the other man was all the way in the vehicle. The cove was cursing and carrying on!" He gave a delighted laugh.

"But the other man did get in and they drove away?"

The boy nodded and held out his hand. Marcus took off his other cufflink and handed it over. The boy examined the ivory and gold object with satisfaction and stuck it in his pocket.

"I believe you still covet my coat," said Marcus. "I'm afraid the price for it is a bit higher. Since my rig was stolen, I find myself stranded here. If you can find someone to convey me into the city, the coat is yours."

The boy gave him a dubious look before consulting with his companions. After some hushed whispering, he turned back to Marcus. "We might be able to find someone to help you, but they'll want to know what you'll pay *them*."

"If they can convey me to my home, I'll pay them there."

The boy nodded, then jerked his head toward one of his companions. The young child—who looked to be no more than six, dashed off. "Freddie will fetch Mr. Green," the boy asserted.

While they waited, Marcus decided to find out a bit more about the little band. If nothing else, it would help distract him from his body's distress. "How old are you?" he asked the boy.

The urchin frowned. "Don't know for certain. Thirteen, I think."

Marcus was shocked. The boy seemed far too small and undeveloped to be thirteen. But that age would fit better with the boy's bold, confident manner than the eight or nine-years-old he looked. "What about the rest of you?" Marcus asked.

The other two gave their ages as eight and ten. As the smallest one stepped forward and spoke, Marcus realized it was a little girl. Her dirty rags were just barely discernable as having once been a dress. Marcus felt a sudden stir of pity for these children. Although he didn't doubt for a moment they'd have robbed him of everything he possessed if they thought they could get away with it, he found he couldn't really blame them. They obviously had to steal to survive.

"Don't any of you have parents or other relatives to

look after you?"

The older boy shrugged. "I'm an orphan. So's he." He motioned to the other boy.

The little girl spoke up, "I was staying with my uncle 'til he started doin' nasty things to me." She grimaced.

The oldest boy suddenly looked wary. Taking a step back, he said, "If you was thinkin' of tryin' to snare us and cart us off the workhouse, you'd best think again. We can take care of ourselves, we can."

"I'm certain you can," Marcus agreed, dryly.

The little girl nodded vigorously. "If we can't get food, it's only a penny for a noggin."

"What's that?" asked Marcus.

The girl shrugged. "Some calls it 'ruin,' but it keeps your belly from grumbling."

"Ruin?" asked Marcus. "You mean gin?"

When she nodded, Marcus repressed a shudder. No wonder these children were so small, if they were regularly drinking spirits, and of the cheapest, basest sort. They were lucky they hadn't stumbled onto a bad batch and ended up blind or had their wits permanently damaged.

He questioned them some more, eventually learning their names. The oldest boy was Robin, his brother was Timmy and the girl was known as Fancy. Despite their assertion they could take care of themselves, he felt the urge to try to rescue them from their wretched circumstances. If Penny were here, he felt certain she would feel the same.

A short while later, Marcus spied a light moving toward them. Eventually he saw it was a lantern affixed to some sort of vehicle. The vehicle came in view—a rickety wagon drawn by a mule.

"Your carriage, guvnor," said Robin, chuckling.

Marcus repressed a sigh. In this rig, it would likely take him half the night to get back to the townhouse. Even so, it was better than walking. Was that what Penny had done? At the thought of her making her way alone through this part of London, his stomach squeezed with apprehension.

Robin broke into his troubled thoughts. "I'll have your coat now, guvnor. You made a bargain, you did."

Marcus took off his coat and handed it to Robin. "I'm not sure why you want this. It'll take you years to grow into it."

Robin grinned, his small teeth gleaming in the lantern light. "I ain't gonna wear it guvnor, but sell it."

"See that you buy some food then. For all of you." Marcus nodded to the other children. "Some decent food, too. No gin."

"Of course, guvnor. Whatever you say," Robin responded.

Giving up all pretense of dignity, Marcus climbed into the back of the wagon and lay down. The sparse straw smelled of dung, but that didn't worry him as much as thoughts of Penny. Finally, he succumbed to the lulling motion of the cart and the swirling dizziness in his head and slept.

The driver "Mr. Green" woke him when they'd reached the West End. Marcus sat up and gave him directions to the townhouse. He guessed it was well past midnight when they reached his dwelling. There were no lights visible in any of the windows. After reassuring Mr. Green that he would be paid, Marcus walked stiffly to the door and knocked. He had to do so for quite awhile before a disheveled-looking Mr. Bowes, a candle in hand, opened the door.

The butler let out a gasp when he saw Marcus, then threw open the door. "My sincere apologies, sir, we thought you were staying at Mr. Ludingham's."

"Don't worry about it, Bowes." Marcus entered. "But if you would be so good as to fetch some money from the box for household expenses and pay the man." He gestured toward the door.

Bowes approached the door and looked out. After giving Marcus a stunned look, he said, "Very good, sir. I'll be right back. Then we can attend to you." He hurried off.

Marcus sat on the chair in the foyer and sought to gather his wits. Although his body was desperate for sleep, his restless mind whirled with thoughts of Penny. Where was she? Had she ever made it back to the city?

Despite his worry for her, a part of him felt relief. If Adrian had truly been holding Penny hostage, the note she'd sent him had been coerced. She might still be willing to marry him!

The thought filled him with a wild excitement, but he reminded himself he still had to find her. The horrible dread that something might have happened to her after she escaped wouldn't leave him.

Bowes returned. "I've paid the man, sir. He asked if he could bed down in the cart for a while and I said that would be acceptable, as long as he left by daylight. I can't think the neighbors would care to find him here."

"Probably not," Marcus agreed. Although he knew it would be futile, he had to ask. "I don't suppose there's any chance Miss Montgomery came back?"

"I'm afraid not, sir." Bowes's voice was gentle as he added, "Now, sir, I think we'd best get you up to bed."

"No, Bowes. I'm not going to bed. I need to send Jeremy—" Marcus broke off, suddenly remembering what else Robin had told him. "What about Jeremy? Did he ever come back with the carriage?"

"No, sir, he didn't. That's part of the reason we didn't think you'd be home either."

Where was Jeremy? Had Withersby done something to him, too? *Dash it, all I need is another person to worry about!*

"If Jeremy's not here, you'll have to wake Will and send him," he told Bowes.

"Send him where, sir?"

"To fetch James. I'll need his assistance."

"Tonight, sir?"

"Yes. This is something that can't wait until morning."

"Certainly, sir. But perhaps you could meet with him in your dressing gown." Bowes gestured toward Marcus's disheveled clothing. Whips of hay clung to his garments.

"I should probably change clothes and fetch a jacket and some cufflinks, but I can't get ready to retire yet. As soon as James arrives, I plan on going out."

"Very well, sir. I'll send Will after Mr. Ludingham, then meet you upstairs in the bedchamber. Here's a candle, sir."

Marcus rose wearily and started up the stairs. As he passed Penny's bedchamber, he couldn't resist going inside. He glanced around the room, then paused and closed his eyes and inhaled. He could still smell her warm womanly scent. The effect on him was as profound as ever. A yearning built up inside him, keen as a knife blade. He had to find her and convince her to marry him. He had to.

He left the room and went down the hall to his bedchamber.

He'd barely had a chance to pull off his soiled clothing when Bowes gave his discreet knock at the door. "Come in," Marcus called.

A short while later, once again properly attired, he went down to the library to wait for James.

He turned down Bowes's offer of a brandy, feeling certain it would put him to sleep. "But I wouldn't mind having something to eat. No, on second thought, I'll fetch it myself," he added as Bowes started to leave.

"Sir?" Bowes gazed at him in surprise.

"I can't sit here, I'll fall asleep." Marcus grabbed up a candle and left the library.

While Bowes watched in scandalized silence, Marcus raided the larder. After some searching, he located a chunk of cheese and some bread.

"I could make that for you," offered Bowes.

"I think I can manage to cut a piece of bread. You'd best go wait for James to arrive."

"Very good, sir."

After a few bites of the bread and cheese, Marcus felt much better. His head still ached, but the rest of him was somewhat revived.

He'd just finishing eating when James entered. "You'd better have a damned good reason for calling me over here this time of night!" his friend exclaimed.

After swallowing, Marcus responded, "I do. It seems you were wrong about Penny. But not

Withersby. The man's a cunning little wretch."

He told James what had happened.

"Gads, Marcus! You might have been killed! What if you'd fallen down the stairs and broken your neck?"

"Fortunately, I didn't. When I first woke I wondered about that. I was surprised Withersby didn't finish me off. But I think he was too distracted when he discovered Penny was missing to worry about me."

"What do you mean, Penny was missing?"

Marcus told him the rest of the tale, of how the children had seen Penny fleeing before he and Withersby had arrived. "Clearly, Withersby was holding Penny prisoner there. I found the button from her glove and bits of cloth he used to tie her up with. I don't know exactly how she got free, but somehow she did. Which means..." He gave his friend a smug look. "The note Penny sent me was coerced. Withersby abducted her and forced her to write me the note telling me she couldn't marry me. All your suspicions about Penny were wrong. She was, and is, an innocent victim."

"You called me here in the middle of the night to tell me this?" James snapped.

"No, of course not." Marcus gestured, his agitation growing. "The thing is, I'm worried for Penny. She may have gotten away from Withersby, but where is she? The area she was being held in is quite unsavory, and a long way from here. I was able to barter my way back to London proper. But Penny might not have been so fortunate."

"Why do you think that?"

"If she was safe, wouldn't she have come here? Or gone to your house? I find the fact that neither of us has heard from her quite distressing."

"What do you propose to do?"

"Go back to the East End and ask questions. I got all my information from a band of children who live near the house. If we talk to people who live further west, we might find someone who's seen her."

"And you propose to do that now? It's three hours after midnight, Marcus. The nefarious sorts that lurk on the street at this time of night aren't likely to be any help to us."

Marcus had to admit there was something to what James said. They probably would have to wait until morning to look for Penny. He began to pace. "I hate not knowing. I know it sounds as if I lost my wits, but right now I can't think of anything but Penny. I had all that time with her and I never told her what I feel for her. Now I might never have the chance. Now that I realize how much I love her, it will be too late and I'll have lost her forever."

James approached him and took his arm. To Marcus's surprise he no longer looked angry, but almost pitying. "I didn't want to tell you this, Marcus. I really didn't. Not only because Lily made me swear not to, but also because I hoped you'd discover the truth on your own."

"The truth? What does that mean?"

"The thing is…" James sighed. "There's no easy way to say this. Lily has seen Penny since she left your townhouse two days ago. Indeed, she was with Penny when she wrote the note saying she couldn't marry you."

Marcus jerked back. "I don't believe you."

"Lily has no reason to lie. And believe me, it

wasn't easy getting her to tell me this."

"But it's still possible Penny was under coercion when she wrote the note. Withersby might have threatened her with harm if she didn't do so."

"I'm afraid it doesn't sound like that's the way it was. I'm sorry, Marcus. I'm sure it would be much easier for you if Penny wasn't part of Withersby's scheme."

Marcus faced James defiantly. "Part of Withersby's scheme? What are you talking about? It's clear he was holding her captive!"

"Is it? You said you found some pieces of cloth. Does that really mean she was tied up? Couldn't the strips of cloth have been used for something else?"

"What about what Robin told me—that they saw Penny leave the house hours before I arrived with Withersby? Clearly, she was running away!"

"Isn't it just as likely she was leaving because she'd fulfilled her part in the plan?"

Marcus walked to the settee and sat down. Dash this awful headache! He couldn't think clearly. Somehow he had to make James understand that Penny despised her cousin and would never intentionally collaborate with him.

But was that true, or was it simply what he wanted to believe?

When he looked up, James was gazing at him sympathetically. "Maybe I'm wrong, Marcus. At least about her plotting with Withersby. But I do think she left here of her own accord. I also think there's nothing you can do tonight. You're obviously half dead on your feet. And since you blacked out, you probably aren't thinking very clearly. Penny was last seen hours ago.

How do you propose to pick up her trail now, when everyone you might ask is undoubtedly asleep?

Marcus nodded slowly. James had a point...or several points. In his current condition, Marcus was no use to anyone. "Very well," he said, "I'll go to bed."

****

Penny woke to the sun shining into her room. *I'm home! I'm safe!*

Rising from the bed, she started to dress. She could hardly believe she'd slept so late. But the mail coach hadn't arrived at the station in Harting until late in the evening. Thank heavens she'd known the innkeeper Mr. Boggs for years. He'd had no problem paying her fare and then having his son take her to Horngate.

She smiled to herself as she recalled greeting Mrs. Foxworthy. The housekeeper had impulsively embraced her, then scolded her about the lateness of the hour and her disheveled appearance. But when the housekeeper learned what happened with Adrian, she immediately fetched Mr. Foxworthy. They locked all the doors, and Mr. Foxworthy had vowed to sit watch throughout the night with his hunting gun on his lap.

By now the whole staff knew about Adrian. She'd be well-protected, if a bit of a prisoner. As much as she wanted to go out to the stables to see the horses, she'd have to wait until someone could go with her. Despite the bright sunshine coming in through the window, it seemed as if a dark cloud hovered overhead. Part of it was her fear of Adrian, but adding to it was her sorrow over leaving Marcus.

She'd tried to avoid thinking about him, but could not. What had he done when he got Adrian's ransom note? He'd probably been furious, absolutely outraged at the idea he should pay a ransom for a woman who'd treated him so coldly. He might even believe she was part of Adrian's scheme.

The thought made her sick inside. Penny hated to think he would imagine she was as ruthless and mercenary as her cousin. But it was probably better if he did believe that. Then Adrian couldn't manipulate him and extort money from him. If Adrian believed Marcus wanted nothing to do with her, he'd finally leave Marcus alone and he'd be safe.

What would her cousin do when he realized his plan wouldn't work? If only he would give up his scheming and accept his situation. Marcus would never want to marry her now, which meant she could stay here and run the horse operation. It was fairly prosperous. There should be enough money to give Adrian a decent living. If he didn't gamble it all away.

A futile hope. Adrian would never change. And as long as he was around, she'd never be free to reveal her feelings to Marcus. Not that there was any chance he still felt anything for her.

She swallowed to dislodge the lump in her throat. There was no point grieving over what might have been. She had to go on from here and be happy she was alive and safe. And she still had Horngate. After breakfast, she'd get Mr. Foxworthy to accompany her to the barn. She so wanted to see Tad and the other stablemen. And the horses. Ah, the horses.

****

"It's so good to have you home, miss. Even if the circumstances aren't what we might hope. Do you think your cousin will follow you here?"

"I don't know, Mr. Foxworthy," Penny responded

as they followed the well-worn path from the house to the barn. "Once he realizes that Mar…that Mr. Revington won't pay the ransom, maybe he'll give up. I was a bit overwrought last night. I'm probably not actually in that much danger from my cousin."

"Well, we can't take any chances. I'll make certain everyone knows you must never be alone when you're away from the house."

Penny's heartbeat quickened as they approached the barn. There was nothing like the familiar smell of hay and horses. Inside the barn, Tad was dragging a sack of oats to the main feed bin.

Seeing her, his eyes lit up; he let go of the sack.. "Penny! That is, Miss Montgomery!" He gave Mr. Foxworthy a sheepish look.

"Hello, Tad. It's wonderful to see you."

"And you, too…miss. You look different."

"So do you, Tad." And he did. He seemed taller and more filled out. Was it possible he'd changed so much in less than a month?

"Where's everyone else?" Mr. Foxworthy asked.

"Out in the training pens." Tad motioned with his head. "We're working with Echo's new colt."

"A colt? Oh, I can't wait to see him!" exclaimed Penny.

"Looks just like Hero, he does. Born about a week ago. Everything went well and Echo's a great mum."

"I have to see him," said Penny. "And Hero, too."

"I'll take her down, Mr. Foxworthy," said Tad.

The estate manager frowned, the weathered lines around his eyes creasing. "Maybe I should go along."

"Oh, you have enough to do, Mr. Foxworthy," Penny reassured him. "I'm certain we'll be fine."

"Very well, but keep an eye out at all times," Mr. Foxworthy warned Tad and then started back to the house.

"You don't have to worry about your worthless cousin," said Tad. "He's a lily-livered coward. He'd never dare mix it up with me."

Penny nodded. Now that she was back at Horngate, what Adrian had said and done in London seemed like a bad dream. She'd been alone and vulnerable then. Here Adrian would know everyone was looking out for her.

"What about Revington?" Tad asked as they started walking to the horse pens. "Aren't you worried he'll show up and drag you back to London and make you marry him?"

Oh, if only he would! "I'm quite certain that won't happen."

"Why not?" asked Tad. "I thought he was desperate to get his hands on this place."

"It's complicated. But basically, I suspect he thinks Horngate is no longer worth the trouble."

"See? You did it!" Tad gave her shoulder a playful punch. "The top-lofty swell shouldn't have messed with the likes of you!"

Penny gave the young groom a forced smile. There was no point telling him that Marcus wasn't a "top-lofty swell" and she wasn't at all happy with the way things turned out.

"Wait till you see the little colt," Tad went on. "We named him Raven, 'cause he's nearly all black. Only a hint of white on his forehead. Oh, and Belle foaled, too. Nice little chestnut filly."

"She did? Oh, I can't wait to see them both!"

"They're all the way down in the far pen. And I

have a surprise for you." His brown eyes gleamed with excitement. "I've got Hero all saddled and ready for you."

"Truly!" Penny exclaimed.

Tad nodded, then motioned. "We could cut through the trees. That would be faster."

As they started into the woods, Penny said, "I wasn't certain I dare go riding. But if you've got Hero saddled, I simply can't resist."

"Why did you think you couldn't go riding?"

Penny made a face. "Because of Adrian. I worried he might follow me here. It might not be safe."

Tad made a sound of disgust. "Really, Penny. You should have more faith in me...and yourself. I'd vow even you could get the best of that weak, puny fellow."

Penny nodded. She'd never been afraid of Adrian before. But recalling the look on his face when he threatened to throw her out the window, she wasn't entirely reassured by Tad's words.

As they walked through the trees, Tad filled her in on everything that had happened over the past month. Penny found herself half-listening. She should be thrilled to be home. As Tad had said, this was exactly what she wanted. So, why did she feel this deep sense of loss? This emptiness? As awful as it was to contemplate, she didn't think she would ever be happy again without Marcus in her life.

She struggled against the tide of grief sweeping over her, telling herself she must be grateful for what she did have, not mourn over what might have been. But it was a battle. And it would continue to be a battle, for far longer than she dare think about.

She was so caught up in her thoughts that when

Tad grabbed her arm, she thought he was trying to keep her from tripping. Then he cursed.

Adrian stood on the pathway ahead of them, a pistol in his hand.

Chapter Twenty-Three

Marcus pushed his plate away and sat back. Behind him, Bowes, who was serving as footman this morning, said, "You've scarce touched your breakfast, sir. Is there anything else I could fetch you from the kitchen?"

"No thank you. I'm not hungry."

"Very good, sir," Bowes responded, sounding disappointed.

Marcus repressed a sigh. He wondered if he'd ever have a taste for food again. Or, for anything else. He felt so dashed empty inside...

He rose abruptly, seeking to shake off the mood. "Still no sign of Jeremy?"

"No, sir. Nor the coach either."

Marcus nodded. He could spend the day searching London for his missing footman and coach.

"Send Will for a hansom, Bowes. I'm going to James's."

On the way to James's townhouse, Marcus sought to focus on Jeremy and the missing coach. He wasn't certain where to begin looking. Maybe he should go back to the gaming hell and see if there'd been any sign of Withersby there.

When he arrived at James's townhouse, Vincent took him to the library. Marcus paced back and forth impatiently.

At last, James appeared. "You're an inconsiderate

bastard these days, Marcus. First, you wake me in the middle of the night. Then you appear here at this ungodly hour. I thought I'd convinced you to forget about searching for Penny."

"You did. But there's still the matter of my missing footman and rig. Not to mention my money. I'm rather disinclined to let Withersby steal from me with no repercussions. There was only a few hundred pounds in the valise, but I'd still like to get it back and see Withersby punished."

"My advice, which I've given you repeatedly, is to hire a runner. Have someone trained in dealing with this sort of thing search out Withersby and bring him to justice."

"By the time I hire someone, more time will have passed and the trail will have gone cold." Marcus held out his hands beseechingly. "I'm not asking you to do anything yourself, James. Just lend me your rig so I don't have to hire a hansom to take me all over the city. Besides, driving will ease my nerves. By the time I find Withersby, I hope to be calm enough not to murder him with my bare hands."

James sighed. "Very well. I'll have Vincent get Billy to fetch the tilbury from the stables. In the meantime, sit. Your pacing is giving me a megrim!"

Marcus took a seat on the settle. James sat across from him. "It's not that I don't sympathize with you, Marcus. I know you care for Penny. and this is a hard blow."

"I'm afraid it went far beyond caring for her. I am in *love* with her. Indeed, the very day she left, I was going to come to you and admit I'd lost the bet, that I was well and truly smitten."

"Look at it this way, Marcus. At least you found out the truth about Penny before the two of you got married."

Marcus sprang to his feet, unable to endure James's dark implications any longer. "The truth about Penny? What is the truth? We don't *know* she was part of Withersby's plot. There's no logical reason for her to help him. What did she have to gain? A bit of money? I never observed that Penny had much interest in money. Besides, she has the income from Horngate, which looks to be substantial. The only reason she would have for cooperating with Adrian was if he'd promised her she could go back to Horngate and resume her life as it was before."

Marcus froze, wondering if he'd finally hit on it. Was Penny's love for Horngate and the horse operation enough to make her go along with Adrian's scheme? It might be, he realized. But if that was the case, she'd gone to a lot of trouble for nothing. Once they were wed, he'd planned to live at Horngate and allow her to do whatever she wished with her beloved horses anyway.

What if he told her he didn't want to take control of Horngate? That all he desired was to share her life. To be near her...

He took a deep breath, realizing how far gone he was. Even if Penny was involved in Adrian's scheme, he didn't care. He loved her and wanted her for his wife. Somehow he had find her and tell her these things.

But where could she be? All at once, he realized the answer was staring him in the face. She'd gone to Horngate.

"I hope your footman hurries with the carriage," he told James. "I've got things to do."

****

Penny stared at her cousin, her heart pounding. "Adrian. What are you doing here?"

"Revington only paid me a small portion of the money. I intend to get the rest. And to do that, I need you to come back to London with me."

"Marcus paid you?" A part of Penny leaped with joy. If Marcus had paid Adrian, he must still care for her, at least a little.

"A few hundred quid, is all. Now I'm going to insist he come up with the full amount."

"If he pays it, what will you do with me?"

Adrian motioned dismissingly. "Oh, you'll be free to go off and do whatever you wish. You'll be of no use to me then."

"Don't listen to him!" broke in Tad. "You can't trust anything he says!"

"Shut up!" Adrian gripped the pistol with both hands and pointed it at Tad.

Penny fought a wave of dread. Adrian was clearly desperate and more than a bit unhinged. Tad was right. She couldn't trust this man. He'd threatened to kill her, and there was every reason to believe that as soon as he'd gotten what he wanted from her, he'd follow through on his threat. She had to get away from him…and keep him from hurting Tad.

She shot a glance at Tad, willing him to understand what she was planning. Then she turned back to Adrian. "All right, I'll go with you. As long as you don't hurt Tad or anyone else at Horngate."

"No, Penny, please," Tad pleaded.

She gave him another look. This time, he seemed to grasp her intent.

"That's better," said Adrian. "Now, we'll all start walking. This way." He motioned with the gun. "I've got the rig stashed in the woods."

Penny didn't move. "You have to let Tad leave, or I won't go with you."

"I'll let him go once we're safely away from here. I don't want him running off and fetching old Foxworthy or any of the others." Again, Adrian motioned with the gun.

Seeing she had no choice, Penny headed for the trees with Tad beside her. She could feel his tension and fear. She didn't blame him. Adrian had always disliked Tad.

If Tad weren't here, she'd have taken her chances and set off running. She doubted Adrian was a good shot, and he might hesitate a moment or two, aware she was his only hope of getting more money from Marcus. But with Tad involved, she couldn't risk bolting.

In a clearing in the forest stood a carriage with two horses hitched to it. As they drew closer, Penny realized it was Marcus's phaeton—with someone sprawled across the back seat. She raced to the vehicle, dreading what she would find. It wasn't Marcus lying there but Jeremy. Thankfully, the footman was alive, although bound and gagged. "Dear heavens! What have you done to him?"

"I figured with him at the ribbons we'd make better time," Adrian answered. "We can have him drive back as well. With a pistol in his back, I imagine he'll do a fine job."

"But the poor horses!" Penny gazed in horror at the

team. They were both covered in dried sweat and their heads drooped as if they could scarce go on. "You have to let them rest. If you force them on now, you might kill them." Then, knowing Adrian wouldn't care about the animals, she added, "If one of them goes down on the road, we could end up stranded miles from London. I doubt you could explain this to any passerby who might aid us."

"You're exaggerating," retorted Adrian. "You always did coddle your horses. The team's had a chance to rest. We'll drive them into the brook and let them have a drink and then they'll be ready to go. If they're not, I'll take the whip to them myself."

Penny shuddered. She couldn't let Adrian kill these poor animals. She confronted him, as furious and determined as she'd ever been in her life. "I mean it, Adrian. I won't go with you unless you get a fresh team. I don't care what you do to me, but I won't let you treat two animals so brutally. We don't even have to go back to the barn. There are several horses in the pasture near here. We'll go and get two of them and Tad will harness them."

Adrian stared at her. "You're utterly daft, aren't you? You really do care more for those bloody horses than for your own life."

Penny crossed her arms over her chest. "It may be daft, but that's the way I am. I can't bear to see animals suffer. At least if you shoot me, I'll have a quick and easy death."

Adrian stared at her a while longer, then said, "We'll probably make faster time with fresh horses. But you and I and Tad will all go together to fetch the horses. And remember, I'll have the pistol at the ready every second."

They made their way through the peaceful oak and ash forest until the horse pen came in view. Several horses stood in the far corner, while Hero, saddled and ready for Penny to ride, was tied to the fence by the gate. The sight of the stallion filled Penny with determination. She wasn't about to lose everything she'd worked so hard for.

"Stay here," Adrian ordered when Penny went to greet Hero. "You." Adrian motioned to Tad with the pistol. "Get the horses. Hurry up."

"I can't lead two animals back to the carriage by myself," Tad protested. "I'll have to have help."

Adrian looked at Penny, his eyes narrowed. "Go on. Get one of the horses. And don't do anything foolish. I'll have the gun aimed at your little friend the whole time."

"I'll open the gate," said Tad.

Penny followed. As she helped him swing the gate open, their eyes met. Gone was the fear Tad had exhibited earlier. Now his expression was angry and determined. Penny gave him the slightest of nods in return. She knew what he was thinking. They must wait for the right moment and then take off.

Tad took a halter from the tack hanging on the fence and approached one of the geldings, while Penny grabbed another halter and headed toward one of the mares, a bay named Whisper. The mare was a little smaller and Penny knew she'd have to get onto the animal's back quickly, as soon as they were out of the pen.

Since she hadn't worked with the mare for several weeks, it took a while to get the halter on, and she could tell Tad was waiting, fumbling a bit with the halter so they could get out of the gate at about the same time. She guessed that once they were outside, he meant to take off.

"What's taking so long?" Adrian called.

"We're coming," she responded. Finally, she got the halter on and they led the animals toward the gate, moving leisurely.

"Hurry up!" cried Adrian.

As soon as they were both through the gate, Penny turned to Adrian. "This isn't easy to do. It'll take some time to lead them through the woods."

"You'd better make it easy. I'm not waiting forever," Adrian said.

While Adrian was turned away, Tad used the stepping block to leap onto on Shadow's back and take off. Adrian whirled and gave a cry of rage. "Stop!" he cried, waving the pistol. Penny used the gate to climb on Whisper's back. The nervous horse sprang forward with Penny clinging to the animal's mane. Behind her, Adrian fired a shot and then another.

Once they were out of sight of the pen, Penny sought to slow the racing animal. But the gunshots had spooked the mare and they galloped on. Penny bent low over the horse's withers, struggling to keep her balance. When she finally looked up, she saw they were headed for the woods. A tree with low-hanging branches loomed straight ahead. The horse swerved and Penny felt herself fall.

****

Marcus's stomach churned with foreboding as he drove the tilbury through the stone pillars marking the entrance to Horngate. On one hand he longed to see

Penny again. On the other, he was filled with dread at the thought that James's assessment of her might be true. But he couldn't believe it. She cared for him, at least a little. If he promised she wouldn't lose her freedom or her control of Horngate if she married him, surely she would consider it.

As for everything else, he truly didn't care. Even if she'd conspired with Withersby to develop this whole ransom plot, it didn't matter. So he'd lost a few hundred pounds; Penny was worth that, and more...much more.

He couldn't blame Penny for trying to hold onto Horngate so fiercely, he thought as continued down the gravel drive, lined with lush oak trees. Now that it was summer, the estate was truly beautiful. He could easily imagine living here year-round and only occasionally going to London.

As the uneasiness built inside him, he wondered if he ever wanted anything as badly as he did Penny. He'd long ago stopped being nervous when he was playing for stakes. But this was a gamble of another sort and he wasn't certain what he would do if he lost. The idea of living without Penny filled him with a horrifying emptiness.

He drove the tilbury around the circle drive and pulled the team to a halt in front of the house. Tying the reins to the seat, he climbed out. He was surprised no one had come out to greet him. It looked as if he'd have to knock.

He raised the heavy knocker and rapped twice. The housekeeper he recalled from his first visit came to the door. Her blue eyes fixed on him with what could only be called suspicion. "May I help you?" she asked.

"I'm looking for Miss Montgomery. Is she here?"

The woman regarded him intently, then stepped back to let him enter. "I recognize you now. Thank heavens. I thought you might be someone sent by Miss Montgomery's wretched cousin."

"I'm familiar with the man," said Marcus. "Is Miss Montgomery expecting him?"

The woman nodded. "We're all on alert here. We fear he might come and...do something to the mistress."

If Penny is afraid of Withersby, that means they weren't working together. But if she is afraid, then Adrian had truly kidnapped her, the villain!

"Is she here in the house, then?"

"No, I believe she went out to the barn. My husband, Mr. Foxworthy, is with her, of course."

Mrs. Foxworthy looked to be about fifty. If her husband was near her age, Marcus wasn't certain he'd be much protection for Penny.

"Thank you. I'll check there." Marcus hurried to the barn. He was probably being foolish, but now that he knew Penny was in danger from Withersby, he had to make certain she was safe. In the barn, he encountered an older man. "I'm looking for Penny...Miss Montgomery," he explained.

The man regarded Marcus suspiciously. "And who might you be?"

"I'm Marcus Revington. Penny's been staying with me in London. We were to be wed."

The man's grim manner failed to relent. "Aye. I've heard about the matter. Withersby arranged the match, didn't he?"

"Yes, but..." What could he say? That despite the way things had begun, Penny and he had come to care about each other? He didn't know that was true, except from his own standpoint. "I have no connection with Withersby now. Indeed, I'm here because I'm concerned for Penny. In London, Withersby kidnapped her. She apparently got away, but I'm worried Withersby might have followed her here. Where is she? I understand Mr. Foxworthy is with her."

"That would be me," the man responded. He shook his head. "I'm afraid she's gone off with Tad. I was dubious, but she assured me they'd be fine."

"Gone off? Where the devil are they?" Marcus felt his panic growing. Having encountered Tad, he had little confidence the youthful groom could protect her, even from puny Withersby. "Withersby has a gun," he told Mr. Foxworthy. "And I'm not certain he wouldn't use it."

Mr. Foxworthy looked alarmed. "But that means..." His frown deepened. "I heard gunshots a while ago. I thought it was someone hunting."

Marcus stared at Mr. Foxworthy. "Where have they gone? Where?"

Mr. Foxworthy pointed, and Marcus took off running.

He was poorly attired for such physical exertion. After a few paces, he yanked his cravat loose, then stopped to pull off his coat. He carried it for a while, then threw it to the ground. He had to find Penny!

He halted as he saw a rider. When the horse drew near, he realized it was Tad. "Hullo! Stop!" he cried.

With effort, the youth halted the horse a few paces past Marcus. Marcus rushed over. "It's Adrian!" Tad gasped. He gestured wildly.

Marcus's insides clenched with dread. "Does he

have Penny?"

Tad shook his head. "I think she got away, but he is pursuing her."

"Give me your mount!" cried Marcus.

"Can you ride bareback? Without a bridle and bit, it's damned hard to control a horse."

Marcus gestured frantically toward the barn. "Go and fetch a bridle then. And hurry."

Tad returned with a bridle and rapidly exchanged it for the halter. As soon as he'd gotten it on, Marcus said, "Here now, give me a leg up." Once astride, Marcus called, "Which way?"

Tad gestured.

Marcus took off, his heart in his throat. What if he was too late? What if Withersby had already... No, he couldn't think like that. Withersby needed Penny as a means of bleeding more money from him. He wouldn't kill her.

He finally reached the training pens. His fear sharpened when he saw Hero, riderless, his reins trailing. He rode up to the stallion and demanded, "Where is she? Where is she?"

The horse whickered and seemed to shake his head.

Marcus wheeled his mount and frantically surveyed the landscape. There was no sign of Penny, or Withersby either. Not knowing what else to do, he guided the horse into the woods. They had gone a short distance when he heard a horse whinny. He urged his own mount faster.

At the edge of the trees he saw his phaeton and team. There was no sign of Penny, but someone was lying across the seat of the vehicle.

"Jeremy!" he called as he rode nearer. Quickly

dismounting, he fastened the reins to the back of the carriage, drew his knife, and cut the cloth covering the footman's mouth.

"By God, sir," Jeremy choked out. "I'm very glad to see you."

"What happened, Jeremy? Where's Penny?"

"Last I saw her, she was with Withersby and the young groom."

Marcus cut his bonds.

"They were going to get fresh animals and head back to London. But they never came back."

"Tad was with her?"

"Yes, sir."

Having freed Jeremy, Marcus stepped back. "I just saw him. That must mean Withersby has Penny." But if he *had* caught her, why hadn't he brought her back to the carriage? Marcus's blood ran cold as he contemplated Withersby's state of mind. The bastard was so deranged, so desperate, there was no telling what he might do.

"I'm going to look for her," he told Jeremy.

"I'll hunt for her on foot," Jeremy responded. "The walk will do me good. Help get the cramps out of my legs." He climbed gingerly out of the carriage, wincing as he stood, then shook out his legs. "What direction should I go?"

"Unfortunately, I have no idea." Maybe he should go back for Tad. But he didn't want to take the time. "Look in the woods, I guess. Maybe he's hiding somewhere."

Jeremy nodded and helped Marcus onto his mount. The two men set off in different directions. Jeremy went into the woods while Marcus circled back to the training pens.

A short while later, Jeremy called out. Heart in his throat, Marcus rode that direction. The vegetation quickly became thick and low-hanging, forcing him to dismount and lead the horse.

Finally, through the trees, he spied Jeremy. The groom was leaning over something…a body. Marcus dropped the reins and drew near, afraid of what he might see. He let out a sigh of relief as he realized the body was Withersby's.

Jeremy turned as he approached. "His neck's broken and there are hoof-prints all around. He must have ridden in here and got knocked off by a low-hanging branch."

"It's no worse than he deserved," said Marcus.

There was a rustling of branches, and Penny stepped out from the bushes. There were leaves in her hair and grass on her clothing.

"Penny!" Marcus exclaimed. "Are you all right?"

She nodded and went over to where Withersby lay. "Hero always did despise him."

"What happened, Penny?" Marcus asked. "Are you certain you're not hurt?"

She nodded again but still didn't look at him. Marcus's stomach churned. Something was wrong. Why was she acting so distant?

"What happened?" Jeremy asked. "Did Adrian follow you on Hero?"

"I guess so. I didn't stay around to look. After hearing the shots, I dug my heels into Whisper, and she took off." She grimaced. "We didn't go far before I fell. Fortunately, we were behind the trees by then and Adrian didn't see. He didn't need to mount Hero at all.

He could have gotten to me on foot."

A chill ran down Marcus's spine. Penny had come so close to being killed. How he longed to take her in his arms and crush her against his body. To hold her and never let her go. But seeing the wary expression on her face, he held back. "You're certain you're all right?"

"I had the wind knocked out of me, that's all. I've fallen enough times that I know what to do. You go limp as you fall and it's not as bad." She gave a rueful smile.

"Thank goodness you're safe." Marcus breathed.

She gave him another shy, hesitant smile, then glanced away. "Yes, I'm safe."

Marcus could hold back no longer. Despite her disheveled appearance and stained clothing, he thought she was the most beautiful creature in the world. He took two steps nearer, then sank to one knee. Seizing her hand, he said, "Now that Withersby's dead, I have no claim on you. Not that I ever truly did. But, the thing is…I love you and want to marry you. Will you please do me the honor of being my wife?"

****

Penny couldn't quite believe what she was seeing: the proud, elegant Marcus Revington, kneeling in the grass his dark eyes tender and pleading. She gave a startled laugh, then said, "Yes. Yes, I will."

Chapter Twenty-Four

Two months later

Penny watched Marcus ride up to her, admiring the easy way he sat the chestnut. He looked so graceful and in control.

As he pulled to a halt, he asked, "Why are you smiling?"

"You ride so well. It's a pleasure to watch you."

"In truth, I haven't had much experience. I'm a much better hand with the ribbons than as a rider." He patted the gelding's neck. "It's Star who makes me look good. I think he's more than ready for the sale."

Penny nodded. "Mr. Foxworthy posted an announcement in the village, but we should probably go to London and find a way to spread the news there. Adrian used to handle all that. I'm not certain how he went about finding buyers."

"It will be easy for me to find plenty of interested parties. Gambling and fine horseflesh are the two vices of many of my acquaintances. But let's not talk about going to London right now. I want to enjoy our day in the country."

Penny motioned to the wicker hamper tied behind Marcus's saddle. "I see you've brought luncheon."

Marcus nodded. "Mrs. Foxworthy made certain we won't starve."

He dismounted and came to help Penny down. After they tied the horses to a tree, they took down the hamper and the blanket Penny had brought, and found a spot for their picnic under a large oak. Penny spread out the blanket, sat down on it, and stretched out her legs. "It's beautiful here, isn't it?"

Marcus nodded. "I never want to leave."

"We do have to go to London occasionally. To arrange the sale and for other business matters," Penny said. "And it will be good to see Lily and James, of course."

"Oh, I forgot to tell you. I got a letter from James. They're coming here in two weeks, after the wedding."

Penny sat up. "Wedding?"

"Yes. Lily finally gave in. James convinced her that they must marry for Charles's sake. It hardly seems like a good basis for marriage to me, but James has always been a practical sort."

"Oh, don't worry," Penny soothed. "They adore each other. The only reason Lily refused him until now was she worried she wasn't good enough for him. It will be wonderful to see them. I've missed her."

"Maybe you can convince them to make their home here. You've managed to convince most of the other Londoners you know to move here."

"I think Maggie likes living in the country. And I know Jeremy does. And we're certainly able to offer a better life to Robin, Timmy, Freddie and Fancy here. I know they're still fighting the notion of going to school in the village, but they took to the rest of it like little ducks to water."

Marcus gave her an indulgent smile. "I don't know whether I dare take you to London any more. I worry you'll convert more city-dwellers to the joys of bucolic living. The manor house is filled to bursting as it is."

"We'll just have to build on an addition then."

Marcus raised his dark brows. "By Jupiter, it seems my fears are real! Who have you targeted to bring here now? Bowes and Will?"

Penny laughed. "I don't think Bowes would be happy here. Or Will either. I was actually thinking that we might"—she lowered her eyes—"might have children someday."

"Are you...that is...?" His dark gaze bored into her, and he seemed to be holding his breath.

She laughed again. "Not so I can tell. But it's only been a month since we wed. For propriety's sake, it would be better if a little more time elapsed."

"Propriety? When have you ever worried about propriety?"

"I suppose I haven't. Otherwise I wouldn't be dressed like this." She motioned to her boots and trousers. "I don't suppose you ever dreamed you'd end up with a shameless hoyden like me, did you?"

"I actually like it when you dress like a boy. I did from the beginning. That sort of attire shows off your attributes quite well. But there's a downside to it."

"Oh, and what is that?"

He gave her devilish smile. "Trousers are a bit more cumbersome to remove."

She frowned at him, trying to look severe. "I don't think you brought me here for a picnic at all. Did you?"

"I'll admit, it was all a pretense." He touched her cheek, then moved his hand to her hair and began pulling out the pins. "I don't mind if you dress like a man, but I prefer your hair down."

Penny leaned back, suddenly breathless. As he ran his fingers through her hair, desire ignited between her legs and spread through her body. When he laid her down and kissed her, her need turned molten. But he was in no hurry. His kisses were long and deep and his caresses leisurely. She drew away with a moan, then stood up and peeled off her clothing. She got her trousers down but couldn't get them over her boots. "You're right," she muttered. "These are dashed hard to remove."

"Lie down and I'll help you."

His movements were smooth and practiced. In moments her lower body was bare. She waited as he took off his jacket and unbuttoned his shirt. When it was off, he undid his trousers, then positioned himself over her.

"You're not going to undress any further?"

"Do you want to wait while I do?"

"Not really."

"I thought not."

He began his slow torture again, his fingers caressing her hips and buttocks, then her inner thighs, gliding close to the aching core of her but not yet touching.

"Please," she whispered.

"You are the most impatient little vixen."

"Vixen?" she demanded, then let out a groan as he finally brought his hand to her heated center.

He teased and fondled until she was near blind with pleasure and yearning. Finally, she decided she'd waited long enough and wriggled out from under him. She flung herself at him, knocking him on his back, then scrambled onto him with her legs straddling his thighs. "Ah, this is much better." She grasped his phallus and stroked him with the same slow deliberation he'd used with her. "Now who is begging for mercy?"

"I am," he groaned.

A delicious thought came to her. She moved her hips and lowered herself onto him, gasping as each glorious inch of him penetrated her. He filled her to bursting, and it was all she could do to remember to breathe. He thrust his hips upward. She groaned with wordless pleasure and met his slow, rocking movements with her own rhythmic ones. The pressure built until she arched her back and cried out as the dazzling ripples burst inside her.

She'd barely come to herself again when he slid out of her, rolled her onto her back and entered her again. She gazed up at him, at his wild eyes and flared nostrils, his handsome face harsh with desire. "You've ridden me, now I shall ride you," he whispered.

Penny closed her eyes and let out a wordless sigh of expectant delight.

A word from the author...

I am fascinated by history, as well as Celtic myth and legend. These interests inspire and enrich most of my books, both romance and fantasy.

Raised in the Midwest, I currently live in Wyoming with my husband and four very spoiled cats and a somewhat spoiled dog. I also have two grown children and have worked at the local public library for over twenty years. In my spare time, I enjoy gardening, travel and reading, of course!

http://marygillgannon.com

www.ingramcontent.com/pod-product-compliance
Lightning Source LLC
Chambersburg PA
CBHW071512260626
47170CB00002B/346